horndog blue

Also by Robert Wintner

Snorkel Bob's Reality Guide to Hawaii (nonfiction)

Whirlaway

The Ice King

Hagan's Trial and Other Stories

horndog blue

A Novel By

ROBERT WINTNER

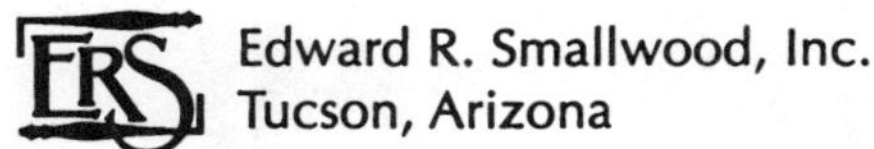

Edward R. Smallwood, Inc.
Tucson, Arizona

Edward R. Smallwood, Inc.
Tucson, Arizona

Published 1995
Printed in the United States of America

01 00 99 98 97 96 95 5 4 3 2 1

Special thanks to Creedence, the Stones, and all those other guys who gave us those great lyrics.

Publisher's Cataloging in Publication
(Prepared by Quality Books, Inc.)

Wintner, Robert.
Horndog Blue : a novel / Robert Wintner.
p. cm.
Preassigned LCCN: 93-087797.
ISBN 1-881334-38-4 — Cloth
ISBN 1-881334-39-2 — Paperback

1. Middle aged men—Fiction. 2. Americans—Europe—Fiction. 3. Midlife crisis—Fiction. I. Title

PS3573.I58C65 1995 813'.54
QBI94-344

To order this and other books by the same author,
call 1-800-905-9908

For saxophonists everywhere

Horndog Blue

Hattie

Hattie said she was hungry. I asked her, "Meat, fish or fowl?" She ignored me. "Italian, Mexican, Chinese? Or French?" She gazed off behind a dramatic exhale. She hated my cynicism. Her smoky whisper, *J'ai faim*, didn't help, and she resented me, too, like I'd tricked her into a stupid charade.

It was Day Two, first week in Paris, *fin de siécle,* 20th go-round, curtains, second millennium, when La Bastille became a gathering place for Les Plongeurs. *Plonge* means plug, as in electrical. Les Plongeurs were plugged in, as in hip. Days of heavy caffeine and nicotine and poses struck in clay, like Gumby disgusted with life itself, were the mode for Les P, who made pilgrimage to Paris, to think.

We began the day wide-eyed and nauseated, because cigarettes and coffee take getting used to those first few days. Hattie was ecstatic, surrounded by potential, new tastes untried. She was focused.

I was disappointed; you can't go back because places get so gone, turn to shit now faster than at any other time in history.

It's the airlines with their cheap fares and hundreds of thousands of punk kids having a big pull on real life, mostly mental. Besides the difference between then and now, another difference took shape—the difference between her and me. I admired her as much as I ever had, and she held up at close range, where most women who want to be physically beautiful can't hide the truth. Hattie didn't need to hide. Good teeth, clear skin, big eyes with a warmth and a sparkle that looked like nothing but fun—she had the spirit. But there we were, she striving for something vague, I nodding to myself in confirmation that there is no suitable woman, only continuing approximation, only ongoing tolerance, understanding and compensation.

But she'd come so close, as close as a woman could come to man, or at least to me. Twenty years my junior, she knew the world differently than girls did when I was twenty-two. Oh sure, the girls were willing then too and maybe more so, since "free love" gave rise to "experimentation" and was a release valve on generations of pent-up demand. But that was just it—demand was so pent up we had our hands full just taking each other's clothes off and having sex as casually as lunch. Don't get me wrong, it was a time, a time it was. But Hattie was different. She sensed things. She was young and often stupid, like stupid was a vogue behavior, and stupid behavior mixed with stupid talk was an elevated plane; beyond intellect I suppose and therefore street-smarter, or something. But she knew things when she wasn't being stupid, where to go, what to touch, what to say or not say. She wasn't intellectual or street-smart but instinctive. I fancied she hung out with me on instinct, that she had her mind moved and liked it, just like I did, just like I felt, in a constant state of wonder, pleasantly inebriated on low-odds reality.

That morning was the beginning of the end, the point where all the vegetables start to move over the bubbles, just before a simmer comes to boil. I stewed in uncertainty, feeling old, cynical and resolute. That was the worst of it, her awful skill at showing my age. Feeling old, feeling young—the feeling was hers to bestow. She'd said, *You really talk neat sometimes, and God, we could blaze with all those credit cards.* I thought that was stupid, not the sentiment but the way she put it, gratuitously stupid, so I could see how the young folk talked.

I looked past the language, accepted the compliment on talking neat, and I honestly loved throwing money down the rat hole, cash or credit, especially with someone like Hattie, young, beautiful, full of spirit and love. I allowed for growth, figured the language would change soon enough, and in the meantime we'd have the fun. And we did, and one thing was so strong it cut through tons of stupidity. I suppose I thought of it as chemistry, which was maybe a delicate word for hormones. No man wants to be a horndog.

The smoke cleared on her bad mood when I said we needed a trip to the money exchange for more money for more fun. Then we would walk the Bois de Bologne, you know, where Henry Miller walked with the hookers. Then maybe we'd swim at Les Halles Piscine. She let the bad mood go. Old guys need exercise.

But the park was scrub weeds, stunted trees, a few acres of greenbelt gone brown, riddled with streets like heart worms in a good dog. Bad breath, gas and smoke wheezed a hoarse bark, death close at hand. Little French cars infested the has-been park like fleas on easy blood. The *piscine* was underground, under a sci-fi shopping mall also underground, no windows. The swimming pool felt stagnant, cloudy, unclean, like a subterranean scum pond. You could hear the subway underwater and wonder what a teensy tiny earthquake would do. I'd had it. By early evening in another cafe like the last cafe, the mood thickened again, like smoke.

I asked her why the Plongeurs looked upset, so disappointed.

"They too feel it, the hunger," she explained.

"I hope they feel something," I said. "They look tired. Too much free time. I think if they were busier, they could shake their funk."

"You miss the point," she said.

"I love it when you say that."

"Their contribution to society is their critique on society, and if they had jobs there would be no critique. Don't you see? As long as they exist, something is wrong."

"Oh."

She said they were an advance group, with time to consider the human condition, time to speculate on human development. "People with jobs don't do that. They don't have the time. And they're too tired."

"Caffeine and nicotine never led to development. Maybe some vegetables and exercise..."

The unspoken question settled in: Why are we here together? I hated the bind we fell into straight-away. It made her sound stupid as ever—and there I was, defending jobs as a concept, when even now the concept gives rise to mild angina.

She said, "Try something new. It's not too late." She lit a smoke, slow, like I was supposed to follow. Fine. I lit one, too. She'd picked up a French inhale in only two days—she pulled hard, held the smoke in her mouth then eased it out, up to flared nostrils. She relaxed, exhaling a smooth stream, smoke rings at the end.

That was all. She wanted me to shut up and make smoke rings, and if I couldn't do it right, then I should practice until I could, because we'd come a long way to get up next to this hip/chic Bastille scene, so it was adapt or perish for me, or at least for my prospects for continuing companionship. I chomped the bit, couldn't help it, French-inhaled a few, went to a teeth clench, cowboy-style on a few more. She looked unsure, mockery or cooperation. I got dizzy and sick. She said, "Let's walk." She went. I followed. I always thought that was a sign of good health, getting dizzy and sick on French smokes and espresso.

In the second block we approached a man, an ashen man with gray skin hanging like a baggy suit, with scabs. His lanky stride was off, shorter now after a life of too much wine, too much smoke, staggering our way. The guy was tall and way fucked—could hardly stand up and quivered in the chest and stomach so you naturally wanted to give him a wide berth in case he decided to puke or drop dead in, say, the next instant. He was a Plongeur in the antique-clothing vogue, his old but elegant suit less threadbare than he was but just as dirty. As he neared he started up, the chest and stomach quivers going into convulsion and reverse-pump mode, spittle-flecks spewing jowls to collar, like a volcano at first burp—he stopped suddenly ten paces out, leaned forward, opened his mouth and waited, like a king-size espresso machine all set to brew. It came. Brown drivel flowed out like from a spigot, a quart or so. This guy was healthy in the gross extreme.

I veered off the curb and crossed the street. Not Hattie. She continued straight ahead, unfazed. Did she want a closer look? Would she check for lumps? Wipe his chin? When the wobble man was behind us, she watched me recross, disgust in her eyes, but not for the pukey wobble man, for the pussy who was her date. "You're so intolerant," she scolded when I was alongside again. I pumped my stomach and chest and made puke noises and wobbled, which caused several people to give me a wide berth. She sped up and left me, which proved my point, I thought, but then it didn't because she was being stupid again, and intolerant.

And it was a good night for tolerance—derelicts, mutants, beggars, criminals with glaring intention. Oh, she let me catch up for the next little neighborhood, no lights. In darkness the identity seekers and lost thinkers joined the undead and desperadoes; like a reef at night, the streets came alive with feeding. Garish tropicals fluttered and scurried in a bioluminescence at once alluring and defensive. My eyes went this way and that, breasts to asses and back again, tolerant. She laid a hand on my arm. "I never want to keep you from anything," she said. "I'd feel terrible."

There, that's what I meant, uncanny instinct. "Yeah, thanks," I said, because cold indifference is your best defense when you're caught hands down, eyeballs reaching for the curves and creases, for the cleavages and contours, for the flesh that will soon be dust, just like you, but for now makes you long for contact—reaching for the street buffet. But she was way too smart to buy a denial.

"I'm serious." She turned to me from the waist, I think on purpose because it stretched her sheer clingy blouse across her breasts, and sometimes I'm smart enough to know what's going on, too. She understood sexual manipulation like a computer understands software; rational man defaults to hormones.

She had big, tough feet because she was a tomboy, always had been, and she said she knew she turned on the homos with her broad shoulders, square chin and high cheeks. She said they loved the combo, called it feminine lumberjack, or rugged bitch, you know. She didn't care who up and downed her all day long, who sent the message: I have power in my dick. She had the real power, made her point. It wasn't a game. It was real, application of her gift. I could look and want. She could look and have. And I suppose she had an easier time making a point, too.

I caught up with her. "Why are you with me?" I wanted the cards on the table, better crying time now than crying time later. Why wait?

"It's one of those things. Don't worry about it. It won't last forever." Miss Shoot-from-the-hip could equivocate and play both ends, and I suppose I liked that, too, most likely loved it, because she didn't even hint for half a heartbeat that I was an old fuck and ought to get lost. So I did worry. Because if she could see me that clearly, that free of the stuff that so often clouds the issue, then she maybe wanted me forever. I thought she was in love.

She pranced ahead, turned with a flourish and announced, "I'll be your slave tonight. Anything you want." She swirled away, leaving eddies of doubt and wonder.

People stared. She didn't care. I didn't know if she wanted me or not, past tonight anyway. I figured she wanted me tonight because she was always horny, but then I wasn't sure about that, and maybe that was another side of her instinct, her ability to keep me guessing. She understood my weakness, my strength, my limitation. I understood nothing except maybe that they were all the same thing, and I followed along, through Paris after dark. She flitted and flirted, smoked and drank and kept moving with tireless energy like my youth passing before my eyes.

High Cafe

It came to one of those mornings way past noon when too much fun in the vast little village led to a headache, brain fatigue, dead weights on the chest, a bowling ball for a head, old bones, noisy lungs. I couldn't breathe, reeked of liquor and smoke. It was unacceptable. I was too far round the bend to confuse optimism with delusion. In the shower she was a wet blur, in a mood, pissed off. I checked my dick for wear. I couldn't be sure, but it looked well rested. She used birth control that looked like giant windowpane acid and once up there in place you couldn't feel it, except it left your dick all crusted over with dried egg yolk.

We'd hit a funky little North African place like hundreds of funky little North African places or Indian, Indonesian, Egyptian, Albanian or Brazilian places. It was a box, architecturally, with no front. She was naturally drawn in, as if deep penetration would accelerate osmosis; as if way in the back was darkest Africa. Stuffiest, hottest and least breathable Africa is what it was. But to the funk she went, and quick.

I stopped halfway back where the air got so thin your lungs cringed, squinted shut because the alveoli could not swap carbon dioxide for oxygen, because oxygen was no more, and why bother changing CO for shit? She pushed on through smoke so thick it was like a pillow on your face—a much-used pillow, no linen, like you get in jail. She came back disappointed, nearly distraught; no vacancy in the vault of souls, deep inside in the grooviest, funkiest recess, where all-knowing, all-meaning lives, where she wanted to be. I shrugged, "Bummer." She gave me the hard cruel stare; she knew malignant sympathy when she heard it, and I shouldn't patronize her by playing along. She eased up on it and slid in to a wall seat halfway back to watch the play. I took the outside seat, to watch her.

A German fellow who looked German sat on one side smoking intensely, staring at the butt with intimacy. He clamped it softly in his teeth, let his lips wrap it gently as his lungs ravaged its innards, its little ember glowing bright in orgasm. He half smiled, held the thought and the smoke, exhaled half and inhaled the rest again, some up through his nose, then exhaled half and inhaled the balance, again and again. Repeat as necessary.

His waxy yellow hair, dull blue eyes and perfectly straight nose were second-glance characteristics. It was his ashen, ocher skin, crude, blurry tattoos, his dirty, greasy, ragged denims and his girlfriend that gave him away; German, no doubt. She too devoured cigarettes, though more from raw addiction than sentiment like him. Her tattoos were from the same parlor as his. And she had two nose rings puncturing one nostril, a stick pin in the other, haute vogue with Deutchlander Plongeurs then. They were revolting, factually. And they inspired discomfort along with disgust—imagine the poor girl blowing her nose in February, the big woolly ones hanging up on the through bolts, freezing quickly to buggery stalactites hanging from her frozen steel nose holes. I couldn't resist, and sat there shivering with the willies.

Hattie slipped into cafe mode, seeking greater truth. The process had a look to it, began in the brain, the only meaningful organ in the body, theoretically speaking. It happened on the fringe—the fringe of society, the fringe of the room, the fringe of rational thought. The only obstacle here and now was me, which was often the case; I stared. Staring is judgmental, a *faux pas.*

But how could I help it? The German guy had a big tattoo spanning his near shoulder and biceps. A line drawing of a woman kneeling, hands tied behind her, three dots and a dash for eyes, nose and mouth, more lines and dots for breasts and nipples and a small but distinct squiggle, like Hitler's mustache, for a pussy, right there on his arm. He talked German to his girlfriend and glanced over at us, maybe in discomfort, you couldn't be sure.

So I turned away, not so much in deference to his sensitivity but more like a bird-watcher who doesn't want to spook his entertainment. I turned toward Hattie, forever sprightly and open-minded Hattie, receptive even then to her companion's insight, thought, idea—ooh, ooh—creativity. Too bad her companion was stodgy old asshole me, who could come up with no more insight than, "He has a pussy on his arm."

"He has a woman on his arm. You think it's the same thing?"

"I have a woman sitting across from me. But maybe she's incomplete, I mean, unbound, with her pussy covered up."

"That's disgusting."

"Yes. We agree."

"It's a statement," she said.

"What? What did you say?"

"It's art."

"A tattoo honey with a squiggly pussy?"

"You're so...judgmental."

"Judgmental? *Moi?*" So we poised again on the verge of conflict, then slipped over the edge. The two guys to the right smoked with an objective: blotting out all oxygen. Like kids whitewashing a wall, they huffed and puffed and pulled hard and blew big in a feverish effort to clear the air of clear air. Deep, long draughts as if sucking on life itself, they filled the room with their own signature dimension. I stared again; it was behavior beyond belief. And again I put it out there, "How could anyone feel good about that?"

A light rain began from the inversion layer outside, the kind of rain that might cause a look up but hardly a run. Someone closed the door and fixed the latch, and the little box got smaller still, darker, closer, less breathable, secure from the torrents of nature. The waiter arrived. I stood up and gave my date the situation. "I can't stay here." I left.

I left quickly, judgmentally, with conviction. I left like a guy leaves a building on fire, because breathing is required for life. Maybe that's where it ended, or started to end, or reached midway in the ending process; it underscored my severe limitation in soulful reality, left her pissed off plenty. Still she was weak for a strong lead. So she sat there a minute breathing smoke thick as drain sludge like it was a normal, casual thing, mostly just to show she could if she wanted to, and moreover that she could think for herself.

Then she split quick and double-timed it two blocks to catch up.

She took my arm—on again—and led me to the next bar up, more of a hole in the wall, off the sidewalk, no door. Thick traffic wheezed by, three lanes of little cars hurrying to their next cafes. She lit a smoke, got a *café noir*, the blackjack demitasse that coats your tongue with hot bitter, puts your nerves on the rack, needs a smoke to cut the edge. It was settled. She was willing again, from the top, with feeling.

But the big, fat piece of shit next to us hadn't changed. He took a break from a butter-and-ham sandwich with a giant ooze of Bel Paise on the side, to hock up the cheese ball from the back of his throat and gob it out almost to the curb, dangling hardly any snot strings at all on his greasy, shit-smelling shirt. Then he ordered another carafe of rosé. I didn't say a word, didn't need to. Even Hattie got the picture, the guy was that good.

So I ordered a carafe, too, tart and cold, and put my arm around my date. "This is living," I said, but we'd reached the point where anything I said was one more smart-ass, snide quip, unless it was nice as a choirboy asking forgiveness. So when she shot me the snake eyes I said, "Really. This is much better. Thanks." She bought it, snuggled in, to my amazement, and said tonight she wanted to get drunk, really drunk.

Inner Meaning

Yamaoka Tesshu said, "Hear the soundless sound, see the formless form. At a glance, control your opponent and attain victory without contention. This is...inner meaning..."

He described a process, a sorting out, leading to one rung or another on the social food chain. I think he identified the phase of development in which children stop fighting each other physically but rather come to know intuitively who among them is dominant, or submissive. Tesshu taught the sword of no sword, by which victory is ultimate, bloodless, still and calm—in all his hundred duels, he never lost, never killed.

A hundred years after he wrote that passage, I was eleven, and scuffling seemed the way to sort things out—until I found Tesshu on Uncle Roland's bookshelf. Uncle Roland was thought to be strange; that role appeals to boys, and then he had books about invisible swords, magical power, old samurai.

Hattie at first glimpse was as far away, as long ago and as mesmerizing as any first glimpse of a reality yet unimagined.

She went beyond hormonal response, triggering that galloping ache across the chest men feel when want approaches debilitation, when desire annihilates the rational faculties. I drove slow one day on Beach Road by the bluff watching waves, considering wave height, water depth and their inverse relation, when I looked down. Hattie pulled her pants off, shimmied her ass and aimed it up at passing cars by the bluff. She bent over, fumbling with her bikini bottom. Into the rough, steering up the sunlit avenue between her legs, I hit the brakes in time, stuck in the tawny haze. Uninhibited and maybe careless, she presented herself in VistaVision. She was immortal, until she felt my eyeballs burrowing up her crotch. She stopped fumbling, stood up and closed the show.

I nodded a friendly hello.

She grabbed a towel and wrapped herself.

My heart pounded again for glory. I wanted to speak, but the wave that broke overhead poured its tons of water, pinned me to the bottom so hard that only a pulse remained, throbbing with the voltage of survival, and it was not verbal. Tongue lay in mouth, six pounds deadweight. It was a love scene from the start with Hattie Summer and me. That's what I thought from the first sight of her bent, bare bottom curving in on the Magic Kingdom, gates open. She felt like a gift that filled my eyes, down to my toes. Seeing her again the same day in a health food store felt ominous. Oh sure, it was a small town, but men past the hustling age know that chance meetings twice are synchronous. I stared again like she was again naked, couldn't help it, under the burden, shamefully, like a pup who knows what the paper is for and still pisses on the rug.

I wanted to tell her: This is no hustle. I am indifferent, but that was a lie and she knew it, so I couldn't.

So I turned away, asked a health food girl about the characteristics of basmati. But among the subtleties—shorter cooking time, softer husks, more delicate flavor—I turned back. She waited.

"I have a feeling..." I said, and I laughed, ran off the road again when she pulled me into the vacuum. Up and down I stared, and I laughed because it was the stupidest thing to do and she made me stupid, moved my brain right down to the end of my dick—I found her eyes quickly, because they're safe haven, and women don't mind that as much. Surely she knew that. Later, she told me it was the opening line—I have a feeling...

Later she said I looked tongue-tied and confused, like I didn't know what to say or something.

I said yes, I was, and asked if that surprised her.

She said yes, old guys never came on to her before. She offered her hand, her warmth. "I'm Hattie," she said.

We took two days. I dropped everything; nothing else mattered. We got some wine and hit the bluff over the beach near where I first saw her. We walked the beach. We had drinks in town and watched the people. She eased me along, sensed my uncertainty, my excitement and embarrassment, my appreciation. She kept the verbal part down. I would have told her who I was, where I'd been, how long and why, because guys in heavy lust are compelled to look normal, are paranoid that silence might give away the four inches of hardcoming love pounding in their pants. They ramble inanities. She shushed me, "Shh. Osmosis."

"Is that like Tantric?"

"Yes. Can you feel it?" I shifted my weight, easing my joint to a new angle. "Can you let go?"

"Not yet."

But then I could. What was only physical made room for something more. We held hands. I walked her home. At her door she looked into my eyes. "I like you."

"Are you free tomorrow?"

"Don't worry about that stuff," she said.

I couldn't have imagined that one day we would travel to Paris together—couldn't imagine that a tomorrow could possibly arrive, on which she and I would share another proximity. So I worried all night, until I rolled around casual just after noon. A note on her door said, *Same place.* I was catching on—I sat down quietly beside her. We didn't speak for an hour, which made the game easy for me, until she said, "That was beautiful."

"Mmm," I went along.

"So many people get to the point where they can't be together."

"You mean where they can't talk?"

"Talking is easy. No, I mean be together and not talk, and still touch."

"Did we touch?"

Stupid question. She didn't answer stupid questions. I went along, followed like a puppy dog after a milk bone. A few hours later she said she had to work at six. I said nothing. I was getting good. She said she'd be off at two. She waitressed.

"Mmm. Late. You'll be tired," I said, meaning I would be tired, or sleeping sound as an old guy.

"Yes." And we strolled easily toward her place. She was fairly impressed that I, white man of reasonable means, could learn so quickly to shut my mouth, calm myself, ditch the chatter. Maybe I was only amazingly patient for the fertile delta, but a woman has to trust her instinct sometimes, and this time looked safe enough.

And that was the size of it—patience for a reward I thought then was as good as it could possibly get. How long would the stifle be required, the hand-held silence, the pose of earthly communion? Forever, because a man must change, if love is in his heart; he must change before the sex. Because that way the change has a chance to stick, to survive even after the hormones get quenched. And if a man wants sexual contact with a woman so bad he can feel it in his chest, then that's the best time to see her and all her faults in the kindest possible light, because no matter how bad she stinks, burps, farts out loud, picks her nose or sinks deep into bad syntax, he still wants her, front and center. Before the fact is the best possible time to practice the wanting, so later he can remember his easy transcendence of her human frailty in the same spirit, with the same zest, the same forgiving lust.

Besides, Hattie was good company between her blissful idiocies. I longed for hormonal liberation, so we could really get to know each other—I mean so we could relax. That was it, the relaxation I longed for, even as I recognized the value of the time we took. Isn't that how it goes? I was clear on the right thing to do, but slowing the action down was as hard as stopping a stampede on the open prairie.

I stayed mum and alert and followed her easily inside where she took off her top. It was easy as doing nothing, but it wasn't sexual, or at least that was the presentation, as if a woman could be so oblivious of a man as horny as I was. Not too likely, although her movement, her awareness, her self-consciousness did not flutter, but maybe she'd had plenty of practice. She was big and rippled taut but with feminine curvature.

She discovered thirst among her window plants, and so she gave them a little drink, filling the water can and pouring just so. She shimmied from her bottoms, bending over just like she was roadside in heavy traffic, like that was practiced too, or natural, or something I didn't quite understand but relative to her free nature in contrast to the fucked-up society we live in. I took it on the chin, felt my legs go weak, never mind. But her cat came in and cried and she was all over him with cross-species intimacy until I tried the same line, "Meow." She laughed. I'd caught on, which gave rise to more affection in the animal realm, to romance, which is what came next. What it was, maybe for the first time, was intimacy, inalienably linked to body parts.

The sex was a gift. She was twenty-two. A man past forty understands the meaning of the end, and that leads to greater reward in all things, by simple virtue of slowing down, smelling the roses, enjoying the details of daily life. And here was life in the grandest sense, stretched to sex warp, crashing the barrier and resting on the far side, not solitary or in small mourning, but different. I felt this relaxation as blissful elixir; I wanted more, in thirty minutes or whenever, but I wanted this interlude too, this balm, this liberation.

So, I thought. And that syllable detailed my total experience in life with love.

"That's not true," she said. "That's not what happened at all." We were drunk by now, in Paris, in a cafe at night, telling a sleazy Pierre how we became lovers, because he wanted to know—*How you become loffers*... He wanted to know just how her labia majora could slip itself over his good stiff self. "It wasn't romantic like that," she said. "We...we just fucked."

"Zuss like dat?" Pierre was on to something, maybe a conclusion on love, or else his own route to the contents of her underpants.

"Okay, okay," I said. "It wasn't like that. I'm a sentimental fool. She didn't offer me her hand, warm or cold. She didn't offer me anything. We didn't walk on the beach or spend hours not talking, none of it, zero, nothing. I made it up, like the guy in the Incident at Owl Creek Bridge who blinked and the rope broke and he hit the river that swept him to freedom, except that in the next blink he dangled. Dead."

"What bridge?" she asked.

"I have read of this book," Pierre said. I liked him better, maybe, but not much.

"She's right, Pierre. I made that up. I fantasized it, you know, at night, when I was masturbating. You know?"

But Pierre too was natural, French, and he said, "Oh yes. Tonight I will myself fuck Mademoiselle just as you did."

"Ha ha," I said. "That's a good one." And I told the story again, maybe for Hattie and me, of Hattie and me and love.

"She made me work. It was all true up to the health food store, but when I tried to talk to her she looked like she'd been attacked."

"I was attacked."

I smiled at Pierre—he understood. "She read me like a book. She knows when a man wants to fuck her."

Pierre showed bad teeth. "Yes. Men want to fuck her."

I hoped she would dislike him for that. It was easy enough to know what Pierre imagined, tongue to clit, banana splits, all-day suckers—I am man. Maybe I was afraid she wouldn't dislike him for it. "I asked her if she wanted to get a beer or something. That's all."

"And she let you fuck her? I will buy her six!"

"No. She looked trés pissed and told me to have a nice day. She walked over to these two guys with ponytails who smelled like goats and hugged each other. To her I was lower than whale shit on the bottom of the ocean."

Pierre smiled and spoke to his wine. "Yes, like when you drove up between her legs, you and the sunlight."

"That's right. I am still no more than flotsam in wave wash every now and then."

She drank. Pierre waited and soon said, "So, you never got to fuck her?"

"No. She wouldn't talk to me. Wouldn't see me."

"But...surely you fuck her now!"

"It's a long story, Pierre. We don't fuck as much as we used to, because of our disease, you know?" Pierre watched his wine, like he did know. "I thought about her all day, all night. You know some women love the goat smell on a man. I couldn't imagine liking it, or wearing it. But I was messed up. In love..." She looked up. "I took a big wet dump the next morning and got in the shower. I'm soaping up my butthole and wondering if I shouldn't. You know, maybe leave some shit smell, go back down to the health food store." He drank. "Give it a shot, Pierre. You got a head start."

"That's disgusting," she said. "And mean."

"It's not meant to be mean," I said. "It's true. If you don't think it's true just say so."

"If you don't want to tell me, it is okay. My name is Étienne, not Pierre."

I finished my wine and asked, "If I don't want to tell you what?"

Hattie turned to Pierre. "Yeah. Tell you what?"

Synchronicity

Letting her go was easy, as long as I didn't see her. I saw her every few weeks or so after failing at the health food store. I'd look and nod, but she'd have none of it. I thought that was good, that when we finally got tight I wouldn't have to worry about her flirting around with other guys. But then it wasn't so good, because her body language spoke rejection over and over again. I got the message. She didn't like me, plain and simple. I didn't know why at the time. Maybe I don't know now, except for the possibility that she didn't like me because I didn't like her, not in the soulful sense, not with love, real love, spiritual love, from the heart. I think about that now. I didn't then; I only wanted to hop in the saddle and ride. But isn't that natural? Isn't that what the male of a species does? I never precluded possibilities for horsefucking over the horizon, for living happily ever after in the saddle, but how could we know if that would be possible without trying it out? Sure I eyeballed up her crotch; big deal. She'd been around guys who made me look like Fred Astaire.

Well, good riddance—that's what I came to, in maybe my closest proximity to real love then, which was love for him who loved me most. She was beneath me anyway, not so much inferior as, well, she was not yet developed, not yet seasoned, not yet able to share the insight of a guy like me who'd been where I'd been, seen and knew and all that. And anyway, she had a boyfriend.

I told myself it was nothing, this juvenile liaison. It would pass—these kids today. The boyfriend was a big galoot, a harmless, simple-looking surfer about her age, maybe younger, who looked like he could fuck her ten or twelve times a night, even if only for a minute or two each time. I saw them out around town. The boyfriend didn't drink. He couldn't dance. He was muscular and stiff. He was on her, all over her, like the security blanket draped over Linus's shoulder. I figured she came with him, but she did the work, most of it anyway, well, she did the tricky part, the soft touch, the finesse, the flourish, the finish; I knew she did. The guy was a stand-in, that was all. I understood these things, I thought, because I went slam-bang plenty myself, when I was younger. I counted women as if sexual contact was measured in quota, by the year or the month—measured so laziness wouldn't set in, so exhilaration could be sustained, boredom avoided. I knew that immersion precedes illumination, and I thought that was the principle at hand. How else could a body know what love is, until it knew what love isn't? How could a man settle in, until he'd roamed the countryside? And these days don't the old shibboleths hold for women, too?

I believe in order, that goodness will prevail. I believe that a busy mind, thinking two or three moves ahead, gets in its own way. She was still a breaking wave threatening collapse, so that I could only stay calm, enjoy the ride, know that this was the height of living, of surviving middle age—knowing that any more than this or less than this could tumble me to the bottom for another pounding. So I gleaned what love I could from the world, knowing that love cannot be contained. I let her go over and over again.

I woke up nights neither groggy nor dazed but thinking of her with my brain in gear—woke up from sleeping soundly, dreaming that we had made contact, knowing we had, just like dreaming of money and trying to bring it home. Then I would lie there long hours telling myself she was a moody bimbo, issuing into the silent night my mantra of no chemistry between us, throwing up the barricades of my self-defense.

Because what I knew was that it didn't matter if she was a moody bimbo or worldly enough and mental enough with enough make-up and composure to anchor the Network News—flat didn't matter because the chemistry in me was so potent it went past want, past hunger, past the hurt in my heart to a stampede across my chest. I wanted to puke, she got to me so bad. Was that drive an extension of hormones? Could I scratch the itch by simply slipping my peepee into her teetee? I didn't think so, but hadn't I experienced more often than not the vanishing act of love? Hadn't I sustained faith in the quota, the roam, the rationale of a horndog getting his share? I was weak with Hattie, and stupid. I realized it wasn't her fault, and if communion was to be, then I must allow it to be; I could not force it; it would arrive or it would not. I must forget her, all thought of her. And I still felt weak and stupid, and tired, and so a process evolved, leading to sleep about sunrise.

Business was good for me then. I'd bought a small apartment building and the house next to it and cut both into tiny cubicles like in Hong Kong. I rented my cubicles to surfers and windsurfers and let them camp six to a box, if they wanted, since most came for only a week or two, for waves and wind. Income was regular, work easy, life stable. It evolved, and days freed up for leisure, away from tedium. It was good, unless the leisure turned to thought, and inward got to be my prevailing direction. I forgot her, but there she was. Plenty of other women came through the place then—young, fit women, women who could roll their eyes around a room scanning potential for the day or night. I could get laid if I was able to talk with a learning disability and ape the postures of the surf boys. I couldn't. It's not easy. Besides, I thought Hattie was different—different because, after all, I'd seen her golden fleece. I needed to get out of town, back into society, among people my own age engaged in daily pursuits toward making a better world.

I planned to travel because getting away seemed so refreshing, and merely making reservations and buying tickets felt like a commitment, a liberation, a giant step toward independence, toward the strength of character and the endurance of not so many years ago. It was then, with thoughts far away and with longings for long ago, on a clear afternoon, I drove down a country road a few miles from town. She walked along the shoulder, carrying a heavy bag. Rainclouds drifted nearby and droplets fell here and there in the cool, moist air. The bag was cloth and stuffed with rags or clothing. I pulled up and opened the door. She looked in. I smiled. She sighed and got in. I drove in silence, but it was a silence resounding with questions, like, Who are you? Where are you from? What are you? And why are you that way? Do you have any ideas? On anything? Do you have anything at all to say, to tell me? What's in the bag? Can I see it again, just one more time, please, the golden fleece?

I did want to know about her, every inch of her and every part of her past, too. She must have known that; she was beautiful. What guy had not wanted to know that, to do that? And all the questions seemed so obvious, so lame, so obsequiously bent on the animal act, so void of spirit or spontaneity, so far from free, so clinging and base; I asked nothing. She offered the same, and though I may have twitched here and there with the droplets on the windshield and possibly squirmed as the drizzle set in, as the electricity between us became as palpable as the rain, I knew the voltage came from me. I kept my eyes on the road, as if she was a cleavage and staring down it would be rude. And there we were sharing the presence of what had become the font of emotional turmoil for me, cruising down a beautiful country road in a spring rain as emotionally detached from each other as the moo cows roadside were emotionally distant from prospects of hamburger.

I asked Hattie sometime after that what she felt then, cruising down that road. "When?" she said. I said, you know. She said, "I didn't feel anything. You gave me a ride. Oh, I was glad I didn't have to walk it. In the rain, too."

If I'd asked her at the time, I would have known the profile fit—moody bimbo. As events unfolded, I came to see the dimension unavailable to me for so long, which was that of purity, simplicity, reality unencumbered by introspection. And even farther down that greater road I can tell myself it's only the old defense kicking in when I know I was right all along; moody bimbo. Maybe I was a moody bimbo, too. But I don't think so. I think she did me not so good. When we reached town she said, "This is okay right here." She got out and looked back in and said, "Thanks."

I shrugged and said, "Sorry." It caught—a moment of difficulty, a crack in the ice. She smiled and walked away again. I let it go again, so it could come back again, theoretically at least.

I saw her two nights later in a bar—two nights after two days of trying to carry on in life two steps ahead of thoughts and images whose suction accelerated like the shrinking spin of a whirlpool. I looked for her, maybe knowing the looking was superfluous. I walked into a bistro looking for a drink, and she sat alone at the bar, slumped over a drink, crying. I sat beside her, ordered quickly, brandy instead of beer, for the extra brace. I played it patient, calming down for half a drink, and asked kind of in her direction, "Hard day?"

She nodded. It was our first conversation—well, first dialogue anyway; or at any rate our first exchange that didn't turn quickly into a dead end. I was exhilarated and finished my drink, to calm down, to constrain my excitement, to hide the problem so common among middle-aged men on the brink of rapprochement with much younger, nubile women, which is that of lunging and grasping, of cloying and clinging, sometimes mixed with angina and/or coronary malfunction. I ordered again, one for her too, casting aside with some effort the momentary doubt on the efficacy of buying a lady a drink; I mean, wasn't that something old guys did? But the world hadn't changed all that much in the short time it took me to hit middle age—she drank and said thanks. We sat. We drank. She said thanks again when I ordered the next round, this time with far more cool, since the bartender was hip to an older guy moving on a major score and kept his distance, eyes open, so only a half-nod got two more on the bar. That was an advantage, I thought, getting that kind of service from years of solid tipping; the young guys couldn't do that.

Oh, we were making good time, I thought, except that every time I thought of something to say, I realized it was only something I'd thought to say, for the sake of saying—small talk—and I knew the kids didn't do that anymore, or maybe I only feared saying something wrong. After awhile she turned to me, "You're probably a good guy," she said.

Good guy? It didn't sit well, it was so...lukewarm. "I don't know about that," I said. She turned back to her drink. "What are your clues?" I said.

"I don't know," she said. "Call it intuition."

"Where you from?"

"Michigan."

"Long way from home," I said.

She stared at me. A tear rolled down her cheek. I'd blown it. She wiped it away and said, "Sorry." I shook my head, drawing a line between us again that I wanted to cross, wanted to lunge over and give her the kind of hug that would banish her loneliness forever, or until tomorrow. But I was a stranger to her, I knew I was, and a hug would only lead to a hard-on and the awful truth of my intention.

She was from Michigan. What, when, who and how would have to wait; if Michigan made her cry, the rest of her resumé could throw her into a sobbing seizure. But the drink was taking hold, and once past the initial emotion of topics too long undiscussed, I felt that she could relax and open up, that we could...get to know each other.

But I am an old guy. Because these kids today don't do

that, either. So about the time we should have eased into backgrounds, thoughts, opinions, assessments, she looked up from her drink and asked, "Will you take me home?" I said sure, thinking of transportation, hoping that our love would not be based on convenience, hoping that I would not become word-associated as the old guy with the car, yet knowing that human contact must be first based on helping each other, taking care of each other—no shit, until we got up, settled up, walked out, got in the car, pulled out and headed down the street, to the left I guess, because that was the direction of my house anyway; until we hit the red light at the intersection and I looked over for directions, and she smiled, little stars twinkling where remnant tears still welled.

Holy shit raced through my brain as the old guy's nemesis, the pounding heart, ran a steeplechase across my chest. She's a nut case, and she wants to fuck—it was at that instant that I fell back to my true niche in spiritual reality. And I resented my weakness, my failure, my base, gross existence all the way to my house—resented it as a mantra, as a flagellation in humility, as a means of keeping the beast at bay. Again I refused to look down, focusing instead on clear light, on helping a friend in need.

I won't say that she wasn't a nut case, but then I wouldn't say that about anyone, or at least anyone with the least iota of imagination. Yet at my house the mad rush slowed down. I opened a medium fine wine, a pinot noir for the damp, cool weather, and poured it, into wine glasses. She was all eyes at this...orgy of sophistication, and at first sip, with no cringe from the turpentine she was used to, she said, "Oh God." I think she meant that the wine was good, that she'd possibly never considered a nice buzz but rather thought of wine as different from beer because it comes in bigger bottles, white or red, and you can get really, really shitass drunk on it.

I found her innocent and refreshing, and on my turf I found myself less plagued by doubt and hesitation. I didn't say any more than I had, but my demeanor must have said it for me. I laughed, shrugged, offered more.

She opened up, gained speed and soon hit a ramble that led to sobbing and more ramble—it was long enough and choked up enough to give me a headache, and maybe that was good for my hormones, seeing her in the light of these faults, these...immaturities. It took no genius to figure the play, and though I resented myself for figuring, for analyzing, for strategizing the surest route to the sweet spot between her legs, I resented her at least as much. For starters, she was out for revenge. No man wants to play serviceman. Still I figured it would be justified this once, to break the ice, which was of course as much bullshit as any justification ever was. I wanted with all my heart to fuck her. So there. Honesty is the best policy, especially with yourself, especially if the end zone is painfully in focus, so near, yet so far—and I knew nothing could be taken for granted. I still had to get loose enough to let her follow through on her impulse. The first twenty minutes she little-girled me, cried like a child with a skinned knee and told the whole sad story.

Far worse, though, was my resentment at her timing. She'd been abused, disrespected, devalued and rejected only that afternoon. I've known for years how much time is spent by men in the most difficult phase of loss and solitude, and through the acute pain, they grow. And how many women I've known on the same rebound, who bounce back so much faster, because a woman seeking companionship, or at least a warm body with a stiff dick, requires simple volition; the get is a function of the want. And here was the woman I'd longed for, weak as a woman ever was, heading in with the first guy who came along in a bar. I would defer. Sorting and judgment could come later, once unbearable distractions were dispensed with. I listened.

Big surfer had chosen another, a beach bunny—"...with these big old floppy tits and a string bikini and you can see the dimples on her ass, I mean really..." The transfer of affection was made shamelessly, publicly, or at least that was Hattie's story for now. She felt wronged, put upon and foolish—and these bad feelings were made worse by the beach bunny's big ass, and I laughed; Hattie was as bad as I was. She sobbed and rambled. I listened, seeking the spirit of communion, friendship, contact.

I listened to her tale of woe, eye to eye with understanding. I required nothing; she was here, in the shelter of a friend, all on the surface, even when sympathy led to comfort, gentle embrace, you know, and me, heart pounding between her legs. I tried to be sensitive to her sorrow, but there between us was my joy. I think she understood. I think she understood more than I did, for who could so completely scratch the vindictive itch in so short a time as she was on the verge of doing? Then again maybe she was only a woman who needed confirmation after a solid rejection; maybe she was plain horny and had been for a long time. Maybe she liked me. I didn't consider that possibility for many months.

She relaxed with all of the above while I, in my understanding of the transitory nature of happiness, felt the curvature of the earth. From our hug of friendship and warmth

I moved across the sacrificial mound. She moved back. That was all.

She changed, went from soft and sensitive to deliberate, practiced, methodical. She shushed me, banned verbal drudgery as I'd hoped she would. Who needs that shit? It surfaces on its own soon enough, when the struggle begins, to keep the mystique intact. She stepped back, peeled off her shirt, dropped her shorts, shucked her panties with her foot.

She smiled sweet as a fairy godmother and pushed me to the bed. "Come on," she said. "Let's get this over with."

"You're using me for sex," I said.

"I didn't think you'd mind."

"Well, I do mind." She stopped. "I'll let it go this time, you know, so we can break the ice." She laughed, and there you go, and there I was, man on a stick, fucking the woman of my dreams as she stopped laughing and burst into tears. It ruined my rhythm, gave rise to the greatest doubt, underlined the truth of my essence. She cried. I humped, ransacking my brain for the fantasy hovering overhead for all the days and nights; this was not it. She nearly canceled my hormones, which would have led to me telling her that that sort of thing had never happened to me. I needed to snap her out of it—"You must not do this sort of thing very often."

Like magic—poof—tears be gone, she laughed again, raucous until she lost control, blew compression farts from the junction. She blushed and stopped laughing. I picked up the pace, but she lay there limp, so I sprinted, like the young guys.

She was relieved when it was done, springing up for a shirt from my closet that made me love her, seeing her looking so good in it. Then for another bottle of wine, she grabbed from the high end, without looking, giggling that she...just loved all this...stuff. We drank more slowly and talked after that, after getting rid of the thing between us.

"You know," I said, pausing after the empty phrase, setting up the delivery, like an old guy again, but now more comfortable with it. "I didn't think you liked me."

"I didn't," she said.

"What? You do now?"

"I don't know. Too soon to tell. Why don't you give it a chance?"

She stole my heart. Why didn't I give it a chance? So I sat there like a bump on a log drinking a merlot from the very high end, knowing that I could not yet make love with Hattie, but I could have sex with her anytime, or at least in the next little while. Well, I thought I could. I hoped I could. I mean, I knew I could, but I hoped she would let me. I mean, I knew she was moody, and though you would at least expect a woman who let you once to let you again, who could be certain? And confused again, I became a bump on a log with a log on the bump. I pulled a blanket over my need.

"Jesus," she said. "You're a fucking animal."

"No," I said. But that was all I said, because I was.

Getting Acquainted

She tolerated me, maybe because she had liked me. Maybe she was stalking quarry, too. My need surprised her, was a jolt to her youthful anticipation—who'd a thunk it, in such an old guy? She was willing to ignore it for the time. I tried ignoring it, too.

She conveyed sincere heartbreak over Big Surfer jilting her. Why do they do that, good women who could take the pick of the litter but lock onto the mangy mutts, like maybe a guy has to be a loser, no manners, no money, no heart, no photosynthesis, to be a good lay. I don't know what they think. I did know that Big Surfer was a certain dolt, a monkey wad, a stiff dick with a lump o'shit hooked on; like I said, a stand-in. I didn't profile him in detail for Hattie. I told her he was no loss, the guy was generic, a good fellow maybe, but easily replaceable, if that's what she wanted. I told her it was the rejection that hurt, not the loss. She asked how to ease the pain. I told her she'd just had the surefire cure.

She said sometimes I was an asshole.

I said, "Sometimes? How often could it be?" We'd been together three hours, or five, but she didn't get it. I told her that beyond the surefire cure, a girl needs to grow up, but I didn't say grow up. I said, "Maybe it's time for some personal development."

"I really love the way you talk sometimes," she said. She could turn on a dime like that, turn on you, turn to you.

"Sometimes? We never shared complete sentences before tonight."

She hung her head. "I know. I didn't realize you were so...funny."

"I guess I didn't realize it myself. That means you do like me."

She laughed. "See. Like that." Humor made affection easier. And affection made my need more natural. She was straightforward and honest from the start. She told me I wasn't invisible to the nubile women at the beach; that all the men who cruised the beach more than once were discussed, at least in passing, by her and her friends. I'd been discussed, not exactly as the old guy with the rentals on the hill over town, but as this guy with big eyes who drifts through once in awhile. That hurt, hearing what I looked like on camera, maybe because a horndog hates to have it show. She read me then, saw the blush. She said, "No. I mean your eyes are beautiful."

She cured self-consciousness in a flash, but then she cured my vanity too. I was discussed in passing, not in the realm of social potential. "Look," she said. "You're different than I would have guessed."

"If you'd thought about it at all?"

"I like it with you. It's different."

"You should see my four-minute version."

"And you're funny. But the girls I know..." She shrugged.

"You mean the young ones."

"Yeah. They don't want to... I mean the main thing is your hair." She smiled.

"You mean they're not attracted to a guy who's thin on top?"

She swung again, right cross. "Man, you're gone on top."

Maybe I was in denial on top. But reality is often easier with someone to accept it with you. "So how can you be attracted? And why tonight?"

She poured more wine. "Don't you think it's a mistake to question stuff like that?"

"Yes. You're right." She'd shushed me again, censoring my weakness, leaving me mute, no place to think to. I liked that.

Maybe she sensed I was a talker, compulsive, mental, and here I was trying something new, silence, because she suggested it. It was another gift. And in that silence, that time of sharing, she reached for the control, shifted once through the gears and up into overdrive for a long cruise down an open road, top down, wind in our hair, making good time again toward zero inhibition, toward what she called natural. She went for the moment, for the now here, for true love in its concurrent natures, eternal and ephemeral. She paused, came up to me and asked, "Do you think I'm too big?"

"No. Not at all," I murmured weakly. "I like a woman I can look up to." And she laughed again, I was such a kick in the ass, and she continued with what all men wanted her to do. She didn't mind.

Life changed then. I'd fantasized a romance, a kiss with this, the woman of my dreams. But the world's best blow job posthaste became detached, an eye-opener, an exercise in sexual control. She was big—five-ten, even if she called it five-seven and a half. She did me up like a dogie roper going for nine seconds flat and was up, towering over me, perky, ready for more talk. "There you go," she said. It shut me up but with discontent, left me like a starving third-worlder after a meal of whole milk and burgers; the exchange was indigestible, too much protein. I wanted more, more than the guys she knew could want. Spelling it out then would have scared her, would have scared me. Now the discontent lingers like a stain—I wanted immortality, even if only for a short time; I wanted twenty years returned to me, through her. I wanted hot, young sex all the time and a woman like Hattie to share those years with once again. Hey, her limitations were laughable and severe, unlike mine only in their nature; I too was paradigm for failure, but the calamity I felt approaching headlong was ultimate, was dust. In all her foolish, promiscuous, naive, ill-advised, tasteless, selfish ways, she could be my salvation.

She took me back, way back, not in time but in the tearing-down process that precedes growth. The fantasy was more than realized, and less. I was satisfied but still restless. I wanted a slow, savored love, forever. But she took the lead and taught me about these kids today. I was the student.

She was a trip, altered reality, and I suppose I wanted that too, just like all those years ago I wanted to drop acid, but then you get to ignition, lift-off, sub-orbital violence threatening delamination on your primary heat shield, and all you can do is grab the armrests and hold on, ride it out. She changed, melted, faded away and came back. From a distance she was perfectly sexual. Curvature, movement, the air about her suggested fervor. She had the stimulators that draw men near for rutting. Up close, sensuality faltered. Her feet were tough and big as a Samoan's who could walk to town with no shoes. Her hands matched, strong, masculine, rougher than mine. Facial features with hard lines—angular bones, strong chin, prominent jaw. She profiled rigid, unsoft. Too much sun had left a coarseness on her face, turned her hair white. Yet the magic rose again from her skin, warm and flawless with no tan lines and a femininity that was for me elixir. I took it in. She basked. Her hopeless attraction for me was simple: Youth. I loved her newness, her spirit, her life, her foolishness, her sense of discovery.

But it was more. Broad shoulders and a muscular back torqued and rippled when she turned. She propped her head on a hand and showed another angle. The mystique was neither breasts nor bush but rather the line, dipping, torso to hips, then arcing up, descending into thighs. The line transcended that which transcends sex. That is, it was nongenital but arousing. It was only a line, a form, and it drew me in. Above it, around it and in it all was her scent, so purely neutral it drew me closer still.

If I had sensed at this level, I couldn't remember when—I was strong defense for older guys; I loved her aesthetically. She knew it, and knew she'd never had it like this before. I looked, smelled, touched, tasted, slowly, as if savoring came in series and never had to end. I loved her past the sex, for no reason at all. Again I thought: Youth. What man wouldn't love the good old days?

She relaxed, fell into verbal mode, let her guard down and told me why she could relate to the wave surfers, really, really relate, and why the windsurfers, on the other hand, were nowhere. I reached for understanding, bolstered myself for nature's sometimes cruel truth, heard my perfect mountain crumble...

"I mean really, they are sooooo fucked."

Old Friends

But it was just like me to fault a child for being childish. Not that she was a child. She played at the beach at twenty-two for the same reason I drank good wine at forty-two, to get away to someplace better. Morning, noon, sundown, never mind—it's the access and the going that counted.

She wanted understanding—the beach was where she lived. It was her society. I listened. For an hour I listened, no interruptions, no nodding off, because I sensed she wanted a listener. She started slow, found her rhythm, and sensing a willing ear with more than half a wit next to it, she opened up.

"The guy I work for now won't pay me what I want," she said. "He gives me $35 a shift. I tell him I'm worth fifty, and he says go get it. I should. I really should. Do you know what he did? He had me driving all the way to the other side for a banquet setup. That's forty miles round trip. He gives me five bucks extra for gas. Then he has me drive all the way down there again next day for cleanup. He gives me another five bucks. So then when he gets a banquet down here I still charged him ten bucks extra for setup and cleanup. He says no no no no no. I'm not paying you that. He gave me five bucks less. He says he can't pay me more. He doesn't have any money because he's building a house for him and his wife."

"Don't you get tips?"

"From surfers? Right." She stared off.

"Why not work in a better place?"

"I like my job." She stared off. "He has the most beautiful lips, the sexiest lips in the world."

"Who?"

"The guy I work for. Sometimes when I'm around him it's very difficult. I'll be right in the middle of something and he'll look at me and I just can't stand it. Those lips. I imagine them between my legs and can't do anything. And it's all bullshit because it'll never happen. He's married and they're between his wife's legs. So all I get is fucked over."

"Sounds bitter." She smiled and sighed. I did, too—how quickly the characters in a dream can change, how poorly we profile in our minds what we want, because we think it's perfect. I veered again from surface truth, maybe reaching for something different, something higher. "What did you feel when I looked at you?" Dumb question—pop fly to second.

"Same thing you felt," she said. "You got your blow job." Easy catch and out. "This guy I'm talking to now about working at his place, he'll probably fuck me over, too. I don't know. All these worthless fuckers. All they'd have to do is read one lousy sex manual to know what to do. I can't believe it sometimes, what these guys' mommies didn't tell them. I get so frustrated squirming around, trying to guide them. One guy rolls over and says: Oh, do it yourself. Then he falls asleep. But not for long. I do it myself and tell him: Get out."

"You fuck this guy you work for?" I wanted to know so I could stroke my compulsion once more, so I could sort out the fuckers, so I could follow the story.

"No. Except for once." That obviously didn't count. "Then you got these guys who think eating pussy means sucking all the juice out of my vagina..."

"Ah! No good," I commiserated, wondering why she said these things. I took a long pull on the pricy sauce to dull the edge.

"I get this guy sucking all the juice out of my vagina and I'm thinking, Oh God. I don't even care anymore. It feels okay sometimes, and sometimes I like the guys so I just spread 'em and let them go in out. It's a favor. But they all think they're great. I fuck this one guy now, he says: I'm the kind of guy who likes to share pleasure with a woman. I'm the kind of guy who likes to let a woman get her pleasure first. He's got a beautiful body and he walks around naked all the time, like it's supposed to turn me on. It does. But then it all gets down to blow job, blow job, blow job. That doesn't. I've never, not once, ever, zero, been fucked right. I might as well charge for it. I doubt I'll get anything else out of it."

She took a break so we could both drink more wine. I worried we would run out before the beating ended. Wine eased the pain, or at least displaced it, and it camouflaged my wince, and it helped me keep quiet. Never ever once been fucked right, I wanted to ask, in all those hundreds of tries? But I was flattered, too, as confidant and confessor. And I'd had my blow job. She rambled on. I recalled dreams of feminine perfection.

"The worst of all was this last guy who practically moved in, a real heavy-hand. What a billy goat. You saw him. But I liked him. I don't know why. I finally got him to the point where he could get me going a little bit. Then one day we woke up and fucked and I left, but the job was canceled so I came back home and he was jacking off. That's the most perverted thing I've ever been through. Using my hand lotion. God, I let him have it.

"But once he let me know he liked jacking off it was like that was okay. He'd get cocaine—the guy never had any money, and he'd get cocaine—and he'd hang around the house all day snorting cocaine and jacking off. Five, six times a day—perverted!

"Then he swore he stopped but I busted him good. I came home...yesterday...and all the laundry was ready for the wash. He'd never done that before. I checked it out. Spruzzo in the dish towels! Shit!

"I kicked him out that minute. He wouldn't get it together to leave though. I told him he had to, but maybe he could come back around. I think I should work it out. But if he gets into my hand lotion or the dish towels again he's out. I told him. And I won't fuck him again. I swear I won't." She tilted the bottle straight up and swilled until bubbles glugged. A little while earlier I'd counseled personal development, encouraged her to view her former date as a lug. Holy shit, she was from another cosmos.

I finished the bottle—fuck it, we opened another. I'd died; this was purgatory—sheer anguish with a hot young woman and very good wine. The dream shattered. It looked laughable now, like what you might see through a lovely kaleidoscope that's been whacked against the wall a few times. Reality is difficult to imagine from a romantic distance. I'd met many women who let a man know quickly about divorces, children, unpleasant diseases, but never a no-holds-barred confession on sexual disappointment.

I was moved. So was the romance—smashed to smithereens. The bed beneath us felt like a bus terminal where her past continued on schedule, coming and going, all directions. I drank the wine.

"What about you?" she said. "What's on your mind? Where you been all my life? Ha ha. I love to talk with smart guys."

I drank the wine. "My past is different from yours."

"Yeah. You're like all guys. You just like to fuck."

"Yes. I'm easy to please. A little traditional squish and I'm a happy man."

"Jesus, it must be great."

"You were great."

She blushed. "You make me shy." That was a laugh.

"It's been different for me. Hustles mostly. They're urgent and important at the time. Then they either fall apart or else you make a few bucks, and they seem like the rest."

"I know just how you feel." She snuggled up with her primary hunger that was maybe what attracted girls like her to gone-on-top guys like me. I was wise old Teddy Bear who would tell her a story. "Tell me what you were doing twenty years ago, no, twenty-two years ago, when I was born." I appealed to her sense of history.

"I was in college. It was Vietnam time. I would have quit otherwise. It was smoking joints and plowing fields mostly."

"Plowing fields?"

"Fucking coeds. It was all fun. Everyone was stoned or tripping, free sex wasn't new, but it was freer than ever before. It was an act of rebellion. We rebelled against everything. It was great for the guys. All we had to do was be there and the girls would fuck us."

"Yeah, we still do that." She laughed a faraway laugh. "Gee, you could have plowed my field if I was around then."

"I just did plow your field. And I got my blow job, too. Didn't I?"

She moped. "That was different."

"It was?"

She hid her face. "You embarrass me."

"How was it different?" She wouldn't budge. "I'm trying to see you on equal footing, but it's not easy. I mean, you sound like you've had more sex. And I've taken twenty years more to get here."

She thought it over. "Equal footing. I love that. The guys I know only talk about goofy footing."

"I've taken twenty years more to get here."

"I fucked a lot of guys. But I only fucked most of them once or twice. You were married. You fuck every day when you're married. I go sometimes a week, sometimes three weeks, without fucking."

"You go longer than that without fucking when you're married, especially when it's winding down. How did you know I was married?"

"I can tell."

"No, you can't. All you can tell is I talk in sentences. And I wash my clothes before I dry them."

"You're not crazy."

"No?"

"Guys I hang around got nothing to lose. They drop into fifteen-footers and stuff. You're not like that. That's all I meant."

"I think you're a fifteen-footer. And you hang around a big crowd of guys. That's all I meant."

She shrugged. “I try them out. Besides, I’m old for my age. Don’t you think so?”

We drank the wine. We cuddled. We slept. She stirred in the night, snuggling in. I moved with the movement and felt it deep. “Boy,” she whispered. “We came a long way in a short time.”

Letting Go

A man's life is two parts, coming and going. The time between the two is sometimes called crisis.

In media-based cultures, the man most often trades his sensible sedan for an expensive roadster. I did that. I went faster, like time. And something still loomed, up ahead, with troublesome certainty. I could face it, or I could wait.

Brahmin men leave family and comfort and go on the road with a beggar's bowl. The road becomes the place where they live, meet the world, give and receive. And what the hell good is life if you can't follow a poetic notion from time to time?

Clarity is a gift; easy-to-read signs said time is now. Bare-assed Hattie bending over, showing the way to Kingdom Come, could lead any man astray. She was the Promised Land, the End of the Rainbow. Yet her steady denial of my existence and the ridiculous dreams of perfection that followed, and at my age, were another clear memo from the Scheme of Things. You are not here, it said.

Clarity became enhanced. I planned a trip, bought a globe with a light inside and spun it slow in the dark, scanning the world for where I would go to become nobody, for sustenance, for the soul, for giving. I passed over Paris and came back to it because I remembered a man in the Metro with no legs whose horn fugue played down the years. I would find him. It was a notion so poetic and unrealistic it drew a laugh, then a sigh and a longing, back again to what you didn't know you had until it was gone. I was drunk in the Metro, lost and late again when serendipity led me to a scene so common there and then that hundreds of people flowed by without looking twice.

But what could they compare it to? A street bum with no legs on a filthy rug with a primitive horn, a corporeal focus out and up, where the notes flowed and drifted in a perfect order, clean, concise, rich beyond market value. The scene stopped me in my tracks then, and again and again over the years, a still life in truth, a reflection of value, a component of the soul; the scene became part of who I'd become. It was set in an apparently Godless world, yet God resided in the fingertips of the legless beggar. That was something, and just as I'd wondered from time to time whatever happened to her, or her, or her, wondered where she is now or what she's doing, so too I fancied a return to a moment, a chosen bottle, a warm buzz, an oblivious crowd, some magical notes and me, en passant, gleaning contact from the very stale, dead air.

With enough kneading, a memory can rise to tangible proportions, as if an event was a place you could go back to. And that was the place I chose, gained animation for, perceived as real and approachable, available and appealing for a man of mobility in middle age.

I set a date—a deadline. All before the line is alive. Once the line is crossed, then all before the line is gone, dead. Daily life became relaxed and calm, which was good; I settled my affairs, like a man who will end his life according to a schedule, a plan, not to die, but for rebirth to a world of wonder. Then something happened, before the line, a gift of sorts, the kind that comes to those who succeed in letting go. She came to me. The line got moved.

She was a novelty, an entertainment, an adventure—another event so frequently longed for but practically remote. She was warm, instinctive, instructive and so fresh. She became a habit, then an addiction. She was game, anytime, anywhere, anything. And though she never came on to my money, she loved the special kind of fun money can buy. She tired easily of expensive restaurants, but was pleased to get it out of her system. She was indifferent to expensive hotels, except for room service. She said they must have room service in Heaven. She invited bellhops to stay for a drink. Anything she asked for I allowed, because she did the same thing. I told her I wasn't rich. She said I had more than enough for her. Then she asked if I thought she was greedy. I said no, only hungry, and besides, immersion often precedes reconciliation. "God," she said. "I love the way you talk." And we moved ahead with further immersion.

Sexual relations were exquisitely enhanced by early recollections. A man past forty may be more capable of perceiving beauty, may have his values more aligned with truth, may not be, for better or worse, at peak sexual readiness all the time, like he was, say, at twenty. That is, I could see her naked and see something other than naked Hattie. I knew enough to realize genuine affection, feeling from the heart; I acquired the habit that becomes a bond that begins in time to become the purest kind of love, which is love of her company, her self, which is more akin to parental or sibling love and may in fact be the kind of love that dooms a romance after so many years.

But I could as well recall her bending over at the beach, parrying my hungry stare with a death look back at me. I could recall her rejection, her sudden spin and exit—the days, weeks and months, and the nights of lovesickness, and my passion would heighten. Maybe it was the conquering male inside me. So what. A few still shots from square one while we went at it, and the little piston that could would find new life, new fervor, higher r.p.m. Her death look had told me the score—she knew about one more hustle, another piece of ass. Now her eyes shone between sparkle and madness in the thrill of upset victory. Another stud got fucked, and he was me, I thought but never said, because that language was for guys getting laid, really laid, and we'd reached the high plateau, making love—the summit at which I should have dispensed with stills from square one. I didn't and didn't resist the pleasure of having such elusive game front and center. Those thoughts aroused me, led to fervor and acceleration.

She liked the change of pace, I thought, uncertain after her lecture on women faking pleasure. She believed most women most often did, for social acceptance, or domestic peace, or something. Her lectures became oppressive with lines like, "I've fucked a lot of worthless assholes lately. Maybe I'm getting old."

"Do you like the way I talk?" I asked. She gave me her stupid-you look; she often said she did, so I needn't dig for compliments. "I'm sensitive to that," I said. She understood.

"I'm very fond of you. That imagery is unsettling."

She laughed. "Imagery. Very fond of you."

"Fucking assholes."

It was a strange, oblique communion, the best contact between generations, and it was continual, because we enjoyed it, like players of equal skill enjoying a volley, enjoying it more because it was mixed with sexual innuendo, sexual contact. We brought each other up, brought each other along to the way of the other, we thought. We helped each other let go of what each thought was junk in the other.

We had fun. Cruising one day without speaking, I had a feeling; she was a good person, honest and loving and without guile; her sexual past was not devious but innocent. The feeling was guilt, and I didn't know why. And then I knew why. "Hattie?" She looked over and waited. "If you had a sexual fantasy, would you feel comfortable sharing it with me?"

She blushed. "Maybe."

"Can I share one with you?"

"Maybe."

I unzipped and wiggled my pants to my knees, which makes driving difficult, and can kill you if you need to clutch or brake in a hurry. My dingdong bonged the steering wheel. "I fantasize a blow job, you know, going down the road. Beach Road, you know, where we first...kind of met."

She shrugged. "Easy." And down she went.

Near the apex, breathing hard, I said, "If we...ever...break up, I want you...to tell...your new boyfriend...about this." Clever me.

She stopped and sat up. "Break up? Are we going together?"

"Can we decide in a few minutes?"

She got her faraway look and said, "God. My old boyfriend, what he made me do. He was so weird." She'd made her point. She watched me drive down the road with my dick thudding the steering wheel. "Boy. You know you really look funny. I wish we had the camera. That would be great, wouldn't it?" She rummaged the glove box.

"I don't think it's in the car," I said.

"Oh well." She watched the scenery, teaching me new meanings of humility and stress, and foolishness. She had eased my guilt on her own terms, iced me down with fantasy delivered.

She helped me quit the old school. I sought to return the favor. Farther down the road I told her: "I'm leaving." She looked at me with no reaction then turned away again, out the window.

"Forever?"

"No. For awhile."

She turned back. "Why?"

"It's a personal thing. A trip I have to take."

"If it's personal then you can tell me."

"It's... I have to get away."

"Away from me? You don't need to leave."

"Not away from you." She verged suddenly on tears. I was gratified, old school. "I have to go to Paris."

She lit up, bright-eyed and happy again. "Take me!" It was another still I would save, of her perfect youth and beauty, all her want aimed at me. It was restaurants, hotels, room service all in one, a trip to Paris.

But it was more—"C'est plus, plus beaucoup," she said. She'd lived in France for two years, seventeen to nineteen.

She'd had her heart absolutely crushed in France by the most beautiful Arab boy you could possibly imagine, who for some reason after they fucked the first time couldn't get it up ever again, she never knew why, but she had to go back, just had to. My turn to stare, as if staring would allow these new images to dissipate, as if looking hard enough I could see that yes, she too, was an old soul, world worn but world wise, understanding what events of the past were imbued with magic and worth seeking again. I stared, speechless, wondering if the imagery of her past would ever change for me, ever move apart from men, from unnatural practices, from no hard-ons or too many hard-ons, hard-ons too numerous and too tumultuous for one little beautiful girl to absorb. Oh she was old all right, at least as old as me.

And she was fluent. She dreamed of the place, oh, please.

A Fork in the Road

A departed soul can haunt a place or move on; attach itself or accept the line—no return. Home is now here.

She could have her way with me. She had sexual power and knew it. She was magic, youth and beauty, with a dash of intrigue that kept me guessing. She was a homecoming to the long lost.

I had a similar power, money. I was security, no more toil, death to tedium, gone the bullshit jobs, vanished the bullshit people who ran them. I was creature comfort. She was naturally attracted. Old guys have that advantage.

Yet our two wills interfaced like oil and water, or like sex and money. We loved each other. We gave, each to the other and enjoyed the giving, to a point.

Planning the trip was a first test. I wanted carry-on. This trip was no lark but was rather a quest, a voyage, a test in free spirit, in weightlessness. I would hitchhike to the airport one morning and go, peacefully, without notice or pain, the way a happy man should go.

It was different prospects for her. She studied maps, recalled adventures, planned itineraries and places we had to see. The pilgrimage became a vacation adventure, not what the doctor ordered. Cutting lead time to a month, and then cutting two weeks off that and another three days off that—we leave in five days—cured the problem significantly. Still the problem arose, like storm clouds on the horizon.

It rose again with luggage. Youthful and free-spirited, she got down to bare bones travel at ground level—a duffel bag at seventy pounds and another thirty in an overnight case. It saddened her, traveling so bereft of extra shoes, dresses, pants and slacks for various occasions, fluctuating moods. "God, I got to admit it's good hanging out with someone who understands how important this stuff is to a woman." She had me, and I loved it when she called herself a woman. I carried the overnight case, until it wouldn't fit the little rack at security—baggage-check was a half mile back. Baggage claim would be another hour on arrival.

We didn't discuss it, so potent was the airport mood, the stifling swelter, the stale air, the asses and elbows of the place. I was pissed. She was imposing on my life. She was pissed and further pissed that I got pissed so easy. "Put your mind somewhere else," she said.

"Ha."

"Look, I'll give you a blow job in the bathroom, okay?"

She wasn't kidding, so nobody laughed. She set us up for the hard truth—I took the bait, since some risky fun would get the trip rolling. "You're on."

She said nothing, slid into the cattle-car body-crush of the friendly skies, fell asleep for three hours and woke up in pain, announcing to sixty passengers in a ten-foot radius, "Shit.

Great time for a period. Excuse me." They say you don't know a person until you travel together. She slid heavily past me and asked, "Are you coming?"

Arrival was equally difficult. Jet lag and baggage claim were compounded by culture shock, trail fatigue and a taxi line at Orly maybe four blocks long. The French crowd pushed and shoved like grocery hoarders before a storm. It was that old fuck you, far from home. I let go of assessment and difficulty. I surrounded us with being, in my mind, as we shuffled along in line in tiny steps, close formation. She surrounded us with elbowroom, swung around and yelled, "Jesus Christ, just back the fuck off!" Even the French understood. Again she wasn't kidding.

The hotel was refuge, but it was small and cramped, eked out in centimeters, its essence striving for parsimony. We called it Bleak House and shared a single chuckle, bleakly. It offered shelter and nothing but, the single window overlooking a noisy, hot street that wafted black spume up and in—car exhaust, the rich, visible kind, with lead, because the French want to go, and now, as fast and cheap as the meager franc can take them. It felt on first flush like a city of lust, a city of survival, one grub to the next, a city without reflection, far removed on the surface from what the hometown crowd calls Le Grandeur that is Paris.

We slept all day. I went for French groceries—baguettes, cheese, nectarines and horse meat—in the room I said I thought it was cold cuts. She said it was cold cuts. It used to neigh. We drank a bottle of red table wine and two bottles of water and slept all night.

Dawn was foreign, like a tiny splinter, but priming up on a coffee jag, the spirit returned. That much raw caffeine calls for movement, and we moved another day or two, but without direction.

Sexual contact was her initiative, but it too was without purpose, more as a palliative than a passion. Sure it was her period. She was doing the right thing. I responded in kind, physically, like taking out the trash.

We waited like anxious family for word to come that the patient would survive. We waited, we coffee jagged, we drank wine and smoked cigarettes, trying to arrive.

The cafe sitters sit, and we sit, too, with the sitters in the cafes, thinking: I am. Ain't I? I think I am. I think I can't move, stuck on this carousel for the wax museum.

At least that's what I thought. I thought she approached the Swing of Things, the delusion in that little burg that the enviable place to be was there, sitting in rickety chairs, elbows on rickety tables, smoking the tits off charcoal cigarettes, drinking blackjack coffee at three bucks a half cup and gazing off, with a brain on overdrive toward real meaning. I have sat, have emptied the vessel and joined its contents for hours, felt life ease away and let it go, felt it come back, just like true love is supposed to do.

I've traveled a path of no thinking, no reaction, no process, neither baggage nor burden of material life. I've shed to the point of nothing, which goes away as easy as it is attained, and so I've shed and shed again and stayed focused on relaxation and letting go and so stayed on the path to Nowhere. From there it's anybody's guess where the road may lead; I prefer movement with the planets, spinning fast but slow, floating free.

But this cafe stuff, with the heavy caffeine and nicotine choke and overwhelming preponderance of pondering, this sub-orbital debris with eyes blazing on the verge of rational... conclusion... Well, it ain't the same.

I tried but couldn't get it. Maybe I was compelled to fit in, to please her and have as much fun as she apparently thought was fun there to have. So I tried again and couldn't get it, and I didn't know why not, but of course I knew.

It wasn't working. She never asked, What's wrong? Or, What do you want to do? I was grateful for that. Patience was her virtue. She could wait, no need to press, until she couldn't wait and got down to the work at hand, things to do, sights to see. I went along because the splinter hurt and itched but was too tiny to reach. She got tickets for a show—Ray Charles—which was more than a dose of fun, it was a great gesture, considering the cost and the paltry funds she'd brought along.

We had wine and light fare in a cafe, and took the Metro to the concert hall. We had good seats, but alas, one seat over was a thinker, high cafe. We'd seen this guy—he sat the Bastille circuit, two p.m. to closing. Six days a week, sometimes fourteen hours a day, with a rare night off for a concert, he'd sit there thinking, rolling his eyes, arching and knitting his beady brow, nodding, tilting his head one way and the other, working it out, alighting now and then on frail twigs of resolution, briefly, before flitting off again in cerebral gyration. He'd fresh-shaved his head for the concert and added a handful of earrings on either side, and he wore a puffy silk blouse, no collar, buttoned to the neck like a high-fashion ascetic, or Zippy the Pinhead. A beautifully painted woman with great big tits that were lifted, spread and served on a platter was all over the guy, stroking his pinhead, his chest, his thighs.

Ray Charles came on, much older and slower than on his album covers, and began with a few standards. Zippy hunched down with intensity and rocked his body and soon hyperventilated with the rhythm and soon was gasping and flopping around like a man possessed, like a real thinker having an experience—he had the feeling. The music was inside him. Kee-riste, I don't know why but I couldn't stop gawking the guy. Maybe that's what he wanted, but I didn't want it, he was just such an unbelievable pain in the ass. I reconnoitered some empty seats a few rows back and down a way. I said I wanted to move. She didn't look up but aped the shaved head's intensity. I moved. She came around a few songs later.

"Isn't he something?" she said.

"Yes, he is."

Later that night was romantic as an empty cup, a full ashtray. At least I had my poke to look forward to, just like I looked forward to the feel of cool sheets and a nice snooze. Wrong again; asleep already is what I was. But I woke up with her denial. She put me off, woke me up, surrounded us with sadness. She turned off the light and lay back. "We have to stop sex. I love you too much. Something's wrong. I know."

She had balls, cutting off her meal ticket like that. Maybe that was the draw. I inhaled deep as if to speak, and over the hump I started to ask, "For how long?" It was the Philistine response; I caught it in time.

Instead she got the great long sigh of a cafe sitter considering life. Maybe she liked it. I said, "All right." She rolled away and soon softly snored. Women can do that.

She woke up early, refreshed and resolute. She made a phone call and talked twenty minutes, laughing, recalling. She hung up and sighed; we would part company, air out, give ourselves some space, some breathing room, to see if that helps, maybe, for a few days.

Deadline

They say you know a language once you dream in it. It's not true. I dreamt in French all night and didn't understand. A few syllables lit up: *jamais, comprend pas*, and so on. But the context was lost. I woke up cold, muddling through imagery for meaning, reaching in the fog. Clarity had come and gone, like it and happiness do from time to time. But then again these wants and suppositions are analytical, intellectual, introspective and rational, which exercises are common to the high cafe, where I sat, where my path this day led and ended.

It was only a day but felt so long ago that she left. We'll meet up again, later, we agreed.

"But here's your ticket, in case...," I said.

"Yes. My ticket," she said.

I think the foggy French dreams came from confusion, and from the endless French chatter all around me, from the strange place I slept, from this sad cafe I came to first thing in the morning for a strong black coffee and a smoke.

It was dark, old, dirty beyond funk, way into crummy,

long used up, with the same vibration as a junkyard sifted by generations of gleaners, losers and thinkers. Nothing survived but the absolutely unusable, the grossly inapplicable, the scum, shit and dregs; ashes to ashes in flesh and blood; rusty, rotting scraps so far gone that the rats looked bored.

Decomposition ruled, once over lightly with grit and smoke. From the ashes new life can arise, but not here. Here the ash persisted, the people burrowed in, wallowed and sifted again for something organic. Imagination gone, they fed on each other. I think they liked it. I think they persist this very minute.

But then maybe not. Out front, between the debris and the street, on a green bench sat three old men, seventy something, talking German, maybe recalling those few years the world would never forget, the few years of power and meaning in their lives. Now they watched the world pass by bumper-to-bumper. They breathed cigarettes and exhaust. Their heads wagged like monkeys in collective denial, but I knew their heels itched for a crisp click, their haunches ached for a sure spring to stiff attention: *Achtung!* I couldn't help it—you don't get an entire nation following a Hitler without one or two people knowing the score.

But these old Nazi farts were like Europe; they were history, gone, buried under cars and traffic. I think the bicyclists must die young from injury or lung disease, and the only motorcyclists you see race for the highway at 200 KPH for a thrill still reachable, and death will be quick. Soot will rule here until the world runs out of gas. People will die younger and with less to show for it each year until they learn to use rubbers, or take pills, or anything at all. The old Germans sat, recalling a past and greater madness, surrounded by cars—two rows of parked cars between their bench and the drab cafe, two more rows of cars between their bench and the street, where two lanes of cars sped past in both directions, and beyond that four more rows of cars parked on the far sidewalk. Cars and exhaust fumes have taken over here like the Germans once did, invaded against mild resistance. Maybe one day, old wrecked cars will sit where the green bench sat now, sprouting rust and weeds, recalling glory and world domination.

Colette worked like corrosion on my thoughts, classic example of a world gone sour, of joie de vivre stigmatized by need, grown rotten from the inside out, like bad cells. Colette was skeletal and looked old at barely fifty—eye holes and jaws worked a jagged line under the paltry skin of her face. Her cigarette jutting from her jutting teeth that grinned prominently made her look like a skull enjoying a smoke. Her oblong, drooping bosom was last vestige of Parisian youth. She displayed it, working her last attraction for men. Her bookshelf was lined with little paintings, childish doodles, oil on canvas. The bookshelf was designed for paperbacks, so it was the perfect size for her small exercises in finger shmush. They recalled childhood, just after infancy, when form and color are met head-on, on a big cheesecloth on the floor, where I and my little pals got big blank sheets of sturdy paper. We got as many colors as we wanted, by the dollop, which was a first lesson in simplicity. The greedy kids wanted six or eight different colors and dove in, smearing quickly up to the elbows in purplish brown. The more clever, more constrained kids took only two or three colors and worked fingers only, no palms.

I'll give Colette this; in nearly all her paintings she avoided the purple mud. In over half she'd kept her thumbs out, and in a few arose distinct forms; people, houses, flowers. The one by the door suggested a self-portrait—a supine woman with a big, pendulous breast and detailed nipple and no head, under a sun with rays, all in purplish pink. She could have called it Womansong, or The Goddess Within, or The Headless Shrew with One Big Tit, or something bright and creative and topical like that. She was commercialized, hokey and past tense, like Paris.

But she came my way, easily, from her apartment in the back of the courtyard, like the sign on the street said. *Appartement à louer.* The street was Rue du Faubourg St. Antoine, built a few centuries ago for horse carts and small people, now jammed like a box canyon in an avalanche of humans, cars, refuse from posterity and the recent past. Grit, cheap shit, junk, frogs and third-worlders logjam this diminutive gap in the labyrinth, and turning off in any direction at any time leads to more of the same, which can turn any time, any way, for more and more, and outward it spreads.

Maybe the best thing about hitting the road in idyllic pursuit is the thrust back to street-level practicality. I could have called the place filthy, ugly, gone and unfit for habitation in a wink. But I needed a place to stay, and though the sign looked as dirty as the street, like tenancy turned over quickly, and the doors looked unwashed since the Jacobins staggered through drooling drunk and bloodstained from a wonderful afternoon of beheading, and the atmosphere matched the dirt, and the dirty feeling was more than ambient, it was pervasive, down to the lungs, I walked in, walked through the tunnel that felt like purgatory back to the open courtyard surrounded by four floors of apartments with open sky in the middle and windows festooned with dirty laundry, empty, pots and ugly, sad, distrustful faces standing back in shadow watching, watching. But hey, it wasn't nearly as shitty in the courtyard.

Among the bent necks perched high in the windows was Colette's; she swooped, came up behind me quick and quiet, her feeding instinct blended with formality—"Are you wanting for a place?" I smiled. She led me up, as if on cue.

Hattie was gone. Sitting was difficult, walking it off was much better. She'd messed up my rhythm, but isn't that rhythm's true test? I'd anticipated a pilgrimage, then allowed it to become a love fest. I'd failed to adjust, but you can't avoid adjustment, you can only postpone it. So I walked the streets, long strides, arriving at last at my objective, unthinking movement, left, right, left, right, with an eye on what to give, what to take. I sought refuge, if not solace.

"I wrote for years," Colette said in the first ten minutes. "I was very good. But now I think I'm better at painting. I love to paint. I can feel paint. I take classes now twice a week and I go every summer for two months to the island to paint. It's important you know that a painter mostly paints, that she keep a schedule and that she doesn't deviate or allow interruption..."

I listened to her like I listened to Muzac in an elevator, looking out the window, sorting other thoughts. Stop sex. I love you too much. Something wrong. She was gone—quick as a phone call and confirmation that yes, they would take her in, these...people. She'd known them before, in the south, near Arles. It was best.

Colette's drone found emphasis. "Any interruption at all." She focused the point on me; unspoken was another confirmation: yes, I could have her little apartment up front, and this is art, the be-all of life itself, don't you see, an essence that must continue undisturbed. That is, the rent money is a commitment, a promise you will make that cannot be broken, ever, for any reason. It's already spent, on the island, on painting. She eased off and turned her body toward her little row of swirls and smurfs, possibly so I could comment on their beauty, their spirit, their art. It was an opening, an opportunity for a big step forward toward my goal of giving, so I gave: The Truth.

"Can I read something?" I asked. She looked puzzled. "Something you wrote."

"Ah!..." she shrugged it off. "I never really wrote anything. Not finished, you know, like a...a..."

"Like a story?"

"Yes. Like a story." I nodded and spoke French, the nonverbal expression that means something like, What are you going to do? Or, It's obviously bullshit. You jut the chin out and down, shrug the shoulders and pump air up inside the upper lip until it flaps. She covered quickly—"I would write, for example, about a waiter, how he might move, or serve, or maybe something unusual he might say."

"You mean you would observe and record?"

"Yes."

"And you had this feeling that was clear and certain, that meaning and, maybe, a dramatic point was implicit in these...little sketches?"

"Yes."

"But you never made a story I could read, with a beginning, a middle and an end?"

"No."

"Ah. Too bad." Touché. I was smug—clean kill. The cafes were chuck full of writers.

Colette smiled a sourpuss smile and took over again. "I'm leaving Tuesday for the island. I've been planning it for months." She bent to an unnecessary task, unstacking the paintings that leaned against the wall, more of the same, silly doodles, lining them up for display.

"We can have a look then," I said.

She stepped back proud, and I got her again. I observed her, not her paintings, and I waited; I meant the apartment, not her paintings. She smiled yet another smile from her repertoire—sourpuss sanguine. She described the little apartment up front and the sacrifice, yes, required for its purchase and then its complete restoration to the quaint garret it was—this, down the steps and across the courtyard to the stacked flats fronting the street.

She was full of shit and hostile, on the make for dollars, jugular-minded. But then I was full of shit and stuck too, so I'd lost the best date I'd had in years. I wanted solitude and calm, understanding and tolerance. I said, "It feels very nice here." She looked at me sideways, defensively, ready for another jab, like I was full of shit and nuts.

The steep, narrow stairs were dark and cool, maybe ten degrees cooler than the swelter outside, Paris in July. "You see," she said. "It's much cooler here. Much, much cooler."

By the seventh landing it was dark and hotter. Much, much hotter. We gasped, in a sweat. The apartment was a studio, meaning small box, ten-by-twelve with a small front window, closed, locked, shuttered and curtained, oxygen count: 0, conditions closing in, like just before emergency free ascent. But then, where was anyone to go?

The spring-loaded shade had no spring. Limp and lifeless, unable to fulfill itself, is how it looked. It felt worse—I pulled down and released. It twitched a weak inch. I tried again, and then again, apparently savoring its failure, until Colette said, "It used to work." She brushed me aside. Sweat streamed down both of us; our breathing was audible. "It's cooler with the shade down," she said.

I brushed her aside, pulled the shade again and rolled it up by hand. "You want me to live here," I said. I opened the windows, big awkward casements that required a three-foot radius. I unlatched and opened the shutters.

A hot, smoky, sooty wheeze engulfed us and the tiny room. Rush-hour traffic honked and choked and coughed and sputtered and honked some more through the window as if through a floodgate. It blasted in and swirled thick, black and noisy as a woolly rat, trapped, seeking refuge from the bigger rat, outside.

"Come," she said. "This is your table." It was old, rickety, two-by-two. I felt like a new dog being shown his dish.

With two steps to the rear she continued the tour. "This is your kitchen." It was three-by-three, though a third of it was a shallow steel sink with a cold-water spigot and a one-burner hot plate. Colette went rhapsodic on the rigors, the trials of refurbishment and remodeling, and oh, the terrible, terrible expense—but even with costs so high she'd planned two burners instead of just one, after all, but then, you see, there was no room for two. "It was impossible. Impossible. But, you see, it is tiled!" She twitched her nose and grinned, and caressed the tiles, all four of them.

"I've seen bigger galleys," I said.

"What is galleys?" But I was into the closet with the munchkin door. It housed a toilet, 20 inches square, no shit. The seat, down, held the door ajar. I sat down for a test drive, uninhibited as a Frenchman, knees in the kitchen, dukey chute and shoulders compressed. I couldn't shit here, too tight, and I looked around. I figured the only good shit in the little WC could be urgent diarrhea with enough pressure and torque inside to override the rim squeeze and shoulder hunch outside. But then if it was thin and watery the bedpan she called a kitchen sink might be more comfortable. She read me like a tasteless book and moved to the shower, which was obviously designed by the same architect.

I didn't squeeze into it but only surveyed the tiny dark dungeon that was the bathroom. Unwilling to dwell on the thoughts these fine furnishings brought to mind, Colette turned her back to me, unbuttoned her blouse, removed her brassiere and gasped, "Oh! It is so hot!" She rebuttoned halfway and turned back to me, pumping her blouse like a bellows, rolling her head and eyes back so I could gaze on her fine big tits without feeling self-conscious and maybe forget the penitentiary conditions she called quaint.

It was her little French suggestion, an easy close. It was another finger painting, another need. She would measure her power by my response. I looked, and I tried on her French expression for futility, the smile of the wise old sourpuss who'd rounded that block before. Then I turned away. Great round tits they'd been, with nearly black nipples three inches across that a man should want to suck on and feel them shrink and go pointy right on the tip of his tongue. Greatness was down to vestige, hanging like a memorial in a sad cafe, alone and forlorn, surrounded by fatigue, by more need and sorrowful truth. Maybe she was used to gallantry, or maybe French hormones are more outrageous than my own. It didn't matter either way. I turned away. The bait was rough, too rough, and muddy as a bog. I could tell. I turned away, hoping in my heart that she would learn about aging gracefully.

The little room was hot, smoky, confining and foreign, way past the deadline, and it had come my way. I imagined Hattie watching the French countryside roll past on the train heading south, harking back to the most beautiful Arab boy and her heart, absolutely crushed. I saw a small vent window near the ceiling in the kitchen and reached for its latch. Colette said don't open that, but it was only her natural French aversion to new air. Opened, it sucked the choking heat out, pulling fresh street heat through the front window.

I walked to the front window, around the mattress by the table. I looked out, closed my eyes, emptied the vessel and focused on its contents. *I didn't even know her. How could I? She was so young, way too young. And now she was south, where she'd once lost her heart and maybe she would again, or maybe she'd find it.* Colette stepped up behind me. "It's only three thousand," she said—about five hundred dollars a month. "And I'm putting in a little refrigerator. So you can cook!" I must have nodded—*Hattie was open to adventure, much more than I was, wanting the world in a daily, tangible, living sense. And maybe I was old and maybe stuck, unable to move.*

Colette said, "Good. Well. I'm just on my way for something to eat. You know we have many excellent restaurants in this area. Many excellent restaurants. I can tell you them. Would you like to go?" *It was so much easier for her now though, out in the country, where in fact I should be. But isn't resolution an internal process?* I thought, *yes it is*. I thought, *fuck all this thinking internal process resolution bullshit.*

"Yes," I said. "I'm hungry."

Resolution in Movement

Colette became my friend. The palpable difficulty between us—her bullshit, my bad mood—fell away like an outgrown shell once we settled the deal. For her it was the certain income, let's call it three months for now. She lit up—fifteen hundred dollars paved her way for twice the time on the island, twice as many paintings. She knew her little hovel up front could hardly arouse excitement. She knew straight away that I had cash, was perhaps rich, like so many Americans. She profiled me quick, which is what a has-been on the make gets good at doing, and with an eye on potential—I was a mobile, intelligent, sensitive man with dollars left in his pocket, dollars she could better spend on the island, on art—she sought to buff me out, give me that extra gram of attention and special care, first to secure the deal, then to extend it.

She eased me into my adventure with that light, delicate touch, that vibrant spirit only the French have phrases for; so we strolled down an alley lined with cafes and tiny restaurants, alcoves of music and movement; it was an alley with panache, alive and spirited, and Colette and I walked to a soulful little restaurant where people still practically ate their cigarettes, but élan was there, too, in a light, open atmosphere with linen and crystal. I felt good there, justified in my taste for creature comfort. I liked Colette ordering in French, and I liked the wine she chose. I liked taking two hours over lunch, and I liked at long last talking about books we both knew and overlapping ideas. I liked some of her ideas and insights and felt warmly humbled in my thoroughly different point of view from just a few hours earlier. I liked what I felt with her, which was an understanding that I would neither suck nor feel her tits, because it was best that I didn't, although she left her brassiere off and insisted on hollowing the vortex of her blouse, showing her formerly-splendid tits every little while in her natural, innocent French way. They were, after all, only normal, her tits. And why shouldn't an old girl let her hair down?

And I felt nothing at all about picking up the tab for lunch, since she made no move for it, and she seemed to want that bit of femininity, if I'd allow it. She leaned forward and scrunched her shoulders when the check came and said that I must come up for dinner, tonight, I must. Geoffrey was cooking, and even though he was simply worthless at fixing things around the apartment, he'd become in his way a marvelous cook. A few women they knew were coming too, so I could help balance things out and maybe make some new friends. Lunch and wine were only sixty bucks, and there I was, far away with new, faraway friends. Hattie was south by now, visiting her old friends.

She was gone but it wasn't so bad, now, with a surprisingly good wine, excellent baguettes, extraordinary pâté and a civilized smoked herring under my belt.

Sure I was weak for creature comfort, but here I was, at last, with a first step on my journey. Back in my hovel I could more easily imagine the feel of it improving, with time, with my presence, with calmness. Time would come soon enough for paring down to the bone. For now, easy transition had come my way, and prospects of a dinner party in Paris danced like sugarplum fairies in my head. "A few women we know" took shape too, swirling happily overhead in faint exhaust, their French babble drifting through the window as a well-earned nap came on. I had time for it, time to let the day go, rise again at seven or so and dress for dinner at nine.

A deep sleep transcended smoke and traffic, transformed my lumpy mattress. Dreamless sleep often means repression, a troubled mind, postponement of the sorting process, but the sleep was deep. It ended with the bang of a big bass drum.

I didn't mind. Waking up was sudden, loud and rude, but that was okay, too, over the line. A parade approached. Hordes in the street turned the corner and marched this way—boisterous, noisy people with banners and hats and signs. Most wore T-shirts that said *Stand Up and Shout*, or *Stop SIDA*, or *London Boy*, or *Paris Boy*.

SIDA is French for AIDS. It was a demonstration. Six or eight females marched along with the hundreds of males, who either pranced and skipped and waved pennants and hollered mottoes, or held hands or thrust hands down each others' pants. Or they marched singly, sincerely.

Some embraced. Some kissed, wide-mouthed, tongues groping, in another demonstration, to get us used to that sort of thing. I thought of us and them, but they saw no such separation. Some watched me in my window.

Their jubilation was that of heroes come home, their relief as boisterous as ticker tape following armistice. Open and proud as any conquering army, they marched tall, stood firm, and it looked like considerable cock sucking would immediately follow the parade. It looked like a really fun day of political resolve, victory, glory, heroism, happiness up the ass.

I pulled my shutters and dressed for dinner. The parade outside was a noisemaker, easily forgettable, and I should have forgot it, but I didn't, maybe because it was so demanding—the boys looked vindictive, like now they would correct a heinous crime, underdogs joining forces, in the glory of justice at last. These boys had been made to suffer. These boys wanted to be somebody, and now maybe they could.

I should have forgot the noisy little parade but I didn't. I left it simmering on a front burner, so after cocktails in French and seating for dinner, and more table talk in French the parade became my entree to gentle conversation.

"Some women we know" were two women, both married. Sophie had three children and a husband who cleared his schedule at the last minute and came to dinner. Alouette, or Ali, had left her husband in New Zealand, had come home to see her parents. Mystique was in her long black hair and big dark eyes, and she could stare back better than any American woman I could remember. But then lust has a way of making each new woman more luscious than the last, each one the perfect one, the one you could want forever. All warm and friendly, it was moved and seconded that English would be the language of the evening. They couldn't press home a point without falling into French, but I got most of it—they discussed Geoffrey's prospects for new roles. I had arrived to a dark room, faces glued to the tube. Geoffrey was a country squire, showing Inspector Poirot around the estate—low budget, BBC, Agatha Christie. Geoffrey turned it off after a few minutes, and everyone raved. I asked if I might see the whole video sometime. It was the perfect question. Geoffrey nodded regally as a king granting a wish.

Ali said she had tried the new drug, Ecstasy, and was curious to know if anybody else had tried it. She looked at me, and I said no. Sophie loved it. Her husband thought it bad. Colette said it was just all right.

Ali thought it bad, it made her so tired the next day. "But it is very good when you are coming. And I am coming much more with it." This with compliments on the fish and the green beans. I asked if she had any. She said no, she didn't, "But, I wish that I did. I have forgotten how...difficult Paris can be. I am so...stressed out. I wish I had some drug, for fun." She put her beautiful hand on my forearm leaning over. "Maybe we can find some." It sounded like a wonderful idea. Nobody paid the least heed; ah, these French. I would get laid after dinner, just after cognac and mints, and maybe after some fun drugs. This too came my way, for only accepting circumstance on the level of human warmth and contact. If I could let the fucking go, then the fucking would be foregone, just like it had been with what's her name. But, my God, I did want to fuck this exotic, dark-eyed beauty.

Geoffrey served salad. In his apron, swirling sauces around the kitchen, swilling wine and making merry he became bon vivant. He was English, about my age, an actor, working now and then for the BBC, bit parts in low-budget dramas mostly, mostly underemployed. His years of commitment and his skill deserved better parts, lead parts, and he longed for more money. He'd come over to Paris ten years ago on a short stint and met Colette at a Jim Haynes party. Jim Haynes, Colette explained, was an American who'd lived in Paris for years, and every Sunday he threw a party. You couldn't just drop in, you had to be recommended, but then you went, and you paid, but not too much, maybe ten or twenty dollars... She stopped short in the telling for a split second, which time was enough for me to feel the sometimes knowing feel of another person staring. It was Colette measuring reaction to ten or twenty dollars. She was past hungry, into famine.

At these parties, she said, you meet people. That was their purpose. "And maybe some time you will meet some person you can click with. Maybe not. But you go. You must go. I will call for you."

"Yes, well, anyway," Geoffrey said. "We met at Jim Haynes', and that was that."

"No, it was not," Colette said. "He took me out, for the weekend. Then he left. I thought I would never see him again. But he called back. And now, we are here."

"Do you think you will marry?" The other woman, Sophie, asked. Everyone looked at me.

I smiled. "It's long odds, I think."

"What is long odds?" Colette asked.

"I would need to meet someone I could love, who didn't want to marry. That's long odds. At my age. The only marriages you see past forty are practical. One is rich and fears growing old alone. The other is poor and hates it."

"So, you are a romantic after all," Alouette's eyes opened wide.

"If that label makes things easier for you, sure, I'm a romantic. All I meant was that romantic love is the rare thing. Marriage is incidental."

Colette whispered to Sophie, "What is incidental?"

Alouette's expression and very mood turned downward; her sadness and Frenchness became innately one. "He is right," she said. "When you are young you have ideas, only ideas, but no grasp. So you wait, or you get distracted by your needs. You get a few years older and you get your grasp, but you get depressed, because you realize you can't really get what you want. You get to be thirty and you learn despair, thirty-five can be worse and forty is not too young to die, from sheer sorrow. Fifty can be hell. I know."

"How old are you?" I asked.

"That is a very American question," she said.

"No, it isn't," I said. "It's a very normal question to a woman who claims to be fifty and sad."

She smiled sadly. "I am as old as you."

"You don't look it," I said. She let it go.

"I think you must give of yourself," she said. "I think you must only concern yourself with the happiness of others." She stared at me. Our warm and friendly fuck after dinner now posed a reality threat. Was she real, or was she bonkers?

"Yes," I said. "I've thought that myself lately."

Geoffrey cleared the salad, served the beans and boiled potatoes. "The French love sadness and death," he said, the vibrant host again. He poured more wine. "Everything they say or do is right. It's the best. Do you remember the nuclear accident at Chernobyl? The French news said don't worry, the deadly radioactive cloud has bypassed France. Bypassed France? Do you know why it bypassed France? Because of Le Grandeur. Because: This is France!"

"Those fucking frogs. Right, Geoffrey?" Colette humored him.

He replied, "The fish is served." And he served it.

Eating accelerated, as it can in French, the Frenchies keeping their forks right and upside down, cutting, stabbing, gobbling this and that, frenzied on flavors, down to the last baguette torn in final vengeance at the evil spirit, hunger, vanquished for now. They smeared bread hunks over plates until squeaky clean. Then they relaxed, sat back and pondered cheese.

In that digestive lull I asked, "Did anyone see the parade?" Yes, they had, but no one had further comment, so I told them, "Aggressive, I thought. Nearly hostile."

"Oh, but they have such a terrible struggle," Alouette said.

"Yes, they do," Colette said.

"They've been terribly persecuted here," Sophie's husband said.

"Yes, and in America, too," Sophie said.

"They've really done nothing wrong, have they?" Geoffrey asked.

"Are you a homophobia?" Colette asked.

"I think that's a misnomer," I said.

"What is misnomer?" Colette said.

"It's homophobic," Geoffrey said.

"Phobic means afraid. I think I was more anti-homo. I didn't like them." The rest waited, aghast. "I lived in San Francisco for awhile. It was a shame what they did there."

"A shame?"

"Who did they hurt?"

"Did they hurt you?"

"It was a charming city of charming neighborhoods. I moved into a neighborhood they took over."

Geoffrey smiled, "And so you did in Paris."

An awkward pall put Colette in a twitch until she sat up straight and pointed obliquely left and down. "Norman Mailer," she said. "I want to see it." She meant the rehash movie now playing at the corner cinema, but she was way off beat.

I shrugged. "I'm only honest. I don't like it." The rest agreed in French, honesty was best. "I remember when two guys butt-fucking was considered unnatural."

"What is unnatural about it?" Alouette asked.

"It is not the way of nature," I said.

"Do you not love any man? Have you never loved a man?"

"Oh, yes," I said. "I sailed the oceans on small boats with men I love. I rode two continents on motorcycles with men I love. I've achieved success with men I love."

"So. You are not so honest."

"I honestly never once wanted to stick my dick up their assholes, and I promise you I didn't want any dick up mine. That's honest." She shut up, her sadness pouring over her in disappointment at this limitation in love.

Then slowly, with a bitterness brimming to the corners, she smiled. "I think what you call honest is simply a lack of imagination. You apparently wanted to 'stick your dick' into one hole or another of women's bodies. Didn't you?"

"Yes. You got me there, Ali. But I don't think natural or unnatural is the question anymore."

"Oh, don't you? Well, good for you. I don't, either. The question is one of consent, between two adults who have every right to do anything they want to with each other."

"The question is public or private."

"You didn't mind the homos when they lived in the closet?" Sophie asked.

"No. I didn't. I still don't. But it's not sexual anymore. It's political, because the politicians need the bunghole vote."

"Your language indicates hatred. Hatred indicates fear," Alouette said.

"What is bong haute?" Colette asked

"Your language indicates dogma," I said. "Dogma indicates lack of freedom—freedom of thought in this case."

"Yes. You're right," Ali said. "I think we're both right. And maybe we can yet agree. But you are still not seeing something..." Alouette was frustrated with my ignorance. "The homosexuals are a political force."

"Yes, I do see that. I don't see what politics has to do with sexual habits."

"Nothing!" she said. "It has to do with money for AIDS, and persecution."

"More people have breast cancer than AIDS," I said. "But breast cancer still doesn't get as many parades, or nearly as much publicity. I think the reason is that the people who control publicity are often homosexuals, powerful homosexuals who control, for example, what happens in Hollywood. So if you have powerful media people suffering from AIDS, and the word gets around Hollywood that not only is AIDS directly affecting the power hierarchy there, but it's also preventing everyone else in Hollywood from having the kind of glorious, star-studded sex with each other that they love to have, well then, that calls for more publicity than a cancerous breast. Doesn't it? As far as social persecution over the ages for homosexuals, that kind of persecution is easily avoided."

"Why? Because the homos are white? So they can stay in the closet?"

"Not all homosexuals are white, and not all of them are persecuted," I said, seeking equal, illogical footing.

"Homosexuals are a movement now, a group to join, but the behavior is something other than political. It's social, a need for attention, for identity, for a worthwhile life. It's a shallow attempt at fulfillment. Maybe it's an honest sexual preference, which I think is how you want me to see the thing anyway." She pondered. I steamed. "In English the homos are called gay. That's a misnomer, too. It's like calling a pile of hot turds éclairs."

"What is hot turds?" Colette whispered.

I had the lead, and like a fool, I ran with it. I explained to Colette the fundamental essence of hot turds. She was less than taken by my candor. Ali too became removed from the lively discourse that had degenerated into gutter politics.

"Your language is so hostile," Ali said. "Even if the parade you saw today was loud and public and you didn't like it, that has nothing to do with AIDS or homosexuals. You are afraid of them, for some reason. I know I get as excited as you do, and I may sound dogmatic. But you are afraid of them, when all they do is between themselves, with consent. They don't need your consent, nor should it be required." Ali was irate. "You can get AIDS much more easily from a drug needle. But I would bet you aren't nearly as afraid of druggists."

I smiled, "You mean druggies."

"Yes. Druggies."

"I don't care what the homosexuals do. I've never cared, until they started yelling at me. You know it's also popular now to consider all males as potential homosexuals who won't admit it. When the apologists come to their logical stalemate, that's the turn they like to take. Is that what you're saying, Ali? That I'm only contentious, because deep down inside I want to come out of the closet too, but I'm afraid?"

"I didn't say it. You did."

"No, I didn't. I said I was awakened by a parade that banged its drum too loud."

"There!" she said. "Why didn't you just say that in the first place, instead of letting us know how much you hate and fear the homosexuals? You make no sense. I see nothing unnatural with two people loving each other and expressing their love, especially if they are adults and in agreement. And I don't think the drum woke you up at all!"

Our casual fuck was off. I sensed it. I relaxed—she was mental, depressed, way off the cost/benefit scale. Maybe seeing her as nuts was my way of dismissing my hormonal urge, or rationalizing its departure. Most people look their best when they smile, and her grim countenance conjured something far different from intimacy. Relieved of the burden of charm, free of the bullshit men so often think is key to a woman's interest, I enjoyed a redirected flow of blood; all of it was free now to surge to the head, the one where the mental brain resides. Logic restored often leads to candor, sometimes in waves, with resolve. "I remember the late fifties when people drank red wine by the gallon and the men wore sweat shirts and grew goatees and the fringe of society was so clearly defined that if you hung out in a coffee house listening to poetry and bongo drums and talked like a beatnik, you were different. You weren't just a little bit different, you were a renegade. You said things like 'Daddy-O' or 'Crazy, Man, like it's splitsville on this uncool scene.'"

"These were not homosexuals," said Alouette.

"Touché!" I turned to her. "Some weren't. Some were. It wasn't an issue. And it wasn't an issue when these people and more people thought all that stuff was passé. So they ditched their bongo drums and sweatshirts and goatees and grew long hair and got some beads and smoked dope all the time and took LSD and said things like, 'Oh, wow,' or 'Far out,' or 'What a bummer.'"

Ali sulked. I honed in. "Then that stuff got old, too, and the next social phenomenon to come along was homosexuals—not as homosexuals, but coming out of the closet. It was the next rebellion. I lived in San Francisco when you could walk down a street and see thousands of guys cruising for a trick. It was a happening, a major cultural event!"

They stared at me, one and all. "Where is Splitsville?" asked Colette. Geoffrey fetched the whiskey, such a good row was shaping up. I changed pace, went soft and quiet. "The point here is that anyone can shave or change the way they talk or trade in their bongo drums for some beads. And when that's all over they can move on to something else. The point here is not homosexuality. It's that a bunch of sociopaths are using the airwaves as a compensation for something. Because when a man has sex with another man, even if they both consent, even if they call it an experiment, something changes. And it's extremely difficult to change it back, to get back what was lost. They have organizations now in American cities for men who got caught up in the gay movement, who need therapy now."

Ali's chair screeched on the floor. She had to pee. "The point here," I called after her, "is that the frequency of homosexuality in nature is severely less than it is in society!"

Geoffrey poured for Sophie's husband, himself and me. The women declined. A rugged, revolting, hot cringe accompanied the cheap rye whiskey. "God, I love rye," Geoffrey said.

"Did anybody see the fête today?" Colette asked. And she broke into an explanation, for me, because of me, of another grand demonstration, this one by the farmers of France, who had covered the Champs Elysée with wheat and tractors in a display of France's formidable agriculture and Le Grandeur. "A million people were there."

"Yes!" Geoffrey said. "And they sold more merguez than crepes. It's the new national food!" Then Geoffrey explained: merguez is a hot dog filled with ground lamb, introduced by the Arabs in Paris, quickly accepted by the French. Merguez was more in demand than crepes. And what do you think of that?

Colette spoke of the island and art. Geoffrey said the national gallery was woefully depleted this year. Sophie's husband blamed the farmers. Sophie wanted to know who would clean up the mess. She meant in the Champs Elysée, but it was a cue. The women were up when Alouette returned, and so was Sophie's husband. Geoffrey said no no no, and in three more minutes they were gone.

Alouette's farewell was three kisses, cheek to cheek, lingering on the last one, her cool fingers on one ear, a gently pained sigh in the other. Another shot of rotgut rye seemed in order. I'd won. I watched her go, sadly.

And there we were, Geoffrey and I, swilling paint thinner as if it was fine cognac and we were rich, or rather he was rich. He delved into my net worth posthaste, filling our cups, leaning forward in warmth and manly communion, elbows in crumbs and sauce. The little room was strewn with book racks and cookbooks and low-watt light bulbs dangling here and there or hooded with cheap tin fixtures and clamped to the racks; cooking utensils and a sink piled with dishes looked devoid of definition but settled in half-light, in a late-night kitchen marinade, roughly congealing into pleasantness once the initial kick of the rotgut passed.

Another moment allowed the possibility of guilt, or at least self-consciousness, I had so obviously ended Geoffrey's dinner party. But Geoffrey would have none of it—he scoffed in the French way, pumping air into the upper lip until it flapped, jutting his chin out as if to say What are you going to do, or, It's all bullshit anyway, or, in this case, I felt certain, At least we're not homos, thank God.

I told him I actually didn't mind homosexuals at all and in fact liked most of them I'd met and had come to see their role in an overpopulated world as vital, because they don't propagate. "I only, you know, was having fun, trying to...make some lively conversation..."

Geoffrey waved it off. It was nothing, done and gone. His firewater would have none of it either but rather insisted on its own warmth. It caused a light sweat, demanding attention to itself, allowing us easy disregard for what had been said and to whom.

It was another still from over the line, and since a sense of gratitude is foremost in a developed soul, I loved it, opened my heart and took it in, the light, the warmth, the whiskey that probably was dear to Geoffrey—the evening that had passed. The cheap, river perch sautéed in jug wine and butter, the pound of green beans with garlic and butter, the baguettes and butter, all simple and straightforward, home-cooked and served warm. I would remember this night. I said, "This place has a good feeling."

Geoffrey said, "Yes," in a half-drawl, half-whine, wishy-washy agreement. "I suppose. You're in a place for ten years and it grows on you. I mean I've done it up as best I can, tried to make it a comfort and all that. It's fine, I suppose. I'm glad you like it. It's not for me, though. It's not how I want to live."

"And how would you live?"

"Mmmmm...I want some...some space around me."

"Mmm. A house."

"Yes, with a garden I think. A big garden and more than that some trees and open space, too."

"Like the squire?"

He laughed short. "Well." He drank and repoured. "Tell me about your home. I want to know. Do you have a house?"

"Yes, I have a house, and space and trees, and a garden and warm weather, and a step and stumble to the beach." He laughed again and repoured me. And what did I do, you know, to make a go of it? "Oh, you know, this and that, business mostly."

"Yes. I suppose your business is doing quite well, if you can take a long holiday like this."

"Yes, well I've been very busy the last year or two. I don't really see this as a holiday but...a change."

"Yes, well a change of scenery is good. And you've come to the right place. We're glad to have you—don't think a nit about Alouette. She's always been that way, you know, difficult and all that. About everything, really."

We drank on the forgettableness of Alouette. "I'm afraid I was the difficult one," I said. "It was just that I got woken by the parade, and I thought it was...like I said, aggressive."

Geoffrey jutted his chin, flapped his top lip. We drank some more. We savored the hour, weathered the bottle, agreed that tomorrow would soon be here. And with a warm exchange of welcome, thanks and friendship, we bid each other good night. Geoffrey showed me out.

I crossed the courtyard in the dark, climbed the narrow steps up to my tower dungeon so far far from home that home was no more. Home was in the heart, now, here. I sensed progress, impending success. I'd sought nothing for two whole days, and there I was, perfectly adjusted and at peace, flat on my back in a box in Paris, drunk and falling quickly asleep.

Adjustments

Fitful sleep finally sank deep, frenetic dreams of jungle closing in. Vines, heat and predators thickened over the sound of distant waterfalls, and the trail opened up, gained light as the falls became near. The long night's march through the sweltering, choking chaos was resolved in the crashing falls. Perfect dream logic was in a cool, fine mist circling the torrent like lace over thighs. With dream strength I pressed on, sought deep penetration, the falls. I woke up, arrived. Dirty, horizontal rain slashed sideways through the wide-open window. And a big rubber mallet pounded my skull from the blind side.

Summer storms had stopped the traffic, if not thinned it, so all the hurried Frenchies below stuck in the morning jam did the logical French thing: honked their horns. And they revved their engines, pumping smoke and fumes into the deluge, as if their lives had purpose.

I sat up stiff and sore somewhere between life and death, ready for death if this was it but demanding reason if life was on for another day. Why this pain from the core of me? What pounded in my head? And how? I watched, senseless, as the rain drenched my kit and caboodle until rivulets flowed toward my mattress. I was soaked and worse. Some sonofabitch had stuck a basketball pump in my ear in the night and inflated my head to a hundred thirty pounds. The banging inside was a demon with an urge, trapped, mad for escape.

I found a shirt near the bed and wiped my face. It was mostly numb, and the drip was not entirely rain but included a slow, steady leak from my nose. And barbwire, about six inches of it, was stuck in my throat. The smoky swirl survived the rain; it was immortal, more of the smoke, exhaust, nicotine, carbon monoxide, soot, no oxygen of the last few days. And I laughed one time at nothing at all, just before a choking coughing fit. I laughed again at Geoffrey's Everclear—we'd slammed it back.

Then I got still and freezing cold, stuck again but this time with jackpot consequences—I felt the big D grinning from all corners of the room, happy with my paralysis, my soreness, my ache and pain. Goose bumps multiplied and took over, turning quickly to a shiver, then a tremble, hypothermia coming on—in America you can jump in the shower, but here the shower would only shorten the few minutes left to certain death.

I struggled up, hands and knees, closed the window, toweled off and pulled on last night's pants and shirt, damp at the end of the bed. I leaned over my table and laid myself back down before fainting, but then the cold, sooty mist sat on my chest like a forlorn spirit urging me to hurry up or we'd be late for the grave. I had to leave that place, had to check into a hotel, but all my things were wet and I'd die first of pneumonia, but this was an emergency, dry and warm was do or die. I got up again, shaky and faint and followed instinct quickly down the three hundred steps to street level where the street Frenchies didn't look at me strangely for the first time but looked past me, maybe with acceptance now, the way they saw each other. The shadow was on me.

I looked like a bum, the kind who favors wine, who sleeps outside, even in the rain. In my morning cafe I went all the way back to way back in the back—dark, stuffy, smoky—warm and dry. I ordered up a big black joe and I waited, shaking.

I liked this place because it was blue-collar French, and blue collar is most often the same temperament, the same disposition from one place to another, just like country people are all from the same country; no bullshit, no dog and pony. No soft-skinned mental fuckers here, just hard-working survivors too stupid to quit, too strong to die. A dark-skinned man leaned over from two tables down. He was a regular like me, most likely pale under all his shirts but whose unwashed face was ruddy from drink and dark with dirt and two days' whiskers. He looked my age but showed more miles and many more days in the dirt—dirt in patina on his longcoat, all his shirts, his scarves, his hair, his hat. His eyes smiled. He understood. He didn't make the snooty, once over up-and-down assessment he'd suffered himself in this life of suffering—his eyes didn't separate from the movement of his whole body, his whole being, his intention, his gesture, his giving—he leaned for me, offering a pack of Gitanes in his burly paw, two or three fags sticking out. "*Tien!*" he said. And when I feebly reached and took one, he said, "*Bonjour, mon ami.*"

And I, alone and much farther past the line than I'd reckoned I could get at this tender age, received, lit up, breathed the heinous *tabac*, suffered further the jagged barbs, because all suffering suffers its own death, and just then in a connection, man-to-man, mine took a pause. I loved him. Warmth poured through my bones, and I would have bet the farm that nobody wanted to fuck.

But lungs collapsed on the exhale. I coughed like a bad engine. Tears rolled down my cheeks. The ruddy man ordered me a brandy, hot, and I melted with gratitude again that somebody in that netherworld cared. The man said something in French, like, *Ce n'est que mal chance*. Down on your luck is all it is. The Frenchman was a sage, a prophet, a man at home in the world.

The brandy was unbelievable shit. But it was hot shit. I drank it down, had to stop the shakes. Bones rattled in their joints, and the new friend laughed, recognizing jolt one, reentry. He dropped a few more cigarettes on the table and slapped my back on his way out. And then he was gone, knowing full well I could be dead by lunch.

I sat another two hours, neither meditative nor asleep but numb, soggy and pained. Standing up was also painful, cold and wet, but I had to stand, to begin my comeback, ascertain my survival. I would climb the tower again, walk three blocks with a load of clothing to the laundromat, and I would dry.

I stopped first at the boulangerie for a gooey Danish with syrupy icing and raisins and nuts. I was ready for solid food, carbos and sugar, and egg too, for protein. So climbing the tower again, assessing nutrition, odds for survival, minimum standards for life itself, I unwrapped the little Danish hungrily. Grease oozed from it like a steady sweat. I opened my window and sat. I breathed, calmed myself and ate. And there in the swirl with the syrupy icing and raisins, a maggot squirmed, and then another. I hocked ptooey out the window, flecking chewed Danish over the sidewalk and street. Far below the prune-faced boulanger restocked more maggot Danish out front with a wary eye for hungry thieves. On a better day I would have gone down again from the tower and pointed out the defect to the cheap, miserable fuck, but maybe this was the best day after all, so I only lobbed the gooey, wormy, grease ball crud. I missed but not by much—got it to splat on the sidewalk, anyway. The boulanger looked up squinting. I yelled, "Fucking maggots!" But it was muffled, congested, sniffling, wheezing, weak and American, like me, and I laughed, asking more softly, "What ees focking magote?"

Nobody cared. A guy on the corner slapped the shit out of his kid. The kid yelled a French death threat, and the old man swung again, but the kid ducked and ran. The Danish tossed from way up in the bleachers was history. So was rancor. Hunger went out the window, too, and so did strength. I lay down two more hours, asleep this time, dreaming of people who visit Paris and love love love it. I dreamed of hard times and that I woke up way back, in hard times, way ahead, dream intact. In this dream of wakefulness and delirium, I sought happiness. It was warm and dry. Wet and cold were a faraway place, a purgatory, testing ground for the soul. The knight-errant forgets his mortal strength in the face of death, sheds his armor, because glory is one with spirit, the dragon is only what lurks in our hearts, and death is easy, beyond pain. I woke up still wet, in pain, wishing I was dreaming, sick enough to worry. I gathered my clothing and went for the dryers.

It was aches and fatigue and glands swollen big as gum balls; swallowing felt like flesh tearing, and a daze settled in like fog on a swamp. Three blocks I wandered to the laundromat, hunchback in Transylvania. Inside was dry and warm. I loaded up, settled in and watched the spinning dryers.

A hard-faced, supple woman drifted in with big, frizzled hair and a denim skirt so short and so tight it was made for stand-up sex, no leaning. Her ragged chemise falling off her shoulders and her classic, vibrant torso couldn't up my pulse. Across the line indeed. But like a tomcat too beat up to go again who goes again, my eyeballs followed with the old curiosity, the undying love. Her rhythmical titillation of two Arab boys looked like an old habit, a familiar game. Light as a breeze, certain as death, she promised touchy, feely, squishy squish. Youth with nothing, alive to animal senses in Paris, they were primitive to me. Lust and hunger was what they knew in the world, and I envied their days and nights. They'd most likely grown up together on the same crummy little street, had discovered sex, hunger and fear together as innocent children, knew the value of shelter and warmth. I wanted some. I wanted to play, too, instead of waiting in line with the unchosen scrubs.

I gathered my bundle and drifted back, dried out from the dryers. The sky cleared. Around the corner in the second block, into the alley of run-down cafes with grimy, sooty, hosed-down walls, where tiny French cars banged their side mirrors against the walls or pedestrians, three men swaggered big. Young, unkempt, bad teeth, ashen skin, they swilled pink wine, drunk at noon. Life span looked short for these guys; like the ruddy man who knew about luck, they looked intimate with hard times. A choreography matched their song, too, call it Singing in the Pain; they swung from lamp posts, vaulted car hoods and sometimes missing, they laughed, caroused and bounced off each other. They floated free, beyond what most days held for them, oblivious to the severe and ghastly hangover they would share by sundown. They celebrated nothing and everything. I envied them, too. They moved with life, in the place with no thought.

Laboring up the tower again I thought, I am like a dead man watching the living, envious of their spirited bodies. I want one, too. Maybe this was progress. Maybe envy was a first step. I didn't know what would come next but felt one step closer to life by what I'd seen. And I'd felt close to death. At the top I found a note on the door from Colette. It said Geoffrey was gone to London on short notice on a decent part. Should we have dinner and see a movie? The cold shower wasn't so bad at midday, and dry sheets made it easy to nap till seven. I woke up and got up, pushing past the big head, dripping nose and torn throat. Movement and rhythm felt better. Night in Paris looked livable.

She whisked away my sniffles and sneezes. "That is normal," she said. A "good cold" always comes soon after arrival, what with the jet lag, the adjustment, the place. She took the lead, down the street to the movie house on the corner. At the ticket window she verified the movie and the time and she smiled big. I paid, first for the movie, a slow-paced story without subtitles. I think it was about homosexuals, but it's sometimes hard to tell in France. Colette said it was good practice for me.

Then I paid for dinner, at a new Armenian place she'd been wanting to try. I couldn't taste it, and by eleven the place was packed. By eleven-fifteen it was jam packed, and jam motherfucking crammed up the asshole packed by eleven-thirty. Colette leaned across the table and said now is when it gets good. It buzzed with talk of this, talk of that, talk of talks past and talks to come. Choreography here had no lyric but the white sound of overlapping voice; the step was all hands and arms, animate as time-lapse weeds. Smoke ruled.

She accelerated when I sniffled or sneezed and especially when I blew my nose into my napkin. Who cared? My breathing was loud enough to hear over the din, at least to me, and it took place through clenched teeth. When my napkin got soggy I pulled free a corner of the tablecloth. Great gobs formed in my lungs and I discharged them, just another oyster hanging near the floor, naturally, French, and she sped happily on. She understood human nature, generosity and giving; it was the soul of France and more specifically, when factored with Le Grandeur, the soul of Paris. "This is my home. I was born here. I am Parisian." She attempted pride as people devoid of resources will sometimes do, as if her accident of birth was currency in the world. It was late, the funk was never so big or so loud or settled so heavily, so badly in me, and around her formed the dark, rank cloud.

The barbed wire in my throat swelled and grew new barbs, and just before I spoke to excuse myself, to call it a night, she hunched close, grew gravely serious and said, "You know, we have a problem." I only smiled from the padded, damp cell of my confinement, confident of very little, but confident in the extreme that besides my health I had no problem at all. "We have a problem." She dabbed her chin, raised a hand to the waiter and ordered another round of cognac, the pricey stuff. "You need it."

She hunched anew and said, "We spent so much. Much more than we had." How can you spend more than you have? "The linens." Two sheets. "The dishes." Two bowls—two, in case I wanted to entertain, or else try an exotic recipe. "The silver." A knife, a spoon, a fork, pot metal, used. "It has an excellent view of L'Opera Bastille." We sat then in the bowels of L'Opera Bastille, choking to death, clinging to life. "I think...we need..." Ah, there was the rub. "A thousand per week." The ante was up, from five hundred dollars a month to eight hundred or nine. It was an increase she and Geoffrey had thought through, thought possible for an American of means who hadn't balked yet.

Nor did he balk now. I sniffled, blew my nose and nodded. She took it for assent. "Can you pay in advance?" Odd vonce?

I laughed, which led quickly to a sputter and a choke—I wondered if Colette had the same kind of light-headed happiness I had every now and then when life looked good. I wondered if she really liked me like a girl likes a fairy godfather. I'd stopped at the money exchange after seeing the three dancing drunks in the street. They would be my paragon. A fat wad pressed my hip—the twelve thousand francs, fifteen hundred clams she'd asked for three months. But now it wasn't enough. Revelation was instant, and so was application. "I think I'm very sick," I said.

"That is normal."

"I can't breathe," I said.

"It is very normal. It happens to everybody."

"I honestly don't think I've breathed for a week."

"When I went to New York I wanted to leave every day for a month. I was sick as a dog. As a dog I tell you!"

It was French consolation. "My head is packed with snot."

"What is not?"

"My throat is so sore it bleeds."

She whisked again with a chin jut and a lip flap. The waiter came with the cognacs. We sipped in silence. "I'm leaving in two days," she said. "For the island. For my art. Painting. I've planned this for months. It means everything to me."

"And I'm certain you'll make your trip. You're very resourceful."

She looked worried, like...maybe...I was an impostor. "Yes. Well. Can you pay in advance?"

"I'll see what I can come up with." The brandy was a heavily advertised brand with recoil and a wince. I sipped it once and said, "Now I have to sleep. I know you understand."

"Yes. It is normal. You will see. You know you must learn to give things a try. I have noticed that about you. You are very impatient. Very unsatisfied. You'll never get anywhere if you don't give things a chance. Give it a try. Your accent is getting much better."

She gained confidence, as the French will do if no argument follows a statement. I looked down on her then, not a happy moment for me. She was a middle-aged, disappointed, lower-middle-class woman with left-wing justifications and class-transcendent greed teaching me, a better-read, more worldly, kinder, gentler person with tangible success in several fields, a lesson in life. Me, a man for whom personal development had meant sacrificing material comfort, getting a lesson from this French floozy.

And so she nearly caught me in the act of superiority. But I won, because the lowest form of life often has the greatest lesson to teach, well, sometimes. I hadn't yet come to believe that lesson by way of experience, but it sounded so good I wanted to try. So I lolled my tongue, put my nose forward so it could drip into the cognac, put my voice between my eyes.

"Why, merci bo coo," I said. She didn't like being toyed with.

So I gave her the honesty she sought. "I'm certain Geoffrey can find a new tenant in a few days."

"Oh, no! He can't!" He con't! "Geoffrey is..."

"Worthless?" Life surged inside.

"Oh, no! I would never call him worthless!"

"Why not?"

"Because he is...an actor. He's not...handy, you know. He cannot find another tenant. We have already made the place unavailable—just last night I was asked if I knew of a place for rent for a few months and I said no, I do not. Our place is taken."

"Who asked?"

"My friend, Jim Haynes asked. He knows of your apartment. How well it is located and the view and the rent." I smiled at the rent that was known. "Oh no, it is taken."

I nodded. "I must sleep now, Colette. We will talk in the morning."

"Talk of what? What have we to discuss?"

I shrugged. "We don't need to talk. You seem anxious."

"No. I am not. I'm anxious to leave for the island is all. I was ready to leave two weeks ago."

"But the apartment wasn't rented."

"Yes. Tomorrow we will talk. Can you go to your bank?"

"Of course. Anything you need."

I got up and left. Colette followed close by. Maybe she feared solitude in a crowded restaurant, I couldn't tell. A quick clip with no talk was what we shared, then a scant good night in the dark courtyard.

Sleep came quick, with hardly time for consideration of where next resolution would lead.

Waking was less burdensome, giving credence to a jaded woman's assessment; a man with no patience looks most happily on a day of change. The pain was gone, but the barbwire swamp still had me. I dressed for travel and packed. I crossed the cobblestone courtyard, climbed the wider, fewer, more civilized steps to Colette's apartment and knocked.

She was busy, too, nervous, also packing. She opened the door and turned away as she said, "Come in." She went to the phone and dialed. "Geoffrey asked me to call him." She waited and then spoke quickly in French. She held out the phone. I took it.

"Hello, Geoffrey."

"Hallo! You must be having a wonderful time there! Colette said the Armenian place was very good!"

"A little pricey I thought."

"Sorry about your cold. You know that's very normal."

"Yes. I've heard that somewhere. Still it's difficult to accept. You understand."

"Give it a few days. You know the city is a wonderful place in summer. Blue sky, not so hot as in the south. It changes dramatically this time of year. It's like a...village on the Baltic or something. It has that empty, quaint feeling."

Geoffrey called it "the city", like New York, and I realized then that it is like New York—nearly asked myself aloud what in hell am I doing in New York? Geoffrey said it wasn't so hot as in the south, as if to the south was where he knew a more savvy man would go, because it was better, and so Geoffrey provided guidance: I would go south. Still, listening to this unfortunate man in the idiom of England, who knew that acting the squire and being the squire were exactly the same, except for the money, and who so desperately failed at the money, I liked him. It was his exquisite good manners, there in the midst of his greed, there beside his scavenging wife. He so keenly skirted confrontation. I did, too.

"Geoffrey. I'm leaving you know."

Geoffrey knew. "Yes. Now look. I want somebody in there. Somebody reasonable."

"You want me to find you a tenant?"

"You must find a tenant if you want to leave. The place is yours."

"I don't speak French. I don't know the city. I have no phone. How can I find a tenant?"

"You speak very good French. Colette can help you." Colette packed in a hurry.

"Colette is leaving. Besides, it's not practical. And I don't feel a sense of obligation."

"Bloody Americans!" I had him pissed now, ready for his biggest test. "We agreed!"

"You raised the rent. Unilaterally, as we say in America."

Geoffrey failed at calmness. "If you don't pay, we'll call the police."

Call the police? For a cash rental? Would they guard the border? These and endless other clever retorts were easily at hand. But Geoffrey was beat once again. I let him hear silence. He said put Colette on the phone. I would have said, Yes, thank you, I will, and hung up. But clarity in the Universe was evident; Colette in Paris, on the phone with Geoffrey in London, both in desperation over fleecing a tourist for money made sense. "Colette. Geoffrey wants to speak with you." I stepped back.

She spoke briefly in French, hung up and dialed again. I caught odd phrases; *les gendarmes, allez vite, un voleur.* I split, on cue. It was best.

At first I went slow, since hurrying is a concession to guilt. Then I hurried, happily fitting in alongside the man who knew about luck and the three dancing drunks. She watched from her balcony, watched the unfairness of life, art and deserved vacations on the island; she watched one more *bon chance* slip from her grasp on fleet feet. Up, down and out and humping it double-time to the Metro I was, on the road again. It all happened so quick.

Leaving Paris

Six blocks to the station was too far for a wounded soldier behind enemy lines; a hundred yards to the Metro could be made in a dash. Besides it was underground and crowded—I wore my hat and dark glasses, fitting in at last. Thoughts crowded, too, chaotic as Frenchies in a maze—Hattie, already south, and should I call, or just go, or nothing? Leaving Paris in a hurry was just like last time except now was sober, sans music, no mystique. And last time didn't seem so hostile, so overcrowded, so buried under media chic. Cheap, primitive fare lined the streets, blending easily with need, desperation and resentment. Colette and Geoffrey made sense in modern Paris, and I did too. But I, an American, with money, could leave.

At the platform two blacks on the far side scuffled like siblings sometimes do, rough but playful. But then it lost its playfulness. The big one went about one-eighty, five-ten, the little one three inches shorter, forty pounds lighter. But the little one had some moves—amateur wrestling, and he looked good, quick and clean, shooting inside—the big one swung and missed, too slow. The little one got the take down, the break down, move to the side for the half nelson. But what was he going to do? Go for the pin? No. It was the city, for keeps, underground, and he was mean, so he went for the two-handed head smash, which of course brought his weight too high over the big one.

All the Frenchies on both sides of the tracks watched casually, and I too looked on curiously, contaminated by only a few days in the city, getting by. But I dropped my bags opposite the brawlers and yelled across the tracks, "*Arrêtez! Arrêtez!*" Everyone stared at me. "Stop!" I raised my hands. "What's wrong with you Frenchies? Stop them!"

It was parallel novelty, ugly American in the ugly city, playing opposite two Africans, fighting again. It was street entertainment, nitty-gritty—I yelled, the big one slid back, free, slid behind the off-balance little one and pushed. So the little one leapt with grace, off the platform, onto the tracks. The sudden rancid gust from the tunnel like a ripe fart preceding a big turd got the crowd's attention. Sprawled over the tracks, the little one wanted up, but the tracks tripped him in his panic and kept him sprawled. The distant, faint clack came quick to vibrant thunder. All the Frenchies mobbed the platform edge then, all screaming French advice. Two people held out their hands, and the little one reached for the rare and precious gift.

Lights shone from both tunnels and all the screams got drowned out. Then the little one stopped fighting, got light as a feather and leaped to the hands that pulled him up to the platform. He wanted more fight, but the big one hugged him, then kissed him. The big one had seen a future and was saved from it. The little one was really pissed and wanted more fight, but he'd just been kissed, so he couldn't. Then the trains rumbled in, and humanity flushed itself out.

The few people on my train stared at me, gave me leeway. I told the six or eight of them nearby, "Stupid frog fuckers. At least I know what I'm pissed off about." I didn't mind—let them mull that one over. Besides a thief is better yet if he's a lunatic, too. I breathed hard, wondering why in the world, in Paris, nobody stole my bags. Maybe it was the protective cover, virtue of the unattached. An old hag looked down her crooked bumpy nose at me. I turned her way quick and said, "Boo!" She jumped. I laughed. I had to admit it was fun.

Further thought, lunacy and unattachment were easy in the cafe row facing the station. A ticket south to a small town on the Med on the nine o'clock express was my focal point. Meanwhile meditations went drip drip drip, nose, sky, eyes—breathing and traffic were the same, sputtering, coughing, glands throbbing in sync with the city. Wet was a consciousness, drizzle to rain, to downpour, to respite, briefly, to drizzle. Breathing, nose blowing, tea drinking, watching and waiting, waiting and waiting while the heavy little arms slogged through the seconds, minutes, hours.

Transmigration

I woke from a dream to another dream, where questions floated—who, what, where—and answers led to new questions. I rode a train rolling south. Air was thin, no oxygen, because the door and window were clamped shut and five other bodies breathed deep. Some snored. Damp, clammy and dazed in the dark, I got up, bumped to the door, fumbled the latch, and answered, "It's a'right," when a gruff Italian voice challenged movement.

Two couples and a male cousin shared the sleeper on their way home to Sicily. "Ah," I'd said in slow pidgin English when we met, "You are mafioso?"

They didn't laugh. The male cousin slowly shook his head, bought a beer and handed it over. "Drink this," he said, and I drank.

Just south of the city conditions for life degraded in the post-nuclear wasteland similar to just south of all cities. Industrial slum crept along the earth for miles; mostly Arab refugees here living in the last phase, before the next phase; in decomposition the earth reclaims itself. But countryside and trees were only another hour down the line on the express. Then lungs expanded, sucked hungrily at original air, ran smoother and quieter. Glands shrank, sloughing toxin. I slept, dreamed of health, and it was so. Is Paris so filthy that a country human cannot adapt? I think it is, chemical, toxic, nonorganic and deathly. But who would buy postcards showing that?

Waking was rebirth, rife with new strength, new confusion. Italians, like the French, don't like fresh air, shut everything tight so sleep is secure. Maybe the habit comes from poverty consciousness deep in the culture for hundreds of years, from the fear of winter cold that brought The Reaper, who ruled, who allowed survival for the strong, or the warm. Maybe that was it. Maybe they can't process July.

Leaning on the window in the corridor I breathed deep through the nose for the first time in ages, exhaled slowly through the mouth, savoring control, the return of life. I dragged my bag from the sleeper, in the gaze of the male cousin. I pulled dry clothing from it and in the WC I stripped, cleaned, changed and emerged in first light, amazed and believing again in God. The busy conductor in his service booth boiled water and gave me a train pack coffee, hot, bitter and electric. The sun rose.

A moment passed, and it was midmorning, Genoa. I embraced my new friends from Sicily, laughing but carefully, fearing the kiss, and I stepped out to a different world.

It was different because they spoke a different language, understood a different passion, a different idiom—it was crowded shoulder to shoulder like a science-fiction movie, like Paris. A taxi driver said it was crowded because fifty-six million people have no place else to go. Maybe so, but it was different, this place, because in thirty minutes I would plant my toes in the sand, let the waves wash up. I would dive in and be healed.

◆ ◆ ◆

But it was a world gone awry. Genoa didn't thin out like it used to, heading south down the coast. Buildings got shorter and roads narrower, but density was constant. A traveler leans toward horizons, and here were none; gone was the feeling, around the bend, over the hill, beyond the city, outside town, into the country, freedom. It thickened near the sea.

The taxi driver was proud of the Hotel Continental—four stars, and he was proud too of an American with money, or maybe he was only proud of speaking English, which he did to the concierge on my behalf. I got a real room with a shower and air conditioning and clean sheets and a great view of the parking lot and the choking, sputtering road packed with traffic endlessly hurrying north and south. It was a hundred-fifty a night, dollars. Never mind, this was convalescence. And the fucking wasn't nearly as troubling as it was with Colette and Geoffrey; these fuckers were front and center with their business.

I got Speedos and swim goggles in the gift shop because all men in Italy wear Speedos and gold chains, but I could swim without the gold chains. Old, white men in starched white jackets drifted about the lobby looking for something obliquely, but only for a little while. I learned later it was money—you tip big up front for deference and service, and if it's enough money they kiss your ass, too, and for a few dollars more they wedge their noses way up in there. Or you can travel on the budget plan, no grease in palms, like scum. I didn't mind tipping big, but they hadn't done anything. Being left alone suited me fine, and after the week that was, being looked down on by the help was a pleasant novelty.

A rock jetty fronted the hotel, seaside, and over it was a cement slab for chaise lounges and umbrellas, and on the chaise lounges lay bare-breasted women, greased and glistening. Maybe another wonder of nature is most men's obsession with breasts, the big, round breast-shaped breasts especially, with the nippliest nipples on the end, especially the large dark ones with the little bumps you can so easily imagine a tongue rolling around—wondrous, yes, along with Italian fashion. The women were mostly fat—fat in the hips and asses with bellies big enough to grab, yet basking their golden, still-beautiful breasts, because a woman can go south and still lure men with her breasts. Italian fashion makes the rest look unbelievably proportionate to the breasts. Except on the chaise lounges, where no amount of grease and gold and sparkling gems can hide the truth, and if an American staring at all the greasy fat soon parallels the rock jetty, and all the fat women soon stare back, it's only because of the breasts, the epic buffet of breasts.

I dove in, to cool off, to shock the shit from my system. And I welcomed it, savored it, reached and pulled through the bracing cold and felt the joints let go, the muscles stretch, the water cleave clean as I made distance easily and quickly from the shore. It was relief, purge, deliverance.

I looked down. Only twenty feet or so to the bottom and something odd, something...everywhere, some kind of pollution I thought, but mostly white so it can't be as bad as sewage, I thought. I dove. It was toilet paper, Kotex, tampons, Coca Cola cans to the aqueous horizon. It was plastic water bottles here and there, assorted trash and a few rubbers. It was fucked. I walked on water getting out. The bare-breasted women didn't look nearly as good. I made haste to my room for a hot, soapy rinse. I'd dived with sharks more comfortably. I had arrived at a strange planet, where all the people shit in their own backyards and smelled nothing.

But I calmed down—the hotel was crowded, too near town, that was all. A couple beers and a Campari let the place settle in, let me savor prospects for dressing clean and walking around. I strolled first down to the guy who handled towels and seating by the water. "Is all the water around here full of trash and shit?"

The guy looked down at my hand, looked up and said, "No speak."

I spoke, soft as a caress. "Fuck you. *Capiche* fuck you? Fuck you?"

"Yes," the guy laughed. "I know."

"Good." And fuck him, too. First the frogs, now the wops. I set out, feeling much better with a salt smell in the air and an oxygen count noticeably higher. The yellow haze over the Med spanned the sky and dipped over the horizon. But following the tree line through the old neighborhoods above the town was good. Slow, friendly people lived in that easy groove. I walked an hour, until the buildings thinned. Traffic stayed thick, and the sea stayed a mile or so to the left. I walked another hour, stretching out, maybe reaching for something I hoped in my heart would be there. I breathed deep, making contact with life again. I turned left toward the sea for another try.

In another hour another beach village looked more promising. It had no beach, not with sand, but the smooth rocks above the water line were apparently comfortable, since a few people relaxed on them. But the beach had no access, except through a funky hotel with a restaurant in back. I went. An old man in a starched white jacket stood at the gate and said *Buon giorno,* and looked down. He wanted lire, 22,000, about twenty bucks. I asked what for. The old man's hands drifted over the sea, chest level, palms up, like the Pope.

I laughed. The rocks looked greasy. Flies swarmed on the funky seaweed in the cracks. And here too the women were fat. "I live in a place with sandy beaches for miles with no people, no trash."

The old man smiled. "You are a very lucky man."

"Yes. Thank you." I turned away. It wasn't the money, and it wasn't the point of the thing, I don't think. I just think it's impossible to relax, knowing you just got fucked in the ass. And I needed to relax.

"Excuse me," the old man said. I turned back. "You may go there." He pointed to a cliff around the bay. I could see a few people scattered across its face on a level outcropping, a few more on a ledge just above the water. "The path will take you down."

"*Grazie.*"

"*Prego.*"

Grazie. Prego. It was the language of understanding, old man in starched white jacket to gringo tourist. Understood was the bullshit, although I wondered what the old guy compared it to. How did the old man know it was bullshit? I guess he figured me for bullshit. That was okay. It was a bullshit scene. Still he was a man with conviction and a soft voice, and he knew how to turn a stiff tourist like me: The path will take you down. Practicing the old dago's accent to the top of the path, I went down, slipping and sliding to the ledge at water level.

The water looked good—clear with no scuz foam. I said, "It looks much better here," to the two German girls who sat there on their towels, eyeballing me, waiting to see if I would invade their space. The pale, anorexic one lit a smoke and looked away.

The husky one with more tattoos than a gang of bikers said, "Yes. They clean it very much for two years. Only here..." She pointed at a ten-yard span out from the ledge where debris collected from the waves and current—wrappers mostly and Coke cans, with only a few tampons and flecks of toilet paper. "Only here it is bad. But...you can swim past here very fast."

"Do you swim?"

"Yes. I swim."

"Want to swim across?"

She lit a smoke and inhaled big. "You mean all the way?" The bay was a mile across there.

"No. We swim halfway."

"Yes. I swim."

The two women were naked. I shucked my Speedos, for equality. The big girl smiled—could have been admiration or pity, and I felt good, since either way was okay. "Last one in's a rotten egg," I said. She looked puzzled, but I was in. She was game and a good swimmer for a hundred yards. It was another surge and stretch for me, pulling through the water. But her breathing got loud and then troubled. I stopped. She stopped. "We go back."

"Yes. We go back." We went back. The pale, anorexic

one waited with a towel for the husky one. The women relaxed over a couple more smokes. The husky one held her cigarette up and said, "This. Not good for my swim."

"No. Not good for your swim. Not good for my swim too," I agreed, and it was my turn for pity—mid-twenties and gone, and she looked like a good-hearted person.

"Ah. You smoke?"

"More and more, when I'm having fun." I copped a smoke and lit up. And there it was, life on the trail, give and take. Alone and lonely, tired and tired of it, bored and horny, I easily wanted Hattie. But wasn't that the test, facing solitude on the road? I thought of asking the German girls if they wanted to get drunk and get dinner and then thought it weak and stupid, just like me, and just the behavior that got me, so far, where I thought I'd be. I thought I'd stroll back to the hotel on the shoreline and maybe get drunk on the way. Evening was only a few hours off, and who knew what adventures waited? Maybe I'd wait until dark and call Hattie. I had the number. I thought I might and then I might not. I would decide later. Maybe I'd be strong.

A motor yacht plowed into the shallow water by the ledge, way too fast that close to shore. About a hundred feet long, it threw a big wake and spumed big foam and big exhaust when the idiot at the helm leaned on it in reverse so he could stop. The roar subsided to whoops and giggles. It was homosexuals again, a boat load of the silly fellows, naked, holding hands. Gold and diamonds glittered here and there on the tanned bodies so greasy it looked like the decks were slick as ice. A few at the stern, where the taffrail dipped lower, moved pliant as willows in the breeze. A short, muscular one had a hard-on.

It was sheer defiance, these Italian homos, a mere toll call away from the Vatican. They made great show of their orgy, giggling and shrieking, playfully sneaking up behind each other to plant the goods.

"They will not suck on each other," the husky girl beside me said. "It is not allowed."

"Not in public anyway," I said.

"Yes. Not in public." The short, muscular homo stepped casually up to a tall thin one, turned him around ass backwards and spoke Italian. The tall thin one cowered, giggled and bent over. The short one moved in with a dominant thrust, right there on deck, blue sky, yellow haze. It fit into a pattern that was impossible to ignore, another memo in bold print.

"It is worse on the other side," the husky one said. "The Adriatic. It is dead. Phosphates. Mostly from German manufacture. Nothing can live, except algae, one species of algae."

I'd heard of this sort of thing, seen it on TV. Seeing it up close, swimming in it can make you wonder where to go, how to get home, and if the invasion will soon follow you home. It's a severe and lonely thought, best suppressed on vacation. I leaned over. "Would you and your friend allow me to buy you a bottle of wine? Maybe dinner?"

The husky one smiled, turned to the pale one and spoke softly in German. The pale one muttered, and the husky one turned back. "No. We will stay here. Thank you."

I dressed and left, headed back along the shoreline and made the village by happy hour feeling hot and tired. But something had changed. It was packed. Gridlock on the sidewalks, shoulder to shoulder, ass to elbow. I stopped at a market for two beers and asked why all the people. The man said, "Friday."

"And Saturday and Sunday?"

"And Saturday and Sunday. All of Italy comes to the water." Outside was a celebration of overcrowding. Jam-packed people spewed debris into the harbor, butts, wrappers, cans and plastic bottles mostly. Acute hunger was insufficient motivation for crowd penetration. I went back to the market on the fringe, got a loaf and some fruit and took the highroad again, arriving back at the hotel by ten, weary to the point of depression.

Traffic buzzed outside. The sun seemed stuck on the yellow brown horizon, smoke and crimson framing the stillborn twilight. I shut the terrace doors, pulled the thick drapes, put the AC on sweater weather and called Hattie. No answer. Good. It was only weakness.

Frustration eased up with several beers, sound sleep to sunrise, check-out and a taxi to the station and a train north to Switzerland. Movement calms an anxious man. Italy, like France, fell away behind the line, gone, history; discounted in a blink and a twitch. Clacking rails became a mantra easing me again to sleep, saying somewhere else, somewhere else, somewhere else. I dreamed that the landfill above Beach Road overflowed and covered the earth.

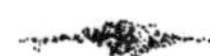

Further Flight

Waking up on a train in a daze and a sweat, packed tight in body smell, is enough to make a man wonder where he is, hope it isn't true. People three to the two seats, crammed in the aisles, braced against potential, luggage and knapsacks by the hundreds overhead, the college kids playing On the Road in Europe with No Money, calling three grand No Money and holding plastic for the cash advance, aping European cool by sucking the tits off their smokes so the air is so thick a sleeping man dreams of asphyxiation and bolts up, no dream. Eighty bucks for a pair of jeans already threadbare, with holes; soul for sale, retail, no experience required. Hey, they only want to feel something. And in the process the road itself gets gentrified.

The window made me look crazy again all at once when I had to grapple with it. It wouldn't open, so I beat on it desperate as a drowning man fighting for air, opened it wide and breathed. A murmur rose, like resentment, like the sleepy old guy was nuts or something. I breathed, cooled off, settled back in my rare and valued seat by the window on the train from hell.

Oh, it's not so bad, lighten up. I unfolded yesterday's *Herald Tribune*. The front page said three-fourths of all beaches in Europe are polluted—shit and trash. I left Liguria this morning—the village measured water filth at 6.4 percent, not too bad. But the reporter said simple tests showed a 90 percent pollution rate. The first simple test was counting tampons at the high-water mark. Shit melts, toilet paper flecks out, but tampons are plastic, each representing a durable shit and trash factor, so the tampon measures overall pollution for the general population, since women are a constant percentage, menstruation a function of constant women. How convenient, and what a relief.

The Italian man in the next seat said, "We have no feeling for the sea. It is to us an interference to agriculture. It is a great toilet, big enough for boats. It is a problem."

The man lit a smoke. A woman in the facing seat moved her knee. I moved my knee too. In awhile, she moved hers again. She lit a smoke and we stared, eye to eye. High yellow, mulatto mix with golden skin, curls to match, and a glow, exotic blend of feminine youth, European worldliness. But maybe it was only youth, early twenties like Hattie but different, not so big and hearty but frail, maybe weakened by smoking. She smiled and laughed, maybe reading me clearly, maybe not, and she moved like Hattie, with grace and assurance where a man was concerned.

And I finished the story with one eye, felt the mortal danger the earth was in as her knee slid again across my own. In the late forties after WWII, the young guys faced the prime of life with the wisdom that comes from exposure to unimaginable horror. Coming home with a head full of concentration camps, wholesale slaughter of humanity by the millions, bombs and madness, they knew where life should go instead. So they invented suburbs, split-level ranch-style houses, television and the fifties.

I stared out the window and realized right then that no other epoch had seen three profound changes to the planet. The second was Vietnam, when all the guys who went and all the guys who didn't went and all the women too realized that war could not be won, except maybe briefly for a speech by whatever dull old fart ruled the kingdom when the last bullet got fired. And now it was us in positions of influence and decision in the world, and so the wall came down and the nukes dismantled, and maybe that will be our legacy, forever, as the planet wallows in poison.

The third great change is to end the poisoning. But looking around the crowded train, I fear no balls, no conviction, no wild intent, no do or die. I scanned the paper again, and again she moved.

She showed intent, maybe. Maybe that's what the coming generation has come to—resignation. Resignation and fucking. But all the generations came to fucking, and I wanted to fuck her and yell at her, You've got to do something! Put that goddamn cigarette out and get out there and do something! The train pulled in. She leaned forward to stand up and dipped her calico dress so I could easily dive down to youth and beauty. Would she grow old? Would she get fat? Was I aging like some men drown, grasping? We all stood slowly, slouching toward the exit, sadly, Madagascar at last is what the German soldiers told their passengers. But the Jews knew it was no train to Madagascar. It was a bad day, so clearly did all the bodies on board look resigned to the way of the world. She waited, standing at last up into a curvature of continuing grace. She reached for her valise. The college kids got off here, too, and so did I, what the hell, the place had trees and cool air, and a trail with a scent. I followed her out, thinking what to say, what to say. Ah ha! How far to Lake Geneva?

We moved through the crowd to the platform where I cleared my voice and said, "Uh... Pardon me!" just as a man about my age stepped forward and embraced the girl. A black woman followed just behind. They looked up.

Oh, hello, three great changes to the whole world in our time, you know, I was just looking into prospects for sexual relations with your daughter. "How far is Lake Geneva?" I said.

"Oh!" the father said. "Not far. Only an hour from here!" I nodded. The family left, daughter tossing curls back with wistful eyes. We could have made history.

Instead I sat in the cafe at the station over a coffee and a smoke, savored the trees down the slope and up the far side, into the vast and forever valley. I switched to beer as the afternoon went to silky haze, drank a few more as the haze tinted yellow. She returned, walked right up, sat right down for a chat and a beer, returned several times in my mind for an hour or two, until clouds rolled in and I wobbled inside for a new ticket, a compartment this time, for the ride to the lake and around it to the far end. Dusk was difficult, maybe because it so colorfully illustrated change, drama and death, leading to reflection in the yet undead, recalling life lived less than fully, disappointment, in a day like today.

Not bad on the whole, though. Today underscored the difference. Maybe it's a symptom of the aging process, the belief that things used to be much better, but they did used to be. Take the eight o'clock train, also up from Italy and just as packed with college kids—packed like rats in a box, thick as traffic. They came with checklists the same way their mothers went for milk, bread, eggs. You turn nineteen, you head out with a knapsack, ride the train all over the place, go home and say you've been.

An angry young man sat deep in thought in my compartment, next to his sweet young cousin. They talked like magpies about the cities they'd seen. It was so cool, it was unreal, no way, I'm sure, what a dorky place. The angry boy grunted. He'd been there, too.

Then came the Tubbses and the Snoles from Pighump, North Carolina. I watched with mercy as Noah must have done when the less savory species came aboard, two by two. They came on loud and overbearing because they were, but they'd been bounced around, too, most recently by the porter on the last train, which was the wrong train. The porter wanted sixty thousand dollars for the mistake.

The head Tubbs meant lire, but was so dyed-in-the-wool dumb he couldn't make the adjustment in his mind, most likely had made nary a single adjustment since the very first one, telling himself, "Wuh shit, uhm born!"

"Hell, Ah told at guy, why ere wadn't no way'n hell Ah'd pay'm sixty thousand dollars!"

I remind myself that these people had the initiative to leave home—here was the progressive, imaginative, adventurous faction from Pighump. There was six, eight head maybe of Tubbses and a similar number of Snoles, and they had maybe a seat or two shy of enough, so they jumped around like in musical chairs, yakking loud and the womenfolk shrieking laughter at their foibles here on their European adventure. "Well, don't you know Wayne lost his ticket at the last stop, had it in the wrong durn pocket. Mary Ellen couldn't find the johnny—Haaaar! Ah swear to God!"

"N'en at fella wanted all at cash. Why Ah gave the man four thousand liras!"

That was about four bucks. An older woman Snole sat beside me. "You speak English," she eked out between her shrieks of comical delight.

"Mmm," I shook my head. "*Pas beaucoup.*"

"Oh. Well." But her disappointment was brief, since the oldest Snole bellowed how teed-off he was, missing Monaco now 'n all 'em nekked women. "You boys are all talk," the woman said. "Why, you wouldn't know what to do with it if it was set down right there in front of you."

That shut the boys up, for a minute, until they got all boisterous again about good times ahead in Marsales, Lion and Paree. They weren't real sure about Amsterdam, heard it was cold, course now they did want to have a look-see at the whores. They asked the nice young man traveling with his cousin if he knew about Amsterdam and maybe some about the whores.

The nice young man got up and told a displaced woman of the Tubbses to have a seat, and all the Tubbses and Snoles murmured niceness. The angry young man lit a smoke in the passageway and got meditative. He said, "Well it's...it's...beautiful. It's really beautiful."

"We hard it was whald!"

Shoowee! Yahoo!

"Yes. It is. And... And I just... I saw so many young people there..." He choked up. He looked like a missionary realizing unequivocal rejection of Christ in the native population, pagan passion coming on. "...destroying their lives!" He smiled. He frowned. He smiled, still friendly, dead serious.

All the Tubbses and Snoles shut their mouths for some respectful cogitation. Then they all shot stink-eye my way quick when the conductor came for passports and mine was a U.S.A. *So your shit don't stank?* was what they asked in their hearts.

The train belched and got underway and I split for a stretch and some air. Nobody sat in my seat. The nice young man was smoking between cars, lighting another off the butt. He was intensely pissed off, mental. He looked like a suicide by thirty-five, or else he could move to North Carolina and run for Senator. He already had a following, but he wasn't cagey enough. No, I could much more easily see him strung up by his rep tie. It just seemed more likely, unless he went back to Amsterdam and destroyed some of his life. "They still sell hash in Amsterdam?"

"Yes. Everywhere."

"You didn't try it?" The angry boy made a harrumph. "I was there a long time ago," I said. "Lost ten days I was so stoned." The angry boy smoked hard and looked down. I wanted to tell him it's okay to be pissed. I was pissed. But I didn't tell him anything. I went back to my seat. The Tubbses and the Snoles had doused the lights. The women read romance novels under the seven-watt lights. The men snored.

Everyone got off in Geneva, but it was too big, so I got another train to Montreux, because jazz is a tradition there, and when you got nothing to go on, you might as well go on jazz. I drank a few beers, scored a gram of hash off another young man, just as nice but not so pissed, and felt good just having it tucked away safely in my wallet, no more borders to cross.

It was Montreux just after dark, a nondescript hotel and a road fatigue that felt like a gift. I thought I'd call Hattie but lay down just for a minute and fell asleep quick.

When You Least Expect It

Maybe I was adapting—I got to where I didn't mind a couple smokes and some straight-up joe the next morning to get going, think things through, maybe head out from there into a walk to see what I could see, stretch the legs and maybe run into something good for a change.

And it would be a change. Something was wrong—a series of wrongs was stacking up and needed a breather—Hattie, the world, me, the trip. I didn't care if I cashed out and headed home, but I'd give it another few days. I'd come so far, it was such a pain in the ass getting here, here being the bigger-than-life ashtray that is now Europe, such a pain in the ass being here, I knew the chance loomed big that I could get home and feel the gnaw again inside, and maybe know it was maybe me, and maybe it was me for certain. I'd only been out a short time, but it seemed an epic hallucination. I've known for years that heroes need heroic odds, and time turns in on itself, especially far from home. Given time, victory is unavoidable. Throw in the towel too soon, and you may have to start all over, square one, throw your shoulder out again trying to reach that same goddamn itch.

I knew this journey, unformed and unplanned, would present obstacles, and I hadn't overlooked hardship, even though you can't fill in the details on that sort of thing from home, with a bellyful of groceries cooked just right and no one to blame but yourself, with an overflow of alpha waves on the idiot box and a couple cats who like you even on days everyone else knows you're an asshole—as long as you feed them. If you could know what the specifics would be on the downside, adventure would be as easy as all the bubble-headed college kids chalking up miles like points. Because precaution would be easy if you knew what to look out for, but you don't. Sometimes you get lucky. I was on a bum roll, and the shit kept stacking up, and I wasn't sure why.

I'd arrived far from home—time stretched out, dimensions changed. But perceptions changed, too, fogged up, and a continent stretched like a mud bog where once a romance, an adventure, a journey had been. Strong coffee and a couple smokes timed these thoughts with proper levels of caffeine and nicotine, so adjournment came on an energetic note if not a happy one. I would reconcile in a day or two, maybe three, or else head home, relax, maybe spin the globe again, maybe not. I'd been wrong about Europe, and so far as I could tell it wouldn't change from north to south or east to west. It was all a picture postcard lie, a beautiful still life that got packed and filthy on play mode. Scandinavia suggests cleanliness, but reality showed up in the daily damage report; North Sea fish and mammal kills at a historical high were no longer attributed to exotic bacteria flourishing in natural phase, but were rather caused by pollution—shit and trash again, and oil, but mostly shit, because it takes many times the shit to hit the same stink level in the cold. Oh, I could easily imagine a travel agent saying, You simply must see it!

And the only difference between Spanish beaches and Italian beaches would be the accent and the currency.

Two smokes and some stiff joe helped sort things out in overdrive, clarified the world: it was so used up with people, cars and shit that a trip like this, a pilgrimage, wouldn't work anymore in many places. Somewhere far west and below the line may be all that's left. Somewhere maybe in the South China Sea or between the Philippines and Tahiti, where enough ocean flowed to keep it clean and even if all the shit got pumped straight in it wouldn't matter because how much shit could a few hundred people make? And cars? Ha.

I headed out feeling good, thinking far far away from far far away, as an anxious man will do, letting the nicotine dizzies and coffee jag ease on into long strides down to the lake. Its shore was a hundred feet from the traffic, separated by big lush trees that made remarkable sense there in a world of short-term convenience. A sidewalk lined the shore all the way around, so its quiet cleanliness could be savored for miles by a road-weary soul. It looked clean and smelled clean, and though the morning haze lifted to a low ceiling and hung there, the cafe operator and the newspaper man both insisted, "Not pollution! No, no. Not pollution!"

But Switzerland is small and riddled with valleys that become wind tunnels for the exhaust of the hundred million cars in Europe. It was pollution. It passed the tampon test but registered singe on the deep-breathing scale. Ah, fuck it. It wasn't yellow and it was up there a few hundred feet and the view was still like ice cream over crap compared to Paris or the Mediterranean, so why not look level and let all the bullshit go?

Which is what I did, walking easily a mile or two, ditching my jacket and then my shirt and going a couple more, to a sweat and a place that felt for the first time in days like the good kind of tired. A lakeside bar with four stools and an awning looked like a good place to rest, and though it was obviously closed, a woman arranged glasses and setups in back. Maybe I could get a cold drink.

She wore a baggy silk blouse untucked over black stretch pants with multicolored chevrons outboard up the calves. She bent over an old steel cooler in back, displaying massive bulk—but she heard me slide a stool and turned around with a sparkle that continued the morning's pleasant syncopation. The place was empty, the water shimmered, and she spread a smile across her face like sunrise on the lake. She was full—full-bodied and full-spirited with full lips and good teeth and a bosom I will recall as extraordinary, even for a big woman, to the end of my days, the last of recollection, resolve with all bosoms. It was huge and scoffed at gravity. She was animate with warmth and welcome, not sexual but loving. She had the gift of giving and the ability to surround another being with a giddy feeling that was no less than cognizance of love and caring. She moved aslant like adding a dash of sexuality to the broth.

She asked in French what I would like. I asked for *un boisson froid.* She moved with deliberate grace, as if my cold drink would be anticlimax to her hot pirouette. A teensy tiny sweat lived on her brow, above her lip, on her cleavage. She dabbed all three with a tissue, looked up with a sparkle just after, showing off this angle and that. Her black hair shone in its thick wild radius. Her fair skin was smooth and hairless in contrast. Her translucent chemise outlined her enormous breasts.

I think I understand a man's weakness for certain things, but a weakness does not make a man bad. Sure I was attracted to Maria's bosom; I thought getting in there for a good tongue-lashing and some barrumsky would be fun—hey, I'm an old-fashioned guy. I remember my ex-wife in a few poses that stand out, including one of her staring sadly into the mirror, holding pencils under her breasts. She'd slipped the pencils up onto the line between breasts and rib cage, took her hands away voila: anti-gravity, for the pencils, not the breasts. It was a milestone, she said, crestfallen and forlorn. I leaned on the doorjamb—she wasn't self-conscious, only foolishly reacting to the breast test she'd read in Cosmo or on a wall. I told her my nuts practically dangled in the water when I sat on the crapper; life was hell. She gave me that look—I was an asshole and making fun of something serious and I knew it and she knew it and now I knew she knew it. I asked what difference it would make, the pencils. She didn't say anything, but she didn't come back with any looks either. I asked her what she was doing for dinner? She grinned. We went out, blew a wad, had a great time, and I gave her a pendant with an emerald I'd been saving for an occasion.

Maybe the terminal indicator was that she'd read *Cosmo,* believed it and responded to it, since a man who understands bullshit can only live so long with a woman who takes *Cosmo* tests to heart. But the pencil test was forgotten. We got romantic then for a few weeks and stayed married another couple years. But I remember the sad look on her face, watching herself in the mirror with her pencils, no hands, looking like her dog just died.

"*Je m'appelle Maria,*" the big woman said.

"*Enchanté,*" I said, trying not to stare. She smiled with understanding; she knew about men's eyes and where they fell. Maria would one day hold a few pen and pencil sets in place, along with a blotter, assorted office supplies and maybe a small credenza. But not today—today a wisp of straw could be nestled into place beneath the cornice, under the great ledge, smooth and firm and broad enough to rub a cheek against, and it would drift away. These guns aimed to kill, and they did, erasing all sense of decorum or tact. Stuck on her cannons I realized it was a classic case of eyeball paralysis, or as they would say on the coast, hormonal polarity. I could not pull my eyes away without great effort. And once achieved, the distance askance soon failed. Focus zeroed shamelessly when images got stuck on the tip of my tongue. She giggled, turning away, letting me wonder if she'd been writhing, or was that only me?

And turning away she became again a great, big, warm woman. The warmth was the thing, I thought—the warmth and the softness, pulling me in like quicksand. Maria seemed snug, like a safe place to be. Yet she transcended form and spirit; she was anomaly in nature, gargantuan if not grotesque. She was nearly a caricature of the female figure, perhaps what the Greater Order had placed in my path, what my "need" had conjured. She attracted my eyeballs like a black hole sucks light. I craved contact—then came the surprise.

She served an orange drink over ice and watched with pleasure as I drank it down. She served another and rattled on in French until I slowed her down—*s'il vous plait, parlez plus doucement*—please speak slower.

"*Ah? Vous êtes Italien!*" She was pleased and off to the races in Italian.

"*No. Je suis Americain.*"

"*Non!*"

"*Mais oui.*"

"*Mais votre francais c'est très bien—c'est très très bien!*"

"*Non. Je ne crois pas. Je parle française touristique!*"

"*Française touristique? Ah! Ah! Ah!*"

She liked my jokes.

It was chemistry.

It was on.

It was strong—we conversed another hour in languages we didn't share and agreed by virtue of a pidgin miracle that a rendezvous after sundown was a good idea—*après le soleil descendre* was my shot at that one. She lit up like a handful of sparklers, went red in the face and nodded like a piston. It was more chemistry.

It was hormones.

It was international currency, universal language—for me. For her it was another shot at the big prize, true love, another chance that a man would love her for her breasts and the rest of her grand stature, and once allowed free rein, that man would sustain that love. That love would be true; that man could be me.

She turned around to her cooler. Big, cellulite saddlebags wobbled down her thighs. She opened her stance leaning forward and reaching deep for the wine, splaying the big jelly roll like a butterfly fillet. She found the wine and found me too when she sprang up and turned around with a laugh so glowing that it transcended instantly the fat some women spend fortunes having surgically removed.

It was a rare moment of growth; I didn't care about the fat. I've never not cared about the fat. I didn't care about the dimple or the wobble. I wanted her naked, smothering me, or else bouncing me off her mound like a play toy. I wanted the works. She said she was twenty-nine, but she sounded like Jack Benny when she said it. She looked young anyway, the way anyone surrounded by happiness and a generous spirit will look. She said she'd never been married, and she had no children, but she took care of her nephew. She said she wanted to get married someday, oh yes, if only the right man would...come along.

She said my French was good. I said I knew better. She said she only wished she spoke English like I spoke French. I told her if she did it would sound like, I meet you with, sun descend, after. "*Oui!*" she said, "*Comme ça!*" She spoke seven languages—Portuguese, Spanish, German, Italian, French, Yugoslavian and Arabic and of course body, which she didn't count, but she tittered madly when I imitated her dreamy shimmy.

I asked if she had a boyfriend—*Avez-vous un ami?*

Non, non. She had no time.

"I find this difficult to believe, you get such prime exposure here by the lake, outdoors, with so many thirsty men passing by. And you do look like the friskiest fuck I may have seen, ever in my entire life."

The puzzlement on her face relaxed into embarrassed gratitude. "*Oh, merci.*" She laid her hands on mine, first touch, with the electric effect that surprised nobody but delivered the voltage nonetheless. She was big, so big, with panache to match. She was open and warm, calm and comforting as snug harbor ever appeared to be. She was shelter from the storm, and the minute or two of silence then seemed natural and sweet, the opposite of the awkward lapse between two people who share a hormonal surge and quickly discover they share no more.

Verbal exchange seemed incidental—this was the communion I'd learned from my recent travel companion—but old lessons surfaced, too, and my mind went to logistics, to the most efficient route to horizontal, but maybe first to vertical, I so longed for the view from her alpine summit. Even the thought pulled my eyes again. Lost there in the clouds, I sighed. We shared a perfect moment together with no interruption, by chance, so far so fast. I caressed her hands. She leaned forward. I touched her nipples. They rose firm behind the silk.

"My God!" she whispered.

"So, you do speak English."

She shrieked with laughter, pulling away, rationing her bountiful self, sustaining my hunger. I felt that this was love. I strove to imagine tiring of so much spirit, so much woman, and I could not.

I told her in failing French and slowest English that I must have been naive when I left home on this trip. France and Italy were so different from what I'd expected. I'd learned in a hurry that any gratification I might derive from my adventure must be found elsewhere.

"Gra...tifi...cation?"

"Satisfaction. *Satisfait.*"

"Ah!"

"And where now will I search?" I asked rhetorically, leaning over the bar toward the vortex and specific destination.

She laughed, backed away an inch or two and told me it was good that people stay naive. Otherwise no one would ever try anything.

I tried that on and it fit. Just see how suffering had led to rich reward. Good feeling flowed freely through me, and along with it was gratitude. She poured wine. We drank. She poured again. We drank.

I said I didn't know. Maybe this isn't a good idea.

"*Pourquois pas?*"

"Here we are with this new feeling, and you know I'm half crazy to see your tits and feel them, but..."

Unable to follow, she shrugged. I continued, "But we can only talk on the surface. We can't talk about ideas. We have a language barrier." *Nous ne parlerons pas les idêes*, which translates something like, "We will not talk the ideas."

She shrugged again. Maybe. Maybe not. This is something to think about. She smiled sweetly, and I got the message—I'd expressed an idea; she'd replied. We drank; she poured again.

And we talked. We conversed in a free exchange of nuance, innuendo, subtle hint and unsubtle hint, touch, feel and gesture. Patrons arrived—a man at the bar downed muscatel one after another as if trying to catch up. After four or five he relaxed, turned to me and said, "Nah!" with great pleasure.

A family took a table and then two couples arrived. Maria performed her dreamlike dance for me, all for me, catching my eyes in her own on her way out, before and after taking orders, on her way back, prepping, serving. She sparkled, tittered, twinkled sprightly on pixie feet, carrying her tray up high on her fingertips. I laughed. She took it for rapture, for pleasure, for intoxication with her as well as the wine, and I suppose she was right on all counts, although she danced like the hippo ballerinas in *Fantasia.*

But I bit my tongue on that sour note. It was unfair. She was not fat nor in any way like a hippo, except maybe ever so slightly in the hips. She was big, not simply or merely big but big with grace and delicate form, big with the grandeur so vainly coveted by the French. Except in Maria it was real.

It must have been late morning or early afternoon when a tour group came down the lakefront walkway to the tour boats just around the bend a hundred yards away. Two and three abreast they moved resolutely along like a centipede with white noise for a voice.

Once they rounded the bend Maria said she did not like tourists. I shrugged, fairly soused. A well preserved woman in her late thirties and a *très* chic outfit with badges and name tags and a few pounds of big jewelry and shoulder pads skittered down the walkway on short steps—tight skirt, high heels. Pan-Cake makeup, rouge, eyeliner, shadow, blush, mascara, lipstick conspired to hide what appeared to be good skin, fine features. Good legs, excellent ass and oh, yes, what breasts, pressing the large end of the scale, even if they didn't peg the meter like Maria's, drew hormonal interest at once. Weak and easy was I, and drunk and happy, too.

And happier still in realizing it was Maria I wanted more.

It wasn't simply lust. Affection and love had become real. This is a test. Because every man knows his weakness for more and newer women, and though he may understand it as a weakness, a just cause for guilt, and still pursue it, or else he accepts it as natural, even though a good woman waits at home, still he pursues it—in his heart, in his mind, in his pants, they all pursue it. Yet some long for the woman to transcend lust, to bring it home and let it rest, let it focus, let it develop into the sweetest product a life can hold, which is love everlasting. The most jaded among us know this, know the condemnation of all womanhood awaiting public disclosure of our secret wants, know that hope springs eternal that, maybe, this next woman will scratch the itch forever.

"Did a group come this way? A tour group? Are the tour boats this way? Do you speak English?" She was late, nervous, having a bad day, clutching her clipboard. She looked nearly pissed that I was drunk. Maria shrugged. The woman didn't know what to do.

"*Ils sont là bas,*" I said. "*Les bateaux. Peut-être cent metres.*" The woman waved her arms in frustration.

"What? Where? This way?" She walked small circles and twitched.

"Just there. Around the corner," I finally said.

"You speak English!" It was an accusation. I'd toyed with her. I hung my head. She tromped off. Maria laughed and chattered, something about the skinny tour bitch, I think. She poured a victory round. We drank.

Uncritical Love

A man can lose track of time in the best conditions, in summer, late afternoon and evening far north of the equator, when the sun hovers on the horizon from six to ten-thirty.

Waking up from stone drunk, cheek to dirt, twigs impressed across the brow and sprinkled through the hair, drool wicking a snail trail of mud, head pounding, eyes blinded, the question wasn't so much what hour it was. The question was more like, Wha? Nnnuuhh... I sat up in pain—deep pain, great, deep pain. A giant form blotted the sun, bringing both relief and fear. Maria squatted with a wet rag and a little brush. She wiped my face, chased debris from my head, emitted tiny whimpers in her heavy breathing.

She cared for me, leaned over so my nose was nary a sniff from her cleavage. She cleaned and nurtured as if holding a helpless baby. In that condition my head rested on her firmament. She smelled like flowers. I could have slept again.

She cleaned me, brushed me off, caressed my head, rubbed my shoulders, lifted me effortlessly to standing and then by magic infused me with a more reasonable posture, all the while chattering that it was seven o'clock, time for our rendezvous. My brain registered complaint, so far from ready. But who is ever ready? So quietly I went.

Her second job, in the bar up across the road, began at ten. We had three hours, and she knew exactly where we should go, what we should do. Love prevailed.

She helped me up the grassy hill, touching and rubbing where she knew I hurt. And maybe I hurt more, became more frail, knowing she was there to cover. She chattered on, I didn't know what. She eased me into her car, got in herself and headed out of town, up toward the nearest mountain.

Cooler air and glacial mist were elixir to the muddled mind; I rode like a rag doll waking up. To my immediate left was Maria, guardian angel, messenger of love, keeper of my soul. Where I, crass and self-centered, had focused no further than the base logistics of where to lie down so I might more conveniently slide my potency into susceptibility, Tab A, Slot B, she was great and giving.

She pulled off the paved road, wended through the trees and once-restless boulders, penetrated a cooler, wispier, more tangible mist and stopped. Falls in gentle rumble filled a small lagoon that spilled itself over its lower lip. We got out and stood in awe and wonder—at the falls and the cold, naked prospects ahead.

She walked around the car, came to me, unbuttoned my shirt and then my pants, pulled them free like skinning a snake and laughed at the goose bump mob charging over my body, the slack-jowled beast hiding below. She wrapped her arms around me, moaned deep and covered my mouth with hers. She searched with her tongue and I think she could have covered my nose, eyes, eyebrows, forehead and chin as well. She was extreme and intense. And though the experience was not, for me, romantic, it showed her incredible capacity. Standing there in cold, naked pain I wondered as well how so much appetite could be satisfied, since the beast below was shrunk down to the last half inch. She wondered, too, tweaked it thumb and forefinger and shrieked a cackle that bounced off the walls of the rocky ravine.

She had a plan, stood up straight, unbuttoned her top button, then the next. It was here and now at the be-all, end-all of tits, front and center, have and hold. Never mind cold or pain, let go of difficulty and travail. Arrival is now, for once and for all.

The next button was good, the fourth better, until my bones rattled with chill, and I hurried the last two. She tittered and grinned as I peeled back her chemise, one shoulder and the other, unveiling the canvas and cable harness.

Fear struck quick and deep as lightning—what if they flopped to her crotch? So I hurried more, knowing they would not, because a woman who takes the care to harness her breasts in lace with an embroidered flower on the front just over the clasp, and then drips flowered scent into her cleavage, is proud. She likes her breasts, and *voilà,* so do I.

"My God," I agreed. She effused warmth. I dove in like Scrooge McDuck in the loot cellar, went deep, came up for air, tongue trilling hill and dale and under the granite ledge where no pencil could stay and then around to the front for a sudden stop. A shudder so basso profundo, so like the mating call of the humpback moose, from so deep within and sent so far beyond warned of the instincts I could unleash. I eased up, grasped them reasonably with my hands, stepped back and relaxed.

The little soldier stirred in his bunker, peeked up at the ruckus outside. He was ready if he must, but he savored the skirmish in a room with a bed and sheets and some warmth for chrissakes.

She interceded, wiggling from her pants like a fish from a net. She didn't hesitate but took my hand and pulled me to the edge of the little lagoon. She let go and jumped in, shrieking again in delight. I followed and in the next instant knew the meaning of sudden death, cardiac arrest, lungs quickly frozen, limbs stiff as ice. She came up easily, breathing hard but casually, playing, cooling off.

Calling on inner calm and adrenaline I fought free of the gripping cold. I remembered ultimate relaxation, what a man pushing middle age knows he wants to die with. I stayed calm, and slowly, turning purple, waded out. She played in the icy water and triumphed yet again, while I stood trembling and shrunken in the shallows.

I didn't care if she was proving a point, laying claim to superiority, or whether her victory was feminine, Italian, Swiss or personal. I was helpless and didn't care. I wanted more.

She saw it, sensed it, rose to it with the gift of life, rose from the freezing foam, nymphet of warmth and comfort. She wrapped her great self around me, huddled me to her car and wrapped me again in a semi-clean towel from her back seat.

Dried and dressed with dispatch we descended again to lakeside Switzerland in summer. Of course it was different, like a new season in new skin for me, the air tingling with potential, fresh from molt. Here too we shared a communication beyond words, and the silence between us was understood, mutually felt. Warmth and haze descended, too, over us like a soft blanket.

Maria's flat circumscribed her life, three floors over the bar where she worked. It completed her daily orbit, flat to lakeside bar to basement bar to flat. She laid me on her bed gently and with reverence, icon come to life. She fluffed the pillows, stroked my forehead and went to the kitchen, where a few minutes of soft sounds led to steaming potatoes and cabbage, hummus and pita with lemon and oily green olives, sparkling water and tea. It was perfect. She chattered in French something about the Arab influence there on the lake and her love of Arab cuisine.

"*Parles-tu Arabic?*" I asked.

The familiar form of French was not lost on her. My first use of it there casually over lunch nearly startled her, opened her eyes over a smile chattering in Arabic. I asked her to teach me. She laughed and spoke slowly but only for a minute—"*Je suis tard!*" She was late. She stripped, changed and left. I should rest, come down to the bar later, anytime before two, when she would be done.

I lay down again savoring the excellent repast, wondering if I should fetch my kit from the hotel, thinking I would rest first for an hour or two, watching the fire-red sun sizzle into the lake. I closed my eyes on the ticktock clock on her dresser—ten o'clock—amazed at the mutability of feelings as they relate to the time of day here, the strange sensation of sunset at ten.

I woke just after two, pitch dark, lost in space under two Jupiters. A tongue sliding over the south pole proved that there is conflict in the absolute universe. The firmament heaved and swayed, came down on my face like a dream of sweet death. Offshore drilling came next, and then severe tremors, and finally the earthquake. And the little soldier bore in, looking for friendly life in that faraway place.

Describing the Sex

Sexual narrative is a nagging problem, because bodily function rarely enhances a story. Without love, it is only bodily function—shitting, pissing, fucking, butt-fucking, blow jobs, eating pussy, all of it, flesh flexing toward one discharge or another, mere flesh racing headlong to dust. With love, images of fluid exchange become unnecessary.

On the other hand, if intimate contact is glossed over or skipped, in the interest of good taste or inexperience, then the love looks timid, uncertain.

For example, in a book widely read poolside, on trains, in cafes that summer, the author said nothing obvious like: He stuck it in there good and fucked her hard till the cows came home. Nor did he capture the exchange, the whispered wit, the control, its loss, maybe a whoop or a whimper, maybe an original twist, a key to character insight.

The back cover said, "Marvelous... Riveting... A Joyous Read... A Sizzling Page Turner... I Couldn't Put It Down." Why do they do that? But then what else can they say? "A Waste of

Time... Why Bother?... Save the Trees... 24-Karat Shit... What Garbage... I Quit on Page 2..."

But the back cover went one step past standard raves. Consensus of those in the know was that the main character wasn't a nice person, as if the author didn't realize it. I like characters more than I like reviewers, especially characters strong enough to make the reviewers pooh-pooh, so I got the book.

The main character was honest, truthful, courageous and kind. He played hard and fucked hard, which became a problem halfway through—the plot was missionary style. New female characters were new fucks in various eye size, eye color, cheekbone shape, height, accent, shoe size.

The character remembered one woman: "We'd spent a weekend wearing each other out." I could only imagine them shouting orders at each other, then stripping and waxing the floors, vacuuming and shampooing the carpets, washing all the windows and screens. I could not imagine a sexual exchange for two days and nights, even as I watched Maria with tireless contentment. The female in the book was fucked and forgotten after her one big line. "Is okay. Now I will eat you." She dropped to her knees.

She dropped to her knees? Reading it made my knees hurt. I've never seen a woman drop to her knees. I asked Hattie once for a blow job while I sat on the edge of the bed, with her on her knees.

"Why?" she asked.

"Something new," I said. She stooped slowly, first one knee, then the other. Her face was at the height of my shoulders.

"This won't work," she said.

"Sure it will," I insisted. "I read about it." She twisted and bent, but it was awkward.

She stood up, pushed me back onto the bed and said, "This is how it works best. You should trust me on this one." She worked the puzzle quickly with the kind of uninhibited display men fantasize, and it was skillful, but Hattie had another technique as well for making me feel like a dog when I should have felt like a king, or at least like a pleased peasant. One was breakneck speed, finishing me off headlong, no change of pace, no savoring, no soft, slow stroke. The other was her announcement, posthaste, "There you go", or "All done" or "Next".

Hattie was cruel in giving like that; and there was the twist, the cut across the grain. "She dropped to her knees," on the other hand, is a different kind of cruel. It was too hard on the knees.

Sex with Maria was big and golden. She was to women what the Hope is to diamonds. Her physical being was perfect emanation of who she was, what she looked like in the ethereal, spiritual sense; big was the dimension of her every part, heart and soul included.

Sex with Maria

Memories of Maria endure because of the dimensions, the blend of the giving with the love, no before and after. She survives in soft light, so much of her, with a sweet, soft scent. That was all. It happened late and again early. She pulled the shades so it could happen midday. She cooed as I'd heard women coo, pleased, I think, with the long-haul rhythm in a man past forty. Maybe staying power is a gift, a compensation in men with the other, longer-term inadequacy.

Maria was pleasure bent. She leaned into love. She hovered over me dangling her breasts because she sensed appreciation, because she anticipated fulfillment.

Maybe she also knew that hovering on all fours was optimal position for covering her massive ass and jellied thighs. I didn't mind the bulk, which was a milestone for me and certain evidence she'd taken me higher. Massive ass, jellied thighs—these thoughts, these physical assessments, what Hattie would call judgments, passed through unimpeded, flashing bright as meteors but only briefly before hissing out, doused by love and giving.

The rest was conventional. She kept an excellent white Chianti chilled bedside and with it kept me drunk. Maybe she knew it was the buzz that allowed me to transcend her fat. Maybe it was. But her movement was so gentle and careful from the top position she seemed weightless. She focused on the small junction of our communion, and it seemed a good place, hospitable, untrafficked, narrow and delicate for a woman so big.

Her nuance was subtle and flowing; she could follow, she could lead. She could move me with her tongue. She paused, poured wine, put the glass to my lips and said, "Do you like that?" It was a request.

I never ate a big fat woman like that. I think she liked it. She should have. It was brief, but it went slowly with spooky effect for me, like walking into a dark room and freezing when the door closes—her thighs closed over my ears. I froze and opened my eyes. Dimples spanned the horizon across the plains and up to the edge of the jungle. Darkness and wine eased the rational view, which could have led to fear, trepidation—to acid flashback and horrific visions of the vagina that devoured Chicago, to entirely too much of what was way too wanted—to the rude bail-out. But she'd timed it right. I was drunk. It was dark.

I laughed. She asked what was funny. I burrowed in. She shut up. It was like the time I left home and got a job in a lakeside resort that was so big all the waiters and waitresses stayed in their own dormitory, a place called Holiday House where odd shifts at odd hours meant the party never ended. I was only a busboy and only seventeen and got tight with a girl who was a senior in college and kissed with her tongue. And every day or two all the kids would go down to The

Ledge, which was our private spot on the lake because it was only a narrow ledge a foot above the water. A steep, sheer cliff backing The Ledge was scaleable to another ledge twenty feet above the water, and another ledge was forty feet up. Everybody jumped off the twenty-foot ledge, and all the guys went off the forty, at least once, because they had to, burdened by machismo, which the girls resented years later, screaming and fussing over the miserable fucking reality of womanhood.

May be, but the guys had to jump off a goddamn toehold forty feet up, and I'll remember to the end, standing there trembling way too long, until all the kids at The Ledge knew it was a choke, and the watching got quiet, dead serious. I knew it, too, knew that death waited, directly, at water level. And I thought and thought about the launch, the arc, the fall, the crash, until Tom Hughes, a big, muscular, slow-speaking, friendly guy climbed up and said, "Don't think. Don't think for a second. Jump. Jump. Go. Jump." He was from West Memphis and talked as slow as he moved, like syrup. He made me smile. I jumped. My heart slid up to my throat.

Years later I jumped again, massaging those dimples with my ears. Maria prayed, in Italian mostly; I half-expected a chorus of "Ave Maria", but it stayed low key, fervent murmuring of *Dios Mio* mostly. It was big in the jungle, and dark, with heavy dew, and just as the child is father to the man, I felt fear.

It was a specific fear, fear of extinction, of death, I thought, but then maybe it was fear of saturation, of getting enough of that stuff I could never get enough of—and what if I came up full? Wending the acrid path that seemed somehow wrought with danger—quicksand, asphyxiation, night beasts, utter, profound love—I held on, put my fear somewhere else, put it far away, long ago, falling thirty-two feet per second square from the forty-foot ledge and then laughing at the sheer joy of survival in spite of the pain. Neither Tom Hughes nor anyone else had told me to cover my asshole with my hand; water jammed in like a broomstick. I limped for a day, even when my college-senior girlfriend ran up to me back at Holiday House and gushed that she'd heard I'd jumped the forty-footer at The Ledge, and wrapped her arms around me and kissed me with her tongue.

I wonder where she is now, and does she ever think of me? I arched my back and hightailed it farther up the path, searching for her tongue. Maria jammed her thumb up my ass, right on cue. Maybe she figured that was what I wanted. It wasn't. I never liked anything going up my asshole, and the only thing I want coming out is shit, preferably in individual turds of reasonable diameter and density, tapered at both ends. Maybe jumping off the ledge and getting my shit jam-packed is why I still cringe thinking of homosexuals. I don't know, but it was a pain so severe I can still feel it just thinking about impact. Maria flopped like a beached whale in death crisis and then lay there, dead.

Okay, she ate me, I ate her, she pulled me up and we fucked, and I drank about half the bottle from the nightstand and rolled over again and went to sleep. She woke me up in the morning dangling a giant nipple in my face. We fucked again and I slept again, and she woke me up later with a blow job, and we fucked again. By that time the twitches set in. I got up, opened the shade and stretched. She did, too.

I didn't know what happened. Of course now I do, because knowing and hindsight go so well together, and so does the truth of a man's notion of forever—forever varies in duration in direct correlation to hormones. She was still lovely as ever a big woman was, but it hit me that the big was bigger than it had been in proportion to the lovely. Her grace and delicate movement was not an infatuated perception on my part but rather was her gift, maybe her compensation for her size. She flitted happily naked about the flat, turning, bending, shaking, as a big woman who knows she is loved can do. I asked about the lakeside bar, and if she was late. She said yesterday was her last day before her vacation. We would have two weeks together, starting now.

Another fear, this time nonspecific, floated through the room with the shades up, windows open. Daylight and fresh air make a healthy man want to move, to press on round the bend, proceed with the adventure. Prospects for true and forever love seemed more difficult now, with the hormone battalions so massacred. Another suffocation loomed like a cloud in the bright, new day. That's how it is.

Love Test

Two weeks isn't forever. Two weeks isn't forever. Two weeks isn't forever.

Maria made the bed, tidied the flat and began her transformation—what some women do to change the way they look for the outside world. She swirled her hair and stacked it way high, a cross between Paloma Picasso and Inez Washington. She hooked herself into three or four pounds of earrings, big brassy turnbuckles with hefty stones, and clasped on another three pounds of necklaces. She slipped a dozen bangles onto each arm and, still naked, perched a six-inch rhinestone butterfly on her left breast. I gave her a look of satisfaction, but it wasn't ecstasy, so it wasn't enough, so she shimmied. I got a hard-on, God knows why. Her eyes opened wide. She went gaga and shrieked a giggle and pointed and ranted in French something about again after such a long night. She shooed me away even though I hadn't approached. She spun and swooped to her wardrobe and said, *A plus tard, mon ami.* Later, my love.

She fanned through her dresses one at a time and finally came up with a billowing satin number she pulled off the hanger and threw into the air, catching its bottom hem and shimmying again up into it with a wobble like a cauldron of Jell-O.

She fit her tits into place, lined up the ruffles and billows, snugged her hips and aligned the shoulder pads. She was too big for shoulder pads. High heels at least shape a woman's calves, flex her ass so it rides higher and tighter and looks better for fucking, even on a woman with a tremendous ass like Maria.

Shoulder pads looked stupid, especially on a woman with shoulders like Bronko Nagurski's to begin with. All done, trussed, gussied, stacked, piled, frilled and twilled, she spritzed perfume, swirled and presented the new product. She moved like a small building with banners. Come, she said. *Nous allons au Grand Hotel manger le petit dějeuner.* We would brunch at the Grand Hotel.

Brunch at the Grand Hotel was an exercise in linen and crystal, and subservience. It was imitation foo foo, tourist format, what dominance-based mentality conjures as ultimate pleasure. The fare was cream-based and dominated my heart, not my heart of hearts, but ventricles and aortas. The exercise for Maria was one of pride, possibly redemption. She clung to me, she in her finery, I in two-day, slept-in, wadded-up duds with wino shadow on my face.

For me it was anonymity, far away, different language, far removed. And it was fulfilling, an opportunity to give, to a giver. I went along with it. She scanned for people she knew. She waved. I was on display.

First came wine, then salads, then soup, wine, appetizer,

lamb brochette, fruit and cheese, baguette, wine, coffee and a short break before dessert. Choices in living color came from an eight-page menu. Maria chose for both of us, and we soon sat behind globular ice cream mounds pyramiding to sprouting sugar cookies, surrounded by sugar sticks penetrating whip cream clouds. Fruit-layered waves shored up bonbon ledges and slowed the multicolored lava oozing down the slopes. Maria called the waiter and spoke very fast Italian and looked indignant. He bowed, left quickly and came back with chocolate sprinkles.

Then she smiled her most beautiful smile and shrugged in resignation; everything dropped, shoulders, head, posture, which for Maria meant tits—life itself seemed to ooze away on the exhale. She looked at me, no need for words. So you see, this is the happy death we've come to.

It was carnage. She finished hers, dabbled at mine. I couldn't help wondering how much of this sugar onslaught would turn to fat cells lining her labia majora, and what could possibly induce me to lick that sundae again. Never mind—I smiled and drank the wine, maybe to see just how far the sauce could take me again.

Maria sensed my contemplation. She sat up straight, got delicate with her ice cream, angled her shoulders so her billowy satin dress would draw taut across her breasts, and she eyed me wantonly up and down. She understood my weakness, my limitation. She had me by the balls. But she was all right, a kick in the ass and good company, a game companion in the ridiculous repartee so often encountered on the road to some ideal, lofty objective. She practically said with her body, It's all bullshit, isn't it? Let's have some fun. So I fell again in love with yet another dimension to her realm of giving: initiative. She could think and do. I am a bullshitter weak for bullshit better than my own.

"*Maintenant*," she said. "*Nous avons deux semaines. C'est très bien, non?*" Two weeks. It's very good, yes?

"*Mmm. C'est parfait.*" Mmm. Perfect.

She said she had an idea for an adventure, a little trip she thought I might like to take. Yes, I would—the idea of a guide in those strange lands relieved me instantly of the burden of travel logistics. She spoke the languages, knew the territories. She was lively and apparently not inclined to moods. She was very fat. I was amazed, dipping my spoon into the goo.

She wanted to go north, first to Brussels, then to a little town just over the Belgian border to Holland, a seacoast town she'd always heard about.

We could leave today, if I liked, or tomorrow, but first she had to visit an ailing friend who lived in a teensy tiny studio with two others, so it would be crowded, but she wanted me to come along. I sensed another display of me. I didn't mind.

But another night on Maria's trampoline seemed more wearisome than lovely. Maybe I was hopeless; maybe I could not learn to love a woman for her soul, once the pussy was had. Maybe I could—the jury was still out. But in the midst of a new approach to love I did not need severe challenge. Two weeks of it loomed ahead like a high brick wall with barbed wire on top.

Maybe Maria sensed that, too. She took my hand and held it gently, her own hand warm, sweaty.

We walked the few blocks uphill behind the Grand Hotel to the cellblock studios for the waiters and waitresses. Jane was a waitress, had been a waitress for eight years since arriving from London. She'd allowed her longtime friend Julian to stay with her since he arrived, three years ago. But they didn't fuck. Julian was most often too depressed to fuck Jane or anyone. And now he faced a crisis with possibly the most important show of his life scheduled for that very afternoon at the biggest club on the lake—producers and agents in the audience—and the funk sunk into him like mold on cheese, a week's worth of it. It would not go away. He couldn't play. Julian was a pianist, when he wasn't too depressed. He lay lifeless on the sofa as if melted there, down to zero, taking his smokes down to the plastic nub and then chewing.

"He's depressed," Jane said by way of introduction. Bright-eyed and effervescent she hugged Maria, kissed her cheeks left, right and left and then hugged me with three kisses too and a whisper, "Don't you just love Maria?" It seemed like a trick question. She spoke fast French to Maria, who answered with a fast shimmy and an oo la la.

Jane turned to me. "He's a wonderful musician really," she said. "Nobody can play like he can. But he gets depressed and he can hardly move. Move, Julian, so they can sit down." Julian rolled over.

I sat on the edge of the sofa. I'd seen it before. This scene was strange, because Maria and I weren't here just to show me off. It was a condolence call, too. Jane was in bereavement. Julian was dead. But I didn't get a hopeless readout on Julian. He'd already rolled over on command, and they say the hopelessly depressed can't do anything voluntarily. Maybe that's why God made breathing automatic. I thought he had a chance, especially if he was only a confused kid, another European thinker on his way to full nut-case status. I knew what depressed me as easily as I knew what pissed me off.

Maybe my strength was the ability to move on these things without sorting them out. "Julian," I said.

"It won't work," Jane said. "His mother and father are both psychoanalysts and they can't do anything for him."

"You mean they can't figure it out?"

"They say he's manic-depressive. They gave him some pills, but I hid them. If he takes the pills he really can't play. At least this way he might snap out of it. He's not like this all the time."

"That's a relief," I said. Julian grunted. "Julian!" I yelled at him, for penetration. It worked; he twitched. "If I can tell you one little thing to try, to help you ditch your funk, will you try it?"

Julian murmured, "Yes." It was a good sign; he at least wanted to come back.

"You must give," I said. Maria and Jane did a French shrug and lower-lip flap in unison.

But Julian budged an inch. "Give what?" His voice opened slowly like an old, heavy door.

"Just give," I said with an American shrug. Julian grunted. "Just play the piano without asking yourself why you're playing. Give the music, like Jane here gives you a place to stay."

He could relate to that. He loved Jane, or at least he should have. "Why?"

"That's not part of it, Julian. It doesn't matter why. It never has. You may never know why. But you know how. And I promise you you can die as soon as you're done. Now stand up." I stood up, not threateningly, really, but hovering over him I imposed on his peace. He grunted again, in the negative. "Stand up, Julian." I pulled him up, and he stood there, straw man, no spine. "Move your arms and fingers." He flopped foolishly, halfheartedly. I told him, in his face, "People all over the world are depressed. It's only for one reason. All they do is take. Gimme gimme gimme. Here you are taking three seats while three people are standing up. Give. Give us your seats, then give yourself a shower. Then give your legs a stretch and walk down to the goddamn piano and give. That's all there is to it."

Julian stood up straighter, croaked slowly, "Just sit down and play?"

"Ta da!" It was a mockery, a scene of hopelessness and foolishness. Julian could relate to that, too, but only for a moment. He turned sad, and he shrugged. "You're slipping, Julian. You're thinking. Don't think. You must stop thinking. Every time you ease up to a thought, crush it with an act of giving."

Julian hesitated and then smiled again. "I don't know if this will work," he said.

"But at least you don't know! This is progress! Give, Julian! Give!"

"But what if I get..."

"GIVE!"

Julian nodded, shrugged again and said, "I'll try it. But..."

I whispered, "Give."

Julian furrowed his brow and shuffled toward the bathroom. "Give, Julian," he said to himself.

Jane was impressed. She gave me another hug, this time without the three kisses but with the energy exchange popular in the spiritual crowd. Over her shoulder while we shared a gentle embrace and allowed the voltage its natural arc I reviewed a photograph tacked to the wall over the bed, eight-by-ten, the most colorful, possibly most expensive decoration in the place. It showed Julian and Jane together on a dock on the lake on a beautiful sunny day. Julian, scrawny, sunburned, stooped and reserved, sheepishly admitted a smile for the camera. Jane beside him beamed happily, topless, proud and spectacular. It affected the arc. I couldn't help it, I felt it most in the pelvis and chest. I too was impressed. And that night's planned departure became another form of relief. I wanted sexual contact with Jane in the worst way, because she was so beautiful, so alluring that I knew I could not get enough of her. I knew she was unlike all others, and she would never fade. How could she? And how could a woman who moves a perfect quarter inch in such a situation be ignorant of the electricity at hand?

"This is Horst," she said.

"What?"

Amazement came again in the far corner where yet another human lived in this ten-by-ten. Jane was a giver too, maybe more so than Maria—they'd met years ago in the restaurant where Jane worked. They giggled. They cruised. They were soul sisters. The problem at hand was not in the bathroom but in the corner; Jane had met Horst and given just as Maria had met me and given. A moment of pain and wonder overcame me then, that the Universe had chosen Horst for Jane and me for Maria and not vice versa. But it was no time for self-pity.

Horst sat slumped in a small chair in a cloud of smoke that compounded his natural haze. His salt-and-pepper hair was uniformly short on his head and face. He was a mouth breather whose teeth never showed, which was so strange looking I tried hiding my own teeth to see if it was easily effected. It is not. Horst neither pulled hard on his smokes nor chewed the butts, but easily puffed profound billows, so his head looked like a toxic factory in the Rhine Valley. His mouth was a black hole where smoke spewed out.

Taking Jane's ear into it was the picture-flashing past—I couldn't help it. Horst neither smiled nor scowled, neither welcomed nor threatened. Drool flecked his lips, and I knew at once that the drool was natural, too. He wore dago pimp shoes, but he was masculine. All else I knew was confined to *un problème* in the general sense, burdening Jane. The little box shrank smaller still as Horst shifted his weight. A threadbare sofa, ragged from compressed slumping and slouching, an unmade bed, scene of too many bodies, too much traffic, a chair, slumped as a body living in confinement, completed the room. Passageways between the sofa and bed, the bed and chair, were themselves amenities, places to be, despite the requirement to be sideways, standing or passing through. It was a matchbox of life, miniatures of the living.

Horst was macho in the corny sense with a big gold chain and his shirt open to his navel and his chest hair bushy as an Airedale's. But he was real, too. Dirt, not the earthen kind but the sooty, greasy kind from city smoke and cigarette tar, covered him in a film with smudges here and there on his two-day growth. Leathery skin and unevenly big muscles reflected time in the trench rather than time in the gym. Horst had been around. He'd paid the piper, would die young and knew it, was reconciled to it and therein was stronger still, in the physical sense. He was drunk and pulled again on his lukewarm beer. Empties lined the windowsill, each with sedimentary butts. In a sweat, especially in the armpits, wet in a ten-inch radius, he wiped his chin with his furry arm. And above all, he honest to goodness looked like he didn't give a good goddamn. That was the attraction for Jane.

Horst grunted and gave a half nod. Maria stood back, showing yet another side of herself, which was aversion and possibly fear. Jane flitted like a nervous butterfly, relating *le problème.*

She was pregnant.

She watched me, waiting. So did Maria. Horst smoked. I shrugged. "Congratulations."

Horst grunted a short laugh and spoke with a thick German accent. "Do you like to smoke some hash?"

In fact, it sounded to me most hospitable. So I gave the nod and sat back down on the sofa. Horst leaned forward and rolled a joint on the bed. Maria disapproved and scowled by the door. Jane brought me up to date. She'd had three—abortions—but the last one never went away, the soul of it, that is. It lingered still, night and day, noon and dusk. She thought of it—she could practically see it, she said, during work, during sleep, in the shower.

Horst sprinkled dark hash into the tobacco and rolled deftly in the style of the northern Europeans, into a huge spliff shaped like a megaphone. He lit the fat end and burned off the stray fuzz. He took a big hit and passed it over. Penetrating the tobacco required some skill—Horst sucked it all straight down, but he was already coated thick in the lungs with tar and sludge. I took it easy, much slower, and still fell into a coughing fit. Horst laughed.

Jane didn't know what to do, and she didn't know what to do, and she didn't know what to do. Horst and I passed the joint, until her not knowing what to do ran full circle and the words conveyed clearly that she knew perfectly well what to do, what she wanted to do but could not proceed comfortably in doing, without some form of "support" from Horst. She floated dreamily in a mere matter of seconds, delivering the truth in words of untruth. She didn't know what to do.

She didn't know what to do because she knew this baby—the new one—was the same soul as the last one, aborted but lingering. She rambled tirelessly, repeating her mantra until the words became incidental to the feeling. Horst smoked the joint to the nub, achieved his greatest movement, leaning over to wipe the oogies from between his toes. He leaned back on the other half of his butt, relaxed and picked the eczema on his elbows. I looked for anxiety and maybe concern if not guilt and responsibility. But guys like Horst don't have to fuck with that stuff. Eminently visible was a strong desire to get stoned, to be stoned, to stay stoned. Horst wanted out, away, removal to another plane. He didn't want away from Jane, after all, he lived in her apartment. That was fine. He wanted to fuck Jane. He just didn't want to be bothered with anything else. He looked up at me and smiled. "Pretty good shit, yeah?" And I had to admit that it was.

Jane said her friends told her to abort and she knew why they told her that. She knew they loved her and only looked out for her best interest. And she knew she couldn't support herself really on the money she made much less take care of a baby, too, but still. Hadn't she always spent just exactly the same amount that she made? "I mean I've always got by haven't I? I mean I've made more sometimes and less sometimes, but it's been enough hasn't it? I don't want to be a burden to my friends. Maria isn't a rich one you know." She laughed and told Maria neither one of them was rich.

Maria answered in hard fast French. Horst raised an eyebrow. “My God, she’s some fine big tits isn’t she?” He looked over at me for elaboration on firmness, size, color, shape, dark hairs around the nipples and so on.

“Yes, she is,” I said. “Maybe the biggest in the world. And finest. You can’t possibly imagine.” Horst growled on cue.

Julian came forth from the bathroom, spit shined and grinning stupidly. “Give, Julian, give,” he said. He dropped his towel, delivered an ashtray to Horst and rummaged his pile for different pants and a shirt. “Give, Julian, give.”

Jane’s turn came for slumping into the couch, ruminant, stuck there just as Julian had been, knowing what to do, unable to do it. A waitress in a box with a great big heart, her diatribe was pointedly void of discouraging words over Horst. Horst was fact, immutable.

“How far along?” I asked.

“Six weeks. I have four more weeks to decide. I don’t know what to do.”

She gave in further to her slump, let her eyes slump too. Maria watched me like a hen watches a chick, like I might disappear any second. Horst lit another smoke, enjoying his recent lift.

A long half minute passed. Julian mumbled from the bathroom, then scatted a tune. Jane sighed and repeated softly that she was glad we’d come, Maria and me. She was so glad we’d come. Maria smiled sadly and waited.

Another half minute floated by. The hash did its work, but dominant in the dream was an expectation. They watched me, the stranger, as if I had descended upon this scene by way of Providence, with answers. “What? Am I the professor?”

"*Oui,*" Maria said. "*Tu es le professeur.*" Jane smiled. Horst smoked.

"What do you want to do, Horst?" I wasn't sure anyone had yet asked.

Horst didn't hesitate. "I have nothing. I am content to have nothing." It was a perfect answer, somewhere between enlightenment and worthlessness.

"And Jane wants the baby?" Jane nodded. "Then it's easy." A cloud of uncertainty became suddenly darker. "*C'est facile,*" I said to Maria. She shrugged. Jane sat up. Horst smoked. Julian emerged looking like a child ready for Sunday school, innocent and fragile, incapable of meeting the world without parental supervision.

"Oh, Julian!" Jane sat up with new life, new love, and the odd plot thickened, the three-way love surfaced. Julian loved despair. Horst loved himself. And Jane's feeling for Julian was heart and soul. She cared from the core. Horst was nothing, another surrogate stiff dick because Julian could not be. She was up and on him in one movement, caressing his wet brushed hair like a TV model showing how effective a little dab could be. "So handsome! Oh God, this is wonderful!"

She came to me with more gratitude, stoking the coals. Maria fidgeted and said now we must go, quickly.

She meant down and out and down the hill to the club. Julian had under an hour to stretch his fingers, find his rhythm. His scat blended with his new orders—Give, Julian, give—and he was surrounded for the walk, his friends commonly sensing where he lived, on the verge of disconnection.

Horst came to life, stood up and literally shook off his own slovenly morning. He was bigger standing up and moved like a man who'd taken some punches, thrown a few more. I was glad he was a close personal friend and not some kind of criminally insane bum you'd find in a dark alley. Strength showed formidably, was a thorough display of nothing to lose; his company made the rest of us stronger, his squirrelly jounce spread to Julian, too, who in a few steps looked like walking wounded ready to throw a punch. Horst said, "So. We are having a son?"

Julian was probably under thirty but had given in to decrepitude. He smoked less vigorously than Horst but smoked just as much. He was beyond café paralysis; the music expressed his thoughts, conclusions and truths. The music was his gift and his curse; it redeemed him, but he'd forsaken all else for it. At the stage door the truth among our small circle of friends was that Julian would most likely die young, maybe during the matinee. But he read it quickly and interceded on his own behalf—"It's okay!" he said. "Really. It's okay now. It went away. I'm fine."

If this was fine, oy vay.

We pretended belief. I nodded like a man, thumbs up, Maria nearly cried, kissing him left, right, left, mashing her breasts to him as if to share their unflagging fortitude. Jane slid in soft and ghostly with another hug, the kind she'd perfected on the fine line between this world and the next, where Julian lived. Her gift from the other world was invisible, good, happy. It was pure love, gift-wrapped in exquisite form, delicate delivery, cosmic sensuality. It was all she had to give, and it was more. It made my teeth throb. I wanted to get rid of the thing between us and love her forever.

Meanwhile, back in this world, Horst said, "I am starving. Do you have money?" He spoke indirectly to Jane. She said sure, we would go now and get something good to eat.

She touched Julian's cheek and he was gone through the doors to the other side.

Topside on the terrace the haze persisted but the sun shone strong. At a plastic table under a parasol, back, away from the stage, where our applause and appreciation wouldn't look staged but would carry forward like we really loved the guy for his music instead of looking like the hometown cheering section, we ordered up. I wanted a cold beer. Maria hesitated, the kitchen smells were so good, but then she sighed, showing strength and discipline by ordering another cold beer. Jane said she couldn't eat, wasn't hungry, didn't feel so good, you know, a lemonade would be good. Horst got the fried-chicken dinner.

It was two more beers and another lemonade before the chicken came. We relaxed mostly, unbuttoned our shirts and eased into the fresh air, sunshine and the natural goodness of no walls closing in. Julian played scales on stage, unamplified. A small crowd drifted in. The crowd got thick twenty minutes before showtime. "He really has quite a following," Jane said. "He's terrific. Wait till you hear."

The place got hot and packed in short order. Horst's fried-chicken dinner showed up a few minutes before the show. He was hemmed in on all sides by chairs and people standing and in front by a few pounds of fried chicken, steamed potatoes, house salad. He dug in, two hands, open wide and engorge, devour with focus and intent. Horst eating fried chicken was grotesque and nauseating. His absolute unconcern for crispy flecks on his lips, cheeks and chest, the grease pool forming on his chin was difficult to watch, to sit next to, and at the same time he was admirable. Horst once again didn't give a good goddamn.

It became nauseating again when Jane reached over and whisked the debris from his mouth with her lovely finger. Horst moved back, avoided her touch like an irritated child would. "I love it when he looks happy," she said. Horst grunted, going for the jugular on a fat dripping thigh. He came away with a mouthful in his mouth and another mouthful hanging out, the skin of it dangling. He moved like a snake, jaws unhinged, lunging and gulping with his whole body on live game. Failing, he shoved the overage in with two fingers. Jane beamed. "He's happy." He looked like a meat grinder on critical overload.

Maria turned away from him. She spoke low and fast, fake-smiling, quickly frowning. I nodded up, asking, what is it? An announcer on stage announced Julian Hamilton, who began playing along with the crowd's obvious appreciation and applause. Julian slid quick and easy to a melody, a mystique somewhere between jazz and classic. He was suddenly and overwhelmingly alive. He was extraordinary. He drew immediate attention, silence, rapture. "One time I fuck him and he never comes back." This, from Maria, in a whisper, in English. "He is no good. He fucks my good friend, and now she has the baby." She threw a scornful nod over her shoulder at Horst, but Horst concentrated on the bone, taking the end of it between his molars and crushing it off. "No fucking good."

I turned to the music; the music lured me in. Julian scored his journey, his arrival to a reality that cannot be anticipated, his presence across the line where giving must go further than a kindness here, a coin and a crumb there.

Surrounded by souls lost and confused, among them and one of them, I was a stranger no more. The music drew us in, one and all, shared with us its elusive order. Julian too, I then knew, was full of shit; a virtuoso with no body except on very good days. He should be big and strong as Horst, Horst should be frail and meek as he.

Maria should be Jane. Jane should be Maria. I should be somewhere else.

Julian played three hours to standing ovation and looked not much longer for the world. Horst got drunk. Jane loved his happiness. Maria got pissed and rushed me out with the crowd, with no farewell. But I hung back for another hug. I told Jane that we may never see each other again, but you never know, and if ever the occasion arose... "I know," she said.

A very long day stretched endlessly toward evening, reached far north up the highway toward a little coastal town Maria had always heard about and always wanted to visit. We pulled into a small hotel under trees so big and lush they blotted out the stars. I spoke English, only English. "So tell me, Maria," I said. "What do we know about this place?"

We shared a strong, distinct feeling then, Maria and I, that I was only fucking around, that time would soon come.

Saxuality in Repose

Leaving Paris at night, sloppy drunk, late for a train, on a wobble and a spin a man considers space, turning in on itself. The maze flip-flops, French yack bouncing off the walls, down the tubes in waves, like slurred Brie. Hex tiles and monotone melt the dream and make it vibrate.

Arrogant signs say this way, now here, now there...then thin down to nothing but three new tubes, empty, with all new signs. Fucking frogs, you can't help but think, and you send the signal—feets, arms, legs, and they move like magic through the goo. Momentum is another guy alongside whispering grace. What? Let the knees rise, float the arms, altogether, and you feel proud of the coordination possible with a little concentration. You look like a slapstick mime.

There's the stride, sweetly timed—lost soul drawn to a jazz horn like flotsam to a swirl. What's this? It's a man with no legs on a rug with a battered old sax playing in the key of Metro, maybe missing a note here and there but what feeling, what tone, what a mesmerizing sound like Pharaoh Sanders at Washington Square because, after all, the liquor, shit, winos and pushing French mob make any notes sound sweet. I ask him, "*Où est le train de Gare de l'Est?*" He plays on, I think—I think the notes don't stop above the bodies and the rush and filth so thick it too seems part of the din. He plays one-handed, waves the other hand at the sign overhead, the platform straight ahead. You are here. "*Il est ici,*" he says, I think, somehow emitting the words within the waves of people, jostle and noise. I play percussion coins, dropping them on his dirty rug, some of them worth ten francs each, what the fuck, this guy is a clear spring in a mud bog, next stop London.

For years I heard that music, most often wondering why, wondering what was left behind. I hardly ever had a drunk as good as that one, and I longed for years for Paris but realized in the second bottle that drunk was where I wanted to be. It wasn't Paris, dirty, hostile, crowded even then. Maybe it was the time, the fucking filthy moment opening up for beauty. You can't possess that. It's like childhood, once around and gone. You can't go back—everyone knows that. Still you make the trip.

And the going gets you down just like it did first time around, but you forget that the whole world is a trash dump of bad behaviors, until you are reminded. Maria in that light was a compulsive eater compensating for her loneliness, seeking me as the perfect entrée.

By compressing questions of linguistics, mendacity and promiscuity into one simple inquiry, by presenting her with a gentle invitation to speak, without challenging her honesty or her motive, I gave. Here for Maria was an opportunity for narrative elaboration rather than self-defense. Here for me was an opportunity to play the saxophone the way I'd heard it played, with honesty, from the heart.

I can't play the saxophone, haven't really ever held a saxophone. But one time after months of hearing the saxophone in a dream of drunken Metros, after years of yearning for the saxophone, for the chance to make saxophone music, I came close to buying a new saxophone, retail over three grand, repo around a grand, low miles, high sheen, and oh sweet Jesus, what a sound. It felt as free and easy as prelubrication, as magnetic attraction, as true love must feel.

It was step one on the saxophone path, but the path changed, mutated to a different route, because it was also a day of chance.

Chance led from the music shop with saxophone thoughts down a quiet street, a shortcut, toward my car, past an austere little building I'd walked past many times and looked through the windows maybe half those times and seen people inside doing what looked to me like an advanced form of nothing. Years later I would understand the difficulty of the pursuit. But then it was only odd and sometimes comical because the weight lifters across the street came outside between reps so they could air out, cool off and maybe by chance allow a passing woman or weakling to ogle the pumped muscles, the throbbing veins. And the weight lifters warned each other, "Hey, don't fuck with the old Japanese guys over there," in fear and reverence.

It was Tuesday and the place was closed Tuesdays but open that saxophone Tuesday. I went inside and stayed awhile.

I heard stories inside, stories of confrontations with knives and how they were made to dissipate, the confrontations, the knives. My teacher wouldn't talk to me or notice me or say my name or in any way recognize my existence. But that was only the old way, like in samurai days when the new boy had to clean up and shag beer or saki for five years or ten for the osmosis of the thing, or deference or tribute or something. After sacrificing those prime years, the new boy might be blessed by the big teacher, who would show him a secret move or two. Fuck that. Who cared? I didn't. I had better things to do than sweep up. And I made friends easy enough with another guy who'd been there for years already and showed me a few things. And when I showed that I could learn, I was told that only a fool or a monkey would waste a potential for learning, that learning would result in the greatest reward, the richest reward I could imagine.

But it still took all my time and didn't feel much different than cleaning up around the place—I didn't forget my saxophone and meant to go back and buy it, but the hour a day I would have spent practicing got sucked into the vacuum, along with a few more hours besides. I told Frank, my new friend, who didn't understand the real world as well as he understood his own little world down there, but who had an open ear, that I'd imagined for years a state of being, a place where resource and potential would converge and make saxophone music. He shot me his stupid-you look, like I was a fool or a monkey. "It's not so strange," I said, "if you go out into the world and accept it and love it and make the music. I feel great, like no other time when I hear certain people play. I want to make that kind of music. I want to hear myself making that music."

"Sure those guys make that kind of music," he said. "But look at their lives. They're all drunk or drugged up. They usually die young and all fucked up. They lose their shit, gradually and then suddenly. Those guys make music. So what. You can practice saxophone for years and make music, but you won't have inside what movement training will give you."

"I can't form an opinion on that. It sounds rigid. I saw a guy in a subway with no legs playing the greatest horn I've ever heard. You talk like that music cost him body and soul, like leprosy or something."

"Your training should come before anything," he said. "Hear the saxophone in your mind if you want to. But train. Train every day. You'll see."

Five years later I kind of saw it. I heard the saxophone in my mind, but it wasn't nearly as good as in person, and I still wished I held the brass, worked the keys. It got a little better in meditation, in movement.

I heard it going up the road through Germany, France and Belgium. I heard it surrounded by circumstance and events. I'd hit the road with purpose but found chaos. I heard the difference between the two, because if you don't put something in that blank space it will be put in there for you, and it isn't always good.

I heard it in a small hotel on the floor. Maria let me be. She sensed a desire in the little room, and it wasn't the desire she'd hoped for. I wanted away, like Horst, never mind his dirt and bad manners; I understood. It's what most men want. Jane and Maria were the same, because wanting something else is symptom of life, as we know it anyway, and it will never be enough. My craving for Jane was only a blip in the chaos; that it was predictable made it one more random event, another stellar movement. I listened to the melody in the air until way past dark, heard all the notes a saxophone ever had to give, then let the music go away. Maria slept. She didn't stir when I slid in beside her, soft as a single note.

The chaos was more acceptable in the morning, and odds were that I too was easier to bear.

The Last Room in Vlissingen

We went the wrong way somewhere in Belgium. We drove an hour down a road to nowhere, turned around and drove back two-and-a-half hours to Rosendaal to the right road to Vlissingen, a port town at the end of the line. Maria had fingered it for years on her map and said it seemed good, and she'd heard how good it was, the sea, the beach, the salt air.

Two nights of Maria passed before me like a small lifetime. She'd drained my tubes, chafed my nub, put my mind on asceticism. The days were worse, daylight was so harsh to my love, so unkind in its highlight, no shadow, the fat rolling like ocean swells under the rippled surface. Dimpled and stretched, she filled my eyes with her overabundant self, even as she sought to please me, stretching her tongue for what I knew was absolutely positively no chance of cream sauce. Her mass, her sweat, her armpit-hair drove me far away—she had more hair in her armpits than Larry the Stooge had on his head, and the style was the same. I thought of love and gave—twitched and squirmed to please her, just as Hattie had told me women so often do to please men who don't make them come, not really. If I thought of Hattie past her lessons in love, it was briefly, for the uncontrolled moments slipping past my barricade of repression; those pesky images of her bright smile, of her fulfillment after all these years with a lost Arab boy, or short of that with a new boy, since, after all, life goes on. Enough!

Maria's light still shone, but it was all heart. Her great big tits became lazy flab, handfuls of it defying the two-hand grasp, oozing to her armpits. These things came to me and settled on this midday interlude, during a "rest" stop on a solitary side road, on a blanket on the ground near her car. This was vacation, time to relax and enjoy—time for knowing the truth, for better or worse.

We reached Vlissingen at last in late afternoon, hot and sweaty again, facing another painful truth—Saturday, when millions of Dutch and Germans stampede to the sea in waves. The little town so fondly fantasized was crowded with people thicker than burbling maggots in a day-old road kill, no room at the inn. Maria looked bad, like she might drop dead from heat and fat and anxiety. I put her in a cafe on the beach and strolled up, looking, because hotel people say no rooms anywhere in town when their own places fill up.

I knocked at a pension, semi-bleak but acceptable. A tall, gaunt man in a bathrobe opened the door, gave me the up and down and said, "I have nothing at the moment."

I returned the up and down and smiled and said, "I must have a room. I have no place to stay, no choice." I felt good, safe and secure with Maria cooling off in a cafe. She would protect me.

The man in the door smiled now, but his apparent

starvation made it look more like a death grimace. He gave me another up and down and with a little smirk said, "Wait." He made a call on the phone behind the door, spoke Dutch quickly and then covered the mouthpiece as he leaned back to say, "You are very lucky. I have found for you the last room in Vlissingen. It has a *douche*, but the *toilette* is...is..."

"Down the hall."

"Yes. The *toilette* is down the hall. I do not know if it is good. But, if you have no choice..."

"I feel lucky," I said, because sometimes saying it makes it so, like praying sometimes leads to faith. The gaunt man slouched, waiting for a real answer. "I'll take it," I said. Back on the line he rattled off a wordy confirmation. "I'll piss in the shower," I said.

"What?"

"Nothing. Is it set?"

He rattled more, rang off and said, "You must hurry." He was a good man, kind and helpful, and his physical aberration was less ominous once he slouched further, lowering himself to his real level of comfort. He gave copious directions and lingered in a handshake and said, "Why don't you come back here. I will have something in two days."

I said, "Yes, my wife and I would like that." He stood up straight again, backing inside and closing the door with a grunt and grimace; he'd been toyed with. I went back for Maria, more certain than I was moments before that daily life in most of Europe is nonspiritual, revolves around food, shelter, opulence and a hole for your ever-hungry dick.

Maria looked fatigued and forlorn, fanning herself over an iced tea in the crowded cafe. Vlissingen was full up—people crowded the sidewalks and the beaches, standing or sitting, not lying down because there wasn't enough space. I wanted away from the crowd and sensed she did too. She looked self-conscious, for the first time aware of the comical difference between us. People looked and laughed, like I was Stan Laurel on a date with Sophie Tucker. Maria was susceptible to that sort of thing.

The directions to the room were bad and Maria got worse. She poured a heavy sweat and breathed harder as we crept through the traffic-jammed town looking for streets that weren't there, heading up dead-end alleys. She closed her eyes and nodded off.

The little car was a traveling circus with a fat lady, and a thin man who doubled as roustabout and driver. But the real circus had only begun its first weekend on a main canal near the center of town, right in front of the Garuda Hotel. We parked three blocks away, on the edge of it, its noise overpowering and unbelievable. Dozens of fun-rides with individual speakers shrieked cracked disco, rap, funk, bells and buzzers at maximum distortion, all different, all at once. It was a noise never before heard.

I yelled at Maria to stay put just as I'd yelled one time to my partner at the helm in thirty-foot seas, fifty-knot winds, to stay put while I went to secure the rigging.

I yelled my loudest but the message was lost in the maelstrom like a leaf. I got out, telling myself we could not dismast or sink or drift away or drown. But I didn't believe it, couldn't imagine human beings making noise like this without evil intention.

The Garuda was opposite a kiddie fun-ride, little cars on a track, with sirens screaming a shrill, whooping noise nonstop as background to a recorded carnival woman yelling in

Flemish. Surrounding this chaos was more funk, soul and disco music with heavy bass lines, all at warp, loud enough to tweak an inner ear.

A young Japanese man waited inside. He nodded and beckoned me up four flights to a room over the chaos. I yelled, "What time do they stop?"

"What?"

"What time?" I pointed to my watch, pointed outside and slit my throat with a forefinger.

"Oh! The music! It is not funny for you?"

I smiled. "No! It is not funny for me. It is sad for me!"

The manager smiled back, looked at his watch and yelled, "Twelve o'clock! At the very latest half past!" He smiled bigger with a head pump and opened the door.

The room was old European—heavy, dark, stuffy, peeling wallpaper, rickety midget furniture, no lamps, a bed like mush and one window over the noise, eighty bucks. It was disgusting. "Is okay you don't like, because I have no room more. No room more everybody. You leave is okay, too. You go five hundred kilometers is no room more."

"I love the room."

"You pay now!" I counted out the guilders. The manager snatched them up and hurried away. I went again for Maria.

She looked beat, puzzled and also disgusted. We slogged through hell, the heat, the noise, the gravity from the car to the room. She sat on the bed looking forlorn. I sat beside her, put an arm around her and spoke, but my voice was lost. I went to the window, but it was stuck open. I laughed and yelled at her, "There's a reason we're here!"

She yelled back, "What is it?"

"I don't know yet!"

She looked suddenly hopeful, got up and pulled the heavy, ancient curtain, came to me and engulfed me like an amoeba on a sub-atomic fleck.

"No no no!" I yelled. "Not now! I can't!" Nor could I ever again. We couldn't stay, we couldn't leave. We left for the street, for a few blocks distance where we walked the gray and shabby seaport until midnight, when fatigue became louder than the noise. We returned. I fell on the bed in my clothes and slept.

I woke a minute later when Maria standing beside me yelled down that she had to peepee but didn't know where. I pointed toward the door, indicated down the hall. She went, and from down the hall she yelled again that she had to peepee but didn't know where. I laughed at her dark bouncing form down the hallway, yelling anxiously, crossing her legs. I yelled that she should come back, peepee in the shower, or in the sink.

She sensed a game, a change of mood, a playful distraction there in Hotel Hell, and she pranced back shrieking delight over the prospects, at last, for some fun, for some revenge. I doused the light in time for discretion as she hoisted her skirt and eased her abundant ass over the edge of the sink. I closed my eyes as she tittered relief.

I woke at three, in silence. She lay beside me naked, and I saw her then as a pure light, as goodness and giving. A gang of vandals came down the street yelling, kicking cans, beating pipes on walls, rails, fences. Maria stirred awake. I closed my eyes and breathed slowly, audibly. She rolled to me and laid a hand on my dick. I grunted and rolled away, drifting off in sweet slumber. The cease-fire outside had finally taken hold.

We slept late. I cracked an eye open from under a pillow to see if the coast was clear. It wasn't. She lay propped on a pillow, watching me, with love. I faked sleep and rolled over. She rubbed my back. I moved into it, her strong hands easing the knots and strains of the road. She moved down and rubbed my ass, moved around to my thighs on a certain agenda. I've had my share of mornings like this one, when the early fuck is a duty, a drudgery, an unsavory task but is after all the right thing to do, considering the needs of others. I'd given in to spurious giving, but not today. Throwing the cover back I breathed big, bolted out and into the shower, where I also brushed my teeth.

Maria was disappointed but resigned, quiet but good-natured. Breakfast was somber and a consistent, bleak cuisine—Wonder Bread, pig meat, instant coffee. I wanted to explain that time had come; I wanted to rationalize our parting, but the truth was too simple. I could not. The noise began again, and we laughed, briefly. I leaned across the table, took her hand and said we'd been there for a reason. I said we'd met for a reason and traveled together for a reason. And now we would part for the same reason. I didn't know what the reason was, what next to say, but she spared me further struggle.

"I know," she said, whether she did know, or she was accustomed to sudden farewell. She was sad but stoic, and so was I, stoic and sad, and relieved all at once, like waking up in post-op, glad to be alive, tumor safely removed. I told her we would talk soon. She said nothing, with a look that said yeah yeah yeah. I told her I'd be back to Switzerland in two months, maybe only a month. She smiled sadly and nodded her head. One more march back to her car in a fit and a sweat under the burden of bag and baggage, because we end up slaves to our possessions and worse, our passions, a hug and a peck and it was all over but the crying. She pulled out forlornly, and my heart went with her. Is that what happens to great, big-hearted people like Maria? I still don't know, but I'll never forget the exhilaration of the moment; it took me airborne, where I clicked my heels and came down whistling a tune for a brand-new day. It was again base and mean in a life of baseness and meanness, yet gratitude infused the moment, too. Maria brought me up. She'd been my guide. And I'd arrived at last, to the road, alone, giving and taking, ready for a new and sunny day with no direction, no plan.

Back at Hotel Hell I couldn't help but believe that the noise and ugliness of this open, festering wound of a town comprised a chaos I was karmically drawn to; what goes around comes around, but Christ, it didn't have to lap the track in record time.

Besides, now the day was newer still. I was down to carry-on luggage once again. I still had all my credit cards and plenty cash, so I was mobile as any man. And morning and blue sky made a perfect atmosphere for cutting through the crap, for dispensing with bad thoughts, dark clouds, lost boys. What if... What if Hattie rode the train south, thought of me as she looked out the window, adjusted and calmed down on her arrival, had a good visit with old friends and now waited, wondering when I would call? So, I called. She'd given me the number, and I called.

Growing Pains

And the morning grew old very fast, went to ash and then anxiety. She'd left the place in the south of France, so the paper with the number was worthless as a Chinese newspaper. She'd gone away to central Italy, nobody knew exactly when or why, wasn't too sure with whom, although consensus was that a fellow showed up just before she left, maybe Italian, and he did mention going home to see his family in the beautiful hills. She'd left a forwarding number. Of course I thought it was for me.

Finding Hattie became necessary then, because I wanted it, all of it, part and parcel, the whole shebang. I wanted her on the other end of the phone saying yes, she missed me too, and though it was beautiful there in the south, and she'd met some nice people, she was ready for an adventure, maybe we could meet somewhere for some radical fun—maybe the coast of Spain, where we could ferry across to North Africa and smoke some hash and see what there was to see.

Nor was she at the forwarding number. They spoke no

English. I could call back in two hours, when someone who spoke English would be there. They thought Hattie was a city to the west, below Florence. They sounded pleased over my enthusiasm for it.

Outside, way north in the little seaside town of Vlissingen, satanic disco and dervish funk stirred to life, whirled up and down the narrow streets hollering chaos. The carnival woman wound up, her recorded laughter and Flemish taunts grinding into momentum. Two hours passed on instant coffee that tasted like dirt and just couldn't make the connection after the high-octane, fully refined espresso of France. The Japanese manager wanted to know: one more night, maybe? I told him may be. I waited for a direction to come to me, for either foot to move, for the other foot to follow. The greedy little man's head pumped vigorously, "You pay now."

"Go away." He stared while I dialed again. Hattie answered. Relief came in a wave, big and warm and flowing gently over.

"God, I've missed you," she said.

"You have?"

"Of course. I have so much to tell you."

"How much could it be?"

"Oh, you know. It seems like so long. I met all these people, and this place is so beautiful I've never seen anything like it."

"Maybe we should get together for a drink and talk it over." The connection felt instantly welded into place, good and strong, yet the next instant, the next wave, collapsed.

"Claudio's family has lived here over five hundred years. Just about everybody here is his cousin."

It was an exercise in relaxation in the clutch. Who is

Claudio? Where did you meet him? Are you staying with him? Do you fuck him?—all gone, out the window, cast off. "Is his father the judge?" Silly, stupid question, yet perfect in its demonstration of acceptance, of nonpossession, of strength.

"Gee, I don't know." She held the phone away and said to someone else, "Is your father the judge?" And she giggled, sillier and stupider than I had done, and all I wanted was away from the charade, away from the pain that crawled up my chest and gobbed my throat. "No," she said. "But he tells the judge what to do." She giggled again.

"I only called to say hey."

"Hey," she giggled. But it wasn't funny. She was nervous and awkward, which was the very worst for me, since she obviously hid the real issue, which was severe affection for Claudio, no need to belabor her means of demonstration.

"I'll call again...soon."

"Wait. Where are you?"

"Holland. A little town on the coast."

"I love Holland."

"I haven't seen any Arabs here." I couldn't help it. "Is Claudio Arab?" Maybe she choked up, too, for me or a long-lost love. Who knows? "Sorry. So, you think you'll be staying there in Italy?"

"I don't know."

"What do you feel?"

"I don't know."

"Is it a new feeling?"

"Yes."

"Can you describe it?"

"You can probably describe it better." Touché. I had it coming. I loved it when she moved inside. She shut me up like few people could with a pain I wouldn't forget. "Listen. I'm experimenting. That's all. Haven't you ever done that? I don't know what I'm doing. I miss you. I want to see you."

"You're a kick in the ass. You want me to come down and whisk you away from a dago kidnapper?"

She laughed, from the heart. "That would be fun."

"I don't even know where you are."

"I was kidding. I'm not kidnapped. I'm just having fun. I got so bored where I was I thought I'd go crazy. You know. I just need a little time. A little more time."

"Time for what? What kind of experimentation?"

"You got a one-track mind. I think you must cause yourself quite a bit of pain with it." Bull's-eye—perhaps her greatest gift yet, a right cross to the heart muscle. She had me pegged as sexually obsessive, jealous and neurotic, and in a tone of voice suggesting those behaviors were ridiculous, much less uncalled for. "I think maybe there's something wrong with me." She couldn't sucker me into that one. "I think, well...I think...it's hard for me to talk about this, but I miss you so much. You're the only person I ever really talked to..."

"Is that like saying I have a wonderful personality?"

"I love you. Don't analyze. Don't dissect. Okay? Okay. He has a sexual problem."

And Whammo! The kid is on the ropes. But if she taught me nothing else, she taught me springing off quickly. "Mmm. That is tough. And I can see where it would give a girl like you some cause for concern. Have you tried blow jobs? They seem effective in tough cases like this."

"Stop it." I shut up, maybe a minute too late. "He's a good guy. That's all. I just want a little more time."

"What? You want to hang out with him until you can

work it up for him, then quit while you're ahead?" It was a mistake, again, but I couldn't help it. She could be so open sexually, if she was getting it sexually. "Then you want to come back to me, because we can talk, and I get hard-ons easier than I don't get hard-ons."

"I don't think so," she said. "I'm just having fun. I'm only twenty-two, you know. Besides, we weren't exactly getting along."

"So? What? Should I call back in three hours?"

"Give me a week. How's that?"

"Terrific. I won't have any trouble at all with a week. I'm sure I won't think a thing of it."

"Well, you shouldn't. Hey, Holland is fun. You should go to Amsterdam. I want to go to Amsterdam. They have more fun in Amsterdam."

"Is this guy standing right there?"

"Well not right on top of me. Don't worry. He knows."

"He knows what?"

"He knows I love you."

"Jesus Christ, Hattie."

She laughed again. "Nobody ever called me that."

"I gotta go. I'll call you in a week. I'll be in Amsterdam. But how will you find me if you need to?"

"Relax. It's only a week. Hey. You met anyone?"

"Yeah, I did." It was my turn to twist the knife. "I met this fat lady. It's been interesting. She wants babies. I never hung out with a fat girl before. She's really a good person. I don't know. I might send her home. She's from Switzerland. We have fun you know. But she is fat. But I don't know. I don't want to hurt her. She's so nice. So giving."

"But you always hurt someone. You have to, or

you...you're stuck. You know. You stay in a bad place just to save someone from some pain, and you end up getting hurt yourself."

"I got to think about that."

"Call me in a week, okay?"

"You mean like you hanging out there with numb nuts just because you think it'll hurt him if you leave?"

"Call me in a week, okay? And please wear a rubber."

"So you stay there instead of coming up to Amsterdam for fun?"

"Call me."

"And room service..." She hung up.

Fire and Ice

The old, black and battered telephone with years upon years of ear grease shmushed into the ear holes in the earpiece was a perfect totem for the mood, the hour, the death noise outside and the pidgin greed in the manager's face—"You pay now."

Of course hindsight and perspective showed the scales evenly balanced between Hattie and me. Hadn't I spent days and nights surrounded by breasts and thighs? Hadn't I more likely than not engaged in squishy-squish far more than Hattie had with an Italian who couldn't get it up? Yet the fear singed my ear to my brain and down from there to my heart, and I knew it was fear of loss, fear that maybe she would not come away from her Italian experiment. At least the guy couldn't get it up, not yet. Yet it wasn't hard to wonder why I still stood there holding the phone; it was in painful meditation of the resourcefulness at the other end.

"You pay now." The little fellow had his hand out.

"Go fish."

"Yes. Yes. Fish. Dinner seven-thirty. Fish."

Outside Hotel Hell the noise neared its peak. There on the sidewalk in front two carry-on bags got opened, contents reviewed and split into two piles. The noise became a happy score to work by, a melody fit for madness. First impulse was to leave the second bag right where it lay. But the general manager of Hotel Hell watched closely nearby, so both bags got hoisted to shoulders and the long slog out began as all slogs must, with one step forward. The little manager watched with suspicion and scorn. Around the corner and twenty feet down an alley a woman peeled potatoes in a doorway. She was about a hundred-fifty and froze at my approach, like it was 1942 all over again and I had blond hair, blue eyes, the world's best genes and a gun. I gave her the second bag. She knew it was hot, so she stashed it quick and got back to potato peeling. I marched on, no good-bye nor thank you nor regret but one more step forward, for what I'd come for, for emptying the vessel. And when mental residue condensed on its walls into drops that rolled down in rivulets and collected in the bottom and little oogies drifted in to form a kind of soup, call it food for thought, then the vessel would empty again. And again and again, and with luck its pouring out empty would come every third step instead of every second, and with luck it would fill again every tenth or fiftieth step, and in time it would empty on its own and stay empty, like the pain of the single shoulder strap cutting into the flesh or the sweat forming like condensation on the walls of the vessel, gathering into drops and rolling into rivulets—never mind. Poof. All gone.

And arriving at that empty place in the amazingly short span of only a few miles, turning and looking back to the soft din and distant chaos of the carnival called humanity, a man could simply will a thing, like a taxicab. It pulled to the curb as if sensing the clear intent of eyes and will, neither of which strained visibly but rather eased with comfort further into emptiness, completely relaxed, more alive than in days and years. Sliding into the back seat I felt my voice open from somewhere deep, somewhere farther off than it had been. "Train station," I said.

The driver looked confused, maybe because a man arrived at a power and a will after so many miles might look different from the average pedestrian, and I had to laugh because maybe the look was a little nuts, too. "Station of the trains," I helped him along.

"You want to go to the train station?"

"Ah. Very good."

The driver shrugged. "Voila." And he pointed to the building beside us. Not bad, I thought, for will, intent and riding the taxi of no taxi. Maybe I was a little lost, a little nuts. I felt that way, too. But I didn't say anything. The driver spoke quickly, probably something about the fare. I emptied the vessel one mo' time, put one foot forward and went in and got a ticket—Amsterdam.

It was three hours or five, a thousand bodies with beat-up baggage and three thousand more with deluxe, Sherpa brand knapsacks for the very ultimate absolute best in roughing it in Europe—the bodies filing in, filing out, seeking communion with something lost, staring off as if off is where it went to, or staring cross-eyed at the little embers glowing on heartfelt inhalations, and clouds and clouds of smoke over miles of clacking rails. The day stayed one step ahead, and pulling into the soot-black city after so many hours and miles and bodies and smokes, time turned its trick; I was still a week away.

It hadn't changed in twenty years—at least in twenty years, since the last time I left Amsterdam, maybe in more years than that. It hadn't changed, but it had—where twenty years ago hundreds of youth crusaders made the pilgrimage to Amsterdam in denim and leather, now thousands upon thousands teemed in the streets, lived in the streets, or else faded quickly away in the streets. A boy maybe eighteen lay propped against a wall in the big stone station as if downed by life itself. Reverberant in its abundant reality, the great chamber was like a church, tending the needs of coming and going, and the boy, lowly supplicant, had found audience at last with God, or with someone or something that could hold his interest, or at least hold whatever pudding was left between his ears. His head lolled on a rubber neck as if drifting on a slack mooring. His hands sleepwalked into his shirt pockets for papers and tobacco, which he rolled mechanically, obviously on automatic. He prepped a paper with tobacco, stashed his papers and tobacco and with a smidgen more of life dug deeper into a side pocket for his stash. He plucked it from its plastic bag, watched it, felt it, crumbled little bits of it into the tobacco, as if measuring carefully, yet he continued until all of it lay strewn down the paper. He rolled it quickly and deftly as American cowboys must have done in the last century, and he lit up and drew deep and savored the slow-motion twitch his eyes made, opening wider, as if seeing more.

I stood right in front of him, shamelessly staring; his vessel got emptied long ago, and then melted, but his mug filled up then with warm, dark, smoky goo.

A tug on the shoulder brought me back—it was more than gravity digging in. It was a crummy, dirty thief grabbing my bag, trying to steal it right off my shoulder. But the thief didn't know with whom he fucked. Of course the bag wouldn't give, and when the thief felt it stuck tight to where it hung, I gave him the death look to send him on his way. It worked, although the thief said, "Fuck you!" and left slowly, casually, daring a chase.

He carried a knife, which seemed strange in a crowd. And he carried a familiar-looking shirt, too. The crummy little slug had slit my bag in back, liked the shirt, wanted it all. What a town.

I hurried on. A voice on everywhere speakers demanded: Don't put your bags down. Don't stand still. Don't talk to strangers. Keep moving. Watch your bags. Beware pickpockets. Don't put your bags down. Don't stand still. Don't...

Outside was better, but that was easy. Dirt and desperation thinned, had more room to spread out. It's a town at street level, where the rebellion continues in constant movement on the flagstones, where the thousands upon thousands of crusaders literally sit down on the street because down and right on the street is where they want to be to pull hard on their dream smokes, because it don't get no nitty-grittier than right down, down on the soot-black slate of the street—who the fuck are you?

Dam Place is the center, the hub from which the streets angle out like spokes of a wheel, around which in concentric circles flow the canals that freeze over solid in wintertime and look slick and clean enough for Hans Brinker but in summertime thaw to greenshit reality, frosted over with scuz foam and empties.

An empty vessel on two strong legs can drift down these streets, cross the canals and get away from the need warp in the center, but not too far. I stopped at a sidewalk place in an alley with no cars, which was refreshing right off, and the air too in Amsterdam was cleaner, because the town sits near the sea, and the only soot surviving is the heavy soot, clinging to the streets and buildings and to some of the hard-core pedestrians. I got a coffee and an apple torte from a soft man inside and noticed that the staff was all soft, all committed to the specifics of a specific way of life, and so was most of the clientele, but it was outside, daytime, integrated, and I don't mind those guys if they keep to themselves. I double-took on the two fellows at the next table—one stoked a pipe with a chunk of hash. I leaned over and asked if hash was readily available here. The fellow laughed and said yes, just about anywhere. I asked, how about here? The fellow said no. But there, just there, Club Ballou. He pointed to a neon dancing bear smoking a spliff. I finished and walked over.

Club Ballou was what they call a coffee shop, ten-by-twelve with a percolator, four booths and a counter with two stools. A woman who looked Arab, sixty-five, behind the counter asked what. I whispered, "Do you have hashish?"

"What?"

"Do you have hashish?"

"Hashish? You want hashish? Good? Here!" She reached under the counter and pulled up a plastic cassette case. I turned it in my hands, opened it. Empty. She took it back, closed it, and handed it to me again, song titles front and center: Pakistan, Zero-Zero, Spoetnik, Libanon, Premiera, Kashmere, Manali, Maroc-Super, Turks, Caramello, Thai, Skunk, Jamaica, Columbia, Hanoi, Transkei.

I studied it. She studied me. "What's the difference in these?"

"What you mean, difference?

"Say Maroc. Is different from...Kashmere?"

She reached again under the counter, this time pulling up her accordion business file. She pulled envelopes from M and K, opened them for me to smell. The Maroc was the old standard. The Kashmere was sweet, acrid, like hash mixed with incense and glue, and maybe a dash of opium.

"That's it? They smell different?"

"No, no. Maroc heavy. You feel heavy. Very nice. Kashmere is..."

"Light?"

"No, not light but... You feel ever the wool from Kashmere?"

"Soft?"

"Yes. Soft. And thick."

"I like Kashmere."

"Yes. Is very good."

Like the wool, it was twice the price. I liked that, too, most likely from remnant superiority, liked the idea of a difference between me and most of the rest, but mostly liked the prospect of a top-drawer high. At that it was only twenty-five guilders for a gram, hardly twelve bucks.

I left Club Ballou feeling accomplished and in the next block saw a pipe store. Again I whispered for a small, cheap pipe. The pipe guy showed me a baby meerschaum for a hundred-fifty. "No, small pipe for hashish."

"Oh! Hash pipe!" the pipe guy caught on. I looked around but nobody looked back—it was more casual than asking for tampons in a crowd. It was natural, an honest need to fulfill. The pipe guy found a little clay chillum for two guilders and threw in the screen and matches for free.

In a minute I was back in the first place, at the same

table, in the same chair, sitting beside the same two friendly fellows, but this time looking landed, like a man who knows his way around town, casually stoking up. It had been a lovely afternoon with a pleasant project to while away the hours. The two fellows at the next table got a big kick out of the new guy in town, getting way too stoned. They thought I was cute.

Amsterdam Revisited

The big difference between the hashish available in Amsterdam and the marijuana smoked in America is like the difference between sleeping on a pillow or sleeping under the featherbed. Like the woman said, soft and thick, gentle to the touch. It had been years—years of heightened potency, intensified THC in marijuana efforts across America, so a couple hits on a joint was a major commitment to stupid silence, lethargy, fatigue, and sleep.

This hash from Kashmere, on the other hand, was sipping whiskey, smooth as it gets. Why, a man like me—especially a man like me—who'd been around the block, had learned the ups and downs of the ups and downs, knew his limits, his friendly maximums, could smoke this shit all day long. I had another hot joe, loved the world, put vast distance between the vessel and Hattie, stood up and sent the message: feets, forward. Like good dogs, they obeyed. You can tell the new arrivals. They watch their feet, left right left right, in utter amazement.

What felt good was the endless afternoon, so far north, with the sun only half down, and it was already seven. What felt good was the walking, walking, walking. I turned for no reason and walked three more blocks, or ten, and for the same reason looked up and read the street sign: Herrengraat Strasse. I'd been here before, over twenty years ago, when the whole town was famous for two clubs for the kids, Fantasia and Paradisio, and a week got sucked down the pipe, or was it ten days?

I remembered the student hotel—Herrengraat Strasse 88. Here was the 400 block, and with no better direction than that of the past, I sat down, loaded up and started the walk back. I laughed, as people sometimes laugh at extreme personal difficulty years ago, laughed at getting kicked out of HS 88 because my eyeballs kept spinning back inside my head and then my head started spinning back, too, so it could keep up with my eyeballs, and I held on to things, anything after a few days and smoked Drum tobacco and drank draft Heineken till personality function was down to sleep and giggle, giggle and sleep.

I'd paid up three days in advance, but first thing I knew they were gone too and there it was, dark and late and the place was full up, so I crawled under a bed and slept there until the middle of the night when some nazi fucker poked me with a broomstick and kicked me out, into the street, dark and cold and bracingly real with five hours to kill until daylight, and the street boogies desperate for anything of value, anything to eat, prowling the shadows, all eyes and teeth. Fuck this, I figured at the time; these guys don't know about the revolution, that we're all brothers and sisters. These fascist fuckers just want more money. And I left Amsterdam, never to return until twenty-two years later, on an afterthought, by chance.

I swung into the first hotel and didn't give a shit if it was homosexual or overpriced or had bad air, fuck it, I had to ditch the goddamn bag and get back out and know I had a place later to come back to so I wouldn't have to bother with it in the dark, even though the years had left a resilience, a survival instinct for the dark, unknown at twenty; let the beasties come on; the very proximity of their lives to mine was a gift, a wonderful thing for which I could now be grateful, knowing what I knew, through which, both I and the beasties could evolve. And maybe I was getting the hang of the road at last.

The woman behind the counter was no beastie. She was easy, accustomed to guys staring, horny or stoned or both, like she knew I was all lit up and pushed the forms for me. Another blast in the room was nice as the first two, and the place wasn't bad at all, and even though it was five flights up and only a two-star hotel so you had to hump it, it had trees out front, tall ones with leafy tops right out the fourth-floor window.

Hotel Hell and Maria were otherworldly now, in slanting afternoon sunlight, clear, cool air, no noise, no pressure, only long smooth hits of soft and gentle.

But no time for sentiment, not in the prime filet of a beautiful new day, in the matrix of emptiness, in the folds of Kashmere. Down and out and down the street again to 88, but what the hell, the night was yet in infancy, and feeling thirsty and then parched, dry inners and then seeing a bar that looked open and airy and played decent music, because they play good music in Amsterdam... What?

A Heineken draft slid down way too easy but was all right because it tasted so good and filled such a deep hole, and the bartender was right there with another and down it went, too. And there again I sat mumbling no no no no, I can't drink it no more.

The bartender laughed, went out back with the sink still running, maybe to load his own pipe. The sink overflowed onto the floor, so I reached over and turned off the faucet. The bartender came back and said, Oh shit! and drew a round for me and another and another and another for saving the whole goddamn place from such a mess.

I quaffed, considering goddamn places and messes and marginal mentalities. I wondered if the bartender was part of a conspiracy to get me way round the bend, because what else could it be? And, Oh fuck it, I mumbled. It was clear to me then as the nose on my face what the plan was down at city hall. It was to develop a tourist industry unlike anyplace else in the world. Brain-cell euthanasia was to this place what sunny beaches, clear water are to the tropics. And oh how they came for the weather.

Just like old times is was it was. And it was a farewell with sentiment, too, between me and my new pal, the bartender at the Whatever It Was Bar, because I'd saved his bar, kind of, well, a part of his life, or the floor anyway, and he...he..., well shit he gave me quite a few beers. Be back I would. And out again to a brand-new town with a stronger pulse now that the sun was farther down, and a life with verve came awake, just like the new feeling between a man and woman just meeting, just sensing the potential without the limits.

The dirt and trash and shitgreen canals took on an eventful air in twilight, a benign, friendly invitation. Unshaved for two days and feeling glad for the nubs, feeling more adapted to the place and spirit, I realized the town didn't shave, either, in the figurative, half-grubbed sense. More people out now, still in denim and dark leather, still stoned, and along with regular whiffs of fresh bowls stoking came the scent of anarchy in the air. It was another revolution, never ending, of the soul, a coup d'etat.

I stopped at a bench by the canal and stoked up again myself, for the spirit of the thing, for the last few blocks to the past.

A few blocks down, boarded up, under construction, *Verboten Toegang*: HS 88's foyer was open but the door inside it was boarded shut, planks and barbwire, appropriate monument to the war dead and walking wounded surviving these gates to the revolution. I remembered that foyer, like déjà vu easily pinned to its antecedent, since the first time was a waking dream that lasted a week or two. No need to linger, I stepped over the short barricade and eyeballed a Dutch dime, heads up, which stretched a big stupid grin across my face and filled the vessel with lumpy gruel—twenty laps around the sun, I thought, to complete the course long way round to the far side of the coin. Luck had changed, and here I was again.

Next door was a long narrow bar perpendicular to the street. A sign out front showed Woody Woodpecker smoking a megaphone joint, fluffed and fuzzy out the end, with smoke trailing out his ears. The place looked like a hallway and most likely was, until it got squeezed tight with a bar and stools.

I ordered a sandwich, American Filet, because the bartender explained it was a hamburger, then served it up raw, there was no kitchen, but then the menu said nothing about cooking it. Hmmm...raw hamburger. My old man ate raw hamburger all the time, and it could have been the old man's favorite dish, especially with salt and onion. The old man died thirty years ago, and here I was, cold beer, raw burger, just like he'd like it. So the son dug in with relish, feeling a certain presence, considering omens, luck, synchronicities. It was amazing, how the hash opened things up like that.

I put my magic coin with a few more and ordered up, savoring the taste by now. I asked about Herrengraat Strasse 88, and the bartender said yes, finally, it got closed last year after years and years of infestation and drugs, filth and junkies and crime.

I was there, I told him, in the late sixties it was it was. The bartender said he was there, too, used to work there; he turned away and loaded a tape, Creedence, loud, "Bad Moon Rising". He turned back and drew another round, for old times' sake, like we were vets from the same engagement, him and me. And I suppose we were. And for the occasion, reverential as Sitting Bull at Council Bluff, I stoked the pipe for communion, for bonding, for everything that is everything.

"You Americans," the bartender said, "smoke that shit straight. Unbelievable." I offered the pipe and was duly impressed at the billowing clouds the barkeep produced in mere moments. Furrowing his brow in a great display of cumulonimbus the bartender asked, "Kashmere?"

"Fucking A," I confirmed. I think he liked it, he smoked it so hard, until he faded in the cloud. "Hey," I had a thought. "Are you the motherfucker who jabbed me with a broomstick under the bed and kicked me out in the middle of the night?"

"I think so," he said, and we laughed so hard we nearly

cried. He said no shit, it must have been him, he poked so many people under the beds. He turned around, and I thought he was going to show me the broom, which would have been too amazing.

But he turned back with a hand-carved wooden box from the backbar and said, "Try this." From the box he pulled a glass vial with a glass stopper with a dauber on the end. He dabbed a globule of tar into the pipe.

"Opium?"

"No. Not exactly. It won't lay you down. Not right away."

"How long will we have?"

"Oh, easy two, three hours."

That would make it late enough, and here I was making contact in a town making contact. I was a pilgrim, on the road, making mincemeat of day one of seven, no survivors, no remains. I lit the pipe, took a hit and asked, "What is it, exactly?"

"Kind of a hash oil." I pulled hard and the goo flared, so I passed it quickly in the old, undying spirit—hurry—waste not, lest ye be unwasted.

The bartender sounded like a small jet intake and handed it back quickly. But twenty-two years hadn't left me stupid, or quite so rash and impulsive as last time around. I took it slow and easy and told the air in general, "Ten. Nine. Eight. Seven. Six. Five. Four. Three. Two..." Just as I thought—liftoff. I stashed the pipe, laid a few bills on the counter, smiled big and knew I didn't need to speak.

"Flipside, Brother," was the farewell of the man who last farewelled me with a broomstick, which flipside would have been something to think about any other time, like say a time when a thought could hold together better than confetti.

Outside the cool night air was good for walking, and the time too was good for dropping into gear, stretching it out to cruising speed and going. Inventory came quick and easy; it was second-nature time, time to move without thinking, time to use what experience teaches, it was way gone, way way out of town, way way way buzzed. In a brief loss of contact at orbital speed I realized I would never find the hotel. Then I remembered it was just like it was, down Herrengraat Strasse, which I hadn't forgot for twenty-two years, and maybe I wouldn't forget it tonight, too.

I know enough to dodge the alleys, keep to the main streets, even though some are long and wide and unlit, never mind, long and wide means room to move, even with a canal in between. An arched bridge leading over to another section, a separate neighborhood, looked good, so I took that route, following the light, monitoring strength and the cosmos.

Strength was stable, reality incoming in waves and warps and the old quasihallucinovibragrid, tingling, turning the faces in the windows purple and yellow, but maybe that's from the lights, red now, strung up all down the fairway—ah, it's the whores, this must be Amsterdam.

Looking out their windows, more lewd now than twenty years ago when whoring was simply whoring and a whore wanted to get as many sailors into her pussy in a night as she could and she wasn't a tourist attraction like now, when business is down to the infrequent novelty fuck. I remembered an older whore, maybe forty then, who had a hard time competing with the younger whores, and her pitch was Blow job? Would you like for me to give you a blow job? She looked like my old English teacher, who I never really liked, not even for a blow job, so I'd picked a young beauty with bruised tits, so many guys had squeezed them.

It was me and Bumpy Oliver and the revolution on pilgrimage that summer. Bumpy's name was Lewis and he talked slow and sounded stupid, but he had a brain that could set a pace. I met him at a fraternity party for boys like us who wanted to be just like the fraternity boys, and the party was to give the fraternity boys a chance to check us out, to see if we were their type. The fraternity boys bought beer for us to drink, and they mixed grain alcohol with grape juice in a garbage can, but I honestly never thought they expected anyone to drink it. They called it purple passion and drank it very carefully with gusto. Some of the new boys swilled it down in the spirit of something or other and got drunk as college boys on grain alcohol. I had a beer. Bumpy Oliver leaned on a wall nearby, apparently not their type, they so completely ignored him, because he sounded so stupid. He lit a joint and offered me some—my first ever. I tried it out. He said, in his remedial drawl, "You know... Uhh, the Moody Blues say thinking is the best way to travel, but most people would still rather take the bus."

We were friends forever after that. He was a farm boy come to college, and he had more joints in his pocket and soon had an audience, since those were the days when joints were brand new and amazingly hip. He let the other boys try, too, keeping them enrapt with tales of homegrown hemp and animal fucking in the barnyard. Once stoned, the other boys found him exotic, even into his assessment of the best fuck in the barnyard, the chickens, except that he had to stop because his daddy got so pissed off at him because it killed the chickens nearly every time. Some of the boys laughed. Some puked purple. Some looked concerned. Who the hell knew?

Bump and I avoided the draft together, got stoned and wondered what the fuck together, got too stoned and lost, looking for the whores of Amsterdam, for historical significance, a common delusion with college boys, especially then when the reefer and LSD and prospects for Vietnam made us certain beyond doubt that we'd either tame what was left of the Wild West in the world, or else we'd die in a jungle, face down in the mud.

Historically stoned at street level in Amsterdam, we applied method to our approach. Amsterdam was the shore leave of choice then for the sailors of the world, who could blow a month's pay in a weekend on what sailors love best and lack most. But we were college boys, so we shopped before buying. Bumpy theorized that jacking off into a canal would help us get our money's worth—about six bucks then.

I laughed. I didn't think I could jack off on a canal in the dark. Bumpy gave it up, allowing it might work if we had some magazines and flashlights or something.

So we walked on into the night, drank more beer and walked some more, thinking, pursuing our campaign of maximum efficiency. At war with our heroic impulses, we got stuck in the thinking—I blame it on too much shelter, too much comfort, too much college. It'll ruin the spirit of any boy who finally gets out into the world, down to street level.

Years later in the here and now on those same loveless streets I wondered what barriers had dissolved, what essence did the adventure now make. How often do you read of the vale of tears, of the tough row to hoe, of the difficult path of life? And at what age do you believe it? At what phase of development—or is that degeneration—do you know the disillusionment in your heart is the forever balance to the love

love that may also reside there? I stopped, sat on a bench, alone and far away as ever I'd been, still and dark as the far side of the seventh moon of Jupiter. I stoked the bowl and waited for meaning to catch up, for resolution, or at least acceptance, to join me there.

We salvaged that night long ago as well with another bowl of hash and let volition take the lead. It got easy then, no thinking required, just left right left behind the movement of the night, along with the twinkling lights and shimmering shitgreen canals, into the arms of the last whores open for business, who sincerely seemed to like us, who wanted us to come into their rooms for some meaningful ficky-fick.

The pick was easy. Bumpy got the old lady, because he'd had her for English too and said this was a much better deal. Mine was young but looked tired but was glad to see me, because I was young, too, and intelligent and good-looking and obviously sensitive. What a refreshing change from crazy sailors night after night. Why else would she titter so? Not only that, she came, no shit, with a twitch and a whimper and a plea and a squirm. I let her have it good but couldn't get behind it because the rubber was the same gauge as my frog flippers. She went limp in ninety seconds flat and spoke English: "Come on come on come on." In fact I couldn't get off at all, but finally made it when she said, "Time's up," pulled me out and went manual, no titter no whimper, only nurse retrieving sperm sample.

Bumpy and I had a laugh after that, agreeing the adventure would stand retelling without recollections of jacking off into a canal. We'd stoked a bowlful back on the street, raised a toast to the beautiful, bounteous-breasted women of Amsterdam, who would open their thighs for your big salami for only five dollars and fifty cents. What an amazing deal, and what a time it was that we toasted, that kept us toasted, kept us cognizant through our incoherence that such a confluence of magic and anarchy would be a long time coming again.

We lost the seams between day and night for a week and a half in 1969, yet that time survives like a beautiful dream, foggy and imprecise but as full of clarity and insight as any lucid memory ever was. I'd just turned twenty-one, just begun the steep ascent of knowing, of wishing I'd known it only a few weeks before—I recalled for Bumpy a girl in the campgrounds at Pamplona where we'd all gone to drink red wine for only seven pesetas a quart and smoke kif delivered daily by brothers and sisters just up from Morocco. She was from California and knew everything—I knew that just by looking at her, but I didn't know anything else. I was from Indiana. She had a perfect figure and long blond hair and a face as pretty as a cameo, and she asked me if I'd take her for a walk up the hill to the old, abandoned church. I told her no, I didn't like churches. And I really didn't feel like a walk. Three days she asked, until she finally asked a guy from Oregon. He knew what to do and did it for another two weeks, until Pamplona got all used up and the campground got piled high with empty wine bottles and the sewage system got so backed up the whole place smelled like shit.

So we all hit the road again. I say "we" as if we traveled in the same group, because we did, mixing and matching, weaving paths because the road then was a single place, with as many adventures, stops, romances, highs, risks—with as much fun as you could want. We were brothers and sisters.

I'd run into Bumpy Oliver in a sidewalk cafe in Athens a

few weeks after Pamplona, so we got drunk and caught a boat to an island and then flew to Rome and hitched a ride north to Amsterdam, via Lausanne and Munich, and there we were, stoned in Amsterdam, just after sexual intercourse with real, live women—his third, my fourth.

I stoked the bowl and raised another toast to Bumpy twenty-two years after that, wondering if he ever toasted me. He sold big-ticket real estate in Denver, closed them slow on a drawl and a twang, sounded stupid and made a mint.

I got up and walked down the street, into the night, the forever endless night.

How in the world could I have been so stupid, so selfish as to say no to a simple request for a walk up a hill to an old church? Even if I didn't like churches, why wouldn't I have just gone for the walk? Her name was Jane, not Jane Alexander or Mansfield—it was Burnee or something like that. I looked around for a pay phone so I could call California information and get the number of Jane. It's Jane Burnee or something like that, the one who was in Pamplona in '69—we smoked a load of kif and drank way too much wine and she fucked some dud from Oregon for two weeks straight but it was me she wanted to hang out with. I wondered where she'd be now, if maybe she wouldn't be able to fly on up to Amsterdam for, you know, old times, maybe a little walk.

I wondered how many women from the years and years ago I'd wondered about, wondering if these same faces in these same windows all these years later for better or worse, for wiser or dumber, would lead as well to some resolution, some reconciliation between the drive and the spirit.

I thought it would. I thought that if Jane Burnee or any of them could materialize right there beside me that I'd be happy as a lark at the prospect for a walk through Amsterdam with her, way past midnight and stoned to the gills, remembering the way it was, so free. Free of consequence, free of fear, free of constraint—as free-spirited as ever a time and rebellion ever was.

Only the night laid its emptiness out before me, only the void remained, loomed endlessly beyond, in which a question took form and orbited like a stellar body, and the question was love. Is it anywhere? Can it last, even with lyrics by the Beetles?

I laughed again with gratitude. At least I loved myself, or I was game for the growth process anyway, with a generous capacity for sheer, dumb naiveté. And I laughed again for my complete lack of bearings on a black night on a foreign planet, step left, left, left. I would have turned back from that wide, dark street with a canal in the center, but turning back is a wrong behavior to show night beasties who swaggered my way in a troublesome threesome, arms swinging too high, too far, legs bowed and overstretched as if reaching for something unavailable, longing, practically lunging.

It was suddenly present tense, twenty years after our wonderful anarchy, our beautiful dream. One of the boys coming my way veered and squared before an empty can and kicked it with vengeance and laughed at the clang and clatter. The others grunted threats and woofed at other cans, and one of them side-kicked a garbage can, just the way he'd seen it done in a martial arts movie. They woofed and howled some more, kicked the garbage down the street and spoke predation in body language, sixty yards and closing.

A gift came to me then, rolled over like a wave, filled and surrounded everything in sight. Subliminal longing come to the surface is what it was; a man ponders love, too drunk and badly stoned and far away as nowhere, he finds himself at last, at home. And what do you know but resolution joins hands with the question, and there in the crux came the blessing, the golden rule I always knew and had preached to others but maybe forgot about myself; it was the greatest gift, attainable only by sending what is wanted most, which is love.

The blessing was a memo from the past and the future, coming home, here, now, like a melody on a saxophone.

Somewhere near, the night dogs fought over scraps. Maybe I could calm them down.

East Meets West

My wrestling coach said I was a scrapper in my head with no goods to back it up. He meant I was a punk. We both went five-eight, but he went two-twenty; I wobbled in at one-o-three. He had a stupid grin all the time. I scowled.

Now here's what I want you to do, he said, laying a forty-pound arm on my eighteen-ounce shoulders. Get some weights, a hundred pounds or so. Lift every day.

He had nothing in the lighter weight classes. I was the best of the twirps. But if I bulked up, I'd gain weight. "You just lift. We'll worry later about too much muscle." Too much muscle. I liked that. I wanted the girls to sigh, wanted the guys in awe. So I blew twenty bucks on barbells—big money then, but I put it together. I wanted to win.

I lifted nights to the radio—two years for thirty pounds, so I was thin instead of skinny. Taller than most, I could still beat the muscle guys—with my legs. Other coaches warned their boys to avoid the legs. I watched them whisper and sent the stupid grin, wondering if the other boy got as puked-out scared as Spiderman did. I was sixteen and winning with a mystique. I believed it too, posing like a spider before matches, rubbing all my arms and legs, spinning a lie to fight the fear. I was winning. I hated it.

"Never mind. The more scared you get, the less scared you'll be. Scared is what this stuff is good for. Use it up and you won't be scared anymore for the rest of your life. Smile."

Pretty heady shit for a fat bastard like you to lay on a kid like me is what I thought, but Spiderman gave it a go—the fear became necessary, like the fear was a basic move to get to the other moves. When I lost, Coach showed me where I lost. When I won, he showed me where the other guy lost. He thought winning was natural, given, until thrown away. Then he died, brain tumor. Spiderman grew up and gained another thirty-five pounds.

I remembered the smile, led with it, opened with warmth, got to thirty-five and still smiled when people said they didn't know what I did for a living, but it didn't look like much. I liked to say it's not. I liked to twist the smile, so people would know my good nature was in fact a dare to anyone who thought they could rub two nickels together and come up with fifteen cents. Why don't you try it?

It led to floating hostility. But a person who survives by his wits must know that the world is not the best possible place. It only reflects convenience.

At forty things change; the end comes into view. I knew I pressed too hard, hurt people when I only needed to make a point. I didn't need a shrink, I needed a coach, or something. Something to vent the pressure.

So I stumbled into a place that reminded me of the old wrestling room. The old guys there said I was amazing, so full of piss and vinegar. I was proud, but they hadn't meant to praise. They said I was a long shot, but I had a chance.

What?

I got harped on, preached at, yelled at, whispered at, told to relax. Do nothing. It's a non-concept and I couldn't get it, which was no surprise. Here too immersion preceded understanding—they got me down to mush. Then came sense, whacking me on the head one day when I figured out they didn't mean don't do anything. They meant Do Nothing!

Some of my new friends sat for days in the country with the Roshi and came back with a smile that looked familiar. The Roshi didn't want anyone to sit who wasn't yet thirty-five. I was forty—nobody know de hustle I seen—and I'd seen it all. He smiled—"Why don't you try it sometime?"

I can't tell you what happens, whether it's two hours or two days or ten days. You pass through pain, anxiety, restlessness, some of all of life, but then you get something new, which is profound at forty. It goes away, just like sexual satisfaction goes away. Meditation isn't hormonally motivated, but people over thirty-five who feel another hunger often go for more. It's easy on a daily basis, easier than lifting weights. It can change the mind and body, turn the action and the oomph into something else. My teacher said we have only one competition—against ourselves. He finally threw me when he got tired of my head banging; he was seventy-two. He barely touched me. I flew. I came up grinning, "Do that again." He laughed, walking away.

I took a few more years trying to do nothing, which is about the hardest thing to do. You meditate, then try to bring that feeling into movement. Still a scrapper with the goods was a hard nut to crack; I still moved for the take down and pin.

My teacher said something was wrong, that my mind was not calm. I hated that. "You must sit. Don't think bad thoughts. Smile." I already sat, I told him, and he yelled, "Not enough!" So it was a few more years of sitting, letting concepts trickle like water through fingers, felt and lost, felt again and lost, until the trickle became a submersion, and the smile was in the eyes, just like the two guys I had no choice but to listen to.

I saw three boys at night in the city walking my way. I heard dogs barking. I imagined them as pups, wagging their tails. I smiled and thought, What interesting lives these boys must lead. I didn't have to think Boy oh boy oh boy am I ever fucked up or what? That was clear as the night, twinkly as the stars.

They joined ranks, their woof and cackles ceased. They came my way, pressing their prey to the canal. I stayed my course, held my pace and smiled bigger. The most aggressive segment of their mind stepped out, stepped ahead for the mark, for the lunge. It came at shoulder height with a grunt and another woof and a snigger, as if I was responsible for the shit that was his life and this was revenge, would be fun, not to mention feeding. He smiled, too.

I turned to baby mush so my new friend wouldn't have to feel anything. The move was basic, get out of the way, first my own way and then his way, or rather be out of the way, or some esoteric shit you can't ever really get right, can't ever do without somebody harping in your face no no no not like that. But even if you do it wrong thousands of times, which is about how many times you do it over the years, well, even a scrapper can scrape together a little mush. I gave the guy as much hospitality as I could, because I knew he needed help without him telling me. I moved okay from the hips, out of his line and then joined him kind of like Arthur Murray joined Katherine in the samba. I could have kissed the guy, but I wasn't that fucked up, but I was that close to him. And I guess my smile was maybe less than sincere until that moment, which was one of those rare moments, of truth, and I remembered Coach, who was the guy who first showed me the one-armed pancake but never dreamed of delivering it with so much nothing, no bump, nary a touch. I felt pretty certain the guy I just threw would want me to try that again, but one of his asshole buddies came on pretty quick, so I turned to him and he veered off, spooked, which was okay, too.

I don't know, maybe I smiled too much, maybe it didn't matter because maybe the last one was the craziest of the bunch—he just stood there smiling back, and I honestly felt he meant it from the heart, and the knife. The second one got his nerve up again and came in with two hands low, already off balance. I went to mush again and this one stopped short to see what the fuck. But too late, no stopping allowed, not him or me or the stellar bodies, and maybe not some of the goods too because you never get rid of all the stuff, and we all had time to keep, ally oop and up with him, into the greenshit ditch.

I took years learning a few simple moves with no scrapping, or at least as little scrapping as I could manage. The first guy might have sensed something wrong with the usual predatory situation he'd grown accustomed to. He hung off, moved to the opposite side of me from the third one, who slashed his knife in front of him and moved slowly toward me.

That's when my asshole slammed shut, my heart went triple time and I knew the illusion was over, the big D was right there with them.

It was a scene you can talk about from time to time and belabor all the way to tedium. You can't process it. You either go to preprogrammed behavior or you die. In fact you have to die in your head and your heart, step up to the line and know beyond doubt that death is foregone, which it is anyway, and if you're lucky and you experience small death on a regular basis then all death becomes small, the big D gets shrunk down to proper perspective, because time doesn't matter when you're dead. Never mind, now let's see who's got what. The Japanese call it *shinken shobu*, do or die, and don't think for a minute it doesn't help to be all fucked up.

It was another scene in a heartbeat—the one where my teacher one day long in the face said a woman he knew who had trained for years but who was still headstrong like some people stay, took a trip to China to show the real way to a group of kung fu students. "That was her first mistake," he said. "You cannot impose your way." He was upset because a kung fu student didn't use a wooden knife, but a live blade and cut the woman from the wrist to the fingers.

I asked, "Well? What happened?"

"What do you mean, what happened?"

"Did she take the knife away from him?"

"Of course she took the knife away from him."

"But she trained what? Thirty years? And she got cut. What the hell?" I'd missed the point again.

The old man said, "If someone attacks you with a knife, you will get cut. If that bothers you, you will die." It wasn't the cut that troubled him, it was the etiquette of the thing.

So this maniac comes in swinging his knife and his pal is blocking my exit. I never played Russian roulette but I think pulling the trigger must be something like moving into a maniac with a knife, with baby mush and love and all the weird shit that courses through your brain when you know you're about to die, and you got one chance only for a swan song, and even if the swan sings it's going to get bloody. I don't know, maybe some thoughts are self-fulfilling—I practically gave him my forearm like a sacrifice. He splayed it all right, and in the next split second all the questions arose in a more or less screaming curiosity: How deep? How severe? How bloody? How damaging? Will I die? And vanished in the same split second, because the maniac was right on line.

I never was as relaxed as the model student, but there's nothing like getting the bloodletting out of the way to calm you down, getting rid of your head, going south to the abdomen where you can bring the Universe in by half and again half and half again, don't fuck it up boy, which thought gives rise to another smile, maybe at boyhood and all that whole-life stuff passing before your eyes, quickly now, and let that go, too. You must present a target, bait the trap, show the predator the prey, the easy kill, like an invitation.

RSVP was right on time, and with a wisp of a turn that took up no more room than a turn of the Earth in the Universe, a tiny turn that couldn't help but feel good, until it too gave up its cup of blood because it too wasn't quite right, leap year maybe, I reached alongside the lunging arm, behind the blade. Farther out and gently down, like a dance, my lead, how do you do? I stepped back now in a sweep and a stretch, until the beast's hand turned in a way never before turned by the beast. My teacher called it love but said never mind in the street—break the bone. The beast went down, where he flopped on the street as much as he could but stayed pegged by his arm that I held by the twisted wrist. It hurts more until the knife falls free, until you know, just like a kid who just won a match, that finally you got it close to right.

I'm no bad ass and can't take a punch unless I'm drunk. And I know stories about winning fights are weak, base and unhumble. But this wasn't a fight, not really, it was a big nasty memo and maybe I needed it and maybe I missed something but I felt good about hurting this guy—even felt good about it later, when I saw that he too was only human, emotional, sensitive, vulnerable and weak. Fuck him. I'll show him a neck move next time, unless I can grow out of that rude emotion in the meantime. I just got lucky, that's all, or maybe I got really unlucky but it wasn't yet my time to die.

I try not to think about it, but you cannot separate a man from a move that worked, from the savoring over and over—the weapon take-off once the wrist and hand are torqued past anatomical limits—I missed the knife, too, because he dropped it sooner than I figured and even though it fell between me and the guy who still hung off I must have learned something in there in the clutch because I kept him off with another smile. I guess a smile gets more effective with a bunch of blood and gore showing. And then there was the pretty convincing crunch of the knife guy's wrist breaking and the crack after that that we could only suppose was the shoulder, on around. Adrenaline clears out quite a bit of liquor and residue but maybe quite a bit remained, and of course the blood showing makes you crazy, too, because you know you got to wrap this thing up before you pass out. So I break this guy's wrist and then his shoulder with these nauseating sounds and then I look up to the guy still hanging off uncertain whether to come in or not, which I'm pretty sure would have been the death of me. But you can only get big-scared at the big D once in a short time span, because you use up your adrenaline and have to wait awhile before you can fire off another squirt, like fucking, or just after fucking, when death becomes small and more acceptable, with the rush and jumble, the hormones and adrenaline out of the way. So I look up to the guy still on his feet and sing low, "Wrist bone connected to de...shoulder bone," and the guy sees the light and takes off running, which is much funnier now than it was then.

So the one guy ran away. The guy in the canal swam away. The guy on the ground slept sound as a baby.

What a vacation. Where was I? I asked the night and got peace and quiet for an answer. And something about love. Wasn't it? I shuffled off, wondering if this wasn't hit-and-run.

Around the Clubhouse Bend

A custom in Dutch hotels right at water level (two-star) is the tea and coffee amenity, bedside. It adds mere pfennigs to overhead, with a teapot, two cups with saucers, some handy packets of instant coffee or tea bags, more packets of sugar, both white refined and turbinado and a few packets of powdered milk—china too, no plastic. It's so convenient, mornings, especially after a binge and a knife fight last night, when a hangover threatens life itself, and the old resilience is way long gone, and your guts ooze out your belly.

And a hot cup of joe is important in the morning, for comfort.

I needed a drink real bad. But me and pain were just getting it on there in bed so I wasn't about to head out to the liquor store. The coffee helped, even though I was afraid the warmth of it might melt the wound that was mostly congealed at last. I sipped it left-handed, felt my right arm stiffen. I knew I couldn't meditate all the way to recovery, but it seemed the thing to do for a few minutes anyway. I was stabbed twice and shook-up bad, and my head hurt and buzzed too with difficult questions. The execution was sloppy, the injuries severe, the aftermath spoiled with blood and another fear. The shakes were ambidextrous and came on with the thrust and parry and two breaks again and again. I lay still and silent so it could go away. Still and silent, and when that didn't work I eased the scene on its way with another little bowlful. The stuff is so amazing, so efficient, soft and gentle, its residual fog so light.

The nurse said don't worry. The arm was cut deep, but no tendons, and it would heal quickly with antiseptic, stitches and a bandage. Not deep on the stomach, only a slash—and I got scared again at what might have been, because setting the fear aside is only a postponement. I reviewed the moves slowly, presented the target, pivoted on the balls of my feet, followed the blade and led. The crummy little fuck tried to kill me. It could make a guy wonder about the world.

The nurse didn't wonder. Emptying the pockets of my bloody pants she looked scornful at my little clay chillum and baby ziplock of Kashmere. "You know it is very easy to avoid this kind of trouble in Amsterdam." It was the middle of the night. I was drunk, stoned, half-dead from a knife fight and the endless walk to the only cab in town still running and the bumpy ride to the hospital. And now I was getting a lecture, once again, on getting things right.

"Amsterdam or anywhere," I said.

"Especially for someone like you."

"Why me?"

"You have nice things. Why do you go to the bad places?"

"I made a mistake. A series of mistakes." She smiled. Maybe she expected resistance to her little lecture. She didn't mind my staring either while she undressed me, dressed the wounds.

At mid-forties her beauty lingered like mine did, though her warmth was far more constrained. Her composure, her neatness, her long, silky blonde hair pulled into a bun suggested years of caring; she was a good nurse, a nurturing soul, clean and efficient. "Do you make house calls?"

She laughed. "It is very expensive."

"I'm rich." She was Christine. The planets spun. She did me up in an hour or so and told me to wait. When she came back with pain pills a few minutes later, post-trauma had given way to libido, don't you know; the horndog would live. "Do you work every night?"

"No. It changes."

"Well, I... I'd..."

"We have the man who cut you." I moved into good posture, reflective. "Do you want the police?"

"I think that would be best. Don't you?"

"Yes. I do. But you must come back to identify him. Tomorrow maybe."

"Back here?"

"Yes. He'll be here a few days. You broke his wrist in three places, broke his arm and put his shoulder in severe dislocation. He may lose some use of his right arm."

"You mean he won't be able to stab so well?"

"You don't seem like a violent man."

"No, I don't think I am." I shrugged. "I just got lucky." She laughed the healer's scornful laugh.

She called another cab and helped me dress. She asked if one o'clock would be all right.

"I don't feel so good."

"You won't for a few days."

"Great."

"One o'clock?"

"What one o'clock?"

"Here, one o'clock, to identify the man who stabbed you."

"Well, he didn't stab me very good, did he?" She waited. "One o'clock. See you then." She'd walked herself to the door of the little room and now she turned and closed it behind her—turned in a way that women turn, which is different from men, no matter who says what. I watched the space where she'd been, certain that her practiced body language could never be accused of availability indicators; yet it couldn't be ruled out either.

I was beat, half-bled, filthy and forlorn, so I only filed nurse Christine for later. And I laughed at this, my contact with the living. Then I didn't laugh, blaming this base physical condition on Hattie. I wondered where she was then. And was she sleeping? Or laughing? And laughed the mirthless laugh again—hey, I'd killed three days already. Or was it only two? Or one?

Sleep was painful, fitful. The hash helped more than the pills, but it was still a bloody scene. Bathing took an hour of careful movement with a wet rag. I was back at the hospital on time, asking for Christine, but she was home, of course, until tonight. They showed me the knife guy. He was severely drugged and in a cast from his right hand to his shoulder with a metal brace from his collar bone to his wrist, so the whole sculpture was elevated in front of him. A Dutch cop asked if this was the man who attacked. I said yes, no doubt about it, and he had two friends, equally vicious. The cop said yes, he knew them, and he left. The suspect's good hand was already chained to the bed. I leaned close to his barely opened eyes, and I sang to him, "Hello again." The beastie flinched and most likely moved his cast and brace, making me wonder again about the world and the forces within its atmosphere.

I didn't feel so good. The hospital was less than two miles from the hotel, so I walked back slow, would stop on the way for a cappuccino and a Spoetnik and while away a few hours, give peace a chance. What a town. A place around the corner had a story sign, three frames. In the first a pirate-hippie-looking man with curly ringlets and Captain Hook's long nose, cleft chin, handlebar mustache and dark dimple had his tongue wrapped around a megaphone joint. Smoke wisped from the spark. In the second frame a cloud, formed from the smoke, covered the man's face. Across the cloud were the words: Wham! Shit! In the third frame only a neck stalk remained, gooey and dripping, just after the explosion.

The fourth frame was the doorway to this walk-in closet cum "coffee house." A study in soot and grit and furnished to match and peopled like a morgue is peopled, with stiffs, sitting upright, their neck stalks similar to that in the third frame, their eyeballs gazing vacantly out.

A block farther down, the street was cleared, the sidewalks crowded because two street entertainers had successfully called attention to themselves, got an audience and begun to perform. Two guys in leotards and foolish swim caps, ratty, bogus swim goggles and fins to match faced each other from opposite ends of the block. One lay on his belly and frog kicked while the other pranced down the block like a fairy. The crowd was patient and maybe pleased, it was hard to tell, but it looked devoid of imagination or talent—maybe the entertaining aspect was the swim fins that made the two guys look so awkward. What else could it be? They commandeered the entire block but had no skills beyond that. The prancing fairy set out a hat, for audience appreciation, or charity. I would have chipped in if they'd sat there quietly in their civvies, but they looked like that neat trick would have been way beyond their means. And worse—their antic made a travesty of the old and most noble form of man imitating fish.

A few blocks down was a more sophisticated smoking cafe, meaning it was big enough for more than three tables and the front window was painted in filigree with flowers and mists and swirls suggestive of the smoky dream, which was easier to bear than Captain Hook's head blown off. A man's face painted in profile among the flowers, mists and smoky swirls was smoke pale, fleshy with wrinkles and heavy eyes under thick brows and lost thought. Over all was painted a veil changing into a spiderweb changing into wisps of smoke coming from the man's mouth. Before him in the haze were obliquely painted the clear dark eyes and full red lips of a woman, young, nubile, with all of life to give. Subtle shading and a stroke here and there for facial features and hair made her part of the dream.

I watched her like the man in profile, then went in to see if she held up from the inside, and for another little bowl. Of course she did, because the window artist understood the importance of both sides of the coin, of coming and going, of converse reality, of keeping the groove intact. The scene was repainted inside, which meant matching layers of paint down to the milky white center. From that razor-thin dimension and the love of good art, the obvious tack was easily down to the left pocket for the chillum and the bag. An easy nod to the waiter got a cappuccino coming, and in no time the man in the window was me.

A guy out front sat down on a stool on the sidewalk and played acoustic guitar in a different league than the idiots down the street, in perfect harmony with the buzz, the joe, the artwork and the razor-thin center. He made music as sweet as music is made, and I wondered if the little clay chillum unlocked the heavy gate in my heart, from where good feelings come. Nah—the two idiots down the street were pegged. The guy out front was good. I was still in proper perspective, which made it easy to tell the waiter yes, I would have a look at the hash list, perhaps sample a new flavor or two.

The fine points got lost, so deep in the fog—Kashmere becomes Booneville, it was all Maroc; stoned and then stoned some more and then stoned to the gills, all the way to way too stoned again, to where the eyeballs lose their heavy underside and roll over like boats with no keels. What the fuck, it was only a day far faraway, time to give to the healing process. Eyeballs dilated so big that reading became a dizzying workout in optical flex, a classic example of ocular disparity, but it was nature's way, because the best book was right out front, somewhere between the eyes and the next tangible object. Being becomes a pastime, and it ain't that bad.

A titter rolled across the dreamy cafe, faint but real, when a man strolled past the front window in a three-piece suit, black with pinstripes, a smart necktie with a protuberant Windsor and a diamond stickpin. His smooth gait and debonair coif put a radius around him—here was a man of means, a visitor from that other Amsterdam that must exist somewhere, in which a commerce and culture thrived, where people met for cocktails and discussed world events and their professions and sat on furniture that matched. How difficult that would be, so close to so much fun. But the polished stroller showed championship form, clear-eyed with steady intent, no a.m. bowl for him, and none after lunch, either. People laughed like he was a Martian clown. I did, too.

I think the best possible world would be on a tropical island, and Amsterdam would be a thirty-minute drive up the road, a narrow road, bicycles only. Or maybe it would be a short sail away on flat water with a steady breeze. If I'd had my globe there I would have begun the search in earnest.

I hadn't eaten in two days, well, a day and a half, well, no. Last night was raw hamburger, on a bun with a slice of lettuce. I thought I should eat.

But I sat in amazement, wondering how this town could develop the way it did, that legal hash and some kind of cosmic vortex for denim and dark leather kept it going day and night all these years. Twenty years ago it was fairly outrageous that the kids who were us could sit on the sidewalk in front of the American Express office and smoke our pipes, and cops would step gingerly over our outstretched legs and smile down and say excuse me. It was only Paradisio and Fantasia then, instead of block after block of so-called coffee shops. The streets were far less crowded and the population was twenty years old, and the dark leather and denim had fringe and tassels and long hair, beads, bangles and brotherhood. It was the revolution and all of Amsterdam was R & R for the troops. Bumpy Oliver and I went to Paradisio and got past the scurvy junkies out front selling inch bits of rawhide leather they'd soaked down and dried out stiff and called the very best from North Africa for only two bucks. Fuck that, we were copping whole matchboxes of *Kif*—the fine, fluffy, golden stuff like pollen or something—for three bucks, and that shit was the crème de la cognac of smoke.

They had a gymnasium or something mostly dark with mattresses all over the floor and speakers all over the walls, so you could sit up and smoke or lie down and groove—Creedence or Stones or Cream or Moody Blues. They always played the good stuff at Paradisio, the heavy downbeat stuff, maybe in response to the collective pulse, or maybe it was the collective coma. Bumpy and I got stoned to giggle mode, couldn't talk, when this fat chick with no underpants stands up by Bumpy, turns around, goes wide stance straddle over his legs and shakes her booty to "Who'll Stop the Rain?" or something. It was so big and fat it hung in layers like dough, shook just like a giant gob of goo.

I leaned over to yell at Bumpy that I hoped she wouldn't cut the cheese, but we both giggled so hard we nearly choked, and Bumpy said later he knew what I was trying to yell, felt the fear at the same time.

It's like this stuff, smoking hash and Creedence and the Stones was going on all this time, every day and every night, through all the time I was married, during the times I sailed across the oceans—when I dove a hundred-twenty feet for lobsters. This shit was going on during the whole time I lived on either coast and every day of my drift across a continent and a life.

It was like all this stuff going on in that little, smoky room, was strange stuff, an unnatural agglomeration from all time and all place that had gone on forever, as if the smoke itself was what the linear time had come to.

The moment was keen for insight—for knowing why hashish is illegal in most developed nations, because you can completely entertain yourself without buying anything. Then again they could justify it by letting the pharmaceutical companies control it, requiring a prescription from a licensed physician. With enough profit, anything could be good for society, like cars, cigarettes, television.

But it would never work, because of the truth this stuff came to, which was not a pretty truth or a pleasant resolution but was instead a resounding denouncement of all endeavor on the material plane. The stuff went on and on with no stop or pause or notice of anything else in the world.

I worked in a match factory at eighteen where the whistle between the shifts was the only time you could really tell the machines from the automatons. But I got so pumped at prospects of a dollar-ninety-eight an hour that I spent six months' pay six times over in my head before the end of the first week. And it was even before the first week was half over that I got suffocated by another truth, which is the death a life can sustain so long before it's over, if you're not very careful to live. It was a mechanical dream in a building as big as a football field, a bastion of bricks and pipes, machines with many arms that exhaled noxious fumes. The end product was book matches, so you could light up, or get a high school diploma, or be reminded of chic imagery with your dinner. The workers had a union and always wanted more. They had no idea they'd lost it all.

I was assistant or apprentice or main boy or something for Frank, who worked the rewinder, who could no longer speak in sentences but mumbled his industrial mantra while four rolls hummed through his machine—fifty-pound, hundred-foot rolls of uncut matchbook covers.

"Thirty-four years," Frank said. "Thirty-four years. Quack. Quack quack." A roll could jump the hub at sixty and tear across the plant like sanity run amok, or you could stop it and lose a finger. Frank had six left. But he'd saved hundreds of rolls, saved the section-shop from loss, made more money for the working stiffs who could spend it on appliances for a better life.

"Thirty-four years," Frank said. "Working like a duck. Quack."

"Hey, fuck you, Frank!"

"Quack! Quack quack!"

"Hey, Frank, why don't you go fuck yourself, you fuck!" They loved him, he was so good; hey, fuck you was their expression of appreciation, really.

"Thirty-four years."

Frank was my boss. I asked him what to do. He said, "Thirty-four years."

I asked around; what was I supposed to do? I was told Frank would let me know.

At lunch one of the other guys told me Frank liked me. He said Frank wanted to keep me for his assistant, and that hadn't happened before. Some of the other guys said Frank was filthy fucking rich, he was a goddamn millionaire, richer than a Jew, he was so rich. He never spent a dime, except for coffee, milk and potatoes, which was all he ate, even at lunch, alone, by the rewinder. He lived alone in a box on the third floor.

He left his cubicle for work and socks. The other guys said go ahead and get to be friends with Frank because he must have fifty thousand dollars stashed in his room, because he cashed his check every week and never bought nothing but milk and coffee and potatoes. And socks. What, he puts the cash in the socks?

No! He jacks off in the socks, but he never uses the same socks for jacking off twice, you know, he throws them out the window, between six and seven—you never want to walk under Frank's window between six and seven because he jacks off in a sock and throws it out the window.

All the other guys laughed, then went back to their stations tired and complaining about no pussy from their wives and not enough money from their jobs. But what could you do? Many were fifteen-year men, or twenty, all junior to Frank, who came off lunch break with new steam, four rolls on, humming full speed and quacking his head off, until somebody yelled, "Will you shut the fuck up!"

And Frank would cringe and mumble quacks, "Working like a duck. Working like a duck. Quack quack."

I lasted a week, which was good for sixty bucks take home. I spent it quick on retreads and a fill-up, thinking for months about Frank at the rewinder. He was there for the duration of the Korean War, on the day I was born, for Hiroshima and Nagasaki, on the day Pearl Harbor was bombed—back to the day the first deuce coupe rolled off the line. For years from far faraway I'd look at my watch for those certain hours I knew Frank was still at the rewinder.

He couldn't still be. Frank had to die, just as all this has to fade away, I thought.

It looked outside like I felt inside, overcast, thick and muggy.

I don't know how anyone could do that, show up at the same place at the same time every day of the week for thirty-four years and stay eight-and-a-half hours every time, relating to a machine until it turned their brains to a duck pond—or worse, relating to sterile cubicles with no windows, water coolers and cheap, burned coffee day in and day out, humping their butts and kissing asses to scrounge up enough dough to clothe their children, and the only escape of the day is the solace between the legs, the exhilaration of genitals rubbing together until that too fades away. People do escape in other ways, like affairs or suicide or sudden dropout. But escapees are rare, heroes rarer still.

Frank was the exception, not a hero but certainly an escapee; from his solitude, his confinement, his fleshy cell, he became a light beam, easing on out between the bars, way past reason and maybe past pain long before he died. At least Frank made contact with something fantastic, found a new reality and grooved there, four rolls rewinding full speed all at once—oh, Frank lost rolls, too. I watched him crank the eight-hubbed beast to redline so the four big rolls flew so fast hub to hub that the friction strips rumbled a bass vibrato like the word, deep and low, Om.

I saw Frank lose four rolls at once, just let them rip because he too needed to feel his limits, needed the blessing of mortal constraint, as if love for the foolishness of his paltry life could best be shown by chasing thousands of flying matchbooks down the aisles, just to blow off a little steam.

I hadn't thought of Frank in years. But he popped up then, decades later, maybe because of the spirits swirling in that smoky little room—because if he'd walked through the door then I wouldn't have asked him what was up or how he's been because he answered those questions for eternity a long time ago. I wouldn't have bought him a drink because he didn't drink and wouldn't have made small talk because Frank didn't do that either, not for one syllable, except for quack. I'd have stoked him a bowl though, a big one, would have lit a whole book of matches firing it up.

Dogs and Cats Together

It's going on right now, if not with Frank at the rewinder then with another lost and lonely soul. I can't believe what people are willing to do, how readily they wear the blinders, how surely their brief lives pass with hardly a glimpse at the great wide world.

I stoked the bowl for Frank and me as a family of gypsies came in, led by their patriarch, Jabba the Hutt.

Look at this guy, another fat stiff with chipped teeth top and bottom most likely from gnawing pork ribs, or maybe from eating nieces and nephews who refused to smoke. At least he looked relaxed, most likely would stay relaxed right up to the last gasp. And he could chew a cigar, too, until the butt looked like a fish spleen spewing detritus. He was obviously Big Uncle, high mucky-muck of the Hungarian clan, top goose, standing aside while they pushed tables together. He got fatter standing there, coughing into a rag.

At least the guy had flair. But how could he let his body turn into a big tub of shit like that? How could he do anything?

How could he pass his days except oozing over a couple chairs, trying to fart? He used the Hungarian inhale on his stogie, sucking big, exhaling a major cloud—then he breathed in deep again as if reaching for more smoke and came up with two more clouds, all from the same hit of the stogie. It was another source of the homage the family owed him. He shot orders at the nieces and nephews.

They gathered round and with ceremony lit their cigarettes, twelve or fourteen of them, from Uncle Fat at maybe seventy, who set his chewed stump aside for the ritual, right down to the tender teens. They smoked filter cigarettes, maybe because they were health conscious. Then the little Hungarian family inhaled with devotion, serenely, like a family that understood the value of smoking together. At least they had flair—and a family tradition, reunion with nicotine, all the cousins, aunts and uncles firing up at once, gaggling and ordering up. But my God, the place had no windows.

So suffocation, pain, nausea and blood converged quickly with one more whack to the head. I stood up like walking wounded, reminded myself that I forgot to eat, bore up under the stares of the smoking gypsy clan, who looked around their family circle, too—hey, who stabbed the white guy? Wading through their cloud on rubber legs and semi-swoon, I knew I wasn't that bad off, really, if I could only make the door and the air outside and find a place to sit down soon.

Around the corner was a Chinese place on a busy street, and the crowd was mostly tourists, so the Chinese guys didn't depend on repeat business and more specifically didn't care a pinch of shit if you ever came back. But this place looked like it might be all right, because it was a place, and it was open, and a little Chinese guy in the door scurried zigzag looking for a table in a shadow, because guys who came in alone have a strange vibe, especially limping and...is that blood?

But bad, this place. The tea was warm, the rice puffed and the Shrimp Fu Chow or whatever was...slimy. How unfortunate, slime, like snot from a nose, slime, hot and aromatic with pungent red pepper sauce. It steamed and was well-balanced with color, celery and carrots and good things. But it was slime. This too was another hit, and I wondered what I'd wondered the last few days, if perhaps a cosmic jig was up, what with this series of clouds and goo that seemed to be what remained of reality.

Never mind. I splayed the putrescence, thread the slime over the edge so it touched the tablecloth—linen, but with that stiff stay-press film on it. This place took American Express. I stood up again without quite so much difficulty and took my leave. The little Chinese guy ran up and said, "*Quang chuck mau fung?*"

"It's slimy. Slimy. The shrimps is slimy." Ling Choy was pissed. So I told him, "Oh fuck off, you little peck." I hate to have to talk like that.

Out in the street again I wondered if I am a violent man, and again with ease and natural inclination I thought I was not. It was only that so much hostility coming my way from the world had found my limit these last few hours and days. And sometimes a man is only human. Then I wondered why it came my way.

I presented a target and pivoted again and maybe could see a little easier now that the target was removed too far, so the beastie had slack between the blade and my belly. The skin stretched and hurt like crazy. Maybe I needed that, too. I wondered if I could clear the knife tonight, and I thought maybe I could with so much strength gone, with less speed and not nearly the goods, I could move much lighter, much cleaner, much farther from the goods.

I could be wrong, but I didn't think so. I thought I could move better tonight by virtue of two knife wounds and less strength. And I knew without thinking where sundown would lead, knew that the afternoon's deliberation, smoke, rationale and memory would lead to where a man must follow, sometimes limping.

It was like this guy I knew who was actually a good friend of mine, maybe one of the closest friends I've had, and who was actually a cat, but I thought of him as a guy, because he was for the most part. Pete's quest for fire was pure and strong. I loved Pete, and the love was returned, I know it was, even when Pete lost the playful spirit, lost his peace of mind, gave up home and comfort, the contentment and goodness available to him. He walked away casually from scientifically-nutritional food, a three-tier scratching post, permanent nap space on the bed, easy access door, chase the paper wad—all that goo-goo kitty bullshit. He gave it all up in search of more, in service of the great spirit, and I suppose it wasn't casual. It was compulsive. We were blood brothers, Pete and I, kindred spirits, and I know Pete loved me, even when his life focused on a single, terminal goal.

He came home after a night or three nights out, looking like he'd fought the pickle slicer, ears chewed up or a bit more chewed off, face gnashed and nicked like a punch-drunk fighter's, paws abscessed with puffy soft spots oozing yellow goo. He dragged his sorry ass home covered with cat whiz and tar, came home humble and weak with a whimper when touched and another when fed and another when lifted gently into the sink. He sat still for the warm soft bath and he purred for the soft sudsing. He purred awhile longer until he slept on my chest, wrapped in a towel and the heating pad.

I figured Pete's drive was irrational, not motivated by information. He was programmed, born with the fatal chip in telemetry. He visited the vet for his sixty-dollar, post-fight routine, and he came home shaved here and there, wrapped in sterile gauze and white tape, the ooze now dripping from eighth-inch surgical tubing, dangling from the worst wounds. An hour home he wanted out. Two hours home he craved it. Four hours home he howled, pissed on the couch, tore at the screen. He couldn't have been horny, not so soon—I'd seen him fight. He was twenty pounds at five, a natural heavyweight with incredible speed. I watched him take a challenge once from a tom who came up blindside in a menacing slink and crouch with a vicious swat and a roundhouse right, claws out. Pete waited casually on his haunches. At the swing he only leaned away a half-inch, then followed with a left of his own, just the way fighters are trained to do. Quick and light and straight inside, he connected to the nose, drawing blood easy. The other tom ran, because cats don't need twelve rounds but understand dominance in a move or two. Pete won his fights. He got laid in his prime. He couldn't have been horny so soon after fucking. I never got horny that soon after fucking, especially with a hangover and sleep deprivation.

And it wasn't the fighting that drew him back out. He avoided conflict, made friends easily, plenty to go around, why fight?

It was something bigger, something innate and irresistible, and it wasn't in his nuts, because I've seen cut cats with the same drive to go. It was something big, bigger than his life, because you couldn't keep him from it, even if his life depended on avoidance.

I knew what it was. It wasn't the dominance. And what living creature is more driven to propagate the species than to preserve the self? No, it wasn't horny and it wasn't the good of the group.

Pete came home the last time, near the end of his life, in the worst condition a cat could be in, covered head to foot with punctures, nicks, cuts, bites, teeth sticking out of his flesh, his own teeth chipped and broken and most likely stuck in some other cat's hide. Battered nose to tail, tar and cat squirt obliterating any semblance of fur, matted hard and tacky. He got the bath and the suds, crying in pain the whole time. He got the ride down to the vet, who shaved, trimmed, clean-cut the rest of the ear off, tacked half the nose back on, cut away the dangling third lid from the eye, removed the teeth and claws from his skin, and with a grim shake said, "This is it."

Pete became a kitten then, for a day and a half. When he got the call it was unavoidable. I went along. Pete didn't seem to mind, until a few blocks from home, on the far edge of a field, gaining momentum, I picked him up and told him this is it. We started back, and Pete sunk what teeth and claws he had into my arm, not playfully but dead serious, eyes focused up, saying he knew I was big enough to kill him. So what. This is it. So I put him down, and Pete walked away without looking back, ready to die for another go-round, please God, just one more time.

Nor was it sexual drive that pulled me down the street, thinking of long-dead cats who had to go. It could not be the sex, which eased my mind, put me one step away from Pete the cat, or maybe one step closer to him. I didn't have to go, I didn't think.

I thought it was the contact, but I wouldn't play games, wouldn't explain away my weakness—yes, I wanted to fuck Christine the nurse. Maybe I needed to know that a substantial woman like Christine would consent to that sort of thing with me, because I was worried that most women wouldn't, because Hattie wouldn't, not now. Sure it was some of that, and hey, going the strokes with Christine wouldn't exactly be penance. Would it? There, now the want was said and done, or at least said and marginally accounted for, clearing me up for the higher plane. I figured her about my age, which indicated similar experience with a similar world.

If she was gone or busy or put off, well then, it wasn't such a bad night for heading back to the hotel and taking it easy. Just me, the little room, the handy tea service with its heating coil.

But it wasn't a bad night for a walk, for easing a load, easing past pain and suffering. I could move more easily after dark, when gravity was less visible, when the sooty brick and grime went to shadow, when light didn't spot the filthy truth but only sparkled from infrequent street lamps to the shimmering surface of the canals. Boats tied up looked much cleaner in the dark, glistening from rails and lanterns.

Hattie said in Paris, "This is the city." It was for her a profound truth. "Anything can happen here." I looked for the city in the zigzag bricks hoofed by so many souls hooked on the same mystique. I am deficient in the city, so all I saw was bricks, grit, trash and lonely people.

The world gravitates toward convenience, away from what may be pure or everlasting because those things may also be less comfortable. I remembered Pete for pure drive. Most people get what they need, and maybe Pete did too, right up to the end. So what did I still need? I didn't know, but it couldn't be another woman.

Another light sparkled on the dark green canal. A funky club down a well-lit alley looked good, so I turned in, went down, went inside and sure enough, a down-Mama stand-up bass rolled along on a splendid riff, opened for an easy piano at the high end, a tenor sax up the middle, all convergent on the same exercise, background fugue to another smoke, another drink, snug harbor to the wandering soul. The feeling here was not just down as in get down, funky down. It was gone down, a place of memory, oh yeah, that's the one, that's the way it was, oh yeah, that's the note, the groove, the thing. Memory here was present tense, jazz on a blue note, into the future. It was a place designed for sipping whiskey, a place arrived at, gently, another sparkle in the night. Maybe this was what need had come to, and it was good. But it was gone in the making, like all memory.

And I couldn't stay long, because of the smoke, and because I had to go, to check out the nurse, for the sheer brief sex of it, because my body hurt and the biggest pain was in my heart, and a good offense was a sure defense, even if it was often misunderstood in a guy like me, who understood my friend, Pete.

Outside again the night was different, tingling, inviting to a dog who was wrong again and didn't care, because he had another bone to hide.

Christine the Nurse

People say that recently divorced women are horny in the extreme, but it's more. It's one more hunger in a famished world. Show me a woman divorced at thirty-six or thirty-eight, or forty-five, and I'll show you a woman who is clear on potential's flipside, which is loss; a woman suddenly free at halftime understands what she's missed, kids, no kids, doesn't matter. Divorce becomes a catalyst in women old enough to know, young enough to want.

Christine and I shared that. I sensed common ground, even if she didn't.

Christine, tall, slim, beautiful and poised, showed interest in men with similar attributes. She would have called that interest a natural curiosity, only human. Hey, I could swing with that, let's use some imagination. She called herself thin, but even calling her stretch-thin was a kindness; skinny could stick to her much better. Lanky in the legs and arms but with a few critical curves she did all right, moved herself like a beautiful woman, even that close to the bone. And she crafted, preened and presented herself to maximum advantage. Oh no, it wasn't truth that was her standard. She needed so much more.

She led with her hands, with long, smooth fingers, supple, fleshy palms disproportionate to her thin profile, and elegant nails, long and red with a few rocks in gold on the right hand. Clean feet, soft and supple with no dead skin and good nails with matching polish and no dirt were prettily presented in open-toe sandals—hers had wedge heels, because a nurse can't wear high heels. But wedge heels looked fairly comfortable and still bunched the calves, flexed the ass so it drew diagonal creases across the tight-wrapped skirt in white. So what else is a guy on his back with his pants down supposed to look at? The ceiling?

And she was a beauty, a California girl with Victorian posture. Long blonde hair and simple features, a straight nose and full lips, all delivered with a proprietary cold wave that could give a man the shivers and make him hot, too, because, after all. She wasn't from California or Holland. She was Belgian, and her divorce was long ago, nearly four years already, but she practiced the uniquely European cosmopolitan approach to life. That is, beyond her innate fatigue, her instinctive intolerance, her chronic PMS, she was depressed.

She'd been alone now ten years, well, only four, really, since the crash, but she'd felt alone for six before the crash. She was eaten up with it, wallowed in it, counted and recounted it, clung to it with every breath. Hers was unmitigated, unequivocal, 100 percent pure, thick, analytical, introspective, reflective and ultramental depression. So what chance could survive for contact?

She was very busy, there on the ward, and she could not go out, no, it was impossible. She touched a nerve, since few things in the Universe could be closer to the easy side of possible, since going out was nowhere near impossible but was the simplest of matters, left right left for the door. But a man cannot seek contact, he can only allow its arrival. So the only response to impossibility was just as simple: "Ah. Well. I understand. Thank you again."

And the response to that, allowing of course for the pivot and turn and left right left, was, "We could go for a bite. I'm famished. I have a break in only a few minutes." It was a mixed signal then. Perhaps sensuality surrounded her at one time, but now it didn't. Now a certain handsomeness took its place. She wasn't too old for sensuality. And much later, after a gauntlet of acceptance, denial, letting go, of establishing the idea that physical contact was a matter of profound indifference between us, she performed her striptease, since that's what it was, it was so slow, and led down to lace bra and panties, the see-through kind most women don't wear to work the graveyard shift. Then she was sensual, and how. She did a fine and admirable job of it, too. But the charade of indifference had become a shadow of truth—she wore me out with her mentality. A romp with Christine was like a cup of water after hiking miles through the brambles. It was good, but there wasn't much of it.

But that was much later. That first night she turned my head easy enough with a simple soft yes, ready in just awhile. I waited nearly an hour, which was a pisser and a relief at the same time—a guy sometimes wonders why a woman calls him back, especially a guy who's developed an honesty inside, a guy who knows the women don't look twice like they used to, don't eye him up and down and signal come on like in the early days, a guy who's been around the block enough to know that no matter what a woman looks like, smells like, talks like, feels like—no matter what—she can get laid and pronto. There are that many guys starving to death for pussy at any given moment on Planet Earth. It's strange but true, especially for some odd reason here, where some good-looking, well-groomed, physically fit and handsome men are courting some big bowwows. So a guy wonders why a woman—and a good-looker at that—lets him go and then calls him back.

Of course the reason was simple. Christine was work. And maybe she knew it. She required it. And maybe her simple soft yes was tantamount to I find you guilty—Come with me! The hour of waiting was only a beginning, a measure, a test, should have been a warning, but then these things are so fogged at the front end, so unclear before the cartilage slides in the slippery folds. Ah, there, it's plain to see now.

Finally ready, nervous and apologetic, she led the way in a self-conscious gait, leggy, long steps, quiet and painfully aware of the push people over forty must make, when the effort is so repetitive and so is the result, but we are alive, not yet dead, so stride forward we will. Another Chinese place looked like the last Chinese place, but I didn't mention slimy shrimp, the air was so brittle already.

She was divorced four years but felt like ten because the solitude had been ten, even with the children, yes, three children—she sat up straight for this part. Her stomach was flat despite the children, three of them, they mean the world to me—and it was most likely the loneliness that drove her in the first place to learn about pianos and what makes their wires exactly, properly tense for the right notes.

He'd been a teacher, a professor actually, with quite a name for himself; maybe you've heard of him, Earnst Fischimille or something, in his field, which was, alas, para-French psychiatry as it relates to root canal elective exploration in subgeriatric, integrated subjects of both sexes—something like that. He was at the University, in Brussels. He'd remarried in the same year as the divorce; his new wife had been his assistant of ten years. Christine had been his assistant too, way back when she was just...beginning...as a nurse.

It was a resumé of depression anxiety. I ordered steamed fish with Chinese vegetables and yes, please, rice, and tea, and maybe for starters a cold beer. Christine wasn't hungry, really, some soup would be fine. "She's twenty-seven. Don't you think that's the way it is with men? All men? They get to be middle age and want young girls."

"Not all men."

She forgot her flat stomach, cradled her chin on her beautiful hands, looking weak and forlorn, struggling for the surface like a swimmer too long down, too late, grasping for a breath of air, real air, not just this fake, depressing shit she was forced to breathe. "They're gone now. I had no choice really. I can't really keep them from him. I should be able to keep them from her, though. She has nothing good to give them, nothing to teach them. I don't just say this. She's very simpleminded, you know. I don't like her. I don't like her around them."

She stared down, waiting for a response from her water.

"When did they leave?"

"This week. A month they'll be gone. I have vacation time, but I don't want to go anywhere. I mean...no place sounds good to me. And what am I to do? Go alone?"

I drank my beer, slowly. Europe is shit in summer with

the heat and pollution and overpopulation and cars, but all the women are on vacation. Yet I savored the blessed beauty of freedom, of knowing the next month would not be spent with Christine and her permanent guest. "You mean...you tune pianos?"

"Yes. I love it." And she did, she must. She perked up like a high note. "It's the only work I ever loved. I don't know why. I know it's foolish. Well, not foolish, but it's, well, impractical."

"And that's why you're a nurse?"

"There aren't that many pianos to tune. There are, but not for me. Nobody knows about me. I'm good. I'm very good, you know." I drank. She sipped.

Dinner was served. She watched me turn my steamed fish over, looking for slime. "I never eat anything I don't check out from both sides," I said. "Now this fish looks good." I ate. "Mmm, it is. I haven't eaten in days."

"Days?"

"Well. Hours."

"Do you exaggerate often like that?"

"No. Never." She didn't get it. She looked glumly down, stuck again in a miserable, fucking meal on a dark, sad night in a rotten, lousy life with a chronic liar. I got another beer, ate my fish. She dabbed at her soup, focused on the dead wontons. "Besides tuning pianos, do you have any fun?"

"Fun?"

"Yes. Fun. Meaningless activity. Exhilaration."

"No. No, no."

"Do you want to have some fun?"

"I...couldn't say. I think...fun is for children."

"Did you have fun as a child?"

"Yes. But look, you don't need to talk to me this way."

"Sorry. Just trying to pull you out."

"Please don't."

"No, no. My mistake." An awkward, hateful silence ensued. I focused on fish, Chinese vegetables and rice, followed up with tea. It was good, followed by the heavy, drugged feeling of too much drug, too much liquor, too little sleep, too many knife stabbings. "You know, Nurse Christine. I wonder if..." She was attentive, clinical and patient. "I wonder if you would...call a taxi for me. I...I feel very weak."

"I can see that." She felt my forehead, her hands cool, soft and sudden. "Where is your hotel?" I told her and she laughed. "You're staying there?"

"It's no good?"

"It's not what I'd imagine."

"What would you imagine?"

"Look. You can stay at my place if you like for a couple of days. The children are gone, and I'm afraid you need looking after."

I took her hand. "Do you think I'm critical?"

"I think you're a sick man."

The offer was sudden and unnatural. Take a stranger into her home? But it fit neatly into the column marked Culture Gap. And besides good hands, good feet, decent hips and a fair ass, she was smart. I was weak, this time in the literal, immediate sense. She excused herself and called a cab. She came back and helped me up. Outside she gave me a key, told me where to sleep, told the cabby her address, told me to go, sleep, she would see me in the morning.

The ride was bumpy with many turns. Either she needed a man to fuck, a man who had some money and half a wit minimum and would leave town soon. Or in the midst of her depression muddle she was a nurse overall, who understood what it means to give.

It was neither of the above; it was all of the above. It was a long climb to the fourth floor, or the fifth, and an easy exit, since it wasn't even midnight and the rock and roll at street level would blare another three hours. Everything got stuffed. Check-out led to another marvel, at the sheer nausea and confusion a man can feel in the back seat of a taxi after only two days in town—well, a day and a half really.

I must have passed out. The cabby turned around with a laugh, seeing me so drunk. I came to with a groan and new awareness of mortality, of the presence of eternity, beyond the flesh. Everything was wrong inside me, and paying the cabby way too much I dragged myself out and up and in.

I turned on a single light. The place was middle-class and nice, furnished plush with overstuffed chairs and sofas the children obviously didn't use. The lamp shades matched and the pictures hung in pairs or sets; landscapes, portraits, little birds. The hutch reflected order, sensibility through the years.

So Christine in an overstuffed chair with a drink was the picture, surrounded by so much stuff. I found a blanket in the linen closet and covered the couch with it, in case I bled to death in my sleep, so I wouldn't have to spend the hereafter with guilt over a ruined sofa. I lay myself down and resumed, not falling off to slumber but collapsing into the folds of purgatory between dead and alive, giving in to a homeostasis that would now come up with its best effort in the finals.

I regained consciousness a long time later wondering if I had died or this was only a bad time. A soft, dawn light, most likely similar to the light of the beyond, made the room pleasantly, partially visible.

She languored, crossed her lovely legs and sighed. I rolled toward her. "What time is it?"

"Two." The soft-dawn light was the dim bulb in the kitchen.

"Not so bad," I said. "You got off early. Was it a slow night for mayhem?"

She laughed once and sighed again. She thought it over, or rather she sank lower. "My life must change," she said.

I sat up, took a minute to wake up in the middle of the night in the fog—yesterday scrolled by, the hash, the drink, the hash and more hash, and still the pain. "Yes. Change is good."

"I think you have smoked too much of it."

"Mmm. I think you're right."

She sat up and leaned toward the tasteful end table beside her, opened the drawer and pulled out her kit. She loaded her little pipe, easing into a another context. I laughed once. "For me," she said, "it is only to unwind."

"It's okay."

"I know it is okay." She smoked it with small vengeance, only a few hits, then put it away. "John Kline is coming here. If I can find him, somehow..."

"Who is John Kline?"

She laughed once, got up, walked to a wall of stereo equipment in proper cabinetry. She played a tape, piano, a modern style, classical with an upbeat. She sat back down.

"You want to tune his piano?"

"I met him once. He told me then he would give me a try. You know they always need tuners when they travel."

"When is he coming?"

"I'm not certain. In a few weeks."

Her voice trailed on hopelessness. I floated in a fog, at peace with no bearings, no questions, no wondering why. The overstuffed and tastefully matched parlor practically tingled in a uniquely European non-silence, as if the scene was made of wax, for display in miniature perfection in a bottle or a shoe box. The ticktock clock timed the stillness; it stifled speech then repressed the inclination to speak. The ticktock ticktock perfectly matched the airless inanimacy surrounding us, becoming us.

I felt like Bozo in a funk, pushed my hair back, sat up in need of a major piss. "I need water. And a few aspirin."

"There, by the bath," she said, her voice weak and failing again, without resources, without hope. I got up, never mind appearance. I was middle-aged, sleep puffed and staggering in baggy drawers with a hard-on. "My God." I held my dick flat, smiled at her sheepishly. But she only looked down. It was high time she saw a guy with a hard-on, but I thought of bad stuff so it would go away—car wrecks, slimy shrimp; it didn't work. She said, "I miss them so much. So so much. I would kill myself if anything happened to them." That worked.

I balanced on the sofa arm and got legs to follow feet. "Sounds like a piece of cake," I said, on cruise control to the bathroom. "We get the schedule, get some tickets and get in to see the guy."

"No. I cannot. It is impossible."

I closed the door on that note, took a piss so long it seemed memorable in its net effect on my outlook, taking me from quiet desperation to serene acceptance in two minutes flat. The aspirin, the drink, a splash on the face, smooth the eyebrows, check for zits, rinse the mouth, stomach in, chest out, and I was ready for my date to continue.

In the living room she smoked another pipe—I hadn't in over four hours, which was a novel feeling and let the fog thin a bit, enough to see the clear and present danger of the stuff. Back on the couch, covered again and snug, I watched her ease into it, covering herself, easing in to the snug cloud. She shook her head, "It is impossible."

"It's not impossible. Very few things are impossible. That phrase has no literal translation into English."

"You Americans," she said. "You think you can do anything."

"I don't think I can do anything. I think you can meet John Kline. I think I could meet him tomorrow if it was that important. As it is I can wait. I can meet him when he gets here. I can introduce him to you if you want."

"How can you do this?"

"Magic."

"Just as I thought."

"All you think is negative. I can meet anybody I want. John Kline meets people every day. Why couldn't I be one of them?"

"I already told you, you don't need to talk to me that way."

I lay back, snuggled in, closed my eyes and wondered why I'd given up the sanctuary of the hotel. Oh yeah, it was the nursing aspect of it, and a foolish hope for pussy. "How do you think I'm doing?"

"At what?"

I laughed once. She was depressed but kept a keen edge. Funked out she was ready to spar. What a woman. I slowed my breathing and with amazing ease found myself at home, there on an overstuffed sofa on the far side of the planet in a parlor for the wax museum going tick... tock... tick... tock... tick... Sleep was easy, moving, smooth and soft, quick and gentle, floating the corpse up and blending with the airless calm. A dream of icicles became too real, too cold, and I woke again—her cold fingers laced across my brow and her beautiful face looking askance saying: "You're doing good. You don't have a fever. I think you did have before."

Poised in the act of giving and then giving more, she needed no response, only patience. Yet no patience could outlast her. We stayed there for minutes. She sat beside me on the overstuffed sofa, one hand resting on my arm, the other on the opposite shoulder. How could she not feel the electrical impulse? How could I be so numb to her numbness? I sensed in time the absolute A-OK to go back to sleep. I played it out, closed my eyes, and opened them again to see her sitting still, looking satisfied to sit there all night. "Why did you bring me here?" I couldn't help it, nor could I help regretting it, since only a fool would ask why she'd brought him home, only a fool could not feel her cool hand strip his conscience naked.

Glacial Movement

"Do you want to go?" she asked.

"No. Not now. I'm only curious."

"What is there for you to be curious about? You are sick. You need help. You need a friend who can assist you."

"It was a stupid question," I said. She smiled, her first smile all night. She stood up and turned and walked away. "Are you off tomorrow?"

"Off?"

"Do you work tomorrow?"

"No. My holiday starts tomorrow."

"Maybe I could take you somewhere."

"Where would you take me?"

"Anywhere. Anywhere you want to go."

She thought. Her head broke inertia slowly and gained weight in its wag. Her body drooped, and she sought more in physical denial. She said, "No. I don't think so." And she drifted like a fish gaining depth.

Sleep was not regained so easily but fitfully, in and out

of it, with regret for being there, for asking the wrong questions, for being myself and crowding in, not letting go, anxious and doubtful and above all for wanting carnal contact with this woman for no reason, except of course her elegant good looks and the pleasant friction, the thrill of naked flesh.

What a simpler world it would be, without hormones, a world in which give-and-take could attain the level of pure goodness. But maybe not. Isn't that why missionaries don't fuck? Or at least profess no fucking? Forget the missionaries. And if I could forget the nag between my legs, I could see as well that maybe Nurse Christine was exactly what I needed. Oh, I wanted more, wanted sexual contact with such a lovely one as she, who was my equal in age, my superior in sensitivity. How well I could sleep then, with all the demon hormones drowned like rats in a garbage can; how they would float lifelessly then, then sink slowly, like me.

I'd at least by that first night on Christine's sofa reached the point of wondering what discourse would follow the sex act between her and me. She qualified as a good person, and though my own life had been different from hers, I couldn't very well fault her for her conventional history of marriage, children, material onslaught, divorce and bitterness. It was the bitterness that loomed big in my projected aftermath—the bitterness that could suck me into the column of All Men, meaning bad men, once Christine and I got done with the ficky-fick—oh, she'd know for sure then what was the only thing I'd wanted. Then again, if I wasn't a bad man, maybe I could help her bitterness to go away.

I doubted her bitterness would go away. She wallowed in it, took succor from her uniquely European depression, in the grand tradition of the great depressionists, for whom life itself is a bother, a drudge, a left, right, left.

Or maybe I was too lazy to address somebody else's depression, because I was too focused on my own. I think a healthy exercise in any quagmire is to ask yourself what would play out most optimally. For me then it would have been a lusty session with Christine, in which my piston in her cylinder would release me from the hormonal yoke, for a few hours anyway, and would open her eyes as well to the true meaning of happiness. Then I would race south for a grand reunification with Hattie, my true love.

The problem with an optimum scenario, however, is that like any childish fantasy the playing out is usually only one act. So the kid in the candy shop gets to stuff his gob with all the malted-milk balls, all the red licorice, all the toffee crunch bars, the chocolate kisses, double fudge nut wafers, marzipan fruit slices, gooey-coated caramels and chocolate cherries he wants—and he wants it all, because he's only a kid, too goddamn stupid to anticipate the gut-wrenching puke session round the bend. In fact, he even hurries at the first squishy sound of his stomach turning purple—hurries so he can pack down some more sugary mud before the pain sets in.

I'm still amazed at how much older than twelve you have to be before you know this scheme of things, and how much older yet you have to be before you can remember it and be strong and say, No, thank you to the candy buffet. I mean, Christine had a problem with depression, but maybe it wasn't chronic, maybe it could be resolved. The important thing about Christine was that she was over the hump, past the severe test—well, not past it yet, but she was who she had become, a nurse, a giver, a care-provider, a skilled, nurturing soul, maybe with some residual suburban sludge in her primary consciousness. But who was ever worth a damn who didn't have some shit on their shoes?

It wasn't the first time I wondered who in the hell Hattie would become when she turned, oh, thirty or thirty-five. I'd be round the clubhouse bend by then, in my prime for certain, and most likely admirably intact. She even indicated an understanding; old guys need exercise. She would understand my morning sessions, meditation, stretching, running a mile or two to break even on the day, while she slept late, woke up on a coffee jag and a few smokes and wondered why she didn't hook up with someone like herself, also blessed with the immortality of youth.

But physical needs and differences were small potatoes next to the other question, which posed itself on a scene of Hattie and me sitting at a table with an excellent wine, a great meal and empty talk bubbles.

I'd envisioned that one before, maybe telling myself that the empty talk bubbles in that scene were good, were far better than anything I could...predict.

Or—and I think this was the clincher—maybe the idiot fucking kid knew good and well he'd get sick as a dog on green meat because he'd engorged on the same stuff before but still couldn't resist the...the smell of the stuff, because that's what dogs and kids do. Me, too, I thought, laughing softly, maybe pitifully, but certainly. I wanted to fuck Hattie, right now, or maybe in a few days, after Christine.

So sleep came again, not so much with acceptance as with scenarios leading one to the next, images easing away from hormones into hashish dreams, in which all moving things glitter with no reason, no direction, sense or being.

Waking was neither crisp nor rested, because for every high, there is an equal and opposite low, if the high is externally induced, unless external induction continues. Pungent coffee and the scent of hot muffins woke me. First glance rested on a towel folded on the sofa back. Into the shower and out was good for further waking, and waking peaked in the kitchen—Nurse Christine set the table with exquisite continental breakfast on beautiful china and silver service, in a sheer robe whose translucence allowed silhouette in abundant eyeful, backed by the big window and morning light in the breakfast room. I know now it was a far different scene than the one between me and my true love. Christine was an eyeful, a little stiff maybe as she leaned and poured without losing her posture, yet her spinal integrity was strong, her silhouette was another challenge, another test, another question. I turned away from it, obviously, with lingering pangs of want and doubt creeping across my chest, pangs that would most likely one day take me.

"Good morning," she said.

"Good morning," I replied like Mr. Sunshine. Thoughts of another hotel, a decent hotel some depressed woman might not laugh at, were dashed, dissolved in that clear morning light. And I know now that nurses are the very best for knowing the score, for understanding the intricacies of moods, of life in its intimate detail, its frail proximity to death. How could they not know these exotic subtleties after seeing hundreds of guys with hard-ons, dead ones, too, after seeing so many bald heads and beer guts and nuts hanging nine inches from the vine, after understanding the humanity of half-drunk, too stoned, bleary-eyed, over-the-hill horndogs? They know what life is about, what love is about. One is about nothing but time, which can be filled with the other, if you're lucky.

"Did you sleep well?"

"Like a rock. And you?"

"Yes. I did." She sat down and bade me sit, beautiful automaton programmed for weak men. I sat. She offered cream, muffins, many jams.

"Thank you."

"You're welcome." We ate. It was peaceful, the silence, the breakfast, food for thought.

"How do you feel?"

I thought it over. "Much better. My stomach is...not healed."

"I'll look at it."

"Thank you." We ate some more. "What will you do today, your first day of vacation?"

She laughed once. "Errands. I have so many." I nodded, uncertain what I would do today, uncertain of what was expected. "You should rest today. Try to stay still. The wound on your stomach is in a difficult place. It should heal more quickly if you stay still."

"Still and calm."

"Yes. Still and calm. You might get restless. I can't help that."

"Can I come with you?"

"For errands?"

"For awhile, yes."

"Why must you come with me?"

"You're right. I mustn't."

"Yes. It's all right. For awhile. I am going first to the flea market. I love it there. I haven't been in ages. After that I think you would prefer keeping still."

"All right. The flea market."

"We will leave in twenty minutes."

"That sounds like an excellent idea." She laughed once again, but different this time, this time with humor. The ice cracked.

I felt like a clever dog, learning my first trick. We finished. We cleared.

She wasn't accustomed to a man helping in the kitchen; the former husband was apparently a slug, cerebral and helpless, well suited to life in the wax museum. I could easily imagine him sitting at that same table, tweeded out, seeing himself as Yves Montand in a classic film about a genius who lived in the suburbs, who read the paper while his wife cleaned up, who tolerated her simple mind while fending off the advances of his youthful girl assistant. At least I never wore tweeds and didn't mind helping with the dishes.

"Thank you," she said.

"Thank you," I corrected, ingratiating and polite. Isn't it amazing what turns a woman's head? She paused then, the ice crumbling in great glacial chunks, no wit, no smooth move, no clever ploy, no maneuver nor situation but simply some help in the kitchen. It wasn't all she wanted, but it was so much, she'd been so long without, there in her tastefully appointed breakfast nook.

"Come. Your wound." She sat me on a chair, checked my arm first, regooped and wrapped it. Off with my pants for another clinical go at a cut that wended daringly close to what I really wanted her to see. But did she care? I think it would have been the same to her as seeing the horses in the paddock, which is nothing to seeing them off. God knows I would have removed her panties if I was the nurse and she was the patient, but maybe that's why God worked it out this way. So it was only an exercise in Samaritan goodness, goop goop, rewrap and up, no thrills, no chills, except for one little bitty one when she caught me looking down her robe and pulled it tighter. It felt like a twenty-yard loss, but it was good to see her tits. I felt base, foolish and animalistic and hoped that wasn't why I was there. Well, not entirely why I was there.

"Christine." The sound of it had a unique vibration, a primary intimacy; it was the first time I'd called her by her name. "Do you think, first day of your holiday and all, a little...buzz might be nice?"

"If you want to smoke hash, then you should." And that was that. And because the equal and opposite low seemed so abundantly surrounding, I did. I offered her the pipe. She took it. "Thank you," she said.

And so, stoned again, we dressed for an outing. She was stiff and formal, and seemed laughably absurd once the hashish made us glow. I wanted to call her Miss, proper and courteous. And I would have asked her last name, to better play the game. But then it would be her husband's last name too, which would bring all that bog to mind. She watched me. I smiled stupidly, and she looked away, most likely wondering what made me so idiotic so much of the time.

It was the hashish, of course. But it was good, too, melting brain cells, including those responsible for sensibility and inhibition. She had spacecakes. She didn't know where they were from, suspected a melange spanning North Africa and Asia. We were stoned silly, buzzed out, not present, floating, dreamlike, animated. At least I was. She looked slightly removed.

The stuff was good, even if a steady life of it would melt a brain like ice cream in July. But we weren't wastrels. We were fortyish strays processing direction and its changing ways. I watched her walk. She was elegant, yet she was comical in her efforts to preserve more elegance than she could, stoned stupid. She watched me watch her and looked easily away, easily discounting a bit more foolishness. I drifted alongside her, put my arm around her waist. "Let's go dancing."

She looked at me, snickered and looked away, as if frivolity was the root of her misery—her misery, yes; she looked down, slumped her neck. "No. I don't think so," she said. "I don't want to."

"No. I don't either." I shrugged with an uncertainty parallel to her misery. "Sorry," I said, because apology is plague among self-doubters.

"You are a strange man," she said, and the loss then sustained was hers. I don't like being called strange, especially by someone whose depression defines her life, someone who hasn't been out of a suburban routine any more than I'd been in one. But resentment turned to tolerance, because I forced it to, because I thought that's what you did when personal development was at hand; I tolerated her, and let myself sink again into lusting her. Strange? I could show her strange. She was stilted, rigid and stuck. She moved and spoke like Gort the robot. And she'd issued a verdict: You Are A Strange Man.

"Is not that the attraction?"

"I see much stranger men than you every night. Bigger. Dirtier. Stronger. Much more strange."

I took another look—now we were getting somewhere; those were buzzwords, operatives. On the surface she was still as pond scum. Yet who knew what creature lurked beneath? I thought I knew; it was mutant from years of chilling propriety, years of prescription love, secure and well-furnished, and it was bitter, since the furniture was all that was left, maybe had been all there was in the first place. She caught me staring again.

"Come, please," I said. "Let me buy you a strong coffee." I pushed her elbow toward the funky cafe just to the left. She didn't resist. It was dirty and had a peculiar air. I said to the waiter, "Strong coffee," and she nodded. I searched for a better fingerhold on the sheer wall we clung to.

The cafe was grimed over, but the seats were reasonably clean from ass friction, like the forearm radii on the tables. An Arab teenager served us quickly with deference, because we were older people in untattered clothing and apparently recent baths and money to spend, chop-chop. "You like hashish. All is very very good. Very very cheap. You buy yes what kind?" He presented a hashish menu.

I gave him the nod, pointing to the first selection on his list: Holy Shit. He left at a trot—I called after for two big espressos, because they forget, once you order the hash. Christine had seen it all before, rumdum routine for her, a lifetime of grimy cafes and cleverly-named dirt that makes you high when you smoke it. She stayed deadpan, mannequin in a window display, reality against the grain. Ahab came back quickly with the Holy Shit. I loaded it up, lit it, pulled and tasted sweetness, the dream sustained. "You might like this."

She tried a short one and tweaked her nose. "It will make you sleep," she said.

But sleep is good for depressed people, I didn't say, because I didn't want her to be depressed, or think about being depressed, or anything. Ahab brought the coffee. "This will keep you awake," I shrugged. And she sipped, gaining distance from life itself with every movement, like a humanoid with low batteries. We sipped. We sat. We waited.

"How long is your holiday?"

"I have one month."

"I have an idea. I can take you somewhere." It came out of nowhere; I watched it and heard it as surprised as she was. Then again, maybe I was only confident in her response.

"I have two tickets to Greece..." She stopped short and sudden as a flushed quail looking down the barrel of eternity, whose last, pitiful eep echoes the thin, hollow resignation of futility, mortality, predation. Her two tickets to Greece came as suddenly as her invitation home, as suddenly as my invitation abroad.

It changed our postures, but only as an electric jolt changes the attitude of a body already dead. The air between us settled back down, flat-lined, no pulse.

I tried another charge, recalling Dr. Kildare in the Emergency Room yelling over the defibrillator, Again! Again! "Greece is great!" I said. "You take me!"

"No. I already said no. I don't want to. I can't. It is impossible."

"Why impossible?"

"You are impossible."

Women often complain of the only thing men want—the only thing men really want. But if men didn't want it as bad as men want it, pursuit would cease, which would be one more terrible difference between humans and the other species. A male learns early the importance of ignoring injury, shedding insult; I thought I'd learned as well the importance of selflessness in giving. I thought I was noble. I took her hand. "Christine. When I first came into the hospital, what did you think?"

"I thought you were bloody. I thought you were seriously injured. I learned that it was not so serious."

She missed it. "What did you think when I came back to the hospital?"

"I thought you looked very tired. I did not think your bandage needed changing."

"Why did you come with me to dinner?"

"I was hungry."

"You hardly ate."

She looked down. "That happens to me sometimes."

"Didn't you think anything else?"

"What kind of thing?"

"Any man-woman kind of thing?"

"Oh, no."

"Oh, no?"

"Why should I?"

"Because you're a woman, and I'm a man, and here we are."

"No. Men have tried to do this over the years. Just like you. But it is not possible."

"It is not possible because you won't let it be possible."

"Whatever you like." And so she sat, still life, sadness cast in stone. We smoked, sipped, sat. One urge was for the exit, another urge was for deeper penetration, not for the sex anymore, she looked too far gone, way too down, no spark, little give. Yet it was the give that kept me there, kept me in the way, kept her from me. But that lesson was yet to come.

I smiled at her. "Shall we?"

She looked up, uncertain, untrusting. I stood, and she said, "Yes."

So the gray drab morning stretched to noon, pleasantly

cushioned by too much hash, compensated by strong coffee and a few cigarettes, because they go so well with hash and caffeine. I walked, stretched out, stayed close to this spider woman, fantasizing on those places her extremities led to, glancing at her, causing her to glance back. But I only made her nervous. She was glued to the has-been, the paltry fare of the flea market, rags mostly, with glitter or without. She was sincere in her desire for solitude, secure in her domicile of sadness. She had me convinced.

Near two she showed a sudden glimmer, like an engine cranking that gives up a single sputter, and that's all you get. "I know a lovely place for lunch. Are you hungry?"

"Yes. I am hungry. Are you hungry?"

She smiled. "Yes." It was our first exchange since Holy Shit.

Amino Acids and Electrons

Lunch was a medley of cold fish, also smoked, and indeed lovely. She spoke, gaining momentum over what used to be. I knew it was necessary, this replay on the past, for sorting out, for letting go. And I told myself that she needed to let go of the past, so she could grasp the present, beginning with a grasp on me. I would not admit that the grasp should be delicate, cool fingers around a hot *schwantz,* because I avoided considerations of love in gross terms. And it would be love, I thought—I honestly did, she was so graceful, so available, so alive, at least potentially.

She remembered Brussels, scene of the crime, and she remembered a most wonderful place not too far from town—Bruges. It's a theme park favored by tens of thousands of tourists daily who ass and elbow through the ancient stone streets, soaking up history. Other than being old, the place is just like Disneyland, rated G, Mecca for suburban families, anathema for café elite.

She recalled the old times in terms of habit, custom,

routine, as divorced people often do. She regarded the loss as a death in the family and more, a death in her heart, because the marriage was loved by one and not by the other.

I listened in the spirit of giving, or at least lending an ear—listened to Christine describe a life I could only imagine as miserable for all concerned. The professor cut an image, not a pose like the ultra-chic, butt-chewing, coffee-stained, baggy-shirted, omnisciently-grimacing slouch of the cafe thinkers. The professor was a formal thinker, validated by degrees, advance degrees and some more degrees after that. He'd earned his tweeds, needed his elbow patches, depended on his pipe, for real. He was a licensed heavy thinker, his thoughts qualifying for ink on paper, until anything drifting between his ears became currency for those who would pay attention.

Christine described him as attractive to young women seeking intellectual substance—"I knew that," she said, simmering over what she had known. I had no response; to me he was a cardboard cutout, without daring, without do. They shared stability in a suburb.

Yet he made her happy, or at least she loved the life, loved the stability in which to rear her children. The gap between the mommy and the daddy grew over the years, because the years counted for her, but not for him. She aged. He did, too, but he was the professor, attractive to younger women, so he traded her in on a newer model. She was devastated, as if he'd invented that kind of behavior, all because of her. Christine didn't get it, couldn't comprehend that horndogs can also be professors.

Who knows? Maybe he outgrew theme parks, too. Anyway, he said he wanted more of what he'd never had, even though he wasn't sure what he'd missed. "'What is it you want?' I asked him. He didn't know. Anything, I would have given him. I gave him. I told him I would give him anything, if he could tell me what it was. He didn't know."

She looked glum. The professor hadn't known, but he was willing to throw the bones.

Maybe he gets some credit for breaking out of what was suffocating him. Maybe he was only a horndog.

I wouldn't have minded meeting him for a drink, to find out, to get his views on marriage and on Christine, to observe his reaction to waitresses. But I didn't offer, because it didn't matter, because the damage was already done. The professor had breached his oath of loyalty.

Christine wasn't rigorous on the loyalty issue—not as far as her country or the local football team or any other institution—except for loyalty to the institution that had been her family. I think she too grew restless over the years of marriage, but she dusted it off as she dusted her furniture and knick-knacks, because a marriage requires that kind of work. She never considered separate paths or ending the marriage any more than she imagined cleaning her house with a meat cleaver. Now a great sadness was upon her, was infused into her life, because her marriage had failed, giving rise to critical personal doubt.

I could not condone the professor's flight or his instant alliance with a new woman who was "twenty years younger with breasts like casaba melons," but I understood the hormones and their influence on a man's behavior. Yet, alas, I could not share this understanding, either. Nor could I ask what proof she had that the new woman was a slut with questionable hygiene.

She became animate in her sentiment, her eulogy over the

perfect life that had been thrown away, the well-matched furnishings and regular outings in the station wagon, cast off like litter. She sat up straighter, remembering, speaking to some imaginary audience as if unburdening herself, finding my eyes only infrequently, for emphasis. This posture and animation, this new pulse and freshening vigor, this sparkle in her eyes gave her an attraction that I doubted she had twenty years earlier. Christine had been run hard around the block and was only now discovering that she still lived, that life surged through her, giving rise to new color, a different allure from only a day or two ago, when she was only defeated and aging. Yet again, alas, this impression was best not shared, it was so close to the source of what all men really want.

She clung to her memories for the order she found in them, just as she carried herself with a poise reflecting order, just as she kept her house in order, her furniture at ninety-degree angles. She wanted what was left of her life, but could not open her arms to the living, breathing anarchy that had wended its way into her life and now sat with her at lunch.

Christine recounted the furnishings of her marriage one by one. I tried my best to look interested, and I was, conceptually. I knew she needed the purge, that any comment by me would only be an interruption. I let her ramble, wondering why anyone would cling to such mundane detail, would so stridently repress the truth. I realized suddenly that we were peas in a pod. I stared off. I smiled.

"What?" she said. "What have you remembered?"

I thought how best to present my own dilemma, then I stopped thinking. "I only smiled because I realized that we are similar."

She didn't smile. "No, we are not," she said.

"I meant that our situations are similar."

"Your wife left you?"

"Not my wife. My girlfriend."

"You are too old for girlfriends. You should have a wife."

"You're old enough to know better."

"Why did she leave?"

I shrugged. "Look at me."

"Not that bad."

I laughed. "Well, she was young. She is young."

She laughed with scorn. "Do you love her?"

"I don't know."

She laughed again derisively. "Men only say that to protect themselves. If she comes back, then you can love her. If she doesn't come back, you don't have to. Is that not so?"

I wanted to ask her the same question—it begged asking, but it was too easy, too obvious, and it didn't matter if she said she loved her husband or not. I could win the point but lose the patient. She was severely attached to what was dead and gone. She needed my compliance. "Yes," I said. "That is so."

We poked and nibbled our fish, had some water, wondered what we'd just said. I didn't think I was nearly as attached to Hattie, but then Hattie wasn't dead and gone. I laughed at that, too. She only watched me.

"Why do you think we met?" I asked.

"People meet every day," she said. "They can't help it. Can they?"

We ate slowly, silently, at an impasse in helping each other through our emotional wastelands, across our dispirited tundra of short horizons, low skies.

"Do you think she'll come back?" she asked.

I didn't hesitate. "No." I lied, because I wanted so badly to ficky-fick with Christine, and I thought the lie would ease her way.

But she went straight back to the wax museum, back to the good old days that should have lasted forever. She hesitated, remembering something, a good thing—"...sometimes we would..." But the words played out, died away. I considered this as progress and finished my lunch.

"Please don't stop," I said. "Not now."

But she settled again into silence.

"I think I've come to understand family life," I said. "It's not easy for someone like me. You know, the simple pleasures of watching the children grow up, relaxing with a full belly and fire in the hearth and all that." I had her attention, maybe for recognizing what she'd had, what I did not have. "It's not bad, for a night or two. I don't think it's for me."

"I would be surprised as well, for you," she said.

"And I will be surprised for you," I said.

"I will not remarry. I will not."

"You don't have to," I said. "Nobody has to. Nobody said anything about marriage. You can have a boyfriend. You can have a string of boyfriends." She looked down and blushed more deeply than I had seen her blush. I'd gone too far too fast. "I will only be surprised to see what indulgence you will give yourself, since you are way too young to grow old, and a world of fun is waiting to be had. And I think someone who knows what's what, as you now know, might have an easier time choosing whatever it is you want to do."

She understood, at last—understood that she could be Nurse Christine forever and still break free of the guilt. She could stop looking back in gloom, stop the memories that were so right, before it went all wrong, stop thinking that now her spirit must die.

She looked up, looked at me, into my eyes with understanding, her own eyes welling up. God knows I wanted her to get drunk, get more stoned—wanted to fuck all night, for the give, for the liberation of the thing.

But it was two steps forward, one step back; she regressed on the next inhale, sighing big over how perfect it had been, before it wasn't. "We had a Volvo." She smiled sadly.

She looked serene, like Mother Teresa after saving an entire slum. "It is rare in Brussels, you know," she said. She meant the Volvo. She and the professor and the children had been unique. I listened over hill and dale as she tittered along like a well-tuned engine; recollection was her opiate, and she was all strung out.

We drove the back roads of her lost perfection until the road ended in a swamp. "I think men are so weak for young girls, especially at that age, don't you?" She answered for me. "Oh, yes. You do. Your girlfriend is also what? Seventeen?"

I shrugged. I could have just as well picked my nose—she stared off. "I don't know why we separated," she said. "I think and think about it, and I can't know why. Can anyone?"

She waited, as if for my answer. I lit the pipe and pumped considerable cumulonimbus. "You have values he did not share," I said.

"Yes. That is part of it."

"That may be a bigger part of it than you realize."

"Yes. But he was weak, too. How could he throw everything away for that? He was weak. Men *are* so weak. Look at you. Trying to take me away. You would get me to someplace like Greece and see a young girl with bigger breasts and off you would go."

She had me there. I wanted to swear that it wasn't true, and I thought it wasn't, but a man's heartfelt protest is lost on the wind when the woman knows the hormones and the damage they can do. Men are so weak, some weaker than most. I didn't think I would leave her on a beach in Greece for anyone, because I wanted to have sexual relations with her then more than anyone else. And I believed with all my heart that soon after having sexual relations with her, I would most love to have them again—and then of course again, and so on; satiation seemed incomprehensible. Why is that?

But she and I knew the score, or maybe it was worse than that. Maybe I knew the score, and she sensed it, like a fear from deep inside. Maybe the fear made her nervous, because I was a man and she'd been there. Christine's cross hairs had me centered; oh, she knew—behind her a waitress with a lip quiver and bigger breasts leered our way. They worked together, Christine and the waitress, tag-teaming with accusation and proof, running interference for each other, testing a man's sincerity.

"How do you know all men are weak for girls with big breasts? I think your ex-husband may have been a normal fellow, but from what you tell me, he sounds bored." I was on thin ice, but I could see no other way in. "And what about chemistry? You think people spend time together just because one of them has big tits—I mean, breasts?" She stared at me in awe and wonder. "You have completely denied that it is possible to love more than one person in a lifetime."

Her eyes puffed and her lips twitched. We sat there, waiting for resolution, knowing it would not come. I was worn-out. Our exchange was, to me, exhausted. She had given in her good and nursely way. So had I. I stood up, offered my hand. She surprised me by taking it, amazed me by holding it halfway to the door, until the grip shifted, becoming tangible, until we could feel the mutable flesh between us.

It was altogether too much—my wounds, the hash, her depression, intimations of further contact. I think she understood timing, read my fatigue—I'd stood up to take my leave, and there I was in the same minute, staying. It was a most exhilarating phase of our liaison. But then a horndog's heart beats fastest over pleasures of the imagination.

Her hands looked good but felt rough, her callused palm recalling too many dishes, too much vacuum, laundry out the ass. Yet holding hands briefly with Christine changed everything at once. She initiated it. You could have blown me over. But I knew this score, too—she still needed a man to be good to her in spite of himself.

I thought I was the man for the job. Her needs were natural, and so were mine. We were human animals, playing our parts. She needed kindness and more. Me, too. So we strolled outside and back down the boulevard the way we had come, homeward, pleasantly thoughtless.

The afternoon played on, our growing acquaintance now a concession to the script we would play out, but it was a comfort, too, for me. Christine remained wary, uncertain, apprehensive, as if I was the castor oil, in need of swallowing but so distasteful. I suppose that was natural, too, but I felt sorry for her, for missing a rare chance to relax with a new friend. She'd worn me out, used me up, made me indifferent to whether we fucked or not, well, almost. At any rate, she'd been able to purge a bit of her haunting past, but she still couldn't fully enjoy the afternoon, not like me.

My wounds were leaking, so she parked me at a coffee bar near some shops she needed. She picked up an entertainment tabloid, gave it to me and told me to sit. She'd be back in a few minutes. In the meantime I read about all the entertainers coming to Amsterdam, for the great audience there, for the reality adjustment. John Kline, pianist, would arrive on the weekend.

I saw her reflection in a window, saw her staring from twenty yards, assessing. I turned toward her and she turned quickly to the window display, discounted it and came on back. She tried on a smile for size and fit, stretching it into place. It was a growth moment; only a few hours before it had been impossible.

I excused myself then under gray skies for the pain and fatigue. She busily crossed items off her list, and she amazed me again with agreement. She too had had enough, and she was certain I needed fresh bandages. We covered the last stretch to chez Christine slowly, quietly through the long, hazy afternoon. I focused on her long-legged, easy stride matching mine. When my limp got worse she put her arm around my waist and held me up. She made me smile, and that made her smile. I loved her.

At home she unwrapped me slowly, looked up, looking for pain. She admired my pain threshold and rewarded it with another slow, involuntary smile. Maybe nursing was her gift, the place she best lived in, because she relaxed, briefly, tending to my wounds. She fixed me up slowly, with care. She made tea and poured it and sat across from me.

I savored the comfort, the honest moment of gratitude, which was among the sweetest we would share.

The Hotel Christine

Which is not to deny the sex. Christine was stuck in a past that could not have been as picture-perfect as her memory of it. Her dream disappeared, like mine did, like that of any person will do. Unlike most other people, Christine had chosen to browse the rubble forever. If my approach to romance was behavioral, hers was mental. Her mentality was confined, stuck on small strokes, dark colors, brittle paint; her perfect picture chipped and faded, in spite of her focus on it and fondling of it. I, on the other hand, was simply overbearing with tunnel vision. I was up for some fun, at least, while she was only sad. I thought all happiness faded as surely as life itself fades away, and both must find new forms, must change, must adapt or perish, as ruled by the laws of nature. I thought sadness would settle like concrete if you let it, like Christine had let it, that happiness required initiative and experimentation. That is, I suffered the common doubt of males in close contact with females; I so wanted her clear on my availability.

Christine's depression was deep and immovable. Like her

happiness, I was fading fast. She was focused and strong, dispensing all her resources in the downward spiral and squandering all my tolerance, patience and appetite at the same time—that's what I thought. Her simplest movement, her basic essence, was wrapped tight in disappointment from the bones outward. Her muscles could not stay relaxed. I thought that I could change these things in her.

Not that sex would need to be unfun; some hash, some wine, some reckless abandon—I believed we could get way out of town, much farther than Greece. And once we got past the physical preliminaries, then we could slow down and cruise. I considered long term with Christine, because past a certain age you know the longest term is behind you—you can croak anytime, so it's easy to regard what was once only casual and fun as something to preserve. I was comfortable with prospects for time with Christine. The obvious comparison to Hattie was not difficult. Hattie was so young, so far away. Christine was seasoned, mature, a beauty in her body and her presence when she was calm. Christine and I could find a common path, I thought.

I lay on the couch with these thoughts, staring up, then looking her way. She watched me. She smiled, which was contagious, giving rise to the next thought, which was that my hormonal disorder was chronic, demanding, discretionless. Giving, helping, life, romance, spirit and beauty—all those notions that had kept such polite company in that afternoon reverie now vanished as big Dick Johnson bellied up banging his fist like a wino at a tasting.

I did want to be sensitive and giving, so I faced my weakness, looked down and then up again at her. I smiled again, now with a shrug. Her brow knitted into worry, into seeing different prospects, and she began again softly on the injustice her children had to suffer, the meanness of that woman, what was left of her life. I listened, closing my eyes, losing my vigor.

It went away. I lay there listening to her diatribe yet again, her spousal purge, telling myself that she only needed an ear, only a friendly ear. Then I could get laid. But I no longer believed it.

She was an ache looking for a head to fill, and I realized my dishonesty, because an honest man would have left. I didn't leave because I was strung out on Hattie and didn't believe her, either, and didn't have anything else to do. I wanted sex with Christine like a child wants tit for tat, or maybe just a piece of candy. She rambled, I stewed. I didn't love her anymore, nor was I fond of myself. I knew she was in control.

These things I thought, watching her without hearing her but nodding as if she made perfect sense, then realizing it was my comprehension, or show of it, that got her unwinding, got her easing at last into the concept of the load finally being off her mind. She got to recent days, describing some of the marital problems between the professor and his new, young wife—"He comes to me for consolation! Can you believe that!" Christine couldn't believe it; she was outraged, but she was gratified, too, because of the marital problems. She got lively again, her color rising again. I moved and pulled a bandage. She leaned quickly into fixing it, close enough to exchange scents. She hesitated just as I did; we were a chemical match.

Moving from warmth to intimacy was a hurdle. Christine was formal, graceful, poised. I'd seen plenty movies where the moment of realization is followed by the quick embrace. That wasn't me, for one thing, and a stab wound to the stomach was the second thing. She only leaned back and sat there staring at me, like I would transmute into Manners the Butler or something if she stared long enough. I said, "Christine."

She said nothing, but sat and stared, taking it in, maybe savoring what I thought she could not savor a few hours ago. She was much better than I was at going slowly. I gave up, relaxed, lay back, breathed deep and closed my eyes. It was all I ever needed to do.

"Do you want to sleep in my bed?" she asked, clinically clean and matter-of-fact, like a waitress asking, over easy or sunny-side up?

"Where would you sleep?" I couldn't help it.

"In my bed."

"I *am* feeling tired," I said.

She stood up. "That's funny. You don't look tired." She walked casually from the parlor to the bedroom. She was ready to get it on. Hallelujah, I thought, dragging my sorry carcass from one room to the next, entertaining new thoughts along the way, like calling it off, because every trick has his pride, even though I knew it was only a joke. But that notion too had no more free will than a fly near shit. And big Dick Johnson was ready to rumble.

She leaned in the bathroom doorway, an honest eyeful, an inspiration to newer thoughts, thoughts of long, longer, longest term of all with this woman I could never get enough of. The professor must have been a dunce. I didn't know then if I'd ever been this close to a woman, or felt this attraction. And she went into a striptease, the drab afternoon timed to the grandfather clock.

Down to the filigree, lace and translucence, she stood there staring again. I stared back and would still be staring if she hadn't come to me, taken my hand and led me to the bed. "Poor little one," she said. She was right. I followed.

We lay there for hours, two war dead on the same slab between those times we rose again to life, taking pace, rhythm, touch, scent, vigor, imagination and all the too-often enumerated and analyzed elements of human contact down to a single item: magic. Nature took its course as it sometimes does, creating beauty as if that is the obvious choice. We fit. Moreover, we felt unique in our fundamental friction. I had imagined cartwheels, somersaults, rebel yells, but it wasn't necessary, none of it, not because Christine didn't go in for that sort of thing, nor did we need contortion in the spirit of newness or freshness. It was Tab A into Slot B, plain and simple. I rode on top, or she rode on top, across the great plains, the nomadic tundra, the vast oceans and beyond, we rode until the stars twinkled across the firmament and over all of Amsterdam. In out, in out, in out until the stuff came out, then rest. Then we rode some more. It wasn't me—I hadn't gone like that since post puberty, when eight shots a night kind of got the pressure vented. It was Christine and chemistry. It was that apex of feeling, over and over again. Then we went again.

In the still and silent carnage of so many dead—hormones, memories—with the whimper still between us, the smoke cleared and we realized the world had changed. We had survived. In a twinkling, we had thrived. It was the time after the fucking when all the bullshit falls away. We went way too deep too fast, but we stayed in that new place, because once arrived you can't very well just...go back. We slept, smoked hash, ate, drank, and filled each other up some more, maybe hoping we would get our fill. I knew why I was there, and I couldn't leave. I considered a life in Amsterdam, lounging around Christine's house, staying high and fucking. I knew it couldn't last, knew that I couldn't last, but we'd arrived in another dream. I knew for myself it would be a dream remembered for years, for years savored and longed for, because all dreams end. Maybe Christine knew it, too. She displayed an affection pent up too long. I don't know what we shared then, other than overwhelming love of what time and circumstance had brought us to.

My frame of mind went from dreamy haze to alert sobriety, as if realizing that this was no dream, that I had stumbled onto a warp, a fit and a friction that was no more on the surface than hundreds before. Yet it was brand new. Pressed for specifics, I would have to credit Christine, her presence, her deliberation, sensing down to the square millimeters of membrane, again in control. I surrendered. The professor went from dunce to blithering idiot. Then again, there must be more to life than sex. I tested this theory by moving toward another go-round. Christine was as receptive as a patient in therapy. My theory would have to wait. We moved into day three, or four.

Naturally things changed, just as any marathon runner experiences different phases of the race. Christine went from release to deep release. Her body became a single muscle in drastic flex. I sometimes could only watch as she took what she needed, killing off what ailed her. She drifted for awhile, away from compensation for years without, drifting toward vengeance, performing those functions most men fantasize. But she leaned into kinkiness as if bending to a task at hand, as if taking a sperm sample was part of the dogie roping competition and she wanted it done in nine seconds flat. She gasped, "I've never done that!" The professor became criminally negligent.

We were making up for lost time, but going too fast to catch up. I liked it better in the beginning, in the present tense. I feared she realized at last that cleaning her house with a meat cleaver might be the reasonable thing to do. Look out.

She calmed down when I refused to share her vindictive spirit, but she still could not get enough of the release she craved. She sought a new pace, getting down like life and death. It felt like mostly death, which is good in some things, but this didn't feel like one of them. She groaned. She wailed. She cried. She carried on like a lost soul, or a body possessed. Now I missed the good old days, three days ago, when it was only Christine and me having a nice screw, before the goblins showed up.

Maybe I only set out to get laid as self-defense. Maybe I thought getting laid would shore me up against thoughts of the one I loved, herself getting laid. I wanted to forget Hattie for the week between us, repress her by replacing her, in the flesh at least.

I realized, looking up at Christine in agony, that I longed to tell Hattie about her. I would tell it casually, about the beautiful, elegant nurse I'd shacked up with in Amsterdam, embellishing on the hash, the jazz, the great good times. I rehearsed it, watching Christine ride and grimace, maybe hoping for a smile, surely hoping that she would find what she so ardently sought. And I would tell about the trauma, too, as a dimension in human adventure we had not imagined, Hattie and I.

I feared mortality, seeing Hattie while in the slip and slide with Christine. I was in love, first with this one, then with that one, now with this one again. I regretted that chaos is also part of nature.

We lay in the hush, in the post-voltage quagmire of the sorting process, hers and mine. I sensed her realignment. I sensed my own as well. I'd kept things basic with Hattie, staying simply grateful for a fine young filly allowing me between her legs—me, a non-surfer, thin on top. I had feared the aftermath with Hattie, feared my age, feared rejection. Now I missed her. In a few days I would call her. I knew that much, but little else.

Christine rolled away. Another afternoon wore on, the shades of gray now defining everything between us, all around us, in and out of us. Christine and I had arrived beyond the flesh, where we could see more clearly now. We needed space, air, movement. We lay there, still and silent, listening to the grandfather clock and the thoughts swirling between us. She was soft, sweet, kind and generous. I loved her but hoped with all my heart that she wouldn't be in the mood for another fuck. Oh, Lord, stuck in Lodi again.

The drab and gray stretched a few more hours, to five, or nine. We dozed, waking up from a dream into a dream, into realizing the flesh of our circumstance. After a long time I said, "John Kline will be here Friday." She lay there.

I said we could find him if she wanted to. I asked her if she thought John Kline would remember her. She said no. I asked if she thought John Kline already had a tuner. She said she didn't know. I asked her how old he was, John Kline. She said about our age. I asked her how a piano tuner like her goes about convincing a pianist like John

Kline that she's the tuner for the job. She said a woman has ways. I said that's fine, but what if he goes along with that and then wants to fuck. She said first she would tune his piano, and he would clearly see that he couldn't get along without her.

But what if John Kline didn't see it that way? She said fuck him. We laughed, for real. She'd made a joke, a sobering breakthrough.

I told her about my own showbiz runaround from a bigtime movie producer, who told me I could be great, could see bigtime Hollywood action, but he too only wanted down on the old bunghole.

Christine rolled my way. She stared at me as if something was wrong, as if something else was up, something I hadn't seen. She relaxed, laying her head on my shoulder. Maybe it was a long time since anyone told her a story.

"You have a problem with the homosexuals?"

"No. Not unless they manipulate and come on like that. I have a big problem with anyone who wastes my time trying to fuck me."

"So. It is only natural for them, just like you think it is natural for you."

I turned to her. "You think I'm a homosexual?"

"You wanted to fuck me."

"I didn't insist."

"But you did. Do you think it is invisible, this...way that you have?"

"But you...you brought me home."

"I did not bring you home. I opened my home to you. You are injured." She looked down. "You are relentless."

"But I didn't..."

"No. You didn't. I did. Because, in a way, you are right. I mean, for now."

I wondered what was right, and in what way, and how long would now last? She said, "So, if this person you met in showbiz was injured, you would not try to help?"

"I think I would," I said. She smiled. "I can't tell why you're smiling. Is it because you don't believe that I could help someone? Or maybe you can't believe I ever had anything to do with anyone where my own personal gain wasn't involved?"

"I know you helped people without wanting to have sex with them. But still, I would like for you to tell me about sometime when you did."

"I helped an old lady cross the street once. I carried her groceries, too. She wanted to give me a blow job. But I said no."

She laughed. What a relief. But she didn't stop. "I think you are a highly sexual person. I wonder what you will do when you get old."

"How old?"

She laughed again. We were building a new mood.

"We're getting off the subject. I was only telling you about sex in showbiz. It isn't a common social thing there. It's currency, what you pay for what you get, maybe. I didn't know that before. I knew this guy was homosexual. I didn't care. But he led me on. I made six trips to Los Angeles in a year, took on assignments, wrote screen treatments—those things take time and energy, all of it. And money. And heart."

"So you know," she said, "about being strung along and then losing everything."

"Yeah. I know. You know, too." I put my arm around her. "But I wasn't married to the guy. I didn't want to make a life with him forever. He wasn't after anything but me, bending over."

"What if you could have made a life with him forever?" She sat up. "What if you wrote the script for a wonderful film. And he produced it. And everybody thought you were good. So you and he made another film, and on and on. I think that would have made you happy."

"I think you're right. And it could have happened, if the guy was for real. But he wasn't. He only wanted to put his dingdong up my asshole and pump vigorously while I fantasized Hollywood greatness. He couldn't put a deal together, and I'm not a homosexual, so we broke up."

"But don't you see? Motivation is the same, whether sexual or otherwise."

"You think all motivation is materially based? What about love?"

She laughed harder this time, threatening our new mood with an old mood. "Listen to you," she said. "Love is something people do in the suburbs. Isn't that what you think?"

"No. That's not what I think," I said. "I think love can be part of sex when the people involved are mutually motivated."

She smiled. "I wouldn't have expected you to say that," she said.

"There was a time when I wouldn't have said it."

We pondered love, briefly.

"I had no idea what this guy was up to," I said. "I was young and optimistic, until the guy's receptionist sits me down and tells me our guy is broke, waiting for backing, and in the meantime stroking a string of guys like me. I thought he was jealous, the receptionist, but then he says, 'You seem like such a nice man. I can tell—you're sensitive.' He said he hadn't been paid in a month but stayed on because the producer wasn't a bad guy, except crazy on the make, like now. But all the entourage stayed on because, gee whiz, he'd been so big. I could join the entourage, and hang out and be perfectly positioned when the greatness came back, because positioning is what people do in Hollywood. But screenwriting for pay was not a possibility. He just couldn't stand it anymore, the receptionist, seeing sweet guys like me strung along."

Christine smiled. "What did you do?"

"I went outside. Santa Monica. Where teenage boys on the street want you to fuck them in the ass for money. This street-hag comes up to me and says, 'I'm a screenwriter. Out of work, you got a dollar?' I gave her two bucks and caught the next bus home. I didn't want to fuck her, either. The end."

Christine didn't move. I could hear her breathing and thought she dozed. The gray, drab afternoon got grayer and drabber. "Fuck it. If you want to do something with feeling, and you love it, then tune pianos. Just tune pianos. Let John Kline find you—that was my problem, chasing it around the block." I pondered pursuits, wondering when I'd have my fill, wondering for the first time ever in that phase of life, when I could head home.

Christine wasn't sleeping. "You've been so patient with me," she said.

I couldn't deny it. "No more patient than you've been with me. You're not exactly difficult to be with," I said, realizing the horrible crux of the lie, even as the syllables rolled off my forked tongue. She'd been extremely difficult to be with, I wanted to fuck her so badly, and she would not receive me. Now the confinement set in, my noodle chafed, my bones yearned for movement, I wanted fresh air, new scenery.

"I love you," she said. "I am in love with you."

Oh, God. I had arrived suddenly to where I always wanted to be, hearing the love of a woman whose beauty, grace, generosity and compatibility were proven. Yet the restlessness surged, because compatibility between the legs was the only thing we'd proven, and that was easy, arbitrary, a trick of nature. Now what?

Christine waited too for an answer, as aware as the next human of the shocking potential of love.

Hattie told me once she could hang out with any guy she wanted, which wasn't news, until she said she could turn any guy to stone as well, just by bringing up the L-word. I asked why she thought that happened. She'd said it's because men hate that. I told her she hadn't been hanging out with men. Not men like me. And here I was, in a cringe.

"You make me feel like no man ever has."

I did?

Christine dilated her soul so another burden could unload. Her pent-up demand gushed with intimacy and new momentum. "The way you push it in. So deep. I love that."

I stroked her temples. "I thought you were doing that," I said.

She turned up, stared at the ceiling. "My husband could never do that. His dick was too little."

"Mmm," I said. "That's the worst, when their dicks are too little. Isn't it?" It didn't work. She stared straight up, like a corpse, eyes open. "You know my dick is not unusually big."

She turned quickly, reaching for my dick. "It's bigger than his," she said, and down she went, seeking the impossible.

"And the others?" I asked.

She looked up, amazed—"It's only you," she said. Her

eyes went wide, her intention grim. "And him." And she proceeded, nursing my fantasy, feeding her revenge.

I rose to the occasion, as if with free will. In the next silence, awash with love, the past, the future, good company and hearts unfolding, I remembered what my friend Barry Dorn told me twenty-five years ago, when we were only boys. He said he'd found out that women like to have sex all the time when they get old, like around thirty—that they change completely, and they like the kinky stuff, too, they really do.

I'd found out that too much candy leads to digestive consequences, that sexual appetite increases with the understanding that life wanes, but it gets so complicated, becomes so much more than the squish and the squirt.

I held Christine. I loved her and I think she felt that. But I couldn't tell her I loved her, and she felt that, too. Maybe I should have lied again, but she would have known. We were a chemical certainty, Christine and I. But I saw horizons, felt a loss.

I understood the consequences of losing Christine, that dropping the bone to reach for a bigger bone would make me a classic fool. I pondered Greece, the beach, hundreds of ins and outs with Christine. She could keep me happy on that primitive level where I lived, and she had every potential for discovering the world she'd let pass by. But it wasn't time for decisions—no, never time for decisions. Because I wanted it all, wanted the ability to choose between beauties, wanted the shot every man wants, and with a safety net.

Meanwhile, it was time for goodness. It felt good to be so accepted, so entrusted, good to liberate the professor from her focus, to give her something for comparison, even if it started as basically as dick sizes, even though the spirit of betrayal would haunt her for years.

I loved Christine for her expression of love, loved her critical view of me. And I suppose the professor was liberated in my assessments, too, as I wondered if her rapacious appetite was not new but had been her standard for years. She was my best sexual partner, ever, yet I wondered how long I could last. Never mind, I would next teach her the slow and easy, maybe leading into three times a week, then once. I felt restless again, talking myself into restlessness, fearing slow death, maybe fearing spiritual birth. I don't know. I wanted to fuck until the day I died, and there I lay, planning a more moderate regimen. I was on a downward spiral. I needed help. I needed more criticism. "I've never been called patient before," I said.

"Yes. You are much more patient than he was. Much more." That didn't help. She snuggled in. I feared another go-round. I wondered if I would stay in Amsterdam forever with the nurse Christine, never to be seen or heard from again. I wondered if I should call Hattie and tell her I'd decided to stay here forever, or at least for another week. And among those thoughts nature played its course; we fell asleep.

We woke up in the dark, Christine first, then me a few seconds later, awakened by another nursing. It was a problem, maybe among the happier problems of a life in avoidance with reality.

But it was late, among the hours when life is most easily held at bay, in the time when thinking is most easily postponed. I didn't know anything, except that another invasion of Belgium seemed logical, since we wallowed in acceptance and trust, at last. Now with a little luck, I could get her to slow down.

Time and Tide

Christine eased up on love. I was saddened. I was relieved. After all, we had our whole lives ahead of us, or what was left of them anyway.

We got up, because it wasn't even midnight, so we pursued our distance from reality with more hashish, a little light piano, sparse talk, the ticktock stillness and a new presence there in Christine's living room. We had displaced her former, imperfect life. We'd mussed the sofa, left glasses lying about, hash and pipes here and there. We'd purged ourselves of constraint, immersed ourselves in human contact. She took to this new order famously.

We'd turned a corner, opened up and further shared our private selves. I could still be the man for the job—her furtive glances my way reflected further curiosity, as if measuring me for desire beyond hormone depletion. She looked for that side of maleness she'd learned from the professor, the side that changes for no reason just when everything seems in place.

The aftermath was difficult for me, too, recalling post-hump reverie with Hattie, comparing the two. Christine was different from Hattie; older, more stable, more generous, more poised, more graceful, certainly more tasteful and obviously more my age. But I was a fool—in love, I thought, but it was only lust, for youth. Poise, grace, taste, generosity and experience became incidental to the sheer adrenaline of twenty-two. I could profile my time with Hattie in a single word: Eeeeeeeyihaaaa! Christine only made sense. Besides that, Christine could do better than me. She could choose her mate. She wasn't oblivious to the reaction she caused in men. She was too good-looking, too smart for that. I don't know if she read my thoughts, but once I thought them, we seemed headed in a singular direction: courteous, passionate, spending time together.

So the week passed with growing understanding. She knew there were plenty more men, bigger men, more-patient men where I came from. I was only the first, in the real-life sense, and the conversation wasn't bad.

The sexual part got better, too. She slowed down, eased into rhythm, articulation, developing from a point to a concept. Her age, her physical maturity and nurturing character were new for me. It was a material, crude tally, but such is the count sometimes in give-and-take. We shared biofunction and more, love therapy, yet we knew of love's rise and fall. We shared the quiver, the whimper, the passion that lasts forever. We shared thoughts, sometimes ideas, growing freer, less inhibited, asking more of each other and ourselves as the days passed. We reconciled the jumbles, hers and mine, balanced the scales for a few days; we were due that. We smoked hash, drank wine, had fun.

By the weekend I was punchy from too much thought, too little action out in the world. She didn't feel the same restlessness, because she'd lived a sedentary life for so long, working and homemaking. Relaxation for Christine was a matter of lying around the place.

She loosened up after falling in love too fast. Then she realized her mistake. I was only pyrite. I think I made her realize it, because I failed in those expressions of love most people need at the outset. I only glittered like the real thing before the fucking. I didn't feel guilty about that—I don't feel guilty about that, because hormones make electricity, no hormones make something else. She became inured to my uncertain nature, yet she learned the value of the moment, learned to slow down, all the way to very slow, then to taking a long time for savoring what was hers.

Days and nights passed in ethereal discourse, hash, restaurants and sex. It was our retreat, the vacation we needed, the elixir of a new life.

She laughed often, once like a child who's just learned about what men and women do to make babies. We were stoned again, drinking wine in a restaurant and talking about sex—I pointed at the people seated around us, and said most of them fucked nearly every day. She giggled. She said she had never fucked almost every day—well, never before now. She wouldn't tell me how frequently she got it when she was married, but I suspect it started out as Sundays and holidays and got down to holidays and then down to Labor Day and the Fourth of July. She wouldn't tell me, but she giggled. She'd got used to the medicine very fast, and now she liked it, more than she thought she would. She ventured a question: Did I think she loved it so much because of me?

I didn't know. I was supposed to say something like, *I hope so*, or else, *Oh, no, you will like it that much with others, too*. But I could only muster more uncertainty. "I don't know," I grinned sheepishly as we shared the unavoidable image of Christine doing the do with another, with others, seeking, searching.

"I'm sorry I made us wait," she said. "I didn't know, either."

Much later that night she rolled over, laid an arm across my chest, caressed my face. I pretended to be sleeping.

We rented a paddleboat and cruised the canals with hash and wine. We rode bicycles around the park and town, walked and walked like every day was Saturday, every night was Saturday night. She made another joke. I asked one morning what she wanted to do. She wanted coffee, hash, maybe breakfast and then another day of play. "It's just another Saturday at Hotel Christine." It was a whimsical note, a flourish, a trill in mid-score for a woman on the flip-flop side of life, celebrating her youth and freedom after her marriage and childbearing, facing the years ahead with a first grasp for the world beyond the parlor.

Christine was strong in the face of my weakness, yet she was exposed as well, farther from home than I was, confused, unconnected. She woke up once startled, looking for an instant like it was a dream, an unpleasant one, with a stranger in her bed. She got her bearings soon enough, taking quick inventory of what her life had come to. She needed help, like a child waking from a bad dream. I needed much more—more than the great lay I'd had in mind. I needed to give—to give more than one more journeyman fuck with a minimum half-wit, decent manners and patience.

I didn't think of leaving at the end of the week. I'd mentioned a long time back that I would leave in a week, but we hadn't discussed it since the night we first hit the sack. Thoughts of leaving became increasingly difficult, with sex ever better every day, with her extreme care to avoid claims or questions on my intentions, with her courteous attention and sterling manners.

Every day was Saturday at Hotel Christine, until the day after Friday. It began in the early morning, about ten, after four hours sleep, three bowls, many beers. It was piss call for me, a little later than usual, but in terms of elapsed sleep time a little earlier. It averaged in the wash, washed in the average. So I slough-footed down the low-lit hallway mumbling my mantra of wash and average, average and wash, until I passed the hall mirror, eye to eye.

Many times I'd passed that mirror but never stopped in front of it until that fogbound morning in blinding light, when the U sent its strongest memo in years. *Look at you*, it said.

And there it was, gilt-framed, perfectly composed, terribly-aging me at eye level. Thin, greasy hair matted flat on top, sprung clownwise on the sides, lines and creases and bags gaining weight, eye- and lip-residue, oily skin and big-stuck boogers in both nose holes from too much smoke and soot in the lint traps, each hole lined with scab from chronic inflammation. Squinty eyes, puffy cheeks, grim reality, painful reminder that time won't wait, even on a man whose hormones survive him.

The mirror sent its resounding truth: *There will be no more young beauties,* it said. *Learn to love the simpler pleasures,* it advised. *Nurses know the score*, it testified. *This woman gives more than you realize*, I realized. *She is a catch, a find, a major score. She will spread her legs right now and happily so for the beast in the mirror. She will travel to Greece or Timbuktu with the same aging satyr. So why not go?*

Why not go? I went past the mirror and its echoing truth, sloughing on down to a possible world-record piss, pondering simple gifts coming my way, considering prospects for another morning in twenty or thirty years when I would see a much older man in the mirror, who would know that Christine waited in bed.

It went two, two-and-a-half minutes, a certain record but unofficial without real timing. But isn't that the way with the very best? Out of the blue, unmeasured, spontaneous, it was a piss more alive than a bevy of young beauties, and it was elixir too, giving new strength, opening a new day with resolution.

A quick shower was all the merciless mirror needed; hose off the oil, bags and oogies, comb the hair and presto chango, maybe not thirty, but better, middle age with dignity and poise, maybe.

Back in the sack Christine waited, her sleepy smile an invitation to what I had resolved. I crawled in beside her and came close to her. We'd been over twenty-four hours without, because last night was too stoned, too drunk, too late. "Mmmm," she moaned. "Come here, please." And she pulled me aboard for a wake-up screw, no headaches, no moods, no periods coming on, no need to wash her hair, no anxieties over her children—oh, God, her children! I forgot about that! But sex in the morning with Christine was too good, too strong to interrupt with practical considerations. We could get a nanny and send them to private school and summer camp. We would discuss it later.

I sought her eyes, going slowly. I said, "Christine."

"Yes."

"I'm going to make a phone call this morning." She stopped. "I need to make a phone call this morning."

"I always thought that men could not stand having sex without coming." I thought I caught her drift, so I shut up, proceeding to my morning tremor. "Now you can tell me. How does your phone call affect me?"

"I have to call Hattie."

"Hattie is your...girlfriend?"

"Yes. I'm scheduled to call her this morning."

"Then call her."

Here too was my cue to say something like, *I'm going to tell her that I'm staying here,* or else, *I'll have to be leaving now, to go back to her.* But I could not complete the resolution I had begun; I could only feel the wheels spin, only imagine that my first, honest move toward lasting love could turn to regret so soon, unless I had all the data. All the data? Well, what if Hattie had opened her heart, had seen and felt what I had seen and felt in the last few days, had gained clarity on what we might share? I wasn't saying I would jump at that chance. But then of course I might.

Christine eased me off. "Go now. Make your call. There is a pay telephone on the corner. You can have much more...privacy there." She stared straight up, still and mum. It was our last ficky-fick, our last embrace, our last intimacy, our last sweetness together. Because Christine knew what men do.

Death is best when it comes unannounced, quickly, in sleep. She lay there unmoved with drawn eyes and a sad smile that said, *Now it's time to say good-bye.* We had reached another blessed moment, which was the moment of independence.

I could have said something like, ***I'll be right back,*** or ***This will only take a minute,*** or ***I love you.*** But waves of sadness turned the messy bed into an emotional undertow. So I didn't say anything, pulling on my pants and heading out and down to the corner.

Hattie My Love

I was happier outside, under a blue sky and sunshine, free of long terms, short terms, prospects for Saturday night.

I felt foolish, in such a bind at my age, yet it would soon be over. And I was foolish to be heading out to a pay phone when she had so many phones right there. I had nothing to hide. Well, in a few minutes I would have nothing to hide.

I walked to the corner and found the pay phone near an alcove where some bums smoked hash and shared a bottle on an extended Saturday and foolish condition of their own. You had to love a town like Amsterdam. I dialed all the numbers and waited, feeling pretty good, with a safety net. Sure, it was a terrible thought, and the next one was, *Let her fuck with me—just let her try.*

I couldn't forget Hattie, not ever, and especially not last week, even immersed in sex. I could only repress, could only squelch images of her valiant efforts to get the blood flowing, even as mine surged like never before.

I was attached to her, but now I could let her go, I thought.

I loved her, maybe with a love growing strong enough to survive intimacy. Maybe I was growing strong enough—old enough, weak enough, flexible and smart enough to allow our love to grow. Maybe our love was over. Either way, okay. I was ready. So I waited with verve, with intent, with confidence.

"Hello," she said, too unexpectant to suit me.

"Seven days," I said, because brevity steels a man for rejection.

"I know."

"What else do you know?"

"Very little."

"Need more time?"

"No."

"How's Pinocchio? Signs of life?"

"You don't want to know."

"Isn't that presumptuous?"

"Don't start."

"Are we on?"

"On what?"

"What do you think?"

"Where?"

"Where would you pick?"

"Where do you think I would pick?"

"Probably Paris."

"You're so smart."

"And patient. Don't forget patient."

"Where are you?"

"Amsterdam."

"You went without me! I wanted to go there!" She whined, pissed-off child, cheated again. I relaxed; we were off. This was no comparison to the house I'd just left. A union with

Hattie would mean the end of everything, the end of youth for her, the end of a reasonable adulthood for me. I stood there listening to Hattie's Amsterdam fantasy, there on the street in a strange town, a heartbeat from farewell, wondering how fast I could get back to Christine's, wondering if Christine would take me back. I thought she would.

Hattie wound down, and I waited for her slow, whining refrain that maybe we shouldn't, that maybe it wouldn't be best, that maybe we would see each other again, sometime. But she came on strong, pleading yes, soon, we should meet at once for fun, for adventure, for all the things we'd missed in the last few days. "And we missed so much," she said.

"All of life is a compromise," I told her.

"I miss you."

"I'm grateful."

"Do you miss me?"

"Isn't that a stupid question? Don't worry about that stuff," I said, still playing with fire.

She got cool and intelligent. "The road does you good. I can't help it. I miss you."

"I had to help it. It came down to getting by."

"You could get by and still miss me. It's easy. Find a woman. Once you get rid of the sex edge, then it's fun to miss someone."

"Okay. I miss you. I found a woman. It doesn't work out that simply for me." I couldn't help it now. I'd had enough of her superhuman, impervious-to-jealousy bullshit. Her moment of speechlessness was sweet confirmation of a direct hit for the poison dart.

"What didn't work?"

"Well, you know I never had Pinocchio's problem."

"No. Just the opposite."

"You never complained."

"Would it have helped?"

That stung. "It didn't work," I said. "I'm not as strong as you, or as smart. I can't roll in the sack six days straight sucking and fucking like no tomorrow and think of you and think, Oh gee, that Hattie, what a swell kid I sure do miss her, well, gee, maybe I'll see her next week. That's what doesn't work for me." I engaged heavy artillery, no time for diplomacy—and hadn't she varnished Pinocchio's dowel rod all week? Anyway, it was a direct hit on her primary missile installations.

"Six days?" Nothing to do now but follow up with infantry, occupy the command center.

"Does that seem like a long time?"

"Six days?"

"Hattie. You been down there on the peninsula for weeks!"

"Not sucking and fucking!"

"Who's keeping score?"

"Do you love her?"

"I could."

"Is she beautiful and smart?"

"Yes."

"Oh God..."

"This isn't like you."

"I know." She was crying—crying over the hungover, bleary-eyed, scab-nosed, pale-skinned, snaggle-toothed old fucker in the mirror. All of victory is illusion, and so is defeat. "I want to meet you," she said. "In Paris. I want to..."

"Tomorrow," I said—I heard myself say, that quick, that easy, that fast. "Tomorrow afternoon. Hotel de la Paix. I'll make a reservation. Say around five."

"Why tomorrow?"

"Why not tomorrow?"

"Why not today? Or at least tonight?"

"What's wrong with you?" I asked. "What's happened down there?"

"I love you," she said. "I know that now."

"Won't it wait a day? I have to pack, get a ticket, call the hotel. All that." And farewell sex with Christine.

"I suppose."

"Relax. Get your ticket."

"I hug you."

"Yes. I feel it. I'll see you tomorrow."

"Okay," she said, like a girl with a broken spirit. It was everything. It was nothing. She was a child, lonely, horny, wanting most what had been taken away from her.

Back at Christine's I didn't need to explain. She sat in a funk, in a mood. I thought briefly of progress lost. I wanted to be straightforward, matter of fact. She was ready. She smiled with an offer to help me get my things together. I told her I could leave now, or tomorrow—I told her I was flying home to America, alone. The lies came quick and easy; anything I could use to ease the pain was okay by me.

Maybe she knew. She too was straightforward. She said she was comfortable with me staying another night in her house, although she had to be away, would most likely not return for two days, so she wouldn't see me before I left.

She said she thought at first that she needed time, to think things through, but if I had taught her anything at all, it was that action should preempt thinking. So she'd called a very nice man who had, you know, shown an interest for quite some time. She said she was confused, because she certainly didn't want to get on a sexual merry-go-round. "But I do think I should do something. I let myself get so...dependent. I like this man. I think if I spend a night with him it will, you know, ease the pain. I don't think I could ever love him, so I let myself down with a little kindness. Doesn't that make sense?"

I hung my head. Now what? I should have changed my mind. I should have stayed. I should have said something. And to think, I step out for ten minutes, and she sets up a date.

Christine said she wanted to thank me. I said she was the one to be thanked. She said no, she wanted to thank me for something. I thought she wanted to thank the Handy Man for the medicine, for piston therapy. But she said it wasn't the sexual relations, although she was glad for that. And it wasn't so much the conversation, even though she hadn't talked things over with anyone over nine in quite a while.

"I'm only leaving to tend to my property," I said. "I'd like to come back. I'd like to stay..."

"It's your spirit," she said, and she blushed deep red, as if she'd said, *Thank you for eating my pussy*. "Your spirit is good," she said. "You've taught me what it means to survive. To thrive." She laughed—"You could have spent a week in a cheap hotel, and look where you ended up." I feared her anger. "Don't worry," she said. "I'm glad you came between my legs. I loved it. I loved you."

"The spirit is that of giving," I said. "And it's yours."

"Please. You are strong. You shared that with me." She faltered. "I feel stronger now."

"By stronger you mean more able to share an intimate experience without involving your heart? Because if you do then I've taught you a lie, taught you the opposite of what you knew, what makes you unique. I'm not good or strong. I'm a bullshitter with finesse, that's all." I gained momentum, heading south on a train in the back of my mind, but highballing for the truth here and now, front and center. Maybe I needed Christine to understand my need, my unvirtuous drive, my penance. But I didn't even understand it. Maybe I only wanted her to wait for me. She ignored me and my lies, ignored my request to stay.

"Yes," she said. "You are full of the shit." Then she came to me. She took my hands. "But I do feel better. Much better. I have the pain in my heart, but I feel more prepared to go on."

"It wasn't ever in doubt, was it?"

She nodded and cried. "I didn't know what to do."

"What do you know now?"

She shrugged, "I don't know. I only feel different." I hugged her, kissed her, and in our sweet embrace, I got a hard-on, maybe swelling with pride at last over the noble results of my hot-beef injections. She eased away. "I really must go," she said. I sat down on the sofa, which is what a man with a hard-on salvaging dignity must do.

"Yes," I said, slamming into midmorning, a world away from sunrise. "Yes. Go. We must."

Seven in One Blow

The train ride south was long and arduous as the ride north had been, but southbound bore down on hope and a promise, on a day of doubt and wonder, when anything less than a beautiful destination would have let a tired soul come unglued. Never mind the place—a woman waited there, for me. And a few grams of hash didn't hurt.

The hash didn't help, either, after a point, beyond which a soul finds itself all alone with the questions that no person or thing can help to answer. I think I knew by then I suffered undue anxiety over the gist, the content, the substance of this love trying to evolve between Hattie and me. So far we had fun, only fun, which boiled down to nitty-gritty was only the playful nuance, the hormones, her youth and beauty, and our favorite stand-up comedian, big Dick Johnson. I would have been convinced only a week ago, that such a package would be plenty enough.

Maybe it's never enough. Human consciousness, being what it is, spirals downward with meager provocation. Like my thoughts now, anxious and depressed—fresh-fucked for a week, stoned to the gills, highballing it south under blue skies for another rendezvous with a woman whose fire never went out. Me, now, anxious and depressed, with what, another twenty or thirty years of this kind of fun to look forward to? Or maybe thirty-five, or forty.

So you get a middle-aged man heading south on a train in a cloud of smoke and images, sorting through, looking for delineation where I know there is none.

I imagined Hattie at thirty, screaming at the children to clean up this fucking mess, and someone better get out there right now and bring in the goddamn groceries from the station wagon before they spoil or...or else!

Or Hattie at thirty-five, successful career woman, on the road to international corporate headquarters, talking that talk, wearing overpriced clothing, very high heels, blood-red lipstick, and a gleam in her eyes that says she's accustomed to cutting off balls. Do you need a trim?

Maybe she'd get fat by forty and love me more for staying home with her. I'd be sixty, or sixty-five, but physically fit. We could play tennis to stay healthy and vibrant.

I hadn't played tennis in years, but maybe fitness would come naturally and we could play croquet over a few drinks and a little more hash.

It came down to the big difference between Hattie and Christine, between anyone twenty-two and anyone forty-five. Christine had become herself, had passed the age of defining herself, had weathered the storm, surviving it more or less, had rounded the clubhouse turn into the stretch. She'd done all right, maybe needing only a little time out in the world to realize just how much resource survived with her. Only an hour out of Amsterdam Christine seemed far away and long ago, a real humdinger I'd let get away.

Hattie would become something, someone. She was a child on a learning curve with a sixty-percent slope. Anticipating potentials could be dangerous. Letting things play out with no forethought could be dangerous, too.

That was the note to savor; life is a hazard. We can only strive for fun on a daily basis.

Maybe that was the biggest danger. I had a friend once, Jack Witte, who wanted to have so much fun that it got to be no fun at all. He was pussy crazy, too, like I used to be but worse. Jack was pussy-craziest of all. That was back in the old days, but some guys won't change. He made me look politically astute, like every woman out there was Ginger Rogers and I was Fred Astaire; Jack was Jack the Ripper. It wasn't only his appetite, but his approach, his insecurity, his insensitivity bordering on hostility that made him a dislikable character. But he was still a character, disarming as a pitiful pup, lost and alone with a single certainty; the world was out to get him, unless he made his move first. Money and women were front and center for Jack Witte.

I hadn't seen or heard of Jack Witte in ten years, most likely hadn't thought of him, not a single ridiculous frame of him. Yet his sad, misunderstood visage accompanied the long ride south. Maybe it was in comparison to what had happened to me, to the person I'd become. I hated to think of myself as settling down, and it didn't have to be that way. I felt good to be heading home to a woman I would stay with, maybe for the duration.

Prevailing recollection of Jack Witte—he pronounced it witty, although he wasn't—was the pose: Jack in a slump.

Jack slumped on a bar stool, leaning on his forearms, gazing at his drink like it was a crystal ball. He wasn't stupid, either, and was the first to call his schemes cockamamie. "Still Life in Zero Initiative" could have been his epitaph, "Except for Pussy and Money." He sold time-share. Maybe he changed, too; the doubts are all mine. He had the potential for change. He was that smart. And he never wore the gold-nugget jewelry so popular with time-share salesmen.

I didn't like Jack Witte, but then again I did, maybe in perverse admiration of his profound consistency. His presence triggered the defense mechanism in some people. He swindled and/or fucked the rest. He was a natural, like a big shark cruising, spotting an iffy flutter, too many bubbles, a dash of weakness, illness, vulnerability, and quickly he would move in, only doing his job.

We sat one time in a bar having a few drinks. It was during a liquor time, and calling it a few drinks was like the president of the United States of America calling triple unemployment an economic fluctuation. We were all fucked up once again.

We drank, waiting for things to pick up, and Jack approached a subject like a grinning dog approaches a sofa. He liked the idea of himself on the sofa, but he feared the beating—in this case, he feared the condemnation. I was his friend and moreover his confessor. I understood his need, or at least I knew about it. I protected myself around Jack, for his sake and my own, because Jack couldn't help himself when it came to taking advantage.

Out of the blue, which was where Jack came from on his initiatives, he said, "I got a cockamamie idea...." This with the grin, the teeth showing good-naturedly, close to the sofa. "I bet I can fuck seven different women on seven consecutive days."

I laughed briefly. Jack didn't. "Is this something you've been thinking about?"

"Yeah. For years."

"Why?"

"Why? Shit, man. Imagine. A different one every day. It's every guy's dream."

"Maybe not every guy, Jack."

"Yeah, listen to you. You wouldn't like it? Fuck you." Poor Jack. He couldn't even share a fantasy with a supposed friend without catching some grief. But he had me, caught me red-handed in a pose of my own, self-righteous self-piety. "You mean you'd like to swindle, I mean close seven women, one each day, on the idea that you and each of them shared an intimacy warranting your *schwantz* between their legs. And after each one, you would then discard whatever was between you, and go on to the next one?"

"Fuck you," Jack said. It was his primary rejoinder. "Even the president of the United States of America would get a kick out of having sex with seven different women on seven consecutive days—even if he couldn't admit it on camera. Some of them tried it."

"Do you have a fantasy on selling time-share? You know, like seven weeks of it to seven different suckers, one each day?"

"Sure, but it's not the same." I waited. He drank. "You don't have any love with time-share." I laughed, but he said, "Oh, I make friends with some of the time-share people, but it's not the same. Besides, I got this worked out with women I really like."

"Anyone I know?" I asked.

"Sure. I gotta count Louise. That's fair. She's female." Louise was his second wife. They got along from time to time, even though she was a bitch from square one. Her complaint got louder as her own needs grew. They had nothing but each other, which I suppose for them was security, insulation from solitude, which they feared.

I threw the stick again. "Who else?"

"I gotta tell you. I hardly ever got so much pussy as I been getting. I been running threes and fours practically any week I want." Threes and fours referred either to women or weeks of time-share sold. Both meant gratification and pride. Jack's time-share "resort," was twenty-six so-so condos with brown pile carpet and generic furnishings—cheap rattan, straw baskets stapled to the walls, plastic place mats on Formica tabletops and a "fantastic ocean view" just across the four-lane boulevard. The place was designed for the people who bought in, who took one look at the decor and exclaimed, "Why...this is nice!"

Jack loved his job—he made a grand just for getting his hand into Johnny Lunchbucket's pocket. He got to fuck Johnny's wife twice—these occasions after the husband got so drunk he passed out and the wife said, *Well...* Jack loved those times, loved the recall, the replay, the slo-mo blow-by-blow, the pivot, the turn, the liquor, the lip lock, the whole, unbelievable scene, there in the cheap-shit condo with the middle-class couple who would commit to ten grand in e-z payments in the morning, so they could come back to paradise for this kind of fun every year.

"We got over a thousand weeks of inventory left," Jack said. "Shit, that's another four years of work!" And the Display

Unit worked out perfect as his pussy pad. "How many married guys got a pussy pad? Huh? Huh?"

Jack had called me down to the "resort" a few times so he could point out women he'd been able to fuck. The married ones were rare, a certain highlight; the rest were single women on vacation, mostly agreeing to "a few minutes of your time to share some information about our program here." Jack said it was all programmed from there. "You gotta getum drunk." He favored rum. Once drunk, he asked for sex. Some said, *Wha?...* And some of those Jack got to fuck.

"You remember Simone with the great tits?" I remembered. Extremely attractive with a nasal twang like hard New York, she wore big costume jewelry and said she was from L.A. in what looked like an identity adjustment. Jack got her drunk. He called me down the next day and pointed her out from ten yards and said, "Unbelievable. Took me four hours but it was worth it." I wanted to know what he used for openers. Jack said, screw tops, what do you mean openers? I said no, how did you approach the romance? Jack said he showed her his dick. And what did she say? Jack made gulping noises.

"She sent me a postcard. She's coming in week after next."

"That's two?"

"Yeah. I had four already. I got that little bitch they use for spiffs down at the club." He meant the beach floozy on cheap-rum retainer at the "resort," who fucked the week's "top producer."

"What if you're not high man in two weeks?"

"Fuck it. I'll give her twenty bucks."

"It doesn't count then."

"Fuck you, doesn't count. Who says it doesn't count?"

"Who couldn't go out and buy seven women?"

Gratification was mine then, as Jack Witte's referee, giving him the harsh reality of the game.

He recovered nicely. "No sweat. She owes me. I'll set it up. You're right. No money. And no fatties either."

"She's not fat?"

"Shit, no, man. She looks good. You know, couple six packs, low light."

"That's three."

"That's six."

"Who are the other four?"

Jack loved a challenge. One was Malta, his irregular girlfriend. They drank, smoked cigarettes and talked shit together. I allowed Malta—she was technically female.

Another was Marilyn, an over-the-hill vamp who'd had every nip, tuck, lift, separation, spread, injection and enhancement money could buy. Pushing fifty in denial, she clung tight to the six-inch pumps, plunging necklines, rouge, eyeliner, lip gloss, long red claws, diamonds, emeralds and body language to back it all up. She also sold, focus on the husbands. She let Jack up into her place and allowed him free range for two weeks nonstop one time, which grope she later described as that of a juvenile delinquent at the ice cream buffet—all grab and gobble till the poor little guy have a tummy hurt. In their second week Marilyn gave Jack the ultimatum—leave that scrawny, mental bitch, Louise, the wife, or it was done-for on the sweets.

Poor Jack. What kind of pressure was that to put on a guy? "I thought you and Marilyn were history."

"I told her I was leaving Louise and maybe we could have a drink. She said sure."

"Did you peg her on a specific night yet?"

"Monday. I gotta get her early in the week. That bitch catches on too fast. She could ruin the whole thing."

"You'll miss football."

"Nah! We'll watch it at her place."

"You have thought this through."

"Planning and implementation are my specialties. You know that."

"Sorry. I forgot for a minute."

"It's amazing how things work out." Jack was excited over the sheer synchronicity shaping up, as if Providence smiled on him at last. Sixth on the hit parade was the clerk at the liquor store two blocks down from the "resort." Jack had cultivated her. "I talk to her. She's thirty-two. Just got rid of her boyfriend. He's a bum. No job. She's pretty nice. She said she'd get a drink with me."

"So she's a wild card. You can't count her in the bag."

"I never said it'd be easy." Jack ordered another round. He tallied on a bar napkin.

"Relax. That's six," I said.

Jack grinned again and nodded. "I got to fuck Diane today."

"Who is Diane?"

"From the escrow office. I wanted to fuck her for about three years now. She's an exercise nut. I'd say about forty-five, but you could fit her ass into your hands." He held his hands out, palms up. "And she's got a rack on her you wouldn't believe. You ever notice how older women go for me? She's a cunt. I mean it. So today I'm down there and she asks if I can get away for an hour. I said sure and she says, 'Your place?' I'll tell you the truth, it was the strangest thing, driving to my place not saying anything, walking in, taking all our clothes off and jumping on the bed. Her body was hard as a rock. I mean everywhere—her tits felt like flint implants. It was strange. I put my tongue on her nipples and she just stares at me, doesn't even blink. Three years I wanted to fuck her. Finally I asked her why we were there."

"Unusual question for a guy like you," I said.

"Yeah. She says, 'Because I'm horny.' I told her that's why God invented dildos. She says, 'That's why God invented you.' That's all she wanted. The high hard one, slow, medium, fast, get dressed, back to work. Three years I wanted to fuck her. It was terrible."

"It's amazing. The disrespect."

"Yeah. I didn't even ask her for a blow job."

"Ah, well, she'd have probably said no."

"Yeah. I think so, too."

We drank. I said, "Gee, Jack. You're a sensitive guy after all."

Jack shrugged, allowing at least the possibility. "We need some cocaine," he said, because those were the cocaine days, just after the marijuana and free love days, before the AIDS days.

"Jack. You're not counting Diane from escrow on the list, are you?"

"Yeah. I am. Fuck it. It's a long shot. But I got a plan. I'm gonna tell her I'm sensitive, and she really hurt my feelings."

"And?"

"And I want to fuck again, but nice."

"Ah!" It all came clear in a wink; Jack Witte was out of touch with reality. "You are a specialist."

"Nothing to it. Planning and implementation." He held a forefinger up. "Plan your dive. Dive your plan."

"Goddamn," I said, "a whole week of different women," and I laughed, wishing him well as the vast golden fields flew by, Dunkirk, Le Havre, Rouen. Steel spikes clicked off miles like a metronome; time was distance, closing. I opened the window, fulfilled by warmth and a buffeting breeze—college kids clamored aboard with their knapsacks in a hurry to get a seat or a spot in the aisle and light their smokes. I didn't mind them so much anymore, and I warmed up to knowing where I was, where I was headed.

Transmigration

Jack Witte said he was running threes and fours any time he wanted, but an easy audit showed he'd run a common three—his wife on Sundays, two Sundays in a row now, after football, before *60 Minutes*, even when the game ran late. His girlfriend was a sure shot Tuesday afternoons, when the wife got her hair and nails done—"Every fucking week she has to get her hair done." And the in-house slut was there for convenience, whenever, before lunch, after lunch, just before going home—"I'm telling you it's a real luxury." The regimen got altered by a chance fuck from escrow, giving rise to visions of Empire.

But it was this kind of delusion that Jack savored. His life was a futile scramble for conquest, measured in money and women. So he embellished on his dream by adding another chance, or maybe four more chances, for the thrill of the thing, for something to look forward to, like the finals of the greatest sporting event of all. So a friendly clerk factored in with decent odds. And closer still to the end zone of his mind, he factored prospects for success with another chance fuck who'd demanded divorce and remarriage to her in short order. This was obviously a resource to be used to advantage, Jack thought.

"What happens if you pull this off?" I asked. He grinned, because I so obviously framed a question in the context of success. "I mean, what do you get?" The grin vanished. "Why not go for fourteen? But then two sevens wouldn't really make a fourteen. Would it? I mean, is it ever enough, Jack?"

He drank his drink, lit another fag with dissolute regret over the lot life had given him, with such negative friends. "You know you got a real bad attitude, Harry," he said. He called me Harry when pointing out my shortcomings. "You got a real problem." He pulled big on his smoke, exhaled and packed up his kit, his smokes, his change, his rolled-up bill. He stood up to leave. "You better learn to relax and enjoy life, Harry," he said on his way out. "This is it. You're gonna be dead a long time, you know." And he left.

Jack was never easy company, the liquor, the cigarettes, the bitterness, greed, hostility and unkind approach to life. I enjoyed rattling him, challenging the significance, the merit of his fuck tournament. He tried to convey to me that I'd been unfair, that I could just as well challenge the meaning of, say...football, for chrissakes.

I realized the sporting grid was all he had, and he, too, like every man, woman and child, deserved more. But this is all he got, the answer to his time of need.

I saw him the following weekend. He grinned again, sheepishly, never one to bear a grudge. I asked him if he was taking his vitamins. He said that he was, and that he'd cut back to a pack a day and a few days ago he'd jogged down the street a ways, to get in shape. I told him his strategy was strong enough to make it off the chalk board, but it was weak and variable. He went long in the face, ready to exit again, leaving me to my negativity. I said the single weakest link in his plan was his wife; she could deny him on any given Sunday as surely as the Colts could trounce Dallas.

He said she'd never find out, never. I said it wouldn't matter if she found out. I meant she was the weakest link because she most likely wouldn't even fuck him if she didn't find out. She'd come across two Sundays in a row, but that was fluky; maybe as long on odds as the Colts trouncing Dallas and then creaming San Francisco the following week. And now he was booking the Colts for a skunk over Buffalo?

He hung his head and said it was true, that she wouldn't even give him a blow job anymore, his own wife, for chrissake. Where was that at? Jack and I were friends again. He loved commiseration.

"So?"

He said not to worry. He'd bought her a diamond. It was a fake diamond actually, but it looked real good, and that would do the trick. I told him he was The Master, which snapped him out of his iffy-friendship, no-blow-job funk. He glowed. Jack loved mastery.

In the end he ran neither a three nor a four, much less a seven. Jack scored a one, but a happy one rather than the solitary one he seemed doomed for. After such rigorous scheming, such thorough rejection, his heart and mind were tenderized, made more ready, at the final buzzer, for love.

Louise, the wife, wanted to know what he paid for the fake diamond. Jack said a grand. Just before payoff, she rifled his wallet and found the receipt—ninety dollars. Jack said,

"The bitch. Like ninety bucks is cheap." But he was smart enough to campaign Louise on the Sunday beginning his seven-day run rather than ending it, so that if she failed, he'd have the whole week to recruit another woman, or work on Louise some more, or something.

But Monday his odds worsened—the in-house slut told him, with love, that she was contagious. Never mind; she'd have a week to get over it, well, six days anyway, or five at the minimum.

The attractive woman with big tits from L.A. canceled her return visit; nothing to do now but try to score, hope for the best.

Marilyn, the old fuck, ran into Louise on Wednesday and said too bad about the separation. Louise said take him, please. But don't believe him. He'd never walk out on half of everything. Touché—Marilyn canceled cocktails. Jack needed to get laid now, for the principle of the thing.

But his irregular girlfriend got a new boyfriend and wasn't fucking around, at least for awhile. And the work week ended with the liquor store clerk threatening to call the cops.

In the end it was only flint-hard Diane from escrow who paid on the nose, Saturday night, long shot to win, who told Jack she wanted to fuck him too for more than three years and held back her passion the first time because he was about the best fuck she'd ever had in a long time, and now they were regular, "Every day she wants it, noon to one, and she got nice, too, oh God, you wouldn't believe what she does." He said he felt deep down inside that he really liked her.

I never really trusted Jack, so why were we friends? What did we have in common? He made me laugh, plain and simple, deadpan sincere with his self-pity, his empty life and the cruel world breathing down his neck. The guy was miserable—but could he sell? Top producer thirteen weeks in a row back in '89. That was in his prime, but he could still dive into a pocket with no bumps, sell a Rolodex card for ten grand and make the folks feel like part of the Deal of the Century. He slowed down, like most salespeople do, once all the compression and liquor catch up.

Stunted wheat flowed by, endless as the miles and hours, breaking every now and then for a poverty-struck village or a *campo* in ruins, or a half-crumbled shack you half-expected a mutant to come walking out of. The whole damn world looked tired, overfarmed, overused, spent, gray and forlorn, and this was summertime.

Jack was good, putting it out there with pitiful innocence, then getting a laugh. A few drinks, a few laughs and put the pedal to the metal—that was his M.O.—get them laughing, then, quick, get them drinking, then a few more laughs. He theorized people are most alive, laughing and drinking, most receptive to what it's all about. I think Jack was wrong on many scores. I don't know what Hattie would have thought, but I suppose I hoped she would have seen through him. But I wished him there on that train for a few miles and hours, for a few laughs, a few drinks.

Two hours down, three to go.

I had to move, and it was closing on cocktail hour so I got up, stretched and headed down to the club car for a beer and a different angle out the window.

The old woman who lived in a shoe with so many kids she didn't know what to do stood in a dirt road motionless as tumbleweed at high noon, all her kids huddling around her, like they were waiting for the old woman to shrink some more, or maybe for the world to close in some more, or maybe for the whole scene to grow a little bit more dirty. They looked fresh out of electroshock therapy, staring at the train but not seeing it, like it could run over them and they wouldn't flinch. Then they were gone.

I laughed, imagining Jack trying to sell some time-share to the old woman who lived in a shoe. "You gotta have vacations!" I could hear him say. I laughed again, wondering if Jack would try to get her drunk so he could ease into sexual relations with her, for the principle of the thing.

I wondered if understanding Jack Witte for his moral corruption was a clue to that day of doubt—wondered as a svelte woman in a dress and ample figure leaned on the bar beside me. She turned to me. I drank my beer, let her look, sensing her assessment. Jack Witte sat on my shoulder whispering urgently, *Move! Move! Move! Now!* I turned to her and smiled the pleasant smile as she easily turned away. Did she, too, see the old fool waving his arms, yelling, I'm open? That's not what I meant to convey. I hit the WC for a look in the mirror to see if I was trailing oogies or something. No, just the aging process, the look that hinted mortality without credit cards. If only she knew. I stoked a bowl of hash in consolation, singing, Oh, no, they can't take that awaaay from me.

◆ ◆ ◆

Gare du Nord near the Bastille is an indelible image no matter how much time passes. Seeing it once is seeing it forever, feeling its gritty, ashen air, its thick and wayward crowd, its sense of direction and nondirection, its merciless punctuality, as if the bums and winos and ragtag knapsackers arrive there to find out how late and far away they really are. A small hotel in Paris conjured the same sameness. Generations of work and deprivation maintained this minimal standard, provided shelter for a Frenchman with arteriosclerosis from too much pâté, cheese and wine, and for his workaday daughters and his old, tired wife.

"*Ah, tien!*" the old guy said, happy as a man with faith renewed—I'd come back. His was a spirit indomitable, French, sustained by rich, fatty foods and alcohol. He was free of anxiety, free of worry—what difference could it make if he dropped dead at sixty rather than seventy? Would not sixty be better, with the good food and drink along the way? I had interrupted the old guy's lunch and offered to come back—"*Non non? Pas du tout? Ce n'est rien!*" He lowered his sandwich, dabbed his chin, removed his bib and reached for the registration papers. His sandwich generated its own gravitational field, like the supertanker of sandwiches—a big gob of bread with a big gob of meat with slaw festoons and mayo suppurations, salted like the streets of Paris in a snow flurry. A pound of fries lay on the side under a blanket of salt, beside a carafe of pink wine. He filled in the blanks, remembered my name and nation.

I watched his daughters. They worked hard in a patina of sweat, shyness and blushing. Beautiful young peasant girls with innocent hearts and hairy armpits. I wanted to sink sometime with them in too much pink wine. I wanted to sleep in the barn on a promise.

I waited in the room, sitting on the floor.

In a few hours I realized that the sameness of the hotel, the street, the foul air was not as bad as it had been. I pulled a pillow from the bed and lay down. Maybe I was only adapting, coming to terms with dying a few years less or more because it doesn't matter, if the spirit is at peace, coming to terms with the idea that being well fed and pleasantly drunk accounts for peace in some people. That I needed something more was a milestone, most likely a good one, I thought. And I felt good, better than in weeks, maybe months, there in another matrix, which was one and the same as that of my first arrival, in Paris or anywhere, but now was blessed with another first step, another journey. I realized as well, as if fact was not a function of data but was rather a gift from way yonder, that Hattie would not come. It was a disappointment, an acceptance, an approaching dusk, a dream swirling into form.

She arrived in the same minute in a blush and a swirl. She stopped in the door for the electric arc, the sweet death of anticipation. She drifted dangerously slowly, closing the gap, neither hugging, gasping, clutching or otherwise having or holding. She only arrived, eliminating the space between us, laying her breath gently on my ear.

And in the pixie flutter of her eyelashes on my cheek, her hot, sweet sigh on my neck, in the glistening dew on that sunrise of our love, tingling with anticipation and uncertain whispers, a balm flowed into me that felt like all she had to give. "I want us to be married," it said.

I had imagined it, that was all, heard within a fantasy the words most cherished, most dreaded. Then I knew it had been spoken, from the heart, beyond whim or youth or old age, synchronous merger between two people coincidentally sharing the same years in all the thousands of years people have lived on earth.

"You mean like Elm Street? With kids and a station wagon?"

She said, "No. We'll live at your house."

In a dream a long time ago I saw Hattie at sixty-five. It was easy. She looked good—better than I would have thought. Not that a dream can be trusted. I used to dream of found money, big bucks, wads of dough, knew it was no dream and that now life would change. Then I would awaken to the sad truth: You can't take money home from a dream. I dreamed the old man wasn't dead, dreamed it for years after his funeral. I dreamed I could fly. I dreamed of Hattie at sixty-five, looking sixty-five and looking good. But that wasn't the point, what Hattie would look like at sixty-five. And maybe I could fly.

The point was that I dreamed of sex after a lifetime of it, dreamed that after a lifetime she would retain the essence of herself at twenty-two. Isn't that what we come to anyway, essence? Before or after the dust doesn't matter, does it? Isn't that what love is, the recognition of essence? Is not the avowal of love an acceptance of the essence, only the essence, forever the essence?

I'd arrived at last at the Paris I'd set out for, which was only a frame of mind, but sometimes miles are required to get there. I'd arrived at last at the faraway place in which very little mattered; it was like the small death, *le petit mort* the French say follows the sexual act, the time when letting everything go becomes easiest, because we have just let everything go.

But this was different, much bigger, on a grand scale—maybe Le Grandeur at last, there in a cheap, dingy cubicle at dusk with incessant traffic outside below and a vision of an old woman who was my mate. I laughed—I'd be pushing ninety by then, so some sixty-five-year-old squish should be pretty good, after all.

I never feared the solitary phase of old age that most people fear, the all-alone-in-the-world part. I'd feared the ball-and-chain part, the leather-and-bones part. I felt strong in the basic, human sense; solitude is my friend, and it befriends so few people, so few can process it free of fear. Yet I felt weak and hungry, too, like Jack Witte, if not hungry right now for new and different women, then hungry for Hattie, and if not for her then for more women, or newer horizons, a change in scenery, a reach and farther stretch, clawing up the years at the itch I cannot scratch. I worry about that, because that hunger isn't natural, isn't so easily dismissed as part of life; I fear it's part of death, too, again on a bigger scale than the small one after fucking. I feared the first wisp of a restless spirit seeking, seeking forever on the earth.

All this in a sweet embrace? Well, yes, I suppose it had come to that—the assessment and reassessment, down to the bones, accepting the leather if leather is what it would come to, asking the hardest questions, dredging the long-standing challenges to what I had for so long avoided. All the logic resurfaced then and vanished in the same split second. Affirmative rang true even as the questions melted away.

"What about the hunger?" I asked. Her face moved against mine, into a smile I suppose, maybe a rueful one, as if the hunger was our common appetite, as if the hunger was our common essence, accompanying us and consuming us from now on.

"Stay hungry," she said. "We'll stay hungry together. Lean and hungry."

"What about last week?"

She took my hand, sat me down on the bed. "It was nothing. I was foolish. I know so much more now."

"In a week, because Claudio couldn't get it up?"

"He got it up. I want to tell you, so you know. He got it up real good. But he wasn't you. It was just like you always say, you know, about smelling right and feeling right. No chemistry. He was a nice guy, that's all. He was in love with me. He wasn't a pussy hound, not nearly as much as you."

"He didn't want you to leave?"

"Of course not." We hung our heads.

"Must've been good for him, anyway."

"It wasn't sexual. He couldn't get it up. But then he did get it up. I mean he hasn't got it up in over a year and he didn't know why but he kept on trying and failing and the poor guy wouldn't give himself a break from it."

"What was your secret?"

"Just what you taught me."

Oh, God.

She shrugged. "Just let it go. He couldn't get it up. I said okay, so what. No big deal. I liked the guy. I mean he was fun. So after a few days he let it go, too, and then what do you know one night he just got it up."

Maybe she didn't give him a blow job, I thought.

"Could you see the pulse in it?" I asked, tormenting us.

"Hey. We fucked. Okay?"

"Yeah, fine. No problem here. I'm just curious, you know. Here's a guy, a pet project kind of, and you like him and all that even though he can't get it up, and you're doing all the right stuff like letting it go and still liking him, because you're on the threshold of a kind of new power and 'what do you know,' it works. So the guy gets it up, and you're happy for him and you fuck him like a good nurse... So why couldn't you still like him? And given time why couldn't it turn to love? I mean you must have felt a special attraction to the guy."

"I did. He was beautiful..."

"So?"

"I lied."

"You mean you did love him?"

"No. He couldn't keep it up."

"Oh, great." I was up. "You figured out you love me by default. I keep it up."

"Don't sell yourself short."

"Right. I smell good. I keep it up. What else?"

"Chemistry. Don't forget the chemistry. That's most important. You know, we harmonize."

She had me there, and with the advantage she quickly moved in. "It's not like you didn't get laid," she said. "It's not like your eyes don't turn for every skirt in sight. At least my guy was real."

"Your guy was real."

"What was she like?"

I laughed—"She couldn't get it up." Hattie wasn't amused. "I'm serious. She was good-looking, divorced, a nurse, on vacation." I shrugged.

"Why didn't you love her?"

"It was all pussy, dear, free and easy. You know me. Woof."

"Yeah, I do. But you're not like that. You could get tons of women like that but you don't. It was more than that. I know it was."

I could? I shrugged. "Call it coincidence. We met, had dinner, got stoned and fucked."

"How did you meet?"

"In the hospital. She was my nurse."

"You were in the hospital?"

"Yeah. I got stabbed." I pulled up my shirt, showed her the wound, told her how great I'd handled my assailant, profiled courage, cool with no adjectives.

She nearly swooned and swooped to it, felt it with her fingertips, kissed it. "God," she said. "I'm a sicko. This turns me on."

"You mean now?"

She took off her clothes, quickly, unsensual, but with a confidence we both understood—she was twenty-two. She could arouse any man, even a weary, impotent Italian, or a fresh-fucked sex fiend. "Sure," she said. "Why not? Just don't fight it."

"Fight it?"

"You hurry too much." She stood there naked.

I sat on the edge of the bed. "I hurry too much?"

"I have to tell you that. You have to slow down, to please me." She stepped up, pulled my head to her stomach and held me. "I want it to be good," she said.

"I thought I was patient."

"No. Not at all."

"Okay. Let me try to get this right," I said. And I went very slow, like instant replay on the action scenes, went to the intimate focus with stop action, frame by frame. Hattie wiggled and whimpered her welcome home, but unlike intimacy in the past, this time her eyes swelled. Tears formed, and it was plain to see that something besides genital contact was at hand. A tear rolled down her face, rending the common rhythm, infusing the physical with the spirit. We touched again, yet we always had. I asked if she really wouldn't prefer more passion in love. "I mean, isn't that where you found me...lacking?"

"What do you call this?" she asked.

"I like this. I just thought you missed—I mean, that you imagined..."

"Aren't we in love?" she asked.

"Yes. We are. I meant mad passion, screaming, lusting..."

"You don't have that in you," she said. "You know it and so do I, and I'm willing to have you anyway."

"You'll tire of me so quickly."

Another tear rolled. I feared a tearful momentum, yet reading me like a psychic would, she picked up the pace a bit, whimpered with sadness and stimulation. She shook her head. "I'll always come back to you."

"You mean you want to get married but still fuck around every now and then?"

"Not if you treat me like this. Not if you go slow and pay attention."

In sexual contact, slow and easy, I repeated her request—"Go slow and pay attention." Leave it to the one you finally know is your true love to touch your gaping weakness like it was a nerve exposed, touch it with pinpoint accuracy. I considered Hattie a genius then, and more; she was in touch with the world around her, maybe more than I had been. It was a lesson learned, a process sentient beings find attractive, are drawn into. And then we were done, hunger relieved, lying still and calm as two bodies at the end of life, or better yet, at a blessed moment of resting in peace with a whole life left to live.

Wine Time

A drive along the bluff over the beach and a chance look at a young woman's crotch seems farther away and longer ago than childhood. Hattie Summer and I arrived at a place only fantasized in the past. We slept, woke up, got up, dressed and left the hotel with no words, yet it was the silence of intimacy, of spiritual communion.

She led down the Metro stairs and we matched steps down a walkway tunnel so long it had its own horizon. Floor and ceiling converged to a point. We walked past that to a platform where we boarded and rode clackety-clack until we got off and walked again through another maze. "Some people spend quite a bit of time down here," I said.

"It's so easy," she said.

People hurried past in both directions, mostly with heads bent, eyes down, city people, survival mode. "Mole people," I said. She let it pass. "Think of how far they are from my place," I said. "The orchard. The arbor. The eucalyptus stand. The palms and ferns."

"This is the city, where anything is possible."

"Maybe not anything," I said.

"What do you want?"

"I miss the clean air. The countryside." She let it pass.

"The floor is crowned here. Look—it's a foot higher in the center. Flood control. I wonder how deep we are. I wonder if it's raining." We came to a curve and another long walk to a long flight up. "Must get funky down here in about three feet of water. Bet it brings the rats out good. Back strokers, dog paddlers, frog kickers."

She laughed to keep from scorning me. "You are a bumpkin," she said.

"Rapids, shoals, falls." We plodded up the steps. Outside in the dark the city was finding its stride, after hours, drinking, smoking, talking things over yet again.

We ducked in just anywhere, which was the common decor everywhere. I wanted wine, and then more wine. She went along. We drank.

A tall, well-formed young man came through the place in long strides. I suspected the stride was methodical, designed to match the tight pants and clinging T-shirt, and it gave his long curly locks the perfect swing and sway. The young man strove for the common image, the vogue impression: salt of the earth but dashing—a street-level buccaneer. But he looked made-up, unreal, a result of hours in the mirror rather than miles on the road. But maybe that was only me, rested, confident, cynical again. The young man's long curls framed his golden face. "Tanning lamps and a curling iron," I said. He paused a half-step to take in the view of Hattie. He stared, blinking his big, dark eyes. "Eye shadow and liner," I said.

Hattie looked him over, up and down. "Well?" I asked. "What do you think?"

"I think he's a good-looking guy."

I smiled. "Do you think he's impotent?"

"Why should I?"

I shrugged. "It just seems like you've known quite a few guys who are." She shrugged. "Do you think your experience with...impotence is unusual?"

"No."

"You think that many guys can't get it up?"

"How many?"

"As a percentage of your experience it seems significant."

"I don't think so. Some of them went the other extreme, you know." She was good, very good. She broke my neck, left my head dangling down, answered the challenge with a swift stroke. And she was even better. She took my hand, rejuvenated the neck, brought the head up, eyes to eyes. "Has anything changed?" she asked.

"I think so."

"What is it?"

"I think...life is about to change."

"Yes. It is. That's very good. You're a good boy."

I was a good boy. I asked, "Do you want to get married right now?" She had me off balance.

"Right this minute?" I had her, too.

"Yes," I said.

"How can we?"

"I don't know."

"I don't, either." We drank, ordered again, drank again. She said, "Tell me about yourself."

"To be sure?"

"No. Tell me about your childhood."

"Short, specific memories," I said. I drank and thought and drank again. "All I wanted as a boy was Saturday and summer. Saturdays and summers I went out with my dog far away from home. My mother put my lunch in a sack. Sometimes I took my Ben Rogers bow and arrow set. Once I shot at a black snake. I missed. I was glad I missed. I got good at targets, though. We went for miles, all day sometimes, in a big circle out and then back in. Forest then, never before seen by white people. It's all gone now."

"You were antisocial even then," she said.

"No. I don't think so. That came later. Too many people."

"It manifested itself later. It was there all along."

"Manifested?

"I hate it when you do that," she said.

"Do what?"

"What was your dog's name?"

"Otto. He was me. Alter ego. I was nowhere he wasn't, except school. What a waste. Four in the morning Otto was up and ready. He went with me on my paper route. We sold seeds and cards door-to-door together. We walked to the bus together. In the afternoon, he waited there at the bus stop. All he wanted was fun. He liked to go."

"A boy and his dog," she said.

"That's a simplification."

"Simplification?"

"I told him stuff I never told anybody. Ever."

"Did you tell him you loved him?"

"Sure. But it wasn't necessary. Dogs pick up on the vibe much quicker than on spoken words. Wouldn't it be something if people could do that?"

She suddenly perked up. "I have an idea!" she said, turning her shoulders, her torso, her hips all at once toward the good-looking fellow, or the waiter, I couldn't be sure, but her hand swept into the wine glass. It fell over, spilling onto my crotch.

Paris Arrival

Truth barged in like a cop with no warrant, smashing down the door, filling the room, blotting the light, grabbing my shirt and yanking me up. I sat in a tremble, heart pounding, sweat rolling down the side of my nose in a single rivulet, dripping onto my chest. Tepid pecker juice, crusty on the periphery was the wine spilled on my crotch. Hattie said she had an idea, just now. She said so and turned to tell me and looked right at me.

Her idea was to vanish, poof, gone with the dream. I continued waking. Is this live or Memorex?

Sperm and sweat were merely that, residual precipitation from the dream life of a confused man, condensation formed by dramatically different temperatures on either side of an ethereal plane. On the dream side was the truth; the result of the subconscious sorting process leading to the inevitable, logical result: poof and gone. On the waking side was the struggle through the sweaty, sticky, funk-mugged denial that this was living.

But living is just what it was, and the truth of it was apparently clearer to a twenty-two-year-old female than it was to me—or at least she could accept it better, was better able to continue our dialogue of spontaneity and expectation, our dialogue of action, no conversation. Hattie knew, plain and simple, it wouldn't work, because it was a bad idea, because we could have the pain now, or we could wait and have it later. All that stuff that was rock-solid true got dense as sedimentary strata in that stuffy little cell, until nothing moved, until the lava mold could have rendered a scene for excavation: ancient horndog stuck in denial, crushed instantly by truth.

I could have just as well relaxed. What you get is what you got, no matter how hard you want it different. And it's only the liquids you can bring back from a dream. This was real; oh, I'd known plenty times that this was real, this is no dream, only to fly away with a bag of gold clutched under my arm and then get chased by dragon monsters who couldn't really hurt me, because all I had to do was wake up.

But this was real. This one sat too heavy for figment. I calmed into it, accepted life and its circumstance, easing into oneness again with the man in the mirror. I'm much, much older than I was. My dog Otto died twenty-three years ago. My God, I wish he was here. He was a promise of loyalty, growth and understanding, even if repartee was only a tongue on my face and my childish insistence that he cut it the fuck out. Otto understood tolerance, uncritical love, communion, showing up on time.

I scanned the room, sifting the air for a vibe, a presence, a premonition, for any feeling at all, any sense of where she was or why. I came up empty, resoundingly unknowing, except for the awful here and now of the thing; Paris, two A.M., headed round the bend to solitude in old age, that inevitable end of the line so smugly seen as safe haven only hours ago, when the sun still shone and something different waited ahead.

The little room closed in, but only so long as it took a road-weary man to change pants and find the road again, maybe for the first time free of expectation, with no baggage.

Down and out was déjà vu, like the dream: Paris at home with itself, in the middle of the night, thick with traffic, exhaust, people searching, people sitting, talking things over yet again. In the first of all the places looking like all the rest a table waited empty just inside. A point and a nod brought a carafe and a glass. I drank it, drank it down, not sniffing or tasting or sipping but quaffing as if the thirst was that of a desert, and the pungent redness swigged big was water flowing over cracked earth. I stayed parched but limbs loosened and sure enough a spring flowed alongside the campfire. The first half-carafe was good, the second half better, once the twang and recoil got adjusted to, and another nod was good enough for another go.

It wasn't drunk I sought—drunk was too far out there, too far gone. It was simple removal. Wine was medicine. The third half equaled the first two in efficiency. The fourth half required letting go of all questions, all answers, if the downward spiral was to be avoided. A sailor knows the best cure for the sickness: stay busy. His life depends on it, keep moving, make yourself useful. The waiter asked if I would like a whole carafe. I said no, I liked carafes in halves. He stared at me. I stared back. He walked away.

I might head home soon. I miss it. God knows I'm drunk enough to leave Paris.

But maybe not. A Fifi sat two tables down with golden,

frizzy hair around a round, bright face, supple, I thought, but not fat, no chafe, no sag, with bright eyes and good odds on a strong spirit. And youth, too young to know the bitterness women get to know, as if disappointment in life is only for women to bear, and men have only the happy task of getting laid.

And better yet, on scrutiny she held up. French women don't mind a stare. And she didn't smoke. I sensed it. So it was easy to imagine regular hygiene, too. I leaned across the empty table between us, and like an idiot, drunk, said nothing. "*Bonsoir, Monsieur*," she said.

And I felt my head shake in the negative, heard another string of words in uncertain coarseness explain, "It was big circles, Otto and me. And uncanny, my sense of direction then, you know, younger. You could cover my eyes, turn me around, roll me over. I'd get up and show you north. Not now. No, ma'am." I tasted again the pungent succor of reality gone away. "I'm not so sure of up, now."

"You are American," she said. "I do not speak so good English."

"Yes, you do."

"Slowly, please," she said.

"Yes, slowly."

"Why are you here?"

"Stood up. And you?"

"What is stood up?"

"My true love did not arrive. She wanted to marry me. She was so young. Younger than you."

"And you are so old? I think you are not so old."

"You are kind to an old man," I said. She giggled. "I know where she is," I said. "She's in Italy, with Pinocchio. He couldn't get it up. Then he couldn't keep it up."

"Very much is up with you."

"Yes. I suspect he promised her the villa. I don't know. Maybe he has a brother."

"You are sad?"

"Yes. Yes. Yes." I considered sadness in the warm red liquid flowing down in waves. "I am sad. More sad than I have ever been." She watched my puffy face. I felt my puffy face, my tender eyes, wishing the numbness was less, the tears more. She came to me, took me to her bosom, and it was there in a sobbing fit that yet another light shone, illuminating the goodness waiting on the far side of structure, of order, of expectation.

"My true love will arrive, too," she said. "Here is Philippe." A thin young man with thick dark glasses and a thick black pompadour watched nearby. With a face devoid of emotion, he offered his hand.

"How do you do?"

"*Ça va*," I said, wiping my eyes and my nose. "I am admiring Fifi's ankles from afar. Excuse *moi. Je suis* drunk."

"He is standing up," Fifi said.

"No, no." I stood up. "I've been stood up. My true love did not arrive." I wiped my face on a wobble and a sleeve.

"She will arrive," Philippe said. "In the meantime we will get drunk."

"How do you know?"

"It happens when I drink too much wine," he said. "And I am having thirst."

"Ha ha," I said. I sat. I sank. "You are a funny man, Philippe. I think you could be American."

"No, no. I am not that funny." He pointed and nodded and called in French with *panache, élan, joie de vivre* and extra hot sauce, so that two bottles arrived, the good stuff. Then came *hors d'oeuvres*, out of the blue, hot and cold, sweet and sour, *avec les fromages et les baguettes* with reason from Philippe, "It is best that we eat something when we are getting drunk."

So the night began and ended, with difficulty for me, since the wine quenched the fire, but then stoked it as well. I think Philippe was impressed at my capacity for drink. He said I drank well.

I said I did not drink well at all, that my speech was slurred, my body fairly disconnected from my mind, my thoughts unraveled.

Philippe said it does not matter, the slur, as you say it, or the stumble or the confusion. What matters is the drinking, the sheer volume of the drinking. He said very few Americans understand that. "They know only to say we have a problem in France. And yes, of course we do, but...we also have a...a...I don't know the word..."

"Addiction."

"Ability. We have an ability that most Americans do not have. We can let everything fall away, you know."

"Yes. I know. Just look around." We laughed. "Le Grandeur!" I mocked the French.

Philippe said, "Yes! You understand!"

"*Sacre Coeur*, motherfucker!" I saluted and drank my weight in wine, going for some kind of point, following Philippe's lead, seeing his bet and raising another bottle.

"*Juste!*... Never mind," Philippe said.

I told him my mother made me wear baggy pants like his all through childhood, hand-me-downs from geeky cousins, old man's pants that made me look like some kind of fucking refugee, just off the boat or something. But I got even—oh, I didn't mean even in the vindictive sense but more in the compensatory sense.

"Compensatory?"

I had these petty, bullshit jobs from early on and squirreled away a few bucks so by high school I could go out and buy my own goddamn pants and blow the piasters on pegged legs, too, so tight they looked painted on. I had a big wavy do then just like Philippe's but with more grease.

Philippe and Fifi were rare, exquisite people, sitting there framed and waiting, enrapt without doubt. And when I got lost and confused and pitiful and said, "I... I don't know why I told you that. I forgot what I was going to say," Philippe perked up as if appreciative of the perfect punch line.

He topped off all around with the good stuff. And he said, "Excellent. Excellent. Tell again."

I drank and shrugged and said, "No más. You tell."

Philippe said once when he was a boy he went south to a beautiful little town on the coast where a friend of his uncle's would take him sailing. I nodded, showing my own appreciation of a good sailing story. Philippe said he had to peepee very badly and couldn't wait until the boat was out of the harbor and it was faux pas to peepee over the rail in the harbor so he went behind the harbor office, because France is not like America, where grown men need four walls, a ceiling and a door with a lock just to make peepee. So he was tweaking his little lizard behind the office and this big man with a head like a giant onion with very wrinkled skin across his forehead is suddenly standing behind a bush staring intently at Philippe the boy. Philippe still had a ways to go, and the big man stepped out from the behind the bush, and in his hand was his big big, how is the word, *coq*, which he beat violently while watching Philippe make peepee.

Philippe topped off all around and looked content. "And so?" I asked.

Fifi said, "I have heard this story. And so Philippe finish his peepee and go sailing." Philippe grinned.

It was obviously a cue. "Excellent," I said.

Fifi said she worked in a dress shop, but not a modern dress shop. She worked for a woman who designed dresses, in a very small shop up a very narrow alley. Fifi was an apprentice, a seamstress, and felt that she would herself design before too long. She sat up straight, showing one of her designs.

I topped off all around and said, "*C'est formidable.*"

She blushed. "*Tu es gentil, Monsieur.*"

Philippe said Paris suffered decay of the soul, but that was okay, because its spirit of decay had always co-existed with its spirit of freedom. "And equality and fraternity," I reminded him.

Philippe said yes, but it had changed, the spirit of decay had itself decayed. He could not explain it in English, but it was like, for example, the difference in pollution. "If you step in horseshit, you say, 'Ah, this is dirty.' You say the same thing if you step in green chemical, but it is much worse. Horseshit cannot hurt you, but the green chemical can kill you."

"How do you know this, and nobody else does?"

"It is because I am young. The old ones will not change."

I said it was more, too many tourists, too much media, too much packaging on an image, with the whole goddamn world accessible to too many people, so that an honest adventurer has crowds at every turn.

"Yes. We walk now. I know a good place."

It was three or four. Most places were closed or closing, their fronts locked and hosed down. We took alleys to other alleys. Philippe and Fifi were like guides through the ashen forest after the fire. Philippe acknowledged night people who stood or lay down in doorways, gave them a look and a nod in unspoken French. We came to a big, dark and dirty place where people drank at tables, drank at the bar, drank while dancing to a black salsa band. We drank and danced, danced in far corners, danced in the center, danced in the doorway and in the hall.

We danced fast until no dance was left in our legs. We danced slow, no more than a lean and a stagger, until I could only sit and watch Fifi and Philippe dance, hanging on to the hour and to each other. How often could they pull out the stops and get shitass drunk and dance all night? How could Fifi design or sew tomorrow? How could Philippe study engineering? But the question how did not translate. Nor did any questions; we had come to another place, which was the end of the night, first light. Philippe bought a bottle and we left again, finding new vigor in sunrise and more wine.

They would have taken me to my hotel, but I didn't know where it was, couldn't exactly recall its name. So they took me home, gave me a sofa and a blanket and a pillow. We sat there together for a moment to savor the stupor, apart from ourselves and all time, and Philippe said, "So now you see, my friend, we have come to where we must live."

"I like it," I said, giving the nod to the sparse Parisian flat. With windows at both ends, seventh floor and way back in the courtyard, it was breathable. Five strides from the kitchen to the bath and a WC with elbowroom compensated for the low ceiling and several centuries of sagging, for the chipped plaster and cracked glass, low wattage, burnished grain and threadbare fabric of the place. A person could sleep here, take a leak here. A man could live here, if he must.

"Not here," Philippe said. "Americansky. Here!" He clutched his heart with his hands.

I aped him, clutching my heart with my hands, gasping, like this was the big one. "Here? Froglegs!"

Philippe went cool—"A man from the United States comes to my school for the big speech, you know, engineers and the world and America. He speaks like we are fools. 'You have your whole lives ahead of you!' he says. I tell him it is not so. I tell him, 'Suddenly you are gasping for air. And then it is all over.'" Philippe smiled his big, warm, happy smile. "Could be today," he said. "So. It is here we must live. Yes. But, it is not so good that we are drunk all the time. So. Pay attention."

I waited, attentive. But Philippe was done. "I am waiting, teacher."

Fifi said, "He means we are someplace else. We are drunk. He means this is our...ability. We have changed. Tomorrow we will wake up and maybe remember what we see here. That is why Philippe says pay attention." Philippe nodded off, fell off and snored. Fifi carried him away.

I lay down under a cover of spinning gratitude, dropped an arm off the sofa for contact with the floor, with Planet Earth. The body, made of lead, sank deep and deeper into the old French sofa, sank far beneath the cover as though taking root. The arm overboard gained weight, too, like a limb of one of Earl Izumi's ironwood trees—Earl Izumi tied cinder blocks on ropes onto ironwood limbs and let them hang for fifteen years, moving the ropes here and there every year or two or five, until the normally straight-up trees with straight-out limbs looked like Uncle Wiggly the ancient, decrepit rabbit who hobbled down the road bent nearly double with posture so warped and twisted his crooked cane was three steps out front to support his horizontal upper half, but the guy knew everything. Everything.

This is *bonsai*, Earl said with a smile. I smiled, too, feeling the cinder blocks gain weight, wrist, elbow, shoulder.

And we spun away.

Away into darkest night, deepest sleep, sweetest dream, in which want, confusion, love and loss did not jumble a man's peace but nestled warm and still, until a dewdrop formed into a kiss, still and warm, familiar and arrived from far away, settling on lips, down from the eyes, with happiness. Here at last by magic in Philippe's and Fifi's flat, high up, in back, in a courtyard in Paris, among the ironwoods.

"I was late," she whispered. "I told the old man I'm your wife. I waited in the room. You didn't come, so I went out. Now I've found you. I was late. My trip was delayed."

I dreamed of delay, of running in dream slag. "Delayed. Waylaid?"

"I quit smoking," she said.

"But you never smoked, really," I said.

"But I did. Now I don't. Don't you see?" she asked.

I wanted to see everything. "I hope I will, and soon," I said.

"I know you will. I wish I'd been here, last night," she said.

"Yes. It was fun. I was so out of it. I feel different now."

"I know. Philippe said you would feel different now. I

think Philippe will be best man, Fifi maid of honor. We'll honeymoon in Paris..."

"You've met Fifi? And Philippe?" Light seeped in, glaring as an accusation: You must live, another day.

"Philippe is gone. I must also go. Stay here until you feel well. Philippe will return after this noon. He will like to talk to you then, about what you saw. *Au revoir, mon ami.*"

Yes. Yes, *au revoir.*

Movement is slow and painful in a Paris flat, stark and compressed on a plaster-flecked, cracked and rickety morning. Walking recalls the Tin Man in summer rain, creaking mortality, back to another room, vestige of hope and patience. The old hotelkeeper nods and sadly smiles at my condition. *Bonjour, Monsieur. Bonjour. Bonjour,* from him and the daughters, whose sadness lengthens hearing the remnants of my voice as I ask if anyone came, looking. They shake their heads quickly, *Oh non! Non, non, non!* And no...calls? They shake again.

In the little room I lay again. A passing hour leads to standing up again, packing a bag, making an exit. A block down a small transaction yields baggy blue pants, black shoes and white socks, exactly like the square threads Mother required so many long years ago—and a baggy black T-shirt like the one Philippe wore. And it isn't yet noon so plenty time for an espresso and maybe a smoke, for relaxing awhile in new clothes that don't feel nearly as wrong as once they looked. Recovery is further along than it was an hour ago, and I sit, sipping, smoking, thinking things over, like a French guy in a cafe.

Horndog Blue

Design and composition by
Byron Design, Tucson, Arizona

Text composed in Garamond, a classic, elegantly
crafted typeface exhibiting balance and readability

Printed and bound by R. R. Donnelley & Sons Company
Harrisonburg, Virginia